CATHERINE MARCH
The Brigadier's Daughter

TORONTO NEW YORK LONDON
AMSTERDAM PARIS SYDNEY HAMBURG
STOCKHOLM ATHENS TOKYO MILAN MADRID
PRAGUE WARSAW BUDAPEST AUCKLAND

Recycling programs
for this product may
not exist in your area.

ISBN-13: 978-0-373-30629-9

THE BRIGADIER'S DAUGHTER

Copyright © 2009 by Catherine March

First North American Publication 2011

This edition published by arrangement with Harlequin Books S.A.

For questions and comments about the quality of this book please contact us at Customer_eCare@Harlequin.ca.

® and TM are trademarks of the publisher. Trademarks indicated with ® are registered in the United States Patent and Trademark Office, the Canadian Trade Marks Office and in other countries.

www.Harlequin.com

Printed in U.S.A.

Chapter One

London—10 December, 1876

'Congratulations, dear boy! Well done!'

Captain Reid Bowen rose from his seat in the lounge of the gentleman's club in Mayfair and accepted the hearty handshake from his uncle, murmuring his thanks and waving a hand at the leather armchair opposite. 'Would you care to join me, Uncle Percy?'

'Indeed!' He clicked his fingers at a nearby waiter. 'This calls for champagne.'

Reid demurred, with a modest shrug of his broad shoulders. 'Come now, Uncle, let's not go overboard.'

'And why on earth not, dear boy? It's not every day that my favourite nephew returns from India and is promoted to the rank of major!'

'Uncle Percy.' Reid Bowen laughed. 'I am your only nephew!'

'Indeed, indeed you are.'

'And my promotion is not substantive until the spring.'

'Major Bowen, humour an old man, please!'

They both laughed and a bottle of champagne was ordered. With his usual generosity Percy, the Earl of Clermount, invited a few fellow club members to join them, but as the last drop of expensive and delightful golden liquid was drained and the gathering dispersed, Uncle Percy turned to his nephew with a gleam in his eye, to broach a subject that had long been a bone of contention.

'Well, now, with your posting as military attaché to the Embassy in St Petersburg, you seem to be short of an essential item of kit, dear boy.'

Reid set down his empty champagne flute and looked at his uncle with a puzzled frown. 'And what would that be, sir?'

'A wife, of course!'

Reid laughed, and flicked up the tails of his black evening suit, before sitting down in the leather armchair. 'I had not given it any consideration, but you may be right. I will need a hostess.'

'A wife is far more than just a hostess, Reid.'

His nephew glanced at him with a twinkle in his dark blue eyes. 'Shame on you, Uncle, I did not think you had such thoughts about the fairer sex.'

Uncle Percy blushed, his jowls wobbling as he shook his head and clucked his tongue. 'I was thinking of progeny, my dear boy. Sons, to inherit all that I shall one day leave you.'

Reid Bowen sighed, and nodded his head, yet kept his thoughts within the seclusion of his mind.

Undaunted, Uncle Percy ploughed onwards. 'Now, the Christmas Ball at Lady Westfaling's this evening will be an ideal occasion to see what's, um, er, on the market, so to speak. You did receive an invitation, did you not?'

'Yes, I had the misfortune,' Reid replied drily.

'Splendid! We will go together and I will point out the most eligible young chits. There's the Bellingham girl; pretty, intelligent, a little dull perhaps; and the Tinson-Byrne chit is a fine filly; not to mention the enchanting Packard girl, though she may be a trifle young and flighty.'

Reid gave him a keen look. 'With all respect, Uncle, I think I am old enough to select my own wife.'

'Then why have you not done so, Reid, dear boy?' Uncle Percy returned his glance with one as equally penetrating. 'I believe you will be thirty-four next spring, and it's high time you got yourself down that aisle and acquired what every man needs most in life—the love and support of a good woman.'

'When I find her, I will no doubt rush to drag her to the altar.'

'Well, with that sort of attitude, it's no wonder you're still on the shelf.'

'Indeed, Uncle?'

'The chits today don't much go in for the dragging bit; they much prefer to be courted with respect and devotion. I think you will find that, if you apply as much savvy to courting as you do to soldiering, you will have no trouble in finding a suitable wife.'

'Sasha!'

Miss Alexandra Packard sat before her dressing table as her maid finished pinning up her hair. She glanced in the mirror at one of her three sisters, standing in her bedroom doorway and wailing with a most disgruntled expression on her pretty face.

'What is it, Georgia?' Her voice was soft and quiet, laced with a patience she was frequently called upon to exert.

'I can't find my white gloves. Have you seen them?'

'I'm sure Polly laid them out on the bed, with your gown. Did you not, Polly dear?' Sasha glanced at their ladies' maid, who nodded her head and dipped a curtsy in confirmation of this fact.

'Then someone's taken them!' cried Georgia, flouncing on her heel with a whirl of white petticoats. 'Philippa!'

Sasha sighed and rolled her eyes at Polly, her glance skimming away from her own reflection. Compared to her beautiful sister Georgia, who had inherited their father's blond and blue-eyed features, she felt there was nothing appealing about her appearance, being the only daughter to have the sable-dark hair and black eyes of their Russian-born mother, the Princess

Olga Alexandrovna, now simply Lady Packard, who was also slightly built and somewhat pale. All that her sisters seemed to have inherited from their mother was her temperamental nature, sometimes passionate and full of life, at other times sinking into a sulk that could last for days. After the birth of four children in close succession, none of whom had been the son her parents had hoped for, her mother had been incapacitated by a weak heart and now spent much of her days lying upon a chaise longue, bravely insisting that there was nothing wrong with her and encouraging her daughters to go out and enjoy their own lives to the full.

It was left to her eldest daughter, Alexandra, twenty-three years old and fondly known as Sasha, to see to the girls: Georgia, the prettiest of them all; Philippa, nineteen and ripe for the marriage market, though she was cruelly afflicted by a glandular problem and a trifle overweight; and Victoria, the youngest, who shared her father's passion for the library and spent much of her time with her nose buried in a book.

'Thank you, Polly.' Sasha rose from the dressing table, her fingers briefly touching the maid's arm in an affectionate gesture as she passed to lift her maroon velvet shawl from the bed. 'Don't wait up, I'll see to the girls when we get in.'

Polly smiled and wished her a good evening, rushing off to see to Miss Vic as she called urgently for assistance with her garters and stockings.

'Come along, girls,' Sasha called as she walked down the corridor, 'Papa will be waiting.'

Voices shrieked, doors banged, slippered feet pattered on the thick carpet behind her, but Sasha did not pause or glance over her shoulder. She knew from experience that any sign of weakness on her part would be pounced upon and time would be wasted on whether this bracelet or that ribbon or those slippers were really the best to wear, so she merely glided as serenely as a swan, gathering her cygnets behind her as she descended the stairs to the hall.

Brigadier Sir Conrad Packard looked up as he fastened his cloak, and his eyes gleamed with pride as he watched his four daughters. No one could deny that he was the proudest of fathers, the only hint that he might have experienced some disappointment at the birth of a daughter being the bestowing of the feminine form of masculine names. Disappointment had long since faded, and he adored all his girls, fortified by the firm hope that one day soon he would be acquiring four strapping sons-by-marriage.

There was a flurry of activity as shawls were fastened and reticules clasped firmly about the wrist and then the butler, footmen and their father assisted and chivvied the four Packard girls into the waiting carriage. At last, settled in his seat and rolling his eyes in sympathy with their butler as the door closed, the Brigadier called, 'Thank you, Lodge. We will not be too late.'

'Very good, sir.' Lodge bowed with a knowing smile at these familiar words and turned back to the house as the carriage set off, prepared for a night of rummy and copious cups of tea to keep him going until the early hours of the morning. He would not rest until the girls and the master were safely home again.

A fresh flurry of snow that afternoon slowed their progress as they joined other carriages on the slush-laden roads of London's fashionable Mayfair, making their way to Lady Westfaling's Christmas Ball. They were warm and snug within the carriage, a froth of white lawn petticoats, beneath silk gowns in shades of cream, red tartan and green, billowing as the girls sought to tame their skirts.

'Do you think there will be a treasure hunt like last year?' mused Philippa, offering a small bag of sugared almonds to her sisters.

The girls each selected one, and sucked on the sweet pink-and-white confections while they speculated on the evening ahead with eager anticipation.

Victoria helped herself to another sugared almond, her sister frowning and snatching the bag away, with an envious glance at

Victoria's slim waist. 'I wonder if the Foreign Secretary, Lord Derby, will be there? I would so like to hear if the Turks—'

'Oh, never mind that,' exclaimed Georgia. 'I wonder if Felix will be there? I want to dance all night!'

Their father looked up from adjusting his white bow tie, and offered snippets of advice and admonishments for their behaviour. A military man, he had served twenty-five years before a severe wound had forced him to retire from active service and spend a number of years in the Diplomatic Corps. He was a kind but very particular man, not overly tall and his pate bald of his once-fair hair, but he exuded the strength and bearing of a military officer. He still kept his hand in with the Army by making good use of his knowledge of French and Russian. Having tutored his own daughters, he now tutored young military officers who were in need of these languages. His quiet yet firm voice brooked no arguments and he was not known to suffer fools gladly, the antics of his daughters being no exception. They held him in slightly awed reverence, tempered by affection.

'We'll not be dancing too often with those young gentlemen,' he said, glancing at Georgia with his ice-blue eyes, which seldom missed anything of importance. 'Your mama was quite mortified when Lady Jessop called and commented about your behaviour at her dinner dance.'

Georgia pouted, recalling to mind the scolding her parents had delivered after that occasion, but made no reply as she sat back silently in her seat, peering out of the window as the wheels of the carriage slowed and they pulled into the portico of Lady Westfaling's impressive mansion.

Sasha exchanged a glance with her father and smiled at him reassuringly, her silent promise to keep a better eye on Georgia. A golden glow from the lit hallway spilled out upon the steps as they descended from the carriage, with the assistance of several attentive footmen splendid in frogged uniforms. The Packards joined the crowd of other guests inching along a carpeted corridor to the ballroom, where the major-domo took the proffered invitation card from the Brigadier, rapped his staff upon the marble step and announced in stentorian tones worthy of any parade ground, 'Brigadier Sir Conrad Packard, and the Misses Alexandra, Georgia, Philippa and Victoria Packard.'

They moved forwards, descending the steps to where their hosts, Lord and Lady Westfaling, their son, Felix, and daughter, Arabella, stood waiting in a line to greet them and to hand the young ladies their dance cards, which had tiny gilt pencils attached with ribbon.

'Conrad, my dear,' murmured Lady Westfaling, looking pointedly over the Brigadier's shoulder as she let him kiss the air beside her cheek, 'is Olga still not well?'

'Alas.' He shook his head and moved swiftly on from her cloying perfume and predatory clasp to extend his hand to his good friend, Avery, Lord Westfaling, with the promise to meet him in the library for cigars and brandy at the earliest opportunity. He nodded curtly at young Felix, who visibly blanched as he dragged his eyes from the delightful blonde-and-blue-eyed vision that was Georgia and bowed to the Brigadier, nervously murmuring good evening, punctuated with several 'sir's too many.

Sasha paused for a moment amidst the hubbub as her sisters chattered and looked eagerly about. Her glance fell to the dance card clasped in her white-gloved fingers. Wistfully, she wondered if any gentleman would actually put his name down, or if once again she would be so busy chaperoning her sisters and dancing with her father to have time to dance with anyone else. Most likely she would be overlooked as the gentlemen made their choices elsewhere amongst the vast bevy of lovely and well-bred young ladies present. Unobtrusively she slipped the card into the tasselled reticule dangling from her wrist, and then looked up, with a well-trained smile fixed on her soft mouth.

The ballroom was indeed a magnificent sight, proof that Lady Westfaling had spent a good deal of money and employed numerous people to transform it into a Christmas wonderland. To one side, halfway down the vast room, stood a twenty-foot Scots pine, brought in from their own estate in Scotland, and decorated with red-and-gold baubles, ribbons, gingerbreads and tiny candles. The smell of the pine and ginger was very pleasant, refreshing the somewhat-heavy atmosphere emanating from the odour of perfumed ladies and sweating gentlemen. Sasha breathed in the scent as they moved to examine the decorations, the orchestra playing discreetly in the background before the dancing began. She glanced at the garlands of holly and wreaths and ribbons festooned about the walls, and the brightly sparkling chandeliers that lit up the room so beautifully.

'Who is that?' Georgia murmured suddenly in her ear.

'Hmm?' Sasha turned as her sister's urgent fingers dug into her elbow, looking in the direction of a gentleman greeting Lady Westfaling. He was handsome, tall and broad-shouldered, his ash-brown hair flecked with blond and his face unusually suntanned. Sasha turned away. 'I have no idea, but do stop gaping before Papa notices. Oh, look, Felix is about to mark your dance card.'

'How wonderful to see you, Reid,' Lady Westfaling greeted her guest, her glance slightly disapproving, 'but not in uniform?'

Captain Bowen bowed. 'My apologies, Lady Westfaling. I am on leave, added to which my uniform is sadly shabby. A friend has made me the loan of his tails for the evening.'

Her glance now admiring as she took in the wide set of his shoulders and the expanse of white shirt tapering to a flat stomach beneath a white waistcoat, Lady Westfaling murmured, 'You must introduce me to your friend; from his clothing he seems to be a fine figure of a man.'

Taken aback, Reid narrowed his dark blue eyes as he took the measure of his hostess and swiftly retreated, moving on to extend his hand to her husband farther down the line, casting a wry glance to his Uncle Percy over one shoulder.

'Jolly good to have you back, Bowen,' Lord Westfaling declared. 'Take no notice of the old gel, she's always had an eye for good-looking chaps, that's why she married me!' He laughed, but there was a note of warning in his tone. 'All talk and no action, I can assure you.'

'Of course,' Reid murmured, practising his diplomatic skills by adding, 'I have spent so long out in the field that I have forgotten how…charming ladies can be.'

'Indeed. Now then, what's this I hear about a promotion? Congratulations!'

'Thank you.' He accepted another handshake.

'Must introduce you to our good friend Packard, Army man himself before a damn Abyssinian spear crippled his knee. How's your Russian?'

'Oh, Avery!' cried Lady Westfaling, 'Do stop nattering, you're holding things up!'

The guests were merging in a crowd about the steps, forcing his lordship to curtail his conversation and usher them on, with the proviso, 'Percy, bring him to the library, soon as I've got this damned dancing on the go.'

'Avery!'

They walked away, Uncle Percy purloining glass flutes of golden champagne from a passing waiter, and raising one to toast his nephew. 'Here's to the future Mrs Bowen.'

Reid hesitated before he sipped his champagne, glancing around at the crowded ballroom and the dazzling array of women in evening gowns and glittering jewellery. 'I must confess, Uncle, that I feel a touch nervous. I would rather be facing a hundred screaming tribesmen pouring down the Hindu Kush than entangle myself with any of these mamas and their offspring.'

'Oh, pish! Nothing ventured, nothing gained.' Uncle Percy finished his glass with a flourish and narrowed his eyes as he surveyed the room with a discreet yet discerning eye. 'Let's take a wander round. My advice would be to select two or three young ladies, a few dances, a little light conversation, then leave it at that for the time being. There are plenty more balls and parties between now and New Year.'

Reid laughed wryly. 'Sounds to me as though you have the whole campaign well planned. Is this to be a full-frontal, noisy attack? Or a covert, silent offensive?'

'My dear boy, do not be facetious!'

'Speaking of time, I had a letter this morning from the Defence Secretary to say that my posting has been brought forwards. So I shall be leaving for Russia at the end of April.'

'Damn me!' Uncle Percy muttered. 'It would have to be a whirlwind courtship, then.'

'I am reluctant to rush into anything.'

'So you have said. For the past ten years. Neither of us is getting any younger, you know.' He paused, and lowered his chin as he murmured, 'Now, there's a girl you may want to get to know, Araminta Cunningham-Ellis. Well bred, elegant, plenty of money.'

Reid snorted, helping himself to another glass of champagne. 'I may not be rich, but I have enough money of my own, thank you.' He glanced carefully sideways at the strawberry blonde in question. 'She's rather tall, for a girl.'

They both gazed upon Araminta, Uncle Percy with frank admiration and Reid with amusement. 'Come along,' he urged his uncle, nudging his elbow, 'before her mama cuffs you with that enormous fan she's brandishing.'

'Can't see what you're complaining about,' Uncle Percy muttered. 'Perfect breeding stock for sons—' He coughed and cleared his throat as an elderly gentleman stepped into his path. 'Good evening, Hallam, is it not a splendid do?'

They paused for a few moments in polite conversation and then moved onwards, Uncle Percy pointing out several more eligible females along the way. To his disappointment, and frustration, his nephew seemed little impressed and he could not persuade him to make any introductions. At last they came to the raised dais leading to open French doors and the veranda beyond. They mounted the steps on the pretext of taking in a breath of fresh air, yet from their elevated position they now had a perfect view of the ballroom. Uncle Percy looked towards four young ladies dressed in simple yet charming green, red and cream evening gowns, blending in with the Christmas theme.

'Now you couldn't go far wrong with one of Packard's gels, all of them splendid creatures. And very useful, too, being fluent in French and Russian. Georgia, the one in the green dress, is the prettiest, and about the right age, I would say.'

'How old is she?'

'Almost twenty-one.'

Reid glanced discreetly, and had to admit that Georgia Packard was indeed very lovely, the sort of girl he would be attracted to and the sort of blonde, beautiful girl that in the past had been his mistress.

'And there's Victoria, the one in the tartan dress. She's seventeen.'

'Too young.'

'And Philippa, in the maroon dress.'

'The one in the cream dress, the small one with the dark hair, is she a Packard?'

'Of course, that's Sasha, christened Alexandra after her mother—a Russian princess by birth, you know. Very beautiful, but afflicted by poor health, and somewhat highly strung.'

'Hmm.' Reid mused doubtfully, 'I would prefer a lady who is strong and capable.'

'I am sure in nature Sasha is both of those qualities, but you never know if she has inherited more than just her mother's looks. If it's a strong gel you want, then you would be wise to settle on Georgia.' They both surveyed the young lady. 'Mind you, she would not give you a quiet life.'

'Indeed?' Reid smiled at the prospect of a challenge, as he gazed at the four young ladies hovering near the Christmas tree, blissfully unaware of his Uncle Percy's grand designs. 'What's the papa like? I believe he's an Army man himself, and not to be trifled with by all accounts.'

'He's a splendid fellow! Shall I introduce you?'

'By all means.'

The orchestra began to play and Lord and Lady Westfaling opened the dancing with an elegant polonaise. Sasha felt the beat of the music vibrate through her whole body, her soul stirred by the rousing tune. Beneath the long skirts of her evening gown her brocade slipper tapped in time to the beat.

'Don't look, but he's coming over!'

'What?' Sasha glanced at her sister with a puzzled frown. 'What on earth—?'

'Don't look!' Georgia repeated in an urgent undertone.

Puzzled and curious, Sasha did indeed look. Just for a moment her gaze met the dark blue eyes of the handsome, suntanned man they had seen earlier, before her lashes lowered and she glanced away. She did not know him, but recognised the Earl of Clermount walking at his side, and dipped a curtsy in greeting as her father beamed at his old friend.

'Percy, old boy, glad to see you!'

'Conrad.' After an exchange of bows, Percy turned slightly. 'I'd like you to meet my nephew, Captain Reid Bowen. He's been out on the North-West Frontier for the past seven years, and now that he's returned, bathed in glory and a well-earned commission to major—'

'In the spring,' Reid interjected.

'Quite.' Percy cast him an exasperated glance. 'I am persuading him to enjoy life a little, before he takes up a posting to St Petersburg.'

The Brigadier perked up at this fact, and turned to Reid with hand extended. 'How do you do? Which regiment are you with?'

'The Royal Fusiliers, Seventh Battalion.'

'Fine body of men. Queen's Light Dragoons, myself.'

'I am honoured to make your acquaintance, sir,' Reid responded truthfully, and for a few moments they made conversation on military matters, before Uncle Percy's sharp elbow in his ribs reminded him of his duty. 'Might I have the honour of marking your daughter's dance card?'

The Brigadier smiled, with a mischievous gleam in his eyes. 'Which one? I have four of 'em, as you can see.'

Reid hesitated, just for the blink of an eye, in a quandary as to whether he should state where his interest lay openly, or be more subtle. He plumped for the latter. 'Well, of course, I would be delighted with any Miss Packard who might care to risk my clumsy two left feet. It has been some while since I practised my dancing.'

Before he had even finished speaking Victoria and Philippa had already thrust their cards beneath his nose, and he dutifully surveyed them and pencilled in his name, while Georgia exclaimed, 'Oh, what a shame, my card is full! Excuse me, Papa, here is Felix to claim me for the mazurka.'

'You've already had a dance with him this evening, Georgia,' the Brigadier growled, as his brows lowered upon the anxiously hovering Right Honourable Felix Westfaling. 'Scratch him out and let Captain Bowen take his place.'

'Oh, Papa, that would not do at all!' exclaimed Georgia. 'It would be very rude, would it not, Sasha?'

Sasha felt a warm blush creep up her neck as all eyes turned on her, but she murmured in agreement, 'It may be construed as rather impolite.'

'Besides, Sasha has not had even one dance yet—can't he go with her?'

'I-I've lost my card,' stammered Sasha.

'Nonsense, it's in your reticule.' And with that Georgia whirled away with a flounce of green silk as she took Felix firmly by the elbow and set off to dance around the ballroom floor with him.

The Brigadier felt a brief spurt of annoyance, which boded ill, as his gaze followed that of his errant and impetuous daughter, yet he calmed as Sasha laid her hand on his forearm and murmured soothingly, ''Tis but a phase, Papa, it will soon pass.' She turned to Captain Bowen and smiled politely. 'I would be delighted to dance with you, sir.'

'Me first!' cried Victoria.

Somewhat curious, Reid Bowen held out his hand to take Sasha's dance card. He was puzzled, as he glanced at the blank sheet, and resisted the temptation to cast a perusing stare. What was wrong with the girl that no one wanted to dance with her? Buck teeth? Bad breath? A total bore? From his greater height, his eyes lowered, he looked at her, and though she was no great beauty he could find no fault with her neat features, smooth, pale skin and dark brown eyes that glowed with intelligence. He pencilled himself in for two dances, both of them a waltz, later in the evening, and then he turned to the young Victoria and escorted her onto the dance floor. Despite her initial enthusiasm, Victoria was overawed by the handsome and mature gentleman in whose arms she suddenly found herself, and for the life of her she could not think of a word to say, which suited her partner well enough. At the end of the dance, he returned her to her family and then bowed as he went off in search of a much-needed drink.

At ten o'clock a buffet of the most lavish and delicious food was served. Sasha indulged in a portion of sherry trifle and was licking her spoon when Captain Bowen returned to claim her for the first waltz of the evening. As he paused in front of her, with an amused smile and twinkle in his blue eyes, she hurriedly set aside the spoon and bowl, as he proffered his crooked arm to her.

'Shall we?'

The strains of the 'Blue Danube' made her smile with antici-pation and pleasure, the waltz being her favourite dance. She accepted with a small inclination of her head, and slipped her hand through his elbow as he led her forwards, every part of her aware of his tall frame at her side.

Though he had to stoop slightly, and she had to reach up to place her hand upon his broad shoulder, Reid was not in the least bit clumsy. Indeed, she had never enjoyed a waltz quite so much. She glanced up at his profile, his straight nose and lean cheeks very masculine. His jaw was firm and his eyes, when he glanced at her as he placed his hand on her waist, were a very dark blue. Following his lead, she swayed and stepped in time to the rhythm of the waltz, her feet and legs moving between his own as he guided her. Though she often had to dance backwards with no idea of what was behind her, her long cream silk skirts swirling about her legs, she had every confidence in Captain Bowen and the music as they swayed about.

'You are an excellent dancer, Miss Packard.'

Reid noticed that she bowed her head, with a smile, in a shy yet charmingly graceful gesture, acknowledging his compliment and yet neither bold nor brazen in her acceptance. He noticed, also, the tiny speck of cream at the corner of her mouth, and agonised over whether to mention it, or remain silent. He found himself glancing time and again, as they danced, at her mouth, until she turned her head, aware of his gaze, a slight frown on her well-shaped, dark brows and a pink blush staining her neck and cheeks.

'Forgive me, Miss Packard.' It was unconscionably rude of him to have embarrassed a lady, so he erred on the side of truth and his judgement that Miss Packard favoured honesty. 'But, um, please do not take offence, but you may wish to dab your handkerchief to the corner of your mouth.'

'Oh!' Sasha was instantly mortified. 'Have I cream?'

'Indeed, you do. Just a tiny speck.'

Sasha felt a red-hot heat of embarrassment wash over her entire body, and wished with all her being she could flee. She made a tiny move to jerk from his arms, but he pulled her back and smoothly manoeuvred her through the flowing steps of the waltz.

'Oh, sir, please do let me go!'

'Why?'

'I— I—' Sasha stammered. 'Let me retire to the ladies' cloak-room, please.' In agony she felt her cheeks blaze.

'There is no need.' As they danced into the corner, and his broad shoulders shielded her from prying eyes, deftly, quickly, he reached out with one gloved finger and flicked the offending blob of cream away. 'There now, it is gone. All is well. And no one could see.'

Sasha tried to pull away again, but he held on to her, and she glanced up at him. 'You must think me very…gauche.'

'Not at all.' He gazed down, saw the telltale glimmer of tears in her eyes, and repeated firmly, 'Not at all. And in the grand scheme of things, what is a mere speck of cream? It's not as though you had lost a slipper or, God forbid, a stocking trailed about your ankle.'

She could not help but laugh, nor could she help it as another painful blush warmed her exposed neck. 'You should not speak of such things.'

He smiled, enjoying the pleasant sound of her laugh, and even her blushes, for it had been a long time since he had been close to a woman who could still blush.

'No, indeed I should not.' It began to dawn on him on him then why Miss Alexandra Packard might not be the belle of the ball, for he sensed there was something infinitely fragile about her. To his surprise he felt the surge of a most unfamiliar emotion, as though he would fight dragons and villains to protect her from all harm. He brushed it off, annoyed with himself. This would not do, as many men no doubt felt, judging from her empty dance card, it would not do at all for an officer's wife to be anything other than a strong and capable woman who could take care of herself, the home and the children while her soldier husband was away winning his medals.

At the end of the waltz they parted company, and Sasha wondered, as he coolly bid her adieu, whether he would return for the second. To her surprise and pleasure, he did, and firmly took the lead, moving her slender body about the ballroom with infinite ease and confidence. He made no move to open conversation, so politely she enquired if he was looking forward to his posting to St Petersburg, and from there they enjoyed a dialogue about Russia.

'I must confess, Miss Packard,' murmured Captain Bowen, above her ear, 'that I have not enjoyed a dance quite so much this evening, as I have with you. Not only are you an exquisite dancer, but very interesting to talk to.'

'Thank you.'

They continued the dance until its end—all too soon, Sasha thought—and then he walked with her back to where her father and her sisters sat. He did not depart at once, but lingered to converse with her father about the Army and the possibility of Russian lessons.

In the dark, early hours of morning the clop-clop of horses' hooves and the rumble of carriage wheels roused Lady Packard as she lay dozing, waiting for the return of her family to their home on Roseberry Street. She stirred and reached to turn up the wick on the glass-shaded lamp beside the bed. Beyond her bedroom she could hear footsteps and the bang of a door, and her husband's deep voice as he admonished his daughters to be quiet. She sat up and plumped her pillows, checked her braided hair and turned her face eagerly to the door. A few moments later it opened, and the Brigadier stepped in, tossing aside his white gloves and bow tie as he walked with soundless footsteps across the carpet.

'Did the girls have a wonderful evening?' she asked in her soft, husky voice, even after all these years still influenced by her native Russian accent.

'My dear—' Conrad turned to face his wife, as he shrugged

off his jacket '—you did not have to wait up.' He spoke gently, sitting down on the edge of the bed and gazing at her.

Olga held out her arms to him, and with a contented sigh he pulled her into an embrace, affectionate and yet restrained, mindful of her delicate health. He kissed the side of her neck, breathing in the scent of her skin and stroking back tendrils of dark hair from her temple. 'How are you, my love?'

'I am well,' she replied gently. 'I have missed you.'

'You should have come with us. The Westfalings were asking after you, as well as Percy, and many others.'

Tears glowed in her eyes, her turbulent emotions easily aroused, 'Next time, I promise. Soon I will be feeling much stronger. Did Georgia behave?'

'No.' Conrad could not help but laugh, his annoyance tempered by admiration for his daughter's passionate, if stubborn and wayward, nature. He sat back and pulled off his shoes and stockings, undressing swiftly and then climbing into bed with his wife, a sigh escaping from his throat as he lay back. 'I am getting too old for all of this nonsense.' He turned his head on the pillow and gazed at his wife. 'What a pair we are! It's high time these girls of ours were married off. Their husbands can run around after them and we can enjoy a little time to ourselves.' He mused for a moment, a vision of rusticating at their country manor in Shropshire taking hold in his mind, hopeful that the country air and quiet life would help improve Olga's strength. 'I think Georgia may have acquired a beau this evening, though not the one she would no doubt prefer. Percy introduced his nephew, a Captain Reid Bowen. I found him most personable and highly suitable, more than capable enough of keeping Georgia in line. However, he's off to St Petersburg in the spring, on a posting to the Embassy as military attaché.'

'Oh, Conrad, how wonderful.' Olga turned to lie against him, resting her head on his shoulder. 'Tell me more! Just think, one of our girls married to an officer.'

'Steady on now, my love, they've only just met. Though he did ask my permission to call, and I have invited him for dinner on Christmas Eve. I hope that will not be inconvenient.' He looked down at her with raised brows.

Olga shook her head. 'We were short of one gentleman, so it will be perfect. But what of my Sasha? Did anyone dance with my Sasha?'

'Only Captain Bowen, but as always she kept close to my side and seemed unable to overcome her shyness. I fear she does rather live in Georgia's shadow.'

In her bedroom Sasha kicked off her slippers and padded barefoot to stand before the dressing table, glancing at her reflection in the mirror. Slowly she raised her hands and removed the pins from her hair, avoiding her own eyes and her flushed cheeks, hesitating as Georgia called from the adjoining bedchamber. She leaned a little closer then, bravely daring to look at her own face... How strange, she thought, she looked exactly the same, but she did not feel the same...not since Captain Reid Bowen had held her in his arms and waltzed her around the ballroom...

'Oh, Sasha, darling, do hurry, I can't wait to get this corset off!' cried an indignant Georgia.

'I'm coming.' Sasha turned away from the mirror and hurried to her sister's assistance.

'I don't know why Polly can't stay up.'

'It's two o'clock in the morning,' Sasha replied, nimbly dealing with the ribbons of Georgia's corset. 'It would be unkind to keep Polly awake all night just to unlace us, when we can very well do it for ourselves.'

Georgia scowled and muttered and then stepped out of the pool of her discarded gown, turning to do the same for Sasha. When at last freed from the constriction of their ball gowns and corsets, they laid them out on a chaise longue beside the wardrobe, for Polly to put away in the morning. Georgia flung herself down on her bed and began to brush out her long butter-blonde hair, her sapphire eyes glowing as she exclaimed, 'Was it not a wonderful evening?'

'Hmm.'

'Felix is the most wonderful dancer, and he makes me laugh. I absolutely adore him!'

Sasha sat down and laid cool fingers on her sister's wrist. 'Don't, Georgia, please, don't. You know Papa will never allow a match between the two of you.'

'Why ever not?'

'You know very well why not. Felix was embroiled in that horrible scandal with the, er, *enceinte* governess.'

'He swears that was nothing of his doing. She was lying through her teeth just to snare him!'

'And he refused a commission into the Army, preferring to stay at home with his mama. In Father's eyes that makes him well and truly damned.'

Georgia rose from the bed and flounced away, moving to the far side and drawing back her bedcovers. 'Felix cannot help it if he has an aversion to killing people, and being sent abroad to God-forsaken places for years on end.'

Sasha suspected that Georgia was quoting Felix and not her own opinion. 'Papa says he lacks discipline and is a coward.'

'I am going to sleep,' said Georgia firmly, climbing into bed and pulling the covers up over her shoulders. 'Good night.'

With a sigh Sasha rose and murmured, 'Good night, sweet dreams.'

Georgia grunted, and Sasha knew better than to pursue the matter further. Once Georgia had made her mind up about something, she could be very stubborn indeed. Sasha went to her own bedchamber and closed the connecting door, slipping beneath the heavy covers of her canopied bed and lying awake in the darkened room for some while. Her thoughts wandered back to the first waltz she had danced with Captain Bowen. Sasha squirmed, hugging a pillow in both hands as she remembered the embarrassing moment when he had pointed out she had cream on her face. She rolled over in the expanse of her bed, trying to convince herself the moment was best forgotten. In the grand scheme of things, as he had pointed out, it was of no importance. She remembered the feel of his broad, solid body as he guided her through the maze of other dancing couples, very sure and certain of himself, his voice a steady sound—even the smell of him, a clean masculine tang, lingered in her memory.

Yet whilst he had been talking to her papa, she had noticed him glance several times at Georgia, as she danced, and then as she had returned and chatted animatedly with her dear friend, Arabella. But he had also made conversation with herself, and Philippa, and even young Victoria. He had asked her father if he might call upon them, and her father, much to her surprise, had nodded his agreement and even gone so far as to invite Captain Bowen to accompany Uncle Percy to dinner on Christmas Eve. Sasha closed her eyes, falling asleep on her last, and pleasant, thought—that soon she would see the very handsome Captain Reid Bowen again.

Chapter Two

Despite retiring in the early hours of morning, Reid was awake and up at his usual time, his routine dictated by a lifetime of military discipline. He had declined his uncle's invitation to stay with him and had taken a room in the Officer's Mess of the Royal Fusiliers, conveniently situated for the town and stables behind the barracks near the Tower of London. At nine o'clock precisely his batman came in with his shaving gear and a bowl of hot water. Reid shrugged on a robe and dutifully sat down to be shaved, facing the light of a long sash window.

Through the open curtains of thick, dark green brocade, he could see a square of blue sky. He would take a ride in Hyde Park before luncheon; it would help to clear his mind. He was not a man who usually brooded, or had any difficulty in life that required mental wrestling, but on this bright December morning his thoughts were indeed a little disordered, and that irked him.

All was not going according to plan. The intention was that he would acquire a wife, take her with him to St Petersburg, and settle down to enjoy his career. But here was the rub—choosing a suitable woman was not as easy as he, or Uncle Percy, had thought it would be. In the past he had felt no inclination to acquire anything as permanent as a wife, and, though he was not a man who felt the constant need for a woman, he had enjoyed the occasional, yet discreet, liaison. Always with a woman who was very beautiful, not very intelligent and yet one who understood that she could expect nothing more than his presence in her bed. When the attraction had been satisfied, and one or the other of them had moved on, there had been no great dilemma or drama, as neither had expected any form of commitment. Ah, Reid mused as he rinsed his face clean in the hot water and stroked his fingers over his smooth jaw, perhaps it was the noose of commitment that he could feel tightening around his neck that bothered him this morning.

He went to his dressing room and selected a tweed riding jacket and fawn breeches, a cream shirt and matching cravat, pondering that perhaps it was more than that. Perhaps it was the memory that lingered in his mind of dancing a waltz with a certain Miss Packard. She had been so unlike any woman he had ever met before. Graceful—yes, she had been light as a feather dancing in his arms. Intelligent—undoubtedly, her knowledge of Russia, of languages and music and goodness knew what else had been most apparent, and yet she had not been a bore at all, interspersing her conversation with humorous, wry little snippets and that delightful, husky, almost shy laugh. Yet in appearance she was not the sort he would normally lust after—indeed not! He admonished himself, for Miss Packard was far too respectable to be his mistress! On the other hand, one does not choose a wife according to the standards of a mistress. She might not be blonde and buxom, but there was a certain charm about her dark haired and creamy-skinned femininity that appealed to him. She was certainly intelligent and well read; he could envisage many a cosy evening together and the conversation would be neither boring nor stilted. She was petite, though, which in itself he found quite attractive and he entertained himself with delicious thoughts of carrying her up the stairs to bed, or sitting before the fire and letting her curl up on his lap, a prelude to making love.

However, Uncle Percy had mentioned the importance of producing an heir and he wondered if her small slim frame would be, er, adequate. He frowned, hesitating even within the privacy of his thoughts to dwell on Miss Packard's nether regions. Well, one just wouldn't breed a Suffolk Punch with a delicate little Arabian filly, now would one? It would not do. No, definitely not, he told himself firmly, it would not do at all.

He would be better off if he looked to the other Miss Packard, the blonde one, who appeared to be everything that he desired in a wife—confident, vivacious, and her figure was certainly admirable. Evidently a strong young woman, her speech and manners a little too loud perhaps, a little wilful...selfish, even? He hadn't yet enjoyed a particularly entertaining conversation with her, and she was frequently looking over her shoulder at that damned Westfaling whippersnapper. His enthusiasm began to wane as he dwelled on the attributes of one sister, and then the other, but even as he made his way downstairs, enjoyed a hearty breakfast, and then to the stables, mounted his bay gelding and rode off in the direction of Hyde Park, he could not come to any satisfactory conclusion about either of them.

'Sasha, wake up!'

From beneath a pile of bedcovers Sasha groaned, and shrugged off the hand shaking her shoulder. She burrowed deeper into the bed, in a vain attempt to escape a persistent Georgia.

'Oh, go away, Georgia, leave me alone!' she muttered from beneath her pillow, her heavy and aching eyes trying to sink back into the bliss of sleep.

'Sasha, you must get up.' Georgia marched over to the window and thrust back the curtains, flooding the room with bright sunshine. 'I promised Felix that I would meet him in the park. Do get dressed, I've persuaded one of the grooms to be ready and waiting at ten o'clock.'

'Ten o'clock!' Sasha sat up then, turning to look at the clock

ticking gently in its gilt case on the mantel abo⋯
and then at her fully dressed sister. 'Are you n⋯
just totally insensitive to other people? It's the⋯
and I'm exhausted from last night.'

'Rubbish! It's almost nine and you've had ple⋯
Here, darling, put on your lovely blue riding habit a⋯
for Polly to bring you some tea and toast.'

Emerging from the dressing room with her arms⋯
Sasha's riding habit, she laid it down on the bed and then cros⋯
the room to pull the bell-rope.

Sasha yawned and stretched, seeing that there was no help for
it but to get up. And now that she was awake, and her thoughts
returned to the memory of Captain Bowen, she was far too
restless to go back to sleep. She glanced out of the window at
the clear blue sky, and mused that a ride in the park seemed just
the thing. The snow had stopped and was beginning to thaw,
and though later it would be slushy out, for now it would be
crisp but not too cold or treacherous. She dressed and enjoyed
a cup of fragrant Earl Grey and a slice of toast with butter and
marmalade, ignoring Georgia as she nagged and badgered in
the background. At last she was dressed, and stood before her
mirror to place her top hat on, pulling down the spotted black
netting over her face, and slipped her fingers into kid gloves.

'At last!' cried Georgia, springing to her feet and ushering
her sister downstairs and out to the stables, glancing now and
then over her shoulder.

Sasha became suspicious. 'Papa does know we are going out?
He gave his permission?'

'Oh, yes, of course.' Georgia waved her hand airily, and
beamed at the young groom waiting for them, holding two big,
dappled-grey hunters by their bridles. 'Good morning, Farrell.'

'Mornin', miss.' The young Irish lad tugged at the peak of
his cloth cap and then led the two horses over to the mounting
block.

The Brigadier had trained his daughters to ride long before

or write, and the two girls jumped aboard and
es side-saddle, waited while Farrell mounted his
the trio set off for Hyde Park, Georgia setting the
rt trot.

the day was crisp and bright, there were not many
oad at this early hour, and some families had left the
end the Christmas holidays on their estates. The limbs
rees etched bare and stark along the wide avenue that
rgia led them down, and Sasha called out to her sister to
slow down, but she was ignored. As they came to a long open
stretch Georgia urged her horse into a canter, her skirts and veil
flying on the wind as the hunter obliged.

Sasha sighed with vexation, giving the command to her own
mount to canter, taking a firm hold of the reins and her riding
crop, leaning slightly forwards as they rode after Georgia. She
glanced back over her shoulder, to make sure that Farrell still
followed; though he lagged behind on his ancient hack, he kept
them within sight. By the time she had caught up with Georgia,
her errant sister had dismounted and was happily engaged in
building a snowman with Felix Westfaling. Sasha drew rein,
breathing hard, her horse snorting and pawing the ground, and
she gazed at Georgia with exasperation.

'Your skirts are getting all wet,' she called out, 'and where's
your hat?'

Georgia laughed, her face glowing in the cold air and beautiful against the virgin-white background of the snow, 'Come and
help us, Sasha!'

Felix straightened up from patting lumps of snow into the
shape of an arm, scooped up a ball of snow in the palm of his
hand and tossed it in Sasha's direction. 'Good morning, Sash,
do join us, got to get this finished before it starts to melt.'

Her horse leapt and shied to one side as the snowball splashed
on the path, but Sasha kept her seat and replied, 'No, I will not.
Georgia, please, do put your hat on and mount up.'

Her sister laughed, whirling away as she and Felix pelted each other with snowballs. With a sigh Sasha glanced at Farrell as he sidled up. He merely shrugged and grinned while she looked in both directions to see if they had been observed. There was no one about, except a lone horseman in the distance. What harm would it do? And it did look like such fun. She handed her reins to Farrell and jumped down, her boots crunching through the thick, powdery snow as she walked over to the snowman.

'I say, Sasha, how would you like a toboggan race? A whole bunch of us are meeting over at Birch Hill this afternoon.' Felix was wise to the fact that if he could persuade one sister, then the other would follow.

'I would not like it at all,' Sasha replied tartly, surveying the round ball he was rolling together to make the snowman's head, and then she gasped as a cold wet lump of snow hit her on the shoulder. 'Georgia!'

With cries threatening revenge, she leaned down and made her own ammunition, and the three of them were soon lobbing snowballs, ducking and rolling in the snow amidst shrieks of laughter.

'Good morning, Miss Packard.'

A deep, masculine, familiar voice echoed from behind her. They froze, Georgia and Sasha both turning to stare wide-eyed at the horseman who had halted nearby. Sasha's already flushed face deepened in colour as she recognised Captain Bowen. She dropped the half-made snowball in her hands, straightened her jacket and looked up to reply, 'Good morning, Captain Bowen.'

'Marvellous day.' He waved his riding crop about at the park in general.

'Yes, it is.'

From the corner of her eye she spied Felix and Georgia slinking behind the bulk of the snowman, leaving her to deal with the Captain on her own. Like Georgia, she had removed her hat and veil, and her cravat flapped all askew.

'That's a fine-looking snowman—need any help?'

'Um, er—' She heard a snort of suppressed giggles as her

accomplices ducked. But, undeterred, the Captain had swung down from his horse and was striding towards them. Her heart sank. She must look a sight, she feared, brushing with the back of her hand at the escaped and messy tendrils of hair curling about her face, and the smudge of snow on her nose.

'Miss Packard,' he greeted Georgia as belatedly, and unavoidably, she straightened. 'And young Felix, is it not?'

'How do you do, sir?' Felix flushed and brushed at his coat. 'We were just—'

'Just about to go,' Sasha interjected, reaching to pick up her hat and pass Georgia her own.

'Don't rush away on my account. Please.'

Captain Bowen turned to look at Sasha, and she was struck again by the blueness of his eyes and how very good-looking he was, his sun-bleached hair gleaming gold in the winter sunshine. She could not help but glance at his mouth, the well-disciplined line of the upper lip complimented by the slightly fuller lower, curving into an attractive smile. His shoulders seemed very broad and masculine, and his legs in beige jodhpurs left her in no doubt that he was a well-made man.

Georgia was not one to let her natural effervescence be dampened and, undeterred by the new arrival on the scene, she and Felix resumed their building of the snowman.

'We need some twigs for his hands,' Georgia said, looking about.

'There's a hawthorn bush over there,' Captain Bowen pointed out.

Being the nearest to it, Sasha set off and trudged through the drifts of snow to a nearby flower bed, reaching out to grasp a twig and snap it off. But it was resistant to her efforts and she struggled, leaning forwards and tugging with both hands, trying to avoid the adjacent prickly holly bush, and then she gave a little cry as her feet slipped and she lost her balance. She teetered, but before she fell two hands fastened on her waist and pulled her back against the solid bulk of a very male and warm body.

'Steady on, Miss Packard.' Captain Bowen laughed. 'Can't have you falling into the holly and getting scratched now, can we?'

Sasha blushed, but it was hardly noticeable as her face was already so flushed from the cold and the exertions of the snow-ball fights.

'Try that one over there,' called Georgia with subtle cunning, as she directed her sister and Captain Bowen farther away. 'We need some big pieces and that bush is too small.'

'Oh, Georgia! We really should be going,' objected Sasha.

'Go on!' her sister urged, casting a glance at Felix. 'And find two pebbles for his eyes.'

With a sigh and an apologetic glance up at Captain Bowen, Sasha turned and walked away, round the corner of the flower bed, her eyes searching for anything suitable. As soon as they were out of sight, Felix and Georgia fell into each other's arms, the groom holding the horses discreetly looking in the other direction.

'Here we are, this will do. Captain Bowen—' Sasha turned to him '—would you be so kind? I can't quite reach.'

'Of course.'

He reached up and effortlessly snapped off two long twigs, while Sasha knelt and picked out some small dark stones from the flower bed. She tried to think of some polite conversation to say to him, but nothing came to mind.

'Your father has kindly invited me to dinner on Christmas Eve.' Captain Bowen took the initiative and spoke first.

'Oh.'

'I wondered if you might have any suggestions for a gift I might bring for your parents?'

'Um,' Sasha mused, nerves paralysing her thoughts. 'Well, I'm sure anything will do.' She glanced anxiously over her shoulder. 'We really must get back.' She did not like to mention the fact that she feared what Georgia might be getting up to in her absence and, taking her skirts in both hands, turned about and began to march back to the snowman.

Unfortunately, she was not to know that beneath the snow someone had left a croquet iron; it was against this that her booted foot caught, tripping her up, and she fell headlong and face down into the snow.

'Miss Packard!' Captain Bowen hurried to her side and knelt down as she raised herself up, spluttering and gasping. 'Are you all right?'

Taking a deep, shuddering breath, Sasha brushed off the cold wetness clinging to her face, ignored the offer of his helping hand and rose to her feet. 'I am perfectly all right, thank you.' Stiffly, she walked on, and called out in a tone much like her father when he would countenance no objection, 'Georgia, we must be on our way.'

Her sister, having achieved her objective and realising that she had gone as close to the boundaries of propriety as she dared, made no protest, and quietly picked up her hat and set it upon her head as she walked to her horse. Sasha followed suit and, while Farrell assisted Georgia to mount, Captain Bowen offered his linked hands to Sasha and boosted her up into the saddle. Once the two Packard girls were mounted, he turned to young Felix and gave him a calculating glance before leaping up into the saddle of his own horse.

'I take it you are on foot, Westfaling.'

'Indeed I am.' Felix stared back at him, with a slightly belligerent set to his mouth, elbows akimbo.

'Well, then, I will escort the ladies home.'

'There's no need!' Sasha exclaimed. 'We have Farrell.'

'Of course I must, Miss Packard. I would be failing in my duty as a gentleman if I did not.'

Georgia was having none of this, and with a wink for Felix, she dug her heels in and her horse leapt into a canter towards the park gates, her glance at Captain Bowen clearly challenging with a *catch-me-if-you-can* bravado. Sasha followed after her. It was obvious to him that both the Misses Packard were excellent horsewomen and he set his own horse into a gallop as he went after them, the groom Farrell struggling to urge his lazy hack into a trot and lagging far behind.

'Georgia!' Sasha called, the drumming hoofbeats of their horses smothering her voice.

Her sister thundered on, and only lessened pace as they neared the park gates and she was forced to slow her horse to a trot as they clattered onto the hard surface of the paved road.

'Wait,' Sasha told her sister firmly. 'Captain Bowen will think it extremely rude if we do not let him escort us. I am sure he thinks I am a complete ninny as it is.'

'Oh, don't be so silly, Sasha darling,' scoffed Georgia. 'Besides, does it really matter what Captain Bowen thinks?'

'Yes!' retorted Sasha. 'Yes, actually, it does!'

Georgia was somewhat taken aback by her gentle sister's vehemence, and she glanced back at the fast-approaching Captain Bowen with a thoughtful light in her bold blue eyes. 'Very well, Sasha, we will let him escort us home, and even invite him in for a nice cup of hot chocolate.'

'Oh, but—'

Georgia looked at her with raised brows, her head tilted slightly to one side. 'What, changed your mind? Come now, you can't be blowing hot and then cold in the space of a few seconds.'

'I am not blowing hot! Really, Georgia, you try my patience, you are the most exasperating—' Sasha bit her tongue as Captain Bowen approached, and the girls drew their horses level on either side of him, making a picturesque tableau that drew admiring glances, the two elegantly attired young women on their dappled-grey hunters riding alongside the handsome gentleman astride his big, gleaming bay.

A few moments later they turned into the stable mews near Roseberry Street, and dismounted. Captain Bowen accepted Georgia's invitation and spent a pleasant half-hour in the drawing room enjoying a cup of hot chocolate and the company of ladies, a novel situation for one who had spent years in the rough company of his soldiers in the wilds of the North-West Frontier.

Lady Packard had descended downstairs and was settled on a sofa in the drawing room, near the long window overlooking the gardens to the rear of the house, where she could gaze out and enjoy the warmth of the winter sunshine. A tartan rug covered her legs; she was pale and a little breathless, yet she smiled at Captain Bowen and he soon fell under the spell of her charm and beauty.

'My husband tells me you are posted to St Petersburg,' Olga purred in her sultry, heavily accented voice. 'It is my hometown, you know, I was born and raised there.'

'Indeed, ma'am?' Captain Bowen sat attentively on the edge of his seat, setting the cup of hot chocolate in its saucer as he answered her. 'And you are quite correct, I am due to sail at the end of April, weather permitting.'

'Have you been there before?'

'No, ma'am, I have not had the pleasure.'

'Do you speak Russian?'

'Unfortunately I do not, but the Brigadier has offered to tutor me. I do manage to get by in French, though.'

'Russian is a difficult language, not one that can be learned in a hurry.' Lady Packard frowned, absently stroking her slender white fingers over the tartan of her rug, several ornate and expensive rings glinting. 'I am a little puzzled, then, my dear Captain, as to why you should be sent, having no experience.'

'Oh, Mama,' protested Sasha gently, who sat on the far side of the room near the fireplace, where the light from the front window fell behind her, her figure a silhouette, 'what an embarrassing question.'

Her mother laughed. 'Sasha, dear, I am sure Captain Bowen is made of sterner stuff.'

'Indeed. I am flattered by your interest,' he replied politely, glancing over at Sasha, and then to Georgia, seated to her mother's right and as close to Captain Bowen as she could contrive, flashing her brilliant sapphire eyes at him. 'I believe it may be my experience in Afghanistan that is the chief reason why I have been posted to St Petersburg. The Russians have long been conniving to get a foothold there.'

'And why would they do that?' Sasha asked, intrigued.

He turned slightly to face her, his eyes roaming over her shadowed face as he tried to discern her expression. 'Because, Miss Packard, Afghanistan is close to India, indeed, a crossroads between Europe and Asia, and the routes from one country to the other are much valued, either for trade or war.'

'Oh, I see.' Sasha looked away.

'And do tell us,' Georgia gasped in a breathy voice as she leaned towards him, 'what Mrs Bowen thinks of her imminent removal to such a distant land?'

'Um…' He cleared his throat and looked at his cup. 'Er, there is no Mrs Bowen. I am a bachelor.'

'Oh, pardon me!'

'It's not a disease, darling.' Her mother laughed. 'I do believe you are to join us for dinner on Christmas Eve, Captain Bowen.'

He nodded. 'Thank you, I am looking forward to it.'

'Are you?' Georgia asked, leaning towards him, her eyes soft and moist, inviting, holding his gaze for a moment almost too long beyond the limits of propriety, then her lashes swept down, and she looked away. 'I do so love Christmas, don't you, Captain Bowen? It's a wonderful time of year, all the presents and the tree and the food, and then even better still is New Year. I do so enjoy a good New Year's Eve party, with all the hugging and kissing under the mistletoe.'

'Georgia,' her mother admonished, in a soft voice, laced with mischievous laughter very similar to the sound purring from her daughter's throat.

'Indeed.' Captain Bowen quickly finished his cup of chocolate and set it on a small table, rising to his feet. With a small bow towards Lady Packard, he bade her farewell and gave his thanks.

When he had left and the door closed behind him, Sasha leapt to her feet, exclaiming, 'Oh, Georgia, I am so ashamed of you!'

Her sister looked up with a wide-eyed gasp. 'Goodness, Sash, what on earth have I done?'

With a swish of her skirts Sasha hurried to the door, retorting over her shoulder, 'Oh, you know very well! You were like a cat with a mouse! You are going to toy with him, just like all the others.'

'Rubbish! Why would I?' snorted Georgia with a little toss of her head.

'To make Felix jealous! And just because you are so beautiful, you can!'

'Of course not, darling Sasha.' Georgia smiled, casting a wary, sidelong glance to her frowning mama. 'Anyway, what do you mean? What others?'

'Hamish?'

'Oh, he had red hair and was a terrible bore!'

'I liked him!'

'He was no good for you.'

'Robert.'

'He was French!' Georgia waved her hand in a dismissive gesture.

Sasha rarely lost her temper, but now she made a strangled noise in her throat, her fists clenched. 'Sometimes, Georgia, I absolutely loathe you!'

The drawing-room door banged on her retreat and they could hear her feet pounding as she ran up the stairs. Lady Packard clucked her tongue and gave her daughter Georgia a look that was both a little amused and chastising. Georgia merely shrugged, with raised brows and a demure smile playing on her shapely lips.

In the next few days Captain Bowen was a frequent visitor to Roseberry Street, yet the girls saw little of him, as he spent long hours with the Brigadier in the library, engaged in intensive Russian lessons. Until the day before Christmas Eve, when the Brigadier summoned his daughters to assist him, a not unusual occurrence if he had more than one student. He directed Sasha to sit with Colonel Bellamy and converse with him in French, and Captain Bowen he assigned to Georgia. The two sisters, impeccably dressed in long-sleeved, crêpe de Chine tartan dresses, bustled and bowed, sat down at opposite ends of the room and not for the first time the Brigadier noticed that his eldest two daughters were not on speaking terms. He frowned, hands behind his back as he contemplated Sasha for a moment, and then Georgia, yet he had no idea what ailed them. He returned his grim attention to young Lieutenant Liptrott, whose inability to grasp the basics of either French or Russian would most likely get him killed in some far and foreign land.

Colonel Bellamy, a portly man well into his sixties, sprouting a thick white beard and a monocle from one eye, did not hold much truck with a snippet of a girl trying to educate him on the niceties of the French language. Sasha, too, was not greatly concerned with her charge, her eyes wandering across the room to where Georgia sat with Captain Bowen. They laughed a lot, and Georgia was leaning towards him, touching his arm with her fingers, tossing her blonde head in a most coquettish, annoying manner, Sasha thought. And here she was lumbered with Colonel Bellamy, who clearly would rather be somewhere else, the Officer's Mess, presumably.

'How are we getting on?' The Brigadier stopped by their desk, hands behind his back as he made his enquiry.

'Listen here, old chap—' The Colonel began to remonstrate about his youthful tutor, but he was cut off mid-sentence by the Brigadier.

'Sasha, I wonder if I might have a word?'

'Of course, Papa.' She rose from her seat, with obvious haste and relief.

'Won't be a moment, Colonel.'

'But listen here—' exclaimed the Colonel and then muttered,

'Oh, damn and blast!' What was the point? he fumed inwardly. He might have the advantage of age over Packard, but he was damn well outranked by him!

In a quiet corner of the library, between the heavy curtains and a potted palm, the Brigadier confronted his daughter in his usual direct manner.

'What on earth is going on between you and Georgia?' he asked in a soft voice, his bright blue eyes catching her firmly in their spotlight.

'Nothing, Papa.' Sasha turned her face away and stared out of the window, her eyebrows raised a little defiantly.

'Oh, come now.' Her father was not convinced by this nonchalant denial. 'Something's afoot, you are not speaking a word to each other.'

'I have no idea what you mean.'

'Sasha, tell me at once what is going on!'

'There's nothing going on, Papa.'

'Is it because of that young Felix Westfaling?'

Sasha turned to look at him then, with her dark, soulful eyes so like her mother's, and assured him truthfully, 'No, Papa, it is nothing to do with Felix.'

'Aha! I knew it, there is something afoot.'

'Papa, I really must get back to Colonel Bellamy, he looks fit to burst like a Christmas cracker, and liable to pounce on poor Lieutenant Liptrott at any moment.'

Her father turned then, and with a sigh hurried off to rescue the young cavalryman from a nasty verbal volley. The Brigadier realised that nothing more could be achieved on this afternoon when thoughts were wandering to the Christmas festivities and goodness knew what else. He dismissed the class, with a stern reminder to practise their vocabulary and to return in the New Year. As the three gentleman left, the Brigadier called out, 'Georgia, wait a moment, if you please. Close the door behind you, Sasha.'

Sasha did as her father asked and turned to find Captain

Bowen hovering, and he fell into step with her as they walked to the front of the house. He spoke a few faltering words of farewell in Russian, and she turned, with a smile, answering him in the same language. In the hallway, as Lodge handed him his coat and hat, Captain Bowen bowed to Sasha.

'Your Russian is much better than your sister's.'

'Thank you, kind sir.' She smiled, her hands clasped as she waited for him to depart, but he seemed in no hurry to go. He was quite tall; she had to tilt her head back to look up at him, and the late afternoon sun beaming in through the glass fanlight above the front door gilded his blond hair and shone a light in his dark blue eyes. He was certainly a most handsome man, she sighed inwardly, watching as he shrugged on his coat over broad shoulders.

'I shall see you all tomorrow evening, then.'

'Oh?' Sasha frowned, puzzled.

'Christmas Eve,' he reminded her.

'Of course.' She felt her cheeks heat with a pink blush, and wondered why she always made the impression, with this man, of being a ninny.

'Goodbye, Miss Packard.'

'Goodbye, Captain Bowen.'

He bowed and walked to the door, and then turned back and called out in Russian, 'Until tomorrow.'

She smiled and nodded. *'Da.'* Her heart was aflutter, hardly daring to believe that a man like Captain Bowen would even look at her. Not when Georgia was about.

Christmas was always a special occasion in the Packard home, and that afternoon on the Eve the four sisters spent a happy few hours decorating a magnificent tree in the hallway, despite the frosty relations between Sasha and Georgia, who, beneath their father's watchful, frowning gaze, made the pretence that all was well between them. The house smelled pleasantly of pine, roasting turkey and plum pudding, and great boughs of holly and ivy were strewn in garlands about the walls and stairs and over the mantel of the fireplace. The girls had decorated oranges with cloves and ribbons to make fragrant pomanders, and hung them all about the drawing room and hallway. Presents had been wrapped and placed under the tree and by four o'clock they had hurried to their rooms to dress for the evening's festivities.

When Sasha came downstairs, wearing an emerald-green, off-the-shoulder evening gown and her hair swept elegantly up, she went into the drawing room and checked that all was ready for their guests. A great silver punchbowl with mulled red wine steamed gently by the dancing flames of the fireplace, and a table covered with a snowy-white cloth was being stacked by one of the maids with plates of fresh-baked mince pies, and small silver dishes of dried figs, nuts and pink Turkish delight.

The Brigadier carried his wife downstairs and settled her on the chaise longue near the fire, with a rug over her lap. If it was up to him, he was quite content to spend the evening with just himself and the girls. Yet he knew how Olga loved company and so he had invited a dozen friends to dinner, including Avery Westfaling, to whom he was distantly related, although he had little liking for his wife and offspring. Lady Westfaling had a doubtful pedigree and he considered her to be a loose woman, and her son certainly seemed to have inherited her less attractive traits, being fickle and vain. Why, the boy would squander his inheritance before he was thirty and no daughter of his was going to get involved with a fellow like that!

The guests began to arrive bearing gifts, and the sisters were taking turns to receive these and place them under the Christmas tree in the hallway. The drawing room was warm and noisy with the gathering, the hubbub of chattering voices interspersed with laughter. Olga was surrounded by her favourite friends, who remarked on how well she looked and would she soon be out in the park taking the air? The Brigadier and Sasha hovered nearby, anxious that she not be overexerted by the evening. When Lodge came in to announce that dinner was served, Olga refused to be carried, insisting that she could manage to walk the few steps down the corridor to the dining room.

The long table was beautifully set, with a white tablecloth, silver candelabra, sparkling cut-crystal wine glasses and a splendid centrepiece of winter fruit, berries and flowers. Olga had deliberated long and carefully over the seating, and she had placed herself and the Brigadier at either end with Sasha seated next to Felix, Georgia next to Captain Bowen, Philippa beside the son of a Scottish friend and Victoria, still very young, between Percy and another friend she knew well. They were eighteen sitting down, and Olga looked down the table as she sat at one end, her gaze pausing on each of her daughters, a proud glow adding to her satisfaction.

Sasha was disgruntled about the dinner partner she had been placed with, but she enjoyed herself far more than expected. Felix was in a good mood and she could not help but laugh at his jokes and silly conversation; really, he was such a featherbrain that it was no wonder he and Georgia were so drawn to each other. Like two peas in a pod, they were. She glanced down the table at Georgia as she sat next to Captain Bowen. She thought her sister seemed a little pensive, and she wondered what her father had said to Georgia in the library yesterday. Glancing down the table as she finished her salmon pâté, she noticed that Georgia was listening attentively to Captain Bowen, but was not her usual bright and bubbly self. Sasha felt a pang, and made up her mind to bury the hatchet and make amends with Georgia as soon as possible. Why, there was no man on earth worthy of coming between sisters!

After dinner they returned to the drawing room, where Sasha sat down at the piano and played Christmas carols, the guests gathering around and singing in good voice, liberally loosened by the fine wines enjoyed over dinner. They played charades, enjoyed coffee and mince pies, and then those who were willing to accompany the family to midnight mass donned their coats.

They were a mere few, the Westfalings, except for the son, and most others, declining and departing for their warms beds at home. So it was only Felix, Uncle Percy, Captain Bowen and two fellow officers who accompanied the Brigadier and his two eldest daughters to church, while the officers' wives and the two younger girls stayed behind to keep Olga company.

The Church of St Ann was not far, and they walked in muffled silence, well wrapped up in coats, scarves, hats and gloves. The church bells of St Ann's clanged with dull resonance amidst a fine flurry of snow drifting through the darkness, blanketing the night. The double doors stood open, welcoming the faithful, a golden light spilling out on the street. The vicar's wife was handing out hymn books as they entered, and then they followed the Brigadier to the front of the church, and Sasha found herself standing between her father and Captain Bowen, the former frowning and twisting about to see where Georgia had got to. She was in a pew several rows to the rear, near the door, standing with Felix with as angelic a look upon her face as the alabaster figurine of Mary in the Nativity scene to one side of the altar. Sasha sensed her father's wrath rise rapidly, and she put a soothing hand on his sleeve. But with Captain Bowen standing so close, neither of them could utter a censorious word.

The organ creaked and groaned into the first hymn, and Sasha fumbled to find the page. She was a little short-sighted and peered at the board hanging on one pillar, the numbers slightly blurred.

'Number fifty-two,' Captain Bowen whispered in her ear, leaning down.

She flashed a smile of thanks and then found the page and began to sing. Beside her she noticed that the Captain had a very pleasant baritone voice, and not too loud, unlike her father, who consistently embarrassed his daughters as he bellowed out hymns, tone deaf and oblivious to that fact. She noticed, too, that her father was not the only one glancing over his shoulder at Georgia, and it irked her that Captain Bowen should be so easily smitten by her sister's shallow charms. She began to rapidly revise her intentions about making up with Georgia, but relented as the vicar's sermon rattled on about Christmas being a time for forgiveness and new beginnings.

After the service, the congregation exchanged greetings and well wishes.

'Happy Christmas.' Captain Bowen leaned down and kissed Sasha on the cheek.

She thought how nice he smelled, how warm his face felt against her own as his lips quickly brushed her cheek, the hint of bronze stubble on his jaw a rough and yet not unpleasant sensation. Then she turned to her father and hugged him, wishing him happy Christmas, too, and she followed him as they filed out of the church. Georgia was waiting on the steps for them, but Felix had melted away into the night. The Brigadier said nothing, merely accepted Georgia's wishes, her voice and her eyes apprehensive, and then the party trudged through the thick snow back to the house.

Though the hour was late, they gathered in the drawing room for welcome cups of hot chocolate, the men lacing theirs with brandy. With fewer guests, and those being close friends and family, there was a more relaxed air. Victoria sat in her slippers in front of the hearth, at the foot of her mother's sofa, and Uncle Percy loosened his bow tie as he sat back in an armchair. Feigning a snooze, he watched his nephew, and the delightful Georgia, and the equally charming, though entirely different, Sasha. At last the party came to an end, the Brigadier hinting that his wife was very tired and wishing them all a very happy Christmas Day as he waved the guests goodbye from the front door.

Reid and his uncle settled in their seats as their carriage took off, the light and warmth of Roseberry Street a loss they both felt as they plunged into the dark streets.

'Do stay the night, Reid, no sense in continuing across

London to your mess rooms. Besides, you would only need to come back again in a few hours for lunch.'

Reid laughed, and nodded his agreement. 'Very well, Uncle, as you wish.'

After a few moments' silence Uncle Percy said, 'Charming people, the Packards. Did you enjoy yourself?'

'They are, indeed, and, yes, I enjoyed a very pleasant evening.'

'Superb meal.'

Reid nodded, and glanced sideways. 'Is there something on your mind, Uncle?'

'Indeed.' He hesitated for a brief moment. 'Charming girls, Georgia and Sasha.'

'They are.'

'Made up your mind yet which one of 'em you want?'

Laughing, Reid shook his head. 'I don't believe I have.'

Uncle Percy made a grunting noise. 'I noticed young Felix Westfaling sniffing around Georgia. I'd pop the question to her fairly soon, before the rascal snaps her up.'

'He'd have to get past the Brigadier first, and somehow I don't think Westfaling is up to the job.'

His uncle made another throaty rumble of disapproval. 'Well, time is marching on, dear boy, time is marching on.'

Chapter Three

Sasha retired to her bedroom, weary and yet glowing pleasantly after the enjoyable evening. She undressed and put on her nightgown, sitting down on the edge of her bed to brush out her long dark hair when she heard a small sound. Her hand hesitated, as it swept downwards, and then she rose from the bed and crept to the closed door connecting her room and Georgia's. Placing her ear close to the panels, she listened and heard the soft, muffled sounds of weeping. Quietly, Sasha opened the door and hurried to her sister, who lay prostrate across her bed, crying bitterly. She knelt and laid her hand on Georgia's shoulder, asking gently, 'Dearest, whatever is the matter?'

'Oh, Sasha!' Turning around, Georgia threw herself into Sasha's embrace, sobbing against her shoulder, all thoughts of rivalry banished. 'Papa has forbidden me to see Felix again. Not ever!'

'Shh,' Sasha soothed, stroking her sister's hair. 'What do you mean, he's forbidden you? Is that why he asked to speak to you in the library?'

Georgia nodded, disengaging herself and mopping at her eyes, sniffing loudly. 'Papa says he is very disappointed with me and this "association" with Felix must cease at once. Apparently Captain Bowen has mentioned our little meeting in the park, and then tonight Papa did not approve of me sitting with Felix in church and he gave me another telling off.' With a gulp, Georgia began to cry again. 'Oh, Sasha, how can I bear it? I do love him so!'

Sasha rose from the floor and sat down on the bed next to her. 'Of course you do, he is the best of fathers and is always wise about our welfare.'

'Not Papa!' wailed Georgia. 'Felix! I love Felix! I couldn't bear to live without him!'

Inwardly Sasha sighed, nonplussed in the face of Georgia's stubbornness. She had no doubt that their papa was right and that Georgia's attachment to Felix would have to end, sooner or later. She was fairly certain that Felix did not have any plans for marriage and Georgia would only have her heart broken. Picking up her sister's hand, she stroked the back of it, her voice soft and gently encouraging. 'I know it hurts, but with time you will forget all about Felix. Just as you thought Hamish wasn't any good for me, so Papa is convinced that Felix isn't any good for you.' Glancing at Georgia, she could see the doubt and confusion warring on her face, blotchy red from crying but still beautiful, and hurried to press on. 'Why don't you try, just for a little while? Test how strong your feelings really are for Felix, and his for you? Why don't you do as Papa asks, just for now, and—' though she felt a little stab of pain herself at her own words, she ventured onwards '—and maybe even enjoy the attentions of Captain Bowen.'

'Oh, that man! I hate him! Conniving, sneaky wretch!'

'He seems to like you.' Sasha hoped the painful note in her voice was not apparent.

With a little disparaging snort Georgia shook her head and turned up her nose.

Gently Sasha persisted, as always putting her sister first before her own feelings and desires, adding gently, 'He's a reputable man, and very handsome.'

'Felix is much better looking.'

'Captain Bowen would make a good husband.'

'He's too old.'

'Only thirty-three.'

Dabbing her nose on a square of lawn handkerchief, more in command of herself now, Georgia retorted, 'Well, if he's so wonderful, why don't you marry him?'

That little stab of pain somewhere in the region of her heart was now suddenly more intense, but Sasha merely lowered her eyelashes and refrained from admitting that if she could, she would, replying softly, 'Come now, Georgia, it would do Felix no harm at all if you kept your distance for a few weeks. Let Captain Bowen pay court to you.'

'No, never!'

'Don't make any judgements, dearest, just sit back and let whatever happens, happen. You never know, you might be able to look at things differently then.'

Georgia was not entirely convinced, yet with more gentle persuasion Sasha at last secured a promise from her sister that, just for a few weeks, she would not engineer any secret meetings with Felix. For all her faults and failings, Georgia always kept her word.

Once Christmas Day and Boxing Day were over—quiet family affairs spent opening presents and visiting relatives— there came a few days of rest before the hectic round of balls and dinner parties to see out the old year and welcome in the new. Captain Bowen singled Georgia out at many of these parties, dancing with her frequently, sitting with her in between and talking. They did seem to enjoy each other's company, Sasha noticed, watching as Georgia laughed, not with the same exuberance as she would with Felix, but perhaps it was high time that Georgia acquired some maturity and capped her youthful effervescence into a less fizzy yet just as delightful charm.

Though Captain Bowen was equally polite to her, Sasha, and

danced one or two dances and entered into conversation with her, he did not make her the object of his pursuit. It became obvious to her, and others, that Captain Bowen was courting her sister. She could not at once understand the feelings that jolted her, and thought that the unpleasant sense of envy would quickly evaporate, for how could she not be happy for her sister to be courted by such an eligible bachelor? Why, he was such a contrast to Felix, who was young, fickle, had dark rumours attached to his name regarding the dismissal and unexpected pregnancy of a young governess and only seemed to bring out the worst in Georgia. No, indeed, Sasha mused, Captain Bowen would steady Georgia and be a good influence on her.

On a Sunday afternoon at the end of January, after several weeks of calling, escorting Georgia to the park, the theatre, dances and dinner parties, after luncheon had been cleared and the gentlemen had retired to the library, Captain Bowen asked permission of the Brigadier to marry his daughter. He quietly agreed.

Yet it was not until Valentine's Day that Captain Bowen called upon Georgia, bringing her the obligatory bouquet of roses and a box of chocolates, and formally asked her to marry him.

They were in the conservatory, and the Brigadier had deliberately allowed them to be alone, having waited some two weeks now for an announcement, and a small furrow of anxiety had begun to crease his brow at the lack of one. It was a bright day, the sunshine slanting through the glass and the aroma of orchids and potted palms pleasant enough in the warm humidity of the conservatory. Yet Georgia stood by a window and looked out, her face sombre, her eyes straying across the rooftops of London, to a place far away and only seen in her most private thoughts.

'Georgia?' Captain Bowen took a step towards her, a diamond engagement ring clutched in his fist.

After a long moment, she turned around and gave him a sorrowful glance.

'Well?' he prompted. 'Will you?'

Her silence was unusual, then she smiled and looked up at him, 'Are you sure you have asked the right sister, Captain Bowen?'

'What?' He frowned.

'Have you not considered that Sasha would make you a much better wife than I?'

'I— I—' The self-assured soldier was momentarily confused. It was not the response he had been expecting.

'Sasha is clever, she's brave and always knows just how to behave. Do you not think Sasha is quite attractive?'

Captain Bowen squared his shoulders, and thought he understood Georgia's hesitation. The sisters were very close, and he had given some of his attention to Sasha, perhaps causing some confusion. He took a step closer to Georgia, raised her chin with his thumb and forefinger, telling her quite firmly, 'You are a very beautiful young woman. You're strong, intelligent and resourceful. That is why I have chosen you, and I assure you, Georgia, that it *is* you that I want.'

Suddenly anxious that he was about to make protestations of love and kiss her, Georgia pulled away. She returned to her former stance by the window, looking out, her eyes lifted to the blue of the heavens. What use was offering up another prayer, when none of the others had been answered? Felix had been furious when she had ignored him, flirting with several other eligible young ladies, and she had heard on the grapevine that he had taken himself off to his family estate in Scotland to do some shooting. She had wanted to contact him, by letter or telegram, but Sasha had insisted that it was out of the question, not becoming of a lady or some such nonsense. She had thought Felix would soon come back to her, would perhaps even challenge Captain Bowen's suit, but it seemed he had not loved her as much as she thought. His mama had quite loudly announced at a luncheon of his intention to stay in Scotland for some long while, something to do with the novel idea of establishing a whisky distillery on the family estate and how good it would be for him away from any 'distractions'. The only option now was to forget all about Felix, and change her life for ever, so that nothing would be the same and there would be no memory of happiness to break her heart. She turned then, impulsively taking a deep breath, and held out her hand. 'Very well, Captain Bowen. I will marry you.'

He breathed a sigh of relief, and promptly slid the very expensive diamond-and-gold ring on her finger. He leaned down to kiss her, aiming for her mouth, but at the last moment she moved aside and his lips landed on her cheek. She pulled away and though he would not have credited Georgia Packard as being coy, he felt it only natural for a young lady to be slightly overwhelmed by a proposal and acceptance of marriage.

He filled the awkward moment by saying, 'Shall we tell your family?'

Georgia nodded, and they walked together to the drawing room, her arm linked through the crook of his. The family were all expectantly gathered and the moment they walked through the door Lady Packard glanced at the glinting diamond on her daughter's finger and gave a little cry, holding open her arms to embrace the supposedly happy couple. The Brigadier shook hands with his future son-in-law, and Georgia's sisters all came to give her a kiss and hug of congratulations. Sasha held her a moment longer than necessary, and drew back slightly to look at her sister keenly. In reply to the unspoken question in Sasha's dark eyes, Georgia merely smiled.

'We shall go at once and call upon the vicar,' said the Brigadier, striding to the door, and then paused for a moment as he eyed Captain Bowen. 'I trust you have no objection that Georgia is married from her own home and at the Church of St Ann?'

'No, sir, of course not. I have no family of my own, apart from Uncle Percy. My parents and my elder brother all died in a sailing accident off the Isle of Wight when I was a young boy.'

The Brigadier stared at his feet and murmured his condolences, then he looked up and said in a brighter tone, 'I gather your plans to sail for St Petersburg at the end of April still hold fast?'

'Indeed. It has been impressed upon me by the Foreign Office that I should not fail to make that sailing. They are expecting me at the Embassy as soon as may be.'

'Very good. That means we have just under two months to plan this wedding.' The Brigadier almost rubbed his hands with glee, relishing the challenge of achieving a tricky objective and clearly about to apply all his military expertise to the task.

Sasha and Georgia exchanged a nervous glance, yet already the wheels of a fast-moving train were greased and rolling into action. They were all aboard and as the days flew swiftly by and the train picked up speed, it seemed impossible for anyone to even think about jumping off.

That night it was Sasha who lay upon her bed and cried, but her tears were silent ones that dripped from the corners of her eyes and soaked unseen into her pillow. She chided and reminded herself that it had never been a reality that Captain Bowen would desire her, merely her own little fantasy. Now was no time to be moping and feeling sorry for herself; she knew how much Georgia, strangely pale and listless for a bride-to-be, would need her love and support in the next few weeks.

Georgia would be married at eleven o'clock on the twenty-ninth of April. After the wedding ceremony there would be a luncheon in the Officer's Mess of the Light Dragoons for a hundred guests, and then the happy couple would depart for their ship and set sail for Russia on the evening tide.

The invitations were ordered and sent without delay, and Lady Packard set about enjoying herself as she had not done for many years, poring over dressmaker patterns for Georgia's wedding gown, choosing the material, the ribbons and pearls, the shoes, the veil, and stockings and garter, even the nightgown Georgia would wear to bed. She chose the flowers for the church, posies of pink tulips, cream carnations, baby's breath and ivy to decorate the pew ends, and several large and lavish floral displays to stand on either side of the altar. The colour theme was cream, pink and lilac, which Sasha pointed out would clash horribly with Captain Bowen's bright red military mess dress. Her mother merely shrugged, murmuring that there would be many guests in different military uniforms and they could not be expected to colour coordinate for all of them, surely?

The sisters would all be Georgia's bridesmaids, and their gowns, in palest pink, were also made by the French seamstress creating the bride's. The wedding cake was ordered, five tiers of ornately decorated rich fruit cake, the champagne and the food agreed with the Officer's Mess, *bon-bonnières* of fine net and sugared almonds ordered as gifts for the ladies on the tables, and hymns were agreed with the organist at the church.

The days melted one into the other, and it alarmed Georgia how quickly time seemed to fly. The dark cold days of winter had ended and there was now a warmth and brightness to each day, the evenings more pleasant as dusk lingered, and the gardens were brightened by shy snowdrops and nodding yellow daffodils. Captain Bowen called less frequently, much to Georgia's relief, and when he did suggest a ride in the park, or lunch at a nearby hotel, she always made sure that Sasha came along, too. He seemed much preoccupied with his forthcoming posting to Russia, and now that he had settled the matter of a wife, he saw no need to make a nuisance of himself. Sasha was somewhat chagrined to watch as the now-engaged couple seemed to have little to say to one another. She did not like to mention to Georgia that surely there should be some emotion if she was to spend the rest of her life with this man, share his bed and give birth to his children. Yet she could not say such a thing to Georgia, all too aware how fragile she was, and how much she pined for Felix. On most nights she could hear the telltale sniffs and nose-blowing that indicated Georgia was weeping in the privacy of her own bedroom. She ached for her sister, and there were many moments when she felt guilty for persuading her to allow Captain Bowen to court her.

It was very true that he was a good man, they had no evidence to suggest otherwise, and he was indeed very pleasing to look at, with his blond hair, blue eyes, firm chin and jaw, intelligent brow and his firm yet sensual mouth. Sasha sighed, forcing herself not to think about Captain Reid Bowen, soon to be her sister's husband. Once they were married, all would be well; Georgia would be happy and would forget all about that Felix Westfaling. Though Sasha feared that it would take her much longer to forget about Captain Bowen; already he was part of her thoughts and had found a place in her heart. She tried to remind herself that it was wrong and sinful to have such feelings for a man who would soon be her sister's husband, yet this did nothing to soothe the ache in her heart, aching for a love that she had hoped would blossom between her and this Captain.

On the eve of the wedding, a quiet sense of expectation descended upon the household. There was a hush, as at last all the hasty preparations had been accomplished and all that remained was for the great day to dawn. Gowns hung on cupboard doors, uniforms pressed and medals polished. The sweet scent of flowers filled the air, and the house was full of guests from all over the country.

No one seemed to notice that both the bride and her chief bridesmaid were afflicted by a sense of melancholy and had retired early to their bedchambers. Georgia could not bear all the hearty congratulations and the knowing looks as everyone wished her good luck for the next day, and she went to her room to nurse her sense of impending doom in private. Sasha, too, found the company hard to take; it was much easier to bear her aching heart in solitude. As she sat on the window seat in her bedroom, gazing up at the stars and the pearly glow of a half-moon, she reflected on how she would get through tomorrow and not reveal by so much as a word or a glance how much she envied Georgia: Georgia, the beautiful golden girl, her personality like champagne, bubbly and intoxicating and hard to resist; Georgia, who did not even seem to appreciate how lucky she was and that from tomorrow onwards, for the rest of her life, she would never be alone again. Georgia would awaken every day to the warmth and comfort of Reid lying beside her, in whose arms she would experience the joy of passion. Georgia would have his help in all matters of daily life, and she would have his friendship and companionship simply by mere virtue of being his wife.

Sasha swallowed back another wave of tears, just as a knock sounded upon her door, followed quickly by the entrance of Victoria and Philippa, bearing a dish of purloined marzipan fruits and chocolate peppermints. They giggled and Victoria went to fetch Georgia, who reluctantly allowed herself to be towed in.

With a smile Sasha descended from the window seat and went to join her sisters on the bed. All four girls gathered close together in a circle around the dish of sweets, their nightgowns billowing in a froth of white muslin, long unbound hair swirling in shades of gold and sable, richly glossy against the pale skin of their slender arms. The two younger girls were full of excitement for the drama of the big day—The Wedding—talked about and planned and anticipated constantly in these weeks past. And there was burning curiosity in their round eyes as they looked at Georgia.

Victoria blushed, leaning closer as she whispered in confidence, 'What do you think it will be like?'

Georgia frowned as she licked chocolate from her fingertips. 'What?'

'You know.' Victoria giggled. 'It!'

Philippa snorted and buried her face in the bedcovers as she stifled her laughter, and then she lifted her head and asked, 'Has Mama said anything?'

Seeing the look of puzzlement on Georgia's face, Sasha admonished the two younger girls. 'Leave her be.'

'Oh, Georgia, you are so lucky!' sighed Victoria, rolling onto her back and gazing up at the canopy of the bed. 'I couldn't imagine anyone nicer than Captain Bowen to be surrendering my bloomers too!'

'I don't think it's just her bloomers he's interested in.' The earthy Philippa grinned.

The two girls shrieked, drumming their heels as they laughed in a most unlady-like way, and Sasha gave them each a playful slap as Georgia suddenly went scarlet, the full understanding of what it meant to be married dawning on her. A most peculiar noise erupted from her throat, and Georgia burst into tears, flounced from the bed and ran to her room, slamming the door shut behind her. Her sisters exclaimed, mortified at what they had done and making to rush after her, but Sasha firmly stopped them, pulling them both back.

'Let her alone,' she insisted, picking up the empty dish and placing it on a table. 'Now, you two, off to bed. The sooner you go to sleep, the sooner the day will be here.'

With little squeals of excitement Victoria and Philippa hurried away to their room, and with a sigh of relief Sasha closed her door. Then she tiptoed to Georgia's door and knocked gently on it.

'Georgie, are you all right?'

'Go away!'

'Shall I come in?'

'No, just go away and leave me alone.'

Sasha stood and listened for a few moments to the sounds of muffled weeping, then with a regretful little grimace she went to her own bed and climbed beneath the covers. She lay awake for a while, anxiously wondering if she should try again to go in to Georgia, or maybe it was best to leave her to some peace and privacy…

When Sasha awoke next it was still dark, but a sound had disturbed her from the depths of her dreams. She opened her eyes and gazed about, her glance straying to the curtained window. There was no glimmer of daylight and there was still the heavy hush of night about the house. Yet her ears had been alerted to strange noises, and she listened, her breath tensely held—a bump, and a thump, and the low murmur of voices.

Sasha sat up, swinging her bare feet out of bed, pausing, listening keenly. With a small intake of breath, as alarm bells rang, she jumped out of bed and ran to Georgia's bedroom door, along the way seizing her heavy silver-backed hairbrush as a weapon. She flung the door open and was ready to strike the unknown assailant, her arm upraised, when a startled Georgia and Felix Westfaling turned to stare at her.

'Oh, damn!' exclaimed Felix, setting down two Moroccan leather portmanteaus on the floor and raising placating hands towards Sasha. 'Now listen here, old girl...'

Sasha noticed at once that Georgia was fully dressed; indeed, she was shrugging on her dark wool coat with the fox-fur trim over her going-away outfit of sapphire silk.

'What on earth!' Sasha exclaimed, her eyes flitting between the frozen couple, who stared back at her with guilty, nervous eyes.

Then Georgia came rushing towards her. 'Oh, Sash, please, do be quiet! I beg you, do not give us away.'

Sasha lowered her arm and stared at them. 'What's going on? Felix, how did you get in here? We thought you were in Scotland.'

Felix shrugged, with a defensive frown. 'I've been lurking in the back alley all day and bribed Farrell to let me in through the servants' door in the mews. He took pity on us—the servants don't miss a thing, believe you me. I came back when my mama wrote to tell me about Georgia getting married to that Bowen chap.' He glanced at his beloved with a sheepish smile. 'Only wish I'd come to my senses and got back sooner.'

Her sister grasped both of her hands and gushed an explanation. 'Felix and I are running away. We are going to Gretna

Green to be married and then to Paris for a wonderful honeymoon! Papa gave me all my travelling papers last night, so I can go anywhere in the world that I want to!'

'Oh, no, you're not!' exclaimed Sasha. 'Have you gone completely mad, Georgia? You are getting married in the morning to Captain Bowen, it's all arranged, everyone will be there, everyone expects—'

'No!' said Georgia vehemently, almost stamping her foot, her mouth set in a mulish line. 'I don't love Captain Bowen and I don't want to marry him! I won't! In a few days' time I will be twenty-one and can do as I please.'

'But—'

Felix came towards them, his arm curling around Georgia's waist. 'Now listen here, Sash, old girl, you know I'm besotted with Georgia. Can't bear to see her getting hitched to another chap, just not the right thing, not the right thing at all.'

'But—'

'Oh, Sasha, darling, please, please, I beg you, don't say anything, just let us get away.'

'But—'

'Better get a move on, Georgie, before someone notices the hansom cab lurking in the mews and starts getting nosy,' Felix urged.

As the couple hastened to pick up their bags, Sasha suddenly ran to the door and blocked their path. 'Georgia, no, I can't let you do this! Have you thought this through? You know how impulsive you can be! Why, tomorrow the church will be full of people and Captain Bowen will be left standing there like a complete fool!'

Georgia sighed, and then tugged the diamond engagement ring off her finger and pressed it into Sasha's palm, firmly closing her fingers over it. 'Tell him I'm sorry, but—but, well, just say I'm sorry.'

'I'll do no such thing! Tell him yourself!'

'Come now, Sash, old girl, out of the way, we really must get going,' Felix said, in a soft voice that held a thread of steel in its depths.

Sasha looked at him in surprise, hardly believing that fun-loving Felix was capable of a serious thought for longer than a blink of an eye. The cold hard contours of gold and diamond seemed to burn into her hand, and she asked, looking him directly in the eye, 'Tell me, Felix, do you love Georgia?'

'Yes,' he answered quietly, returning her gaze unwaveringly. 'I do, very much, and I promise that I will look after her.'

Sasha wavered then, as he turned to smile at Georgia, and she saw in that one glance how much they adored each other. How could she stand in the way of her sister's happiness, when it was so obvious that this was what she truly wanted?

'Are you sure, Georgia?' she asked again, desperate to ascertain that this was no mere whim on her sister's part and that she understood all the consequences, 'Captain Bowen will be so hurt; he's such a lovely man, so strong and kind and handsome.'

'Oh?' Felix bristled, with a disgruntled thrust of his lower lip.

Georgia clicked her tongue in annoyance. 'Oh, please do stop, Sash, it will do no good, I've made up my mind. Goodness, if you feel that way, why don't you marry him?'

With a sharp intake of breath, Georgia and Felix looked at each other, suddenly taken by the merits of an excellent plan.

'Splendid idea!' exclaimed Felix, dropping his voice as Georgia quickly hushed him, glancing nervously about. 'Always thought the two of you made a fine-looking pair.'

'Oh, do,' Georgia gasped. 'What a perfectly perfect solution. No one would be any wiser and once you are safely on board ship to Russia it will be far too late to do anything about it. And no one would think to be looking for us—' Georgia glanced slyly at her sister '—and you have to admit, Sash, you are smitten with the man. And he's probably smitten with you, but just doesn't know it yet.'

Sasha shook her head, wondering if she should laugh or cry,

and quite speechless for words. Then, as her senses returned, she glared at Georgia and retorted, 'Why, you really are the most selfish, conniving, manipulative little minx—'

'Steady on, Sash!' Felix objected, a frown marring his brow at this maligning of his much beloved.

With her own brows sceptically arched, Sasha asked, 'And how exactly am I to accomplish this feat? Marrying my sister's bridegroom, that is? Do you think that Captain Bowen will be so overcome by the joys of his wedding day that he will not notice that his bride is slightly shorter than he remembered? And has dark hair instead of blond? Brown eyes instead of blue?'

'Oh, with that ridiculous Spanish-lace veil he won't be able to see a thing,' scoffed Georgia. 'And our feet are the same size, so you can borrow my shoes with the two-inch heels. I am sure he won't notice.'

'Until it's too late,' interjected Felix.

'Far too late,' Georgia agreed.

'And what about at the end of the marriage ceremony, when the vicar says you may kiss the bride?' There was now a heavy note of sarcasm in Sasha's voice, and she felt as though she had stumbled into one of her own dreams, for surely none of this could be real? 'What do I do then?'

'Oh, I don't know, pretend you have a cold or something!'

'And at the reception?'

'Overcome by nerves,' suggested Felix. 'Come along, Georgie, the train for Edinburgh leaves in an hour. We really must go.'

Georgia suddenly embraced her sister, and kissed her on the cheek. 'Goodbye, darling, and thank you.'

'For what?'

'For helping us.'

'I didn't say that I would.'

Georgia smiled, hugging Sasha one last time and smugly replied, 'Oh, but you will, darling Sasha, I know you will.'

And with that, Felix and Georgia departed. The door closed.

She listened pensively to their muffled footfalls, until there was
only silence, followed by the sudden clip-clop of a carriage passing in the street. Sasha ran light-footed to the window, thrust
back the heavy brocade curtain and peered out, catching a mere
glimpse of the hackney carriage bearing Felix and Georgia. It
was cold by the window, and she drew back, pulling the curtain into place. With a shiver she hurried to her own room and
climbed back into bed, pulling the covers high up around her
ears and curling into a ball, her knees drawn up to her waist.

For a while she could not think of anything at all, and stared
blankly into the dark, the first glimmer of dawn just beginning
to touch the window. Then she felt the small round object in the
palm of her hand and opened it, staring at the diamond engagement ring Georgia had relinquished.

A sudden stab of panic and alarm sent goosebumps rippling
over her skin, as Sasha contemplated the débâcle that would
be tomorrow—no, this morning, the great day, The Wedding
Day. Damn Georgia! How could she? How could she do this to
them? To Captain Bowen? She drew in a painful breath as she
wondered just how to tell him. Or should she go to her father and
let him do the nasty deed? Yes, yes, she decided with a sigh of
relief, Papa would handle it all quite admirably. With the matter
settled, Sasha wriggled and snuggled down to sleep, but it was
not long before her lashes flew open and she was again brooding
on the impending doom about to fall upon her family.

It was no use, she couldn't possibly go back to sleep with all
these thoughts raging inside her mind. With a sigh Sasha sat
up, holding her head in her hands as she sat cross-legged in the
bed, her thoughts roaming this way and that. She imagined that
Georgia was most probably boarding her train for Scotland now,
totally oblivious to anything except her own happiness.

Poor Captain Bowen. Would he be very heartbroken?

Would Mama have a fit of the vapours in church, as they
stood waiting expectantly for the bride to appear and walk up
the aisle?

Would Papa have a stroke at the shame of it all? With a gasp she wondered if he would go charging after Felix, no doubt armed with his pair of revolvers. Good God, Papa might even shoot him! Captain Bowen was a soldier, too—why, he might even join Papa and shoot Felix, as well! Sasha pressed a hand to her mouth as she envisaged murder and mayhem in the days to follow.

Unless…she did as Georgia had suggested. She could quite literally step into Georgia's shoes, and the wedding would go ahead, no one any the wiser. All would be as it should be, the bride would arrive on her father's arm, and she would marry the groom. There would be peace and happiness. What had Georgia said? '…*a perfectly perfect solution.*' Sasha's lip trembled as she contemplated such an audacious plan. Could it be done? Would she, could she, possibly have the nerve to carry it off? Sasha chewed her lip, and surmised that it would only be for a day or two, until Georgia and Felix were married, just to keep the peace and avoid a tragic family scandal. For a moment or two she wondered how Reid would react and how it would affect his posting to St Petersburg. Did he desperately need to have a wife at his side? Surely it would not matter one way or another; besides, once he got to the Embassy and the Russian court there were bound to be plenty of beautiful young ladies only too willing to become his bride.

Certainly Georgia's madcap suggestion that she marry Reid in her place was going to be difficult to achieve, but in the circumstances she could see no other solution, none that would not bring dishonour and disgrace on both Reid, Georgia and the Packard family.

Climbing out of bed again, Sasha tiptoed into Georgia's bedroom. She lit a candle and then opened the door of the dressing room to stand and gaze at the spectacular frothy white creation of Georgia's wedding gown. She felt the blood drain from her face as she wondered if she would indeed be able to fit into it. Georgia most definitely had a bigger bosom, but no doubt she could pad the bodice out with a few stockings if it gaped. And the hem would be too long, yet there was no time to alter it. But she could wear the shoes with the two-inch heels; with that in mind, she searched through the shoe rack until she found them. They were beige silk and did not exactly go with the dress, but with the length of it she hoped that no one would notice anyway.

The plan began to form, and one link led to another as she hurried about in an attempt to cover every possibility. She made sure Georgia's door was locked, as well as her own, and when Polly came knocking she would pretend that Georgia had had an attack of the nerves and would see no one except her own sister, Sasha. And then she would have to dash out and convince Mama that she would not be able to attend the wedding; after all, it would be impossible to play both bride and bridesmaid at the same time. But what possible excuse would Mama tolerate on this, the grandest day of her year, her life even? A cold or headache would not be enough, she was sure; it would have to be something nasty, something contagious.

She had an idea and hurried to Georgia's dressing table, reaching for a small bottle of lavender oil that had long been abandoned, as neither of them cared much for the scent and it had given Sasha a most unpleasant rash. Biting her lips, Sasha opened the vial and sprinkled a few drops on her forearms, rubbed it into her skin, and then her neck. Sure enough, within a few moments it began to burn and itch. Her nose tingled and she sneezed, and in a panic she rushed to the washstand, scrubbing with soap and water at her arms and neck. Not even for Georgia could she put herself through this! But it was too late; even though she had removed all traces of the lavender oil, her skin was indeed irritated and would take a few days to recover.

The household was beginning to stir, the maids knocking on doors and delivering trays of tea, drawing back the curtains, the footmen bringing up shoes that had been polished the night before, and jugs of hot water for the guests' morning ablutions.

Sasha realised that she would not be able to dress herself

unaided, there were far too many tiny hooks and eyes on the back of the wedding gown, and she would need Polly to help her put the veil on. She decided to take Polly into her confidence, and when the little maid arrived, she let her into Georgia's room, locked the door behind her, and gave her a very brief summary of the night's events, swearing a shocked, yet loyal, Polly to absolute secrecy.

'Will I be in trouble, miss?' asked a nervous Polly. 'Jobs is hard to come by nowdays.'

'Oh, no, Polly, don't worry.' Sasha hugged the young maid. 'I will leave a note explaining everything, and that you had no idea whatsoever what was going on. Besides, you know the Brigadier and her ladyship well enough, they would never vent their wrath upon you.'

The hardest part was to convince Victoria and Philippa that they could not come in. They wailed, and moaned, and made threats and promises in equal quantities if only they could please, please come in, just for a moment. Sasha was reduced to lying, making false promises that as soon as Georgia was ready they could come in to see her, but first they must go and enjoy a hearty breakfast to keep them going through the long day, and then get ready themselves.

Her mother proved to be an easier case, as she did not appear at all, having herself succumbed to a fit of nerves and was resting in her room at her father's insistence, Polly reported. Her father knocked once upon Georgia's door, and Polly called out in reassuring tones that 'they' were busy bathing and getting dressed.

'Very well,' replied the Brigadier through the door panel, in relieved tones. 'But, Georgia, make sure you are downstairs in the hall at ten forty-five sharp, the carriage will be here then to take us to the church.'

He moved on down the corridor to check on his other daughter, and when Sasha called out in a feeble whimper for him to enter, the Brigadier poked his head around the door with an alarmed exclamation.

'Come along, Sasha, what on earth are you doing still in bed?'

'Papa, I feel very unwell. I think I may have a fever, and look, a horrible rash.' She pushed back the long sleeves of her nightgown and showed him her arms and neck.

'Good Lord!' He edged nervously away, half-closing the door. 'Really, Sasha, how very inconvenient! As if we don't have enough to worry about today, of all days.' He sighed heavily, preoccupied with his father-of-the-bride duties. 'We will send for Dr Symons later, but there's just no time now. Stay in bed, and for goodness' sake do stay away from your mother, you know how delicate she is.'

'Yes, Papa,' Sasha replied in a meek voice, as he began to close the door. 'I'm so sorry, Papa.'

The Brigadier grunted and went off, deciding to keep to himself Sasha's condition, a frown creasing his brow as he went to his dressing room to sit with a brandy and the newspaper before his valet helped him don his best dress military jacket, striped breeches, leather belt and sword, and attached his medals. All he was most concerned with was getting Georgia to the church and married to that Bowen fellow—why did he have this nagging feeling that the girl was going to be contrary?

As soon as the door had closed, Sasha threw back the bed covers and Polly came hurrying in from Georgia's bedchamber. The maid began to help her into the bridal gown and when she was fully dressed, the veil secure, Sasha paused and looked at herself in the mirror. But she cringed, horrified at what she was about to do. She thanked the maid and then sent her to check the luggage was ready for removal to the ship, seeking a quiet moment in which to gather her thoughts, and to sit down at her writing desk and pen a note. For long moments, anxiously aware of the ticking clock, she stared at the blank sheet of cream paper, and then with a tremulous sigh set the pen's nib to write, *'Dearest Mama and Papa, please do not worry or be too angry, but…'*

When she had finished, she folded the page and slipped it into an envelope, rising from the desk and looking about the room for a place to leave the note, where it would be found, but not too soon. Eventually she propped it on the mantelpiece, behind the gently ticking ornate gilt clock. It was twenty minutes before eleven o'clock and with a last glance about her bedroom she settled the veil over her face, leaving the room quickly before she changed her mind.

The carriage conveyed them to the Church of St Ann at precisely five minutes before the bells of eleven o'clock began to peal. When they rumbled to a halt, Sasha stepped down from the carriage, assisted by her father and her two young sisters acting as bridesmaids. The heavy Spanish lace veil was indeed so thick that no one could see her face, but she could hardly see anything, either. Her father was extremely smart in his dark green-and-gold Light Dragoons uniform, yet he was indistinct. She could not see more than a green shadow and she reached out blindly to take his arm as they mounted the steps of the church. She could hear the genteel tones of the organ music; when they came to a halt in the vast arched door way, her heart suddenly lurched and pounded very hard in rapid beats.

This was it. She stood on the threshold of a moment—her life, and the life of everyone else involved in this marriage, was about to change in ways unimaginable.

The organ paused for a moment, and then launched into Handel's 'Hornpipe in D Water Music'. Her father took a step forwards, and she followed, placing her feet slowly and carefully on the dark blue carpet, the congregation on either side a mere blur. That walk seemed the longest of her life and she wondered if it would ever end, but then at last her father halted, and she became aware of another taller, broader shape in a scarlet jacket, moving to stand at her side.

Remembering the rehearsal a few days ago, Sasha turned to Philippa and handed her the bridal bouquet, a heavy and ornate arrangement of lilies, roses, ivy and forget-me-nots that made her arms ache and her nose tingle. She could feel a sneeze tickling in her nose and throat, the scent of all the flowers arranged in the church upsetting her already lavender-annoyed senses. As Captain Bowen reached out to take her left hand in his, she could not stem the succession of sneezes that erupted from her.

The congregation were amused and sympathetic, murmuring gently with soft chuckles, yet Sasha was mortified. She felt the prickling heat of a red-hot blush sear her cheeks and she glanced up nervously to Captain Bowen. But she could not see his face, whether he was amused or annoyed at this lack of decorum, but fortunately the vicar had a pressing timetable and he launched at once into the ceremony.

Sasha whispered the vows, flinching inwardly and praying that she would not be struck down by lightning as she professed to be Georgia Louisa Roberta, who promised that she would love, cherish, honour and obey Reid Peter Michael for all the days of her life until death parted them. At one point, as she sniffed and was tempted to wipe her nose with the back of her sleeve, her mama leaned forwards and pressed a lawn handkerchief into her hand. The vicar had to pause for a moment as the bride blew her nose, but then at last, to his relief and the Brigadier's, he pronounced them man and wife. The final hymn was sung, the bride avoided being kissed by blowing her nose and reaching for her bouquet, and then they departed to the registry to sign the marriage document. Sasha scrawled Georgia's name, albeit illegibly, and now considered it the right moment to swoon and make her escape.

The Brigadier muttered darkly that his eldest girl was at home unwell and feared that it might be catching. Captain Bowen lifted his bride up from where she had collapsed on the stone floor, in a froth of shimmering white organza, silk and tulle, holding her in his arms and somewhat surprised at how small and light she felt as he carried her prostrate form from a side door of the church and out to a waiting carriage. He climbed in beside her and ordered the driver to take them at once to the docks at Tilbury. He feared that his wife's family would insist that she was not well enough to travel, and he could not possibly afford to miss the sailing of the naval warship HMS *Dorset* on the evening tide.

All in all, it was remarked upon for weeks afterwards as the most extraordinary wedding of the year: the bride sniffed and sneezed throughout the ceremony and then fainted in the registry, the happy couple never appeared at the wedding reception, which was thoroughly enjoyed by everyone else, and the father of the bride, usually a most upright fellow, became so drunk he had to be carried home, bellowing 'God Save the Queen'.

Chapter Four

Reid gazed down at the new Mrs Bowen as she slumped sideways in a corner of the carriage. He patted his hip pocket and wondered whether to give her a shot of whisky from the small silver flask he had fortified himself from earlier in the day. But he decided against it—no telling how the girl would react to strong spirits and he certainly didn't want to have to deal with a pie-eyed bride as well as a sick one. With a frown he wished someone had warned him that Georgia was ill.

Sasha longed to fling off the suffocating weight of her veil, and wondered how on earth she was going to keep Captain Bowen at bay. Should she tell him now? How far was she willing to proceed with this charade? Was Georgia safely married at Gretna Green yet? She would be twenty-one in two days' time, and then no one could prevent her from doing as she pleased. And, Sasha had to admit, with a shocked little shiver at her own daring, she rather liked the idea of being Captain Reid Bowen's wife. It had been very pleasant when he had lifted her up into his arms, as though she were a mere feather, and carried her out of the church. His chest and his arms had felt both solid and warm, and he smelled so nice...

'Georgia? Are you all right? Shall I help you remove this veil?' He leaned over her and gently shook her shoulder.

Drat! There was no help for it but to make a reply of some kind, so she croaked an incoherent confirmation and moaned that she might be contagious.

Captain Bowen, realising he was far too close if that was the case, sat down opposite, his long legs in the close-fitting breeches and shiny leather boots very close to her own. They gazed at each other, Captain Bowen noting the way she turned her head to lean against the bolster of the carriage, and his voice very gentle as he asked, 'Are you feeling absolutely rotten, Georgia?'

'Hmm,' Sasha croaked in reply.

'As soon as we arrive on the ship, we can get you some tea, it will make you feel better.'

Sasha stifled a gasp, hesitating, realising that she would have to lift her veil to sip from the cup. Soon there would be no need to pretend illness, as a faint wave of nausea and dizziness washed over her. But still, she did not dare move, for fear he would notice something, anything, out of character. As the moments ticked by, she became aware that he was staring at her intently, with his very blue and beautiful eyes.

'I've been thinking,' said Reid, leaning forwards slightly, his hands clasped between his knees, and his voice lowering to an intimate tone that made Sasha tense. 'Considering that you are not at all well, I thought we might give the reception a miss and go straight to the ship. The Navy surgeon on board can take a look at you and the sooner we get you into bed, the better.'

A peculiar squeak strangled in Sasha's throat as her shoulders jerked with shock and her glance flew to his face.

'I—I mean…' Reid suddenly realised how his words may have been interpreted and hastened to make amends. 'Of course I don't mean, um, er…' He searched for delicate words on an indelicate subject to a young and innocent bride. Failing, he merely murmured, lifting a corner of the blind to look out of the window in a distracted fashion, 'Well, not tonight, anyway.' He let the blind fall and turned his attention back to her. He peered at her, trying to see if she was blushing, expecting a throaty Georgia laugh, but there was only silence.

'At least you've stopped sneezing.' He smiled, with what he hoped was an encouraging tone.

She smiled in return, though all he could see was the faintest glimmer of teeth and the slight movement of her head.

'Must have been all the flowers in the church.'

She nodded in agreement.

The carriage continued on its way, and Sasha sat there, mute as a marble statue, part of her, the sensible logical part, urging her to speak up, to tell him the truth. She had the opportunity, she could not deny that, but the other part of her, the romantic, womanly, playful, lonely part kept her silent. She realised, as the moments flew by, that she did not want to stand up and confess. She did not want to stop being his wife—indeed, she very much wanted to find out what it would be like to truly be Captain Reid Bowen's wife in every sense of the word. And so she kept quiet, and they arrived at the docks.

It did not take very long for her to walk up the gangplank of HMS *Dorset*, pausing on the deck as Captain Turnbull greeted them and shook hands with her 'husband', bowing to her respectfully, agreeing heartily that they were more than welcome to board ahead of schedule; indeed, they were only waiting for them before pulling up anchor.

'Aye.' The ship's Scottish captain grinned, his mouth framed by a thick beard. 'We may as well catch the early tide and be on our way. Save this lot from going ashore and getting bladdered.' He nodded his head at the sailors hurrying about deck. He beckoned to one and told him, 'Show Major Bowen and his wife to their cabin.'

'I don't get my majority until I take up my post,' Reid pointed out.

'That may well be,' replied the Navy man, 'but there can only be one captain aboard this ship.'

The two men laughed, while Sasha clutched at her veil as the wind suddenly snatched at it. She followed behind the seaman, who led them down steps and corridors until they arrived at a cabin towards the end of one corridor. She wasn't sure what she had been expecting, her thoughts had not ventured this far, but there had been a vague expectation of a large hotel-like room. As the matelot opened the door and showed them into their cabin, she was rather dismayed at the small, narrow space. There were two bunks on one side, a bureau with an oak-framed mirror fastened to the wall above it on the other side, a rattan tub chair in a corner, and in between was the porthole, with a narrow strip of dark grey water and pale sky her only vision of the outside world.

Captain Bowen thanked the sailor and then asked him, 'Is your surgeon about? I'd like a word with him.'

'Aye, sir, this way, sir.'

He turned to her as he stepped over the high doorway. 'Georgia, I'll be back shortly. Why don't you get that contraption off so you can breathe fresh air—' he waved one hand at the veil '—relax and lie down for a while?'

She nodded, and then hastened to lock the door as soon as it closed. Taking a few steps over to the porthole, Sasha pulled off the veil covering her face, laying it on the chair and taking great gulps of salty air in through her nose. She looked out at the murky waters of the harbour and above her the cloudy sky. Squinting to left and to right, she could just make out a fraction of the crowded docks, but there was little else to see. There was much noise, a faint vibration of feet running on the decks and the rumble of the steam engines deep in the heart of the ship as all was made ready to depart, stowing luggage and supplies in the hold, preparing the equipment on deck, stoking up the boiler.

She stood still, poised in between two lives, two futures, and the moment had come to make her choice. She could speak up now, at this the very last moment, and tell Captain Bowen the truth, and go back to her life as the lonely Miss Packard who had no suitors. Or she could keep quiet, not say a word, until the ship sailed and they left England's shores. She could step into Georgia's shoes and the role of Mrs Reid Bowen. A memory of his face came to her mind. His blue eyes, his fair hair, tanned skin, the set of his broad shoulders, his warmth, his smile and his voice, even his smell, had already melted into her skin, her blood, into her heart, and she could not, however sensible it might be, do anything to part herself from him.

So Sasha sat down on the bunk bed, and when her 'husband' returned and rattled the door knob, she did not open it. She heard him murmur, and the low voice of another man. She tiptoed closer to listen with one ear pressed to the door.

'Thank you, Doctor. Perhaps you can see her later.' Reid turned back to the door as the doctor departed and tried again. 'Georgia? Are you all right?'

Sasha thought it cruel not to reply, so she croaked, 'Yes. I'm just getting changed.'

As other passengers tried to squeeze past, some with suitcases, Reid Bowen stood and stared at the locked door of his cabin. He supposed that it would be crass of him to suggest that now they were man and wife she was perfectly entitled to dress and undress in front of him. In fact, the mere idea of Georgia in her corset and stockings stirred his blood, but then he sharply admonished himself, mindful of the fact that Georgia was young and well bred and she needed some time to get used to him. 'I'll wait out here. Are you feeling better?'

Sasha thought for a moment. Should she be feeling better? No, then he'd want to come in and goodness knew what that might lead to. What did a man expect from his wife within a few hours of being married? Surely not…well… She blushed… She didn't even dare let her mind wander in that direction.

'Georgia?'

Suddenly the whole situation seemed too absurd and impossible for words, and Sasha began to giggle, as she imagined an ardent Captain Bowen hovering in the corridor, with high expectations of passion from the very beautiful Georgia. And in reality all he had was…her. Great waves of mirth washed over her, a natural release to the tensions of the day, and she clasped a pillow from one of the bunk beds over her mouth to stifle the sounds. With a deep shuddering sigh intended to control her somewhat out-of-control emotions, she realised that she would have to come clean and tell him the truth. Sasha lay down on the bottom bunk, suddenly very weary. She closed her eyes, thinking that she would just take a few moments to mull things over, and then decide. But all too soon her eyelids became heavy, so heavy she could not keep them open, and her thoughts swirled away into a deep dark sleep…

The rumble of engines and the unfamiliar movement of the ship woke Sasha, hours later. It was dark and she sat up, feeling groggy and uncomfortable in the stiff voluminous folds of the wedding gown. Her corset pinched her waist with cruel fingers and she longed to take it off, free her ribs to draw in deep gulps of air. One way or the other she would have to undress, with or without help. She wondered what time it was, and then rose to her feet and ran her fingers through her untidy hair, scattering pins on the floor.

Footsteps sounded in the corridor and Sasha lifted her head, glancing to the door, but the footsteps passed and she breathed a sigh of relief. She started tugging and pulling at the gown, investigating ways and means to escape its constriction, kicking off the borrowed shoes and then searching the drawers of the bureau for a tool to assist her, scissors maybe, anything at all. Several times she heard people in the corridor, but they passed on by. Then the moment came when the footsteps stopped and the brass doorknob rattled in its socket. The man who considered himself her husband knocked, calling out, 'Georgia, open up, sweetheart.'

Sasha braced herself, and slid back the bolt. Swiftly she moved away, hurrying to the far side of the cabin in her stockinged feet, standing in front of the porthole with her back to the man who entered and closed the door behind him. She heard the bolt click home. She sensed his warmth and presence behind her. He smelled of musky maleness, and tangy sea salt, and a faint odour of alcohol... Whisky?

'God, what a day!' Reid flung himself down in the chair, oblivious in the gloom of the veil that he crushed beneath him. He pulled off his leather belt, unbuttoned his jacket and loosened the collar of his stiff linen shirt. Then he sat back, his hands dangling, and glanced up at the shadowy figure of his bride. It was dark, too dark; he could not see her, and he rose to strike a match and light the oil lamp fixed to the wall. Carefully he turned up the wick, and then replaced the glass and moved to stand behind her.

'How are you feeling now? Better?'

Without saying a word in reply, Sasha turned slowly and faced him.

For a moment he blinked, and then looked about, and peered at the bunk beds, and then he took a step forwards and stared at her with eyebrows raised in astonishment.

'Sasha! What on earth are you doing here?' Again he looked about. 'Where's Georgia?'

'I—I—'

His eyes narrowed in suspicion and his hands settled on his hips as he took an aggressive stance. Sasha quailed, the colour draining from her face.

'What's going on?'

'Captain Bowen.' Sasha took a step towards him, and then thought how foolish the formality was. 'Reid.' And yet that sounded far too familiar and she again floundered. 'My sister—'

'Yes?'

'Well, you see—'

Suddenly all the little oddities of the day began to flash through his mind: his bride who seemed so much smaller and lighter than he had imagined, her silence, hiding behind a veil, locked doors, and now this young woman standing here in his cabin, the top of her dark head barely reaching to his chin, when blonde Georgia had been almost level with his eyes. They didn't all add up, and he was still not making sense of it all. He reached out and grasped Sasha by the arm, giving her a little shake.

'You should not be here, Sasha. I don't mean to be rude, but you have to go. I don't intend to start my marriage to Georgia by explaining why I have another woman in my bed.'

Sasha gasped, and pulled her arm free from his painful grip. 'Sir, I am not in your bed!'

'Not yet, but I assume that your scheme is leading in that direction.' He frowned at her, reaching out to try to catch hold of her again. 'Just go, before Georgia sees you.'

'Oh, for goodness' sake!' exclaimed Sasha, quite at the end of her patience. 'There is no Georgia, you idiot!'

'What?'

'And as for scheming to get into your bed, well, I—I wouldn't want to if you were the last man on earth!' Sasha flounced away from him, her chin thrust up and her mouth set in an obstinate pout anyone in her family would have known to be wary of.

'Sasha, explain yourself!'

'No, I won't!'

'Yes, you will!' Reid marched up to her and fastened his hands around her slender upper arms, pulling her towards him and bending his head so that she could clearly see his face, and the anger written on it. 'You surprise me, Sasha, I did not think you capable of such low behaviour, making a play for a man who has just married your sister!'

'You did not marry my sister.' Sasha arched away from him, but this only pressed her bosom closer against his chest.

'Of course I did!'

'No, you married me.'

'But—'

'Georgia has run away to Gretna Green to marry Felix Westfaling.'

For a moment Reid was dumbstruck, his silence absolute while this information seeped into his understanding. She watched the pupils of his eyes dilate as sudden rage at Georgia's duplicity ignited. He swore, most rudely, words that Sasha had never heard before, but she deemed them no doubt to be absolutely forbidden in the presence of a lady. She frowned at him, and then he said, 'Explain to me what the hell is going on!'

She shook her head, not at all liking this Captain Bowen, who was showing a side of his character that she had never suspected. Were all men like that, she wondered, so uncivilised the moment they were presented with something they did not like? Well, he was certainly not going to behave like a rabid animal in her presence! And with a disdainful little arch of her brows and a haughty lift of her chin, Sasha shook her head.

His frown was thunderous. 'Speak!' He shook her, not too hard, but hard enough to make her glare at him. 'Why have I been deceived into marriage with the wrong woman and made a complete fool of?'

Sasha replied, 'No one has made a fool of you. As far as anyone's concerned, you are happily married to Georgia Packard.'

'You can stop talking now. I need to think.'

'Don't speak to me like that! Who do you think you are? Just because you've put a gold ring on my finger doesn't mean you can behave so rudely, and it doesn't mean for one single moment that I would tolerate—'

'Please, do me a favour.' He strode up to her then, towering over her, as he barked, 'Shut up!'

Sasha drew in a sharp breath between her teeth. 'Captain Bowen, I find I do not like you at all and cannot imagine why I thought you a charming man! One moment you tell me to speak, and the next to—to stop!'

'Indeed?' He cast her a sour glance. 'Well, Miss Packard, I find I do not like you very much, either, and cannot imagine why you are here, pretending to be my wife!'

'Because Georgia asked me to. She was utterly distraught without the love of her life.'

'Oh, that's good, blame your sister.'

'Well, of course. It was all her idea.'

He frowned. 'Why would she marry Felix when she's in love with me?'

'She is not in love with you. She loves Felix and always has.'

He grunted as he mused on this distasteful, yet not altogether surprising, information. 'Then why did she agree to marry me?'

'Because our papa forbade her to have anything to do with Felix.'

'Wise advice. Pity she didn't listen.'

Sasha wondered if it was his ego or his pride that was wounded. 'And I doubt very much whether you were ever in love with Georgia.'

His eyes narrowed as he looked at her. 'How do you know? She may well have broken my heart.'

Sasha leaned her head to one side and gave him a sceptical glance and a wry grimace, clearly indicating that she did not believe so for one moment.

'Anyway, I'm not pretending to be your wife. I am your wife.'

'No, you're not. Your name is not Georgia Louisa Roberta, is it?'

For a moment, Sasha was disconcerted, as she realised the truth of that.

Reid contemplated her, with a furious frown, hands on hips, and then sighed with a shrug of his very broad shoulders. 'What am I to do with you?' His glance strayed to the dark glimmer of the porthole. 'It's too late to put you ashore, we've already left the English Channel.' He looked about at the enclosed space of the cabin, and then at her. 'You realise that your reputation will be ruined when this gets out?'

'Will it?'

'Most certainly.'

'Why?'

'Why do you think? Shall I spell it out for you? You are alone with me, in—in—' he waved his hand about the narrow confines of the cabin '—intimate surroundings, and we are most certainly not legally married.' He spoke the last three words very slowly.

'What are we to do?' she asked, in a rather small voice.

'Stay well away from each other. I will ask the purser for a bunk somewhere else.'

'But—' Sasha now began to worry in earnest '—we are supposed to be on honeymoon; if you leave this cabin, there most certainly will be talk.'

'Hmm,' he conceded in a reluctant voice, 'you are right. We must carry on as normal and not arouse any suspicions.' He shrugged off his jacket. 'It's late; let us sleep on it and in the morning we will find a solution.'

Sasha turned her face away as he began to undress, pulling off his boots. She felt the colour flare in her face; she did not know where to look as she glimpsed his chest beneath his shirt, and certainly there was nowhere to hide.

He stopped, realising her predicament, and left on his shirt and breeches, yet his voice held a wry tone as he said, 'It's a bit late to be turning missish now.'

Sasha smiled slightly, her humour robust enough to appreciate the irony, and then she realised that she too must undress, for she could not endure a moment longer in the crushing grip of her corset. 'I would be very glad if you could help me.' She turned and presented her back to him, her fingers indicating the row of hidden hooks that needed undoing.

He stared at the slim width of her back, his elbows akimbo and still a frown upon his brows.

'Please,' Sasha pleaded. 'I can hardly breathe.'

He took a step closer and stooped, brushing aside the long swathe of her dark hair, lifting it over her shoulder. His fingers felt warm against her neck as he inserted them into the high lace collar and tugged. It was easier than he expected, the hooks slipping in rapid succession as he pulled them apart, the heavy lace fabric of her bridal gown gaping, revealing her shoulders. He noticed she had a few freckles between her shoulder blades, and her skin was very soft and pale. A faint scent of roses and female penetrated his nose and teased his senses. The final hook gave way under his fingers and the gown fell down to her waist.

Blushing profusely, hiding her face behind the curtain of her hair, Sasha turned to look over her shoulder at him, as he stood there still and silent. 'The, um, corset, too, please.' Her voice sounded very odd, husky and almost inaudible.

She heard his uneven breathing, and then felt his fingers on her waist as he pulled her closer, narrowing his eyes in the poor light as he peered and tried to make sense of the intricate lacing.

'Don't know why you women wear these contraptions,' he muttered, strangely embarrassed. It was not the first time he had unlaced a woman from her corset—indeed, undressing was a pleasurable part of the act of lovemaking with a mistress—but it was certainly the first time he had ever performed such an intimate service for Miss Sasha Packard. Or was she Mrs Reid Bowen? He frowned again, his fingers tugging ruthlessly.

Sasha tried to speak, quite out of breath for more than one reason. She had to clear her throat to murmur, 'Maybe we wear them because you men demand that ladies be the height of fashion.'

'Oh, really?' He laughed, getting to grips with a stubborn knot. 'I think you are mistaken; men don't give a damn, really, they only want what's underneath.'

Sasha did not think her face could go any hotter, but another surge of colour prickled her skin, and she reached out to steady herself on a corner of the bureau as his movements pulled her slender body about in an effort to free her from the corset. At last it came loose and she heaved a sigh of relief.

'Besides, with your tiny waist, you do not need such a thing.' He tossed the corset aside in disgust, and it landed with a thwack of cotton and whale-bones in a far corner. For a moment he stood gazing at her, wearing nothing more than her thin chemise, frilly drawers and silk stockings. She had a lovely figure, and if this was indeed his wedding night it would certainly please him to reach out and remove her undergarments.

'Thank you.' Sasha moved away, drawing in a deep breath of air, and turning shyly to face him.

They stood looking at each other, both of them acutely aware of their state of undress, and the fact that they were alone in the confines of this darkened cabin. His eyes narrowed as they roamed over her, taking in at a glance her flushed face, her lips, parted as she breathed rather quickly, and the rise and fall of her bosom. He lingered on her breasts, noting that they were small, yet round and firm, her nipples hardened and showing pink through the fine white fabric of her chemise. His gaze lowered farther, skimming over her slim waist and the curve of her hips, down to slender thighs showing above the tops of her cream silk stockings, covering slim yet shapely legs. His impression had always been that she was rather thin and fragile, but looking at her now he found her to be most delightfully formed, slender yet curvaceous in all the right places. He felt his blood stir, yet he resisted the temptation to yield to desire as he remembered their circumstances.

Sasha was all too aware of his examination, and she moved away to fumble in one of her overnight bags for a robe, slipping on the flowered satin and tying the sash firmly about her waist.

'Well…' He cleared his throat, and moved to blow out the lamp. 'We should get some sleep.'

She nodded in agreement.

'Do you want the top bunk, or the bottom?'

'I don't mind,' she replied.

'Well, I don't, either.'

For a moment they stood and stared at the beds, each of them wondering which would be best, to avoid the danger of any further intimacy.

'Damn ridiculous, if you ask me, giving a couple on their

honeymoon bunk beds,' he grumbled, reaching out to pull aside the stiff sheets of the upper bunk.

Sasha smiled, following his lead and leaning down to tug at the linen of her own bed underneath, 'It would make things rather awkward. How on earth would we both fit into the same bed and—and—?' She stopped then, suddenly embarrassed at her own conversation.

He laughed, unabashed as he followed the train of her thoughts. 'I guess we would have ended up on the floor. More room there.'

'On the floor?' Sasha glanced down at the hard surface of the wooden boards.

'With plenty of blankets to lie on, of course. We wouldn't want to get bruised.' He lay back with a sigh, hands behind his head. 'Good night, Miss… Sasha.'

'Good night…Reid.'

She slept a deep and innocent sleep, considering her guilty conscience, not waking until well after ten, and only then stirring at the sound of a knock on the door and the rattle of a tray. Sasha opened her eyes, momentarily confused and wondering where on earth she was. And then her memory was jolted as a pair of masculine legs swung out from the bunk above and her 'husband' jumped down, padding to the door in his underdrawers, bare chested, having divested himself of his clothes some time during the night.

'Good morning, sir,' the cabin steward greeted him as the door opened.

'Mornin'.' Reid yawned, rubbing his chest hairs absently with one hand as he took the tea tray from the steward.

'You've missed breakfast, sir. I was told not to disturb you and your good lady—' the steward winked '—but I've put on some sandwiches and biscuits to keep you going. Lunch is at noon in the dining salon.'

'Very good.' Reid Bowen closed the door and moved to set

the tray down on the bureau, saying with a dry note of amusement in his voice, 'You can come out now, he's gone.'

Sasha raised her head from where she had ducked underneath the covers, mortified with embarrassment, spluttering on her words. 'He—he thinks we—we've—!'

'Of course he does. The whole ship does. We were married yesterday, after all.'

Sasha groaned, diving under the covers again and pulling them over her head. 'I will never be able to set foot out of here until we reach St Petersburg!'

'Nonsense.'

She became aware then of a heavy weight and warmth as he sat down on the edge of her bed and leaned towards her, pulling down the covers. She resisted, trying to pull them back up, but he was stronger and the covers came down.

Sasha stared at him wide-eyed, her heart beating very hard as she covered her breasts by crossing her arms protectively over them. 'You are not going to—to ravish me, are you?'

He looked at her for a long moment, his eyes lowering to the swell of her bosom, a speculative gleam in his eyes, and then he smiled, aware of her tension. 'No,' he said gently, 'not right now.'

Sasha heaved a sigh of relief, but she still sat warily as he made no move to stand up.

'I've been thinking, though, while you've been snoring—' he said.

'I do not snore!'

'Well, snuffling, then, but you do make a funny noise when you're asleep—anyway, we digress. As I said, I've been thinking—'

'Good for you.'

He placed his hands one on either side of her hips, and leaned closer, in a manner that was intended to silence her, and yet was more arousing than intimidating as she became aware of his muscular broad shoulders and strong arms, his skin tanned to a honey colour, and his chest liberally covered with golden hairs.

'Listen to me, please.' He tapped her lips with his forefinger. 'Well, it seems that this marriage thing is three-quarters done, and maybe Georgia was right, I should have asked you to marry me in the first place—'

'What!'

'Be quiet, you are distracting me.' His gaze fell to her chemise, suspecting that she was unaware how her current posture pressed her breasts together and made for a most interesting cleavage, but with an effort he raised his eyes to her face again. 'The fact remains that I am in need of a wife, you are here, of sound mind and body, reasonably attractive—'

'I beg your pardon!'

'And my only option is that I do the honourable thing, and marry you properly.'

Sasha stared at him, bewildered, her senses swimming with a heady mixture of attraction, desire and outrage. 'I—I don't understand.'

'As soon as we get into international waters, most probably around midday, I will ask the ship's chaplain to marry us.'

'But—' she stared at him '—is that possible? As far as he knows we are already married.'

'Don't worry, I will have a quiet word with him.'

'Can we trust him?'

He shrugged. 'I hope so. I know Padre Meares from his days in India. I think I can persuade him to be sympathetic and discreet.'

'What will you say?' Sasha stared at him, and thought how beautiful his blue eyes were, his nose, so straight and perfect, nostrils slightly flared, and his mouth, not too wide, not too thin.

'Leave it to me, I'll make up a plausible tale, something along the lines that you were too ill for the actual ceremony yesterday, but we couldn't miss the ship sailing, blah, blah, blah.'

Her eyes narrowed as she gazed at him suspiciously. 'Will it be legal?'

'I believe so.'

'So—' she blushed, her voice and her eyes lowering, choosing her words carefully '—so tonight, you will not be wanting to sleep in the top bunk?'

His voice was even softer, huskier, as he shook his head and leaned closer. 'No, Mrs Bowen, I will not be wanting to sleep in the top bunk. In fact, I suspect that I will not want to sleep at all.'

Sasha gasped, as his shoulders blocked out the cabin and she felt the heat and warmth of his mouth on hers. It had been a long while since anyone had kissed her, and certainly never like this. His mouth moved expertly on her lips, parting them, savouring their soft pink fullness with his lean male lips, tasting her as his tongue slipped inside. She felt her heart drum and her hands pressed against the rough hardness of his chest, holding him back, and yet she melted as his kiss deepened. His lips strayed then, and pressed to the side of her neck, and down across her collarbone, to the soft swell of her breasts. She shivered, her skin absorbing delightful sensations at the feel of him, and she made a small sound, arching her neck, her hands sliding up over the bulk of his solid shoulders, urging him closer.

He groaned, and it took a supreme effort on his part not to get into bed with her, strip her naked and make love to her there and then, but he pulled back, his breath just as short and sharp as hers, to his surprise, as he had not expected to feel this way about a girl like Sasha.

Sasha felt an emotion stir within that she had never felt before. A feeling of such bliss, and contentment, as though this moment put her whole world to rights. And yet, she knew that Reid did not love her, and was unsure if the feelings she herself experienced were indeed love, or merely the physical effects of a handsome man upon her female senses. She pondered on it, innocent but certainly no fool. She realised with a slow seep of

ice through her veins that she could not possibly agree to his
suggestion. It hurt, deep inside within her heart, but she drew
back and shook her head.

'No.'

He leaned back, pulling up the covers over her breasts. 'Don't
worry, I will do the honourable thing first.'

Sasha again shook her head. 'I—I mean, that is, I'm saying
no to your proposal. I do not wish to marry you.'

'What?' He frowned at her.

'You do not love me.'

'What's that got to do with it? I didn't particularly love Georgia, either, but we would have dealt well enough together.'

She felt tears prick at the back of her eyes, and crowd into
her throat. How could she explain that she did not want to be
'dealt' with, but that she wanted him to love her?

'I don't think that's enough. My—my parents love each other,
passionately, and I don't want anything less from my own marriage.'

'Well…' He sat away from her, not looking at her. 'I can't say
I love you, because at the moment I don't.'

'Very well,' Sasha whispered.

'Hmm.' He grunted, and then slanted her a sideways look.
'What do you propose, then?'

She hesitated, uncertain. 'I don't know.'

'The ship is putting into Copenhagen tomorrow. Do you wish
to go ashore and return to England?'

Sasha considered that for a moment. It was not very much
to her liking, but she could see no alternative solution, so she
merely nodded, not meeting his gaze.

Reid levered himself up, his tone cool. 'Very well, then. I
will speak to the captain.' After a moment's pause, as he contemplated the floorboards and his future, sans wife, he said in
a flat voice, 'I'm going to find somewhere to get washed and
dressed. I suggest you do the same; lunch will be served in
an hour.'

He collected his clothes from a travelling case, opened the door and departed. Sasha sagged back against the pillow, quite astonished at this turn of events. She pushed aside the covers of the bed and climbed out, padding over to the bureau and pouring herself a cup of tea. It was hot and fragrant. She drank thirstily and the rumble of her stomach reminded her that she had not eaten for a long while. She ate a cheese sandwich, dunked several biscuits in her tea, and then set about finding her clothes, humming quietly under her breath. She lurched and lost her balance several times, as the ship rolled on the increasing swell. Sasha went to the porthole and peered out, but she could see nothing except the dark cobalt sea and a cloudy grey sky. The weather had turned, the wind whipping up white caps of foam on the water. She could smell the tang of salt, as well as the odour of the ship itself, a mixture of paint and rust and a musty smell she could not quite identify.

A knock on the door brought the steward with a bowl of steaming hot water. Sasha avoided his eye, murmuring her thanks as he set the bowl down on the bureau and then he departed. It was quite difficult keeping her balance, most disconcerting, as she stripped off her chemise and drawers and washed. Then she struggled into clean clothes, a neat dark blue skirt and a white blouse, with a tortoiseshell belt to draw in her waist, as she had no desire to restrict herself in the confines of a corset. She slipped on warm woollen stockings, fastened them with plain garters, and then put on her shoes. For a moment she pressed a hand to her mouth as a most peculiar feeling wafted up from her stomach. It must be because she had not eaten for so long, and then bolted down food too quickly. A brisk walk on the deck was what she needed, to clear away all the cobwebs before lunch.

She managed to find her way through the warren of corridors and up steel flights of steps to the deck. The smell of salt was even stronger as she emerged, the wind tearing at her hair that she had braided and fastened in a loop at the nape of her neck.

She should have put on her coat, but was loath to return to the cabin, stepping out smartly and taking in deep gulps of air, clutching at the railings now and then as the ship lurched and rolled.

It wasn't long before she became aware of someone calling her name; turning about, she saw Captain Bowen striding towards her.

'What on earth are you doing?' he shouted, his voice snatched away by the wind.

'I'm taking a walk,' she shouted back.

She couldn't hear his words, but she gathered they were not complimentary, even rude, as he grasped her arm and dragged her back inside. In the corridor below he stooped over her, his face marred by a frown.

'You idiot! Are you trying to get yourself killed?'

'What?'

'Not even the sailors are out in this wind!'

'Oh.' Now that she thought about it, the deck had seemed rather deserted.

'You could have been swept overboard.'

'Well, I wasn't. I'm still here.' She tidied her hair. 'Did you speak to the captain?'

'Yes, I did.' He frowned, and taking her arm he led her down the corridor. 'He's agreed to set you ashore in Copenhagen. He wasn't too happy about it, I must say, and I'm not sure that I am, either. But I will take you to the British Embassy and you can stay there until a passage can be secured for you back to England.'

She said nothing in response, and fell into step with him as he led her to the main salon, where several officers in crisp white naval uniforms sat in lounge chairs reading the paper or writing in journals. They stood up as she entered the room, and introductions were made. Then Reid showed her to a tub chair in the corner, leaning over her as he whispered, 'Sit there and don't move. I have a few things to attend to.' He nodded his head at the glass-fronted bookcases. 'Find something to read and stay put.'

Sasha gave him an aggrieved glare, but then he leaned down and kissed her hard and swiftly upon her disconsolate mouth, causing her to gasp.

'I know what you Packard girls are like, up to mischief given half a chance.' He smiled then. 'And that kiss was for the benefit of our audience. Be good now.'

He straightened up and took himself off, leaving Sasha to sit and stare out of the row of small wooden windows, from the corner of her eye noticing the curious glances that came her way. Stay out of mischief, indeed!

Chapter Five

At noon sharp a gong clanged in the hands of an orderly, echoing along the corridors and rousing the officers in the library to converge on the dining room for luncheon. Sasha sat down at a long table, between the Navy men, and across the width of the snowy-white tablecloth set with cut crystal and silver sat Reid. She glanced at him, and he smiled back, with a perusing thoughtful look in his eyes that puzzled her.

A bowl of steaming tomato soup was set in front of her. For a moment she felt the room sway in dizzy circles, a wave of nausea rising from her stomach and choking in her throat. A dew of sweat filmed her forehead, but she breathed in slowly, one hand clenched in a fist beneath the table. It was an ordeal to swallow even one mouthful of soup, and yet she managed to almost finish the bowl before it was taken away. The next course of plump chicken breast in a white wine and mushroom sauce was quickly served. The Captain made approving noises, grasping his knife and fork and attacking his plate with gusto. Sasha hid a shudder as she watched him swallow a mouthful, poked and prodded at her meal, toying with it, gingerly cutting up tiny morsels and placing one in her mouth. The stewards were swift and efficient, the Navy used to eating quickly, and with relief she surrendered her half-finished plate. Next, there was dessert, and Sasha sighed as she eyed a bowl of steamed rum-and-raisin pudding swimming in custard. One of her favourites, and she succumbed to temptation, but was soon to regret it.

Without the presence of a lady the gentlemen would normally pass the port round and light cigars, taking time out for congenial talk. Sasha became aware that Reid was looking at her, with a frown upon his brows. She did not think this unusual, as he quite often seemed to have a look of thunder when gazing at her. But he kept directing his eyes to the door and Sasha realised that he was hinting that she should retire. A great wave of nausea washed over her then, much worse than before, and she prayed that she would make it back to the cabin without disgracing herself.

Reid leaned towards her as he escorted her to the door. 'Are you all right, Sasha? Your face is white as a sheet.'

'Yes, thank you.' But then her stomach rebelled, as the ship heaved and plunged on a steep wave, forcing her body to mimic the action. No matter how hard she tried to prevent it, a dreadful noise erupted from her throat, followed swiftly by the contents of her stomach.

'Good God!' Reid jumped back.

Sasha retched again, clinging weakly but ineffectively to the wall, moaning, wondering if there was any likelihood the ship might sink and save her the embarrassment of having to face anyone, especially Reid, ever again.

The Captain advised, 'Best get your wife down below.'

'You wouldn't think such a tiny thing could throw up that much,' one of the ship's officers commented, as several of them peered with curiosity from the doorway of the salon.

Someone elbowed him into silence, and Reid swung Sasha up into his arms, carrying her down to their cabin. There he closed the door and set her on the chair in the corner, squatting on his heels in front of her as he peered with concern at her pale, sweat-dewed face, and then quickly reaching for a bowl of water on the bureau as she started heaving again. He chucked the water out through the porthole and thrust the bowl under her nose. She was sick again. When at last the dreadful retching subsided, tears crowded in her eyes, and she sniffed, her words muffled as she turned her face aside. 'Oh, please, do go away.'

'Why?'

'It's awful—what on earth must you think of me?'

'Don't be ridiculous,' he chided, his voice infinitely gentle as he wiped her face with a towel she had discarded earlier. 'I'm in the Army, remember? I've seen a lot worse from my soldiers.'

'But you aren't married to any of your soldiers.'

'Well, apparently I'm not married to you, either.'

She smiled weakly at his words, and raised her tear-spiked lashes to glance at him with an apologetic wrinkle of her brows. 'I'm sorry.'

With one hand he poured her a cup of cold black tea. 'Here, sip this. It might help.' He watched as she complied, and murmured, 'No doubt we will both survive.'

As another wave of nausea gripped her stomach and she leaned over the bowl, retching painfully yet producing little, she wondered what he meant—whether they would survive her sickness, or this so-called marriage?

It was a very long and uncomfortable night for Sasha. Reid stayed with her, helping her to change her clothes and put on a clean cotton nightgown. He sponged her face with a cool cloth and tried to encourage her to eat a few ginger biscuits, the steward swearing that it would help to ease her discomfort. But she could not hold them down and it was only as the first flush of dawn touched the horizon that Sasha at last fell asleep, exhausted and drained.

The weather did not improve at all that day, the iron-clad ship bucking on the steep waves, creaking and groaning in a manner that gave even Reid pause for thought, and to take a turn on deck to discreetly check out the lifeboats. The Captain announced apologetically to Reid that it would be impossible to make harbour in Copenhagen and they were going to carry on. He assured his passengers that, once they were out of the rough waters of the North Sea and into the calmer Baltic, things would settle down. Reid, who had been so preoccupied with caring for Sasha through her illness that he'd forgotten he had asked that she be set ashore in the Danish capital, sincerely hoped so. He watched grimly as Sasha stirred and reached blindly for the bowl.

Towards evening of the third day, the waters suddenly calmed and there was a strange peace in the air. The rosy amber hues of sunset flooded a pale blue sky, and seagulls wheeled and screamed overhead. Reid rose from where he had been dozing in the chair and peered out of the porthole, but he couldn't see anything of significance.

'Are we there?' Sasha asked, her voice weak and rough from the abrasion and violence of her seasickness.

Reid turned and knelt beside her bed, looking at her pale face as she lay back on the pillow, her sweat-dampened lank hair twisted into a loop at one side of her neck, soft tendrils curling about the curves of her face.

'I don't think so.' His voice was soft, concerned and wary. 'How are you feeling?'

She smiled weakly. 'Not so bad.'

'Good.' His fingers stroked her forearm in a comforting gesture. 'Here, take this and try to sleep.'

He held a teaspoon of liquid to her lips, urging her to swallow it down. The ship's doctor had prescribed the only medicine he thought would help—laudanum. He commented that he had never seen anyone quite so bad as Sasha and the best thing to do was to remove her from the world, so to speak. Reid had been reluctant, knowing how addictive and dangerous such a drug was. Too much could do more harm than good, but the doctor assured him that the dosage was mild, but enough to keep her unconscious for a good twelve hours, during which time, it was hoped, her system would adjust and they would sail into calmer waters.

It worked like a charm, and Sasha slept soundly all that night, as did he, but he swung down from the upper bunk several times to check on her. His fingers held her slender, smooth-skinned wrist and felt for the flutter of her pulse in the delicate blue veins. He listened carefully to her breathing, recalling to mind the horror of one of his company sergeant majors who had taken his own life by using laudanum, tormented by debt and the loss of his own woman in childbirth. Satisfied that Sasha was safe and well, he watched her sleeping, his gaze roaming over her face, thinking of how she had behaved with the officers of the ship at luncheon, with grace and a quiet, intelligent charm. He wondered how Georgia would have been, his brow furrowing as he imagined her flirting and seeking attention. Was it fate that had taken a hand and delivered Sasha to him? Sweet, innocent, clever Sasha. With a sigh he stroked back tendrils of hair from her forehead, and then climbed up into his bed, and tried to sleep. Yet a barrage of thoughts hammered at his mind and kept him awake.

What of the future? He had some doubts about his post working as military attaché in the British Embassy, preferring to be in the field with his soldiers, but the offer of promotion had been tempting and it would only be for two years. Then they would return to England; his expectations had been that he would leave his wife and children at home and continue with his soldiering, going wherever the Crown chose to send him. But now there was a fly in the ointment—he had no wife. And what on earth was he to do with Sasha? He feared for her reputation and the scandal that no doubt had already broken in London. How long would it be before the discovery was made that the woman posing as his wife was indeed not his wife? The simple solution would be for Sasha to marry him post-haste, but she had refused. He was at first puzzled, and his ego certainly irked, at her refusal, for there was no doubt that there was an element of attraction between them, and she had already conspired to marry him. He was sure that Sasha did not fully understand that people would naturally assume that if she was not his wife then she must be his mistress. With a sigh, he turned on his side, shrugging off his thoughts until at last he, too, fell into a deep sleep. By dawn they were sailing into the Gulf of Finland.

On the sixth day Reid decided that enough was enough, and insisted that Sasha rise from her nest of tangled sheets. The air in the cabin was stale and fetid, the porthole shut against the bitter wind that blew across the sea, the temperature well below freezing and the sapphire-blue waters caked with floating layers of ice, like sugar icing that had come adrift from a wedding cake.

'Come on,' he said firmly, pulling Sasha's limp body from the bunk bed, holding her with one arm while he snatched up his own thick brocade dressing-robe and wrapped it around her, tying the cord sash securely. 'The fresh air will do you some good.'

'Oh, please, Reid, let me lie down,' Sasha begged, brown doe-eyes huge in her wan face, her slender frame swamped by the voluminous folds of his robe.

'No.' He reached for his Army great cloak and fastened it about her, then sat her down on the chair while he rummaged in her bags and found a pair of thick warm stockings. 'You'll feel much better, believe me.'

'I'll be sick.'

'No, you won't.'

'I will.'

'No,' he said with a note of weary patience, 'you will not. There's nothing left in you to bring up.' His large hands pushed up the layers of linen nightgown, brocade robe and his cloak, and then picked up her foot, a frown of concentration on his handsome face as he wrestled her stockings on. 'And you can stop pouting at me like that.'

Sasha gave up then, rendered dumb as she sat there and watched him, all her attention drawn to his strong lean hands, tanned golden-brown, the fingernails short and neat, very clean, his touch impersonal yet gentle as he pulled the stockings up over her legs and fastened them with a plain garter just above her knees. Then he reached for her boots, his blond head bent down as he tied the laces and she could not see his face, her glance straying instead to the broad width of his shoulders.

'There.' He sat back on his heels with a satisfied nod, his hands reaching out for her waist. 'Up you get.'

He lifted her from the chair, and for a moment she hung limply, her body like a rag doll's in his grasp. Then, with an effort, she straightened, levering herself up by grasping the lapels of his jacket. How tempting it was just to lay her head upon his chest, to surrender, safe in the certain knowledge that Reid would put to rights everything that was wrong. She lifted her eyes to his face, and for a moment they stood there, looking at each other.

'You have such beautiful eyes,' Sasha murmured, gazing at him. 'They are blue like the deepest, darkest sea.'

He smiled, his voice just as soft, his smile rueful. 'Don't you know that it's the man who is supposed to pay compliments?'

'Why?'

He shrugged, and then took her by the elbow and manoeuvred her to the door. 'Come on, while the wind has died down.'

Out in the corridor Sasha swayed and moaned, but he was unrelenting as he propelled her towards the gangway and up a flight of brass-and-wood steps to the closed sliding door that led out to the deck. Sasha gasped as the cold air hit them when Reid slid it back an inch, and he was forced to admit that it was indeed far too cold and windy to take her out to the deck. She sagged with relief as he closed it, not realising how near he was until her back came into contact with his warm, solid chest.

His arms folded around her, as he steadied her swaying form. 'We'll just stand here for a bit. Try to stare at the horizon for as long as possible. I'm told by the sailors that it's the best way to orientate the brain and stop the motion sickness.'

'Is that so?' Sasha replied drily, anxiously waiting for the surge of nausea that had plagued her for days to come rushing at her, with all the force and vengeance of an alien monster that had invaded her being.

'Yes, Miss Packard, that is so.' He leaned down, the better to see her face. 'I do believe you have some colour in your cheeks. How are you feeling now? Has it worked?'

Sasha hesitated for a moment, waiting, squinting at the far-off cobalt line of dark blue sea, above it the paler band of the sky. With a note of surprise in her voice, she confessed, 'I don't feel anything.' Half turning in his arms, she smiled up at him. 'Goodness, I feel…completely better! Isn't that wonderful?'

'Excellent.' He smiled, too, and then asked, 'Are you hungry?'

'Starving!'

'I'll get the steward to bring you some tea. What would you like?'

'Hmm.' Sasha thought for a moment, holding thumb and forefinger to her chin. 'A ham-and-tomato sandwich, please.'

He laughed. 'Is that all?'

'And a piece of fruit cake, if there is any.'

'I'm sure the cook can rustle up something. Come on, let's get you back to the cabin.'

That evening Sasha dressed for dinner, wearing a dark burgundy gown with velvet bodice and satin skirts that had been designed for Georgia, an elegant masterpiece that rustled seductively as she moved. When she walked into the officers' dining salon, on Reid's arm, a round of soft applause from the officers' gloved hands echoed about the small room. The Captain himself hurried to draw out a chair at his right hand and, blushing profusely but glowing with delight, Sasha sat down.

'Glad to have you back, ma'am,' Captain Turnbull murmured.

'Thank you.'

The waiters poured wine into crystal glasses and the gentlemen remained standing as they raised their glasses in a toast.

'To Mrs Bowen,' the Captain declared, with a knowing wink.

The officers echoed his salute, and across the table Sasha stared up at the man who was supposed to be her husband. Reid bowed to her, a slightly sardonic smile upon his firm lips.

He raised his glass to her, saluting her fortitude. 'To Mrs Bowen.'

Two days later HMS *Dorset* nosed her iron-clad prow through the thin layers of ice that crusted the waters of the Neva. Sasha stood on deck to catch her first glimpse of St Petersburg on the far horizon.

'The city was built on the orders of the Russian Tsar, Peter the Great, in 1703, and is spread over more than forty islands and dozens of rivers and canals.'

'Yes, I know.' Sasha half turned as Reid joined her, now dressed in his military uniform beneath his cloak, scarlet jacket encrusted with gold braiding and epaulettes, leather belt and sword scabbard attached to his waist, the snug fit of dark blue breeches tucked into shiny black boots. To her eyes he was more breathtaking than the famous city the ship was gliding into. She looked away, leaning on the rails as she peered ahead, the cold wind teasing tendrils of hair from beneath the fur hat she wore to keep warm, her long coat securely fastened. 'My mama has never ceased talking about the most beautiful city on earth since the day I was born.'

Reid smiled, nodding as he drew on his leather gloves, his glance sweeping about the low yet massive buildings crowding the shoreline. 'I forgot your mother is a native of the land. But still, to see it for the first time is quite impressive.'

'Yes.' Sasha smiled in agreement. 'It is indeed the Venice of the North. Look—' she pointed to a slender gold spire rising from the tiers of an elegant building '—that must be the Peter and Paul Fortress. And that other golden steeple must be the Admiralty.'

With a nod Reid gazed in the direction of her finger, but he was not looking at the imposing buildings, thinking rather how exquisite her small and ivory-pale hand was, just like the rest of her. How would she survive in this harsh place? He was sure that her mother had only told her romantic tales of palaces and balls and dashing princes, and that she was completely naïve as to the realities of life here in Russia for the poor and common folk. And how would she react if she ever found out that his job was to spy on the Russian military and report his findings to London? They were a dangerous enemy, he knew from his years of experience in India and Afghanistan, and he would certainly not be falling under the spell of any charming or dashing princes, and as a military wife he must ensure that neither did Sasha.

The ship glided along the wide cobalt waters of the Neva, slowing down and gradually inching its way into the docks of the naval base and mooring at the quayside; Russian sailors scurryed about to fasten the ropes as the anchor was weighed with a rattle of chains and splash of water.

'Well,' said Reid, looking down at Sasha, 'we are here.'

'At last.' Sasha looked up at him for a moment, a blush adding to the crimson colour staining her cheeks from the icy sting of the wind. 'Thank you, Reid,' she murmured. At his puzzled frown she added, 'For looking after me so well in these days past. What will we do now? Where will I stay? How will I get back to England?'

He took her arm, and they began to walk across the deck to the gangplank. 'Let us not worry about such things.' He lowered his voice. 'Just play along for now.'

Her brows creased in a frown as she glanced anxiously sideways at him, but here was Captain Turnbull, waiting to bid them farewell, shaking hands heartily with Reid, and kissing her on both cheeks as he wished them goodbye and good luck.

'No doubt we will see you at the Embassy,' Reid offered, in way of thanks for the Captain's good humour and assistance throughout the voyage.

'A pleasure I look forward to.' He turned to look at Sasha for a keen moment. 'Mrs Bowen, at your service.'

The two men saluted each other and then Reid took Sasha by the arm and guided her down the steep wooden gangplank. She was greatly tempted to drop to her knees and kiss the solid ground as her feet, at last, touched on a base that did not move. Although, she felt as if the ground was indeed still moving, and she looked to Reid to voice this strange occurrence, but all at once they were surrounded by a group of people, several men in dark coats, two in military uniforms, and two elegantly dressed women much older than herself, and there was not a moment for a private word.

'Sir Stanley Cronin, British Ambassador, glad to meet you at last.' The short bald man in dark suit and coat introduced himself, waving to the others in quick succession. 'This is my wife, Lady Cronin, that's John Hartley, my Secretary, and over there is Major Anthony Hope-Garner, whom you are replacing, and his wife, Charlotte.' Sir Cronin turned towards Sasha with a small bow. 'And I presume this is your wife, Georgia—'

'For goodness' sake, Stanley,' interrupted Lady Cronin, 'let's get out of this freezing wind and back to the Residency. We can do the introductions there.'

'Quite, quite, my dear,' agreed Sir Stanley, turning to Reid as they walked along the quay to where a carriage awaited them.'We'll do a briefing later on this afternoon—'

'No, you won't,' said Lady Cronin, ushering a bemused Sasha aboard the carriage. 'Tomorrow will do well enough. They've only just arrived, and only just been married, so do be a dear and give them a chance to settle in.'

A sigh heaved from Sir Stanley's portly jowls, and he shrugged, though there was little amusement in his dark, narrow eyes. 'We will see.'

Amidst the mutterings of the Ambassador and his wife, Sasha was ushered aboard and wedged in between Lady Cronin and Mrs Charlotte Hope-Garner. Opposite sat Reid, between Sir Stanley and the Secretary, Mr Hartley, his broad shoulders turned slightly sideways as the three men jostled for position and settled back. There was a shout and crack of a whip as the coachman set off. The carriage lurched, and Sasha instinctively flung out her hand to grab hold of something, encountering Reid's knee, so close as to be almost between her own. However, she need not have worried about being thrown from her seat as the carriage set off at a cracking pace, for she was firmly bolstered by the two ladies. Her glance went to the window and she peered out, wondering why the other four men had mounted horses and were riding close alongside.

Lady Cronin leaned towards her as she noticed Sasha's curious glance. 'Our bodyguards. We just can't be too careful, you know.'

Any hopes Sasha had of viewing the magnificent buildings of St Petersburg were soon dispelled, as the blinds were drawn and the horses urged on at a fast canter. She raised her eyes to Reid, trying to discreetly impart to him her sense of alarm as they proceeded through the streets as though the very hounds of hell were nipping at their heels, yet without alerting the other passengers to her feelings, but his expression was bland and she followed his cue, holding her tongue and casting her features into a mask of blankness.

'You will be staying at the Residency for the next week or so,' said Sir Stanley, raising his voice above the thunder of the carriage wheels on the cobbled paving. 'When Anthony has taken himself and his family off, you may move into their apartment.'

Reid nodded, and then conversation turned to their voyage, and the weather, and their recent wedding. Here Reid deftly manipulated the conversation elsewhere, bringing in comments about his recent years in India, his progress with the Russian language, until Lady Cronin grew bored with shop talk and announced that they would be holding a ball in a week's time, to bid farewell to the Hope-Garners and welcome the Bowens.

'Of course, it will be nothing compared to the grand affairs they have at the Palace—' said Lady Cronin.

'Well, no,' retorted her husband, 'my pockets are not as deep as the Tsar's.'

Lady Cronin merely sniffed.

It was a relief to them all when the carriage rumbled beneath the arched gateway of the courtyard leading to the back of the Residency. On their arrival, Reid noticed the sturdy twelve-foot gates were firmly barred and bolted behind them. The party stepped down from the carriage and climbed the steps that led to the rear entrance hall of the Residency. Several uniformed servants waited to take their hats and coats, then Reid and Sasha were escorted to their bedchamber. Lady Cronin urged them to return downstairs as soon as they could for refreshments in the drawing room, followed by luncheon at noon.

Sasha fell into step at Reid's side as they followed the maid up two flights of broad marble stairs, lined with a dark emerald-green carpet, the walls of the corridor hung with portraits of the Queen and her many children, as well as military paintings of various battles and flags from different regiments. Sasha glanced about, noticing the high ceilings and how opulent the furnishings were of satinwood chiffoniers and Chinese vases, marble Grecian statues and numerous hot-house plants, giving the impression of luxury and grandeur. It was not at all what she had expected.

The maid dipped a curtsy as she opened one half of a set of tall double doors, standing aside so that they could enter. Sasha stepped in before Reid, and halted as she looked about. The bedroom was the largest she had ever seen in her life, easily three times the size of her own bedroom in London. Two sets of long windows on the opposite wall opened onto small balconies that overlooked the Nevsky Prospekt and the River Neva, filmy white voile screening the windows between voluptuous swags of maroon-and-gold brocade curtains.

'Can I get you anything, ma'am?' asked the maid.

Sasha turned, surprised by the girl's accent. 'Why, you're English.'

'Of course, ma'am. My name is Jane, and all the staff are English, ma'am. It wouldn't do to have them foreign lot in here.'

'No, indeed.' Reid placed his hand on the door, discreetly hinting that it was time for the maid to depart.

She bobbed yet another curtsy, and closed the door behind her as she went out.

'Goodness, Reid!' exclaimed Sasha, wandering around the vast bedroom. 'Have you ever seen anything like it? Look at the size of that bed! I'm sure at least five people could sleep in that.'

'Hmm.' Reid unbuckled his leathers and then peeled off his gloves, glancing sardonically with one raised brow at the four-poster bed in question. 'I could certainly enjoy a good night's sleep in that.'

'Oh, no, you won't!' Sasha flung herself down like a starfish, staring up at the canopy of pleated pale gold silk above her. 'We're not married, remember? You couldn't possibly sleep in the same bed with me.'

'We've just spent quite a few days sleeping in a space the size of a broom cupboard,' Reid pointed out drily.

'True, but we had separate beds.'

He strolled over, leaning a shoulder on one ornately carved and gilded bedpost, his smile teasing. 'What difference would it make? Besides, there are enough pillows on that bed to build your very own Wall of China.'

Sasha turned her head slightly, gazing at the pile of pillows beneath the covers at the head of the bed, relief at having arrived on dry land bringing out a little mischief as she smiled. 'Don't you mean a Wall of Chastity?'

He chuckled, and moved to stand closer, looking down at her

as she lay spread-eagled on the huge bed. 'Your virtue is safe with me, Miss Packard.'

She pouted, and then jumped up as she ran to the wardrobe, a towering edifice of gleaming rosewood. 'I'm sure Russia is a land of giants, look at how huge everything is!' But Reid had wandered over to the window and was staring broodingly out, while another sight had caught Sasha's eye. She opened a door and went into a tiled bathroom. An enormous white-enamel bath stood on brass claw feet, ornate gold taps set into the patterned tiles of the wall at one end. 'Oh, Reid, come and look at this! Oh goodness, how divine, I would absolutely die to have a bath at this very moment.' Sasha groaned, emerging from the bathroom and wandering around the room examining *objets d'art* and the silk wallpaper, the walnut writing bureau set between the two windows, and then she came to a halt at Reid's shoulder and looked up at him.

'It's all so incredible and beautiful.'

He turned his head, catching the note of wistful sadness in her soft voice. The light of Russia had a special quality, a depth and clarity that shone now on Sasha, his eyes lingering on her flawless pale skin and the shape of her pink mouth, the little determined dent in her chin and the line of her delicate jaw and nose. He reached out and lifted her chin with the crook of his forefinger. 'And all this opulence makes you sad?'

'Of course,' she replied solemnly, gazing out at the distant expanse of the wide Neva glimpsed through the voile.

'Why?'

'Because…' She paused for a moment, hesitating, considering her thoughts and the weight of them. 'Because it is all a charming, wonderful fantasy and I must return to reality.' She raised her eyes to him. 'Soon.'

'Where will you go?'

'Home. To England.'

'But that could take weeks to arrange.'

'My mother has many cousins, aunts and uncles in St Petersburg. I am sure someone will take me in.'

'You don't have to do that.'

'Don't I?'

Reid turned then, his hands lifting and settling on her waist, drawing her closer to him. He had to stoop to see her face, so small was she against his taller frame. Beneath his hands her waist felt so soft and slender, and he murmured, his eyes never leaving hers, 'Do you know that we have never even kissed?'

'Yes, we have, on the ship.'

He shrugged. 'You can hardly call that peck a kiss.'

Sasha held her breath, feeling the warmth and strength of his hands upon her waist, holding her firmly, and her lips parted slightly as he leaned closer. She closed her eyes, her senses delighting in the closeness of him, his warmth, his male scent, the promise of pleasure as his mouth hovered close above her own.

A knock upon the door made them both start, and they broke apart, almost with guilty haste as the door opened and the maid announced that Lady Cronin was waiting for them to join her in the drawing room. They stepped apart, with a fleeting glance, and followed the maid downstairs and there gave themselves up to the curiosity of their hosts, though Reid kept Sasha close to his side and fielded any awkward questions with all the skill of a true diplomat. He noticed that Sasha began to wilt, sometimes almost flinching each time she was addressed by the name of 'Georgia'. After luncheon, he discreetly mentioned to his hostess that his wife had been very ill on the sea voyage and begged their pardon. Lady Cronin was somewhat reluctant to let them go but, as 'Georgia' was saying very little, she saw no point in keeping them.

Once he had settled Sasha in their bedchamber, Reid took himself off to meet Sir Stanley to discuss his forthcoming duties.

The afternoon passed all too quickly and Sasha woke as the maid tiptoed in to light the lamps and draw the curtains. She drew a hot bath for Sasha and started unpacking her cases, taking herself off to the laundry to press an oyster-pink chiffon evening gown while Sasha lay back in the hot and comforting water of the huge bathtub.

Gazing up at the high ceiling, she noticed the mural painted on its surface, her eyes widening at the erotic scene of naked lovers reclining upon a grassy knoll in the woods, surrounded by flowers and sunshine that left little to the imagination. She studied the naked buttocks and muscular legs of the male lover as he leaned over the female, and wondered what Reid would be like naked, leaning over her. She glanced down at her own body, not quite as curvaceous and well endowed as the woman in the painting. What would it be like to make love? She felt a heat rise in her cheeks and her neck, spreading down into her belly and between her legs. In the bedroom she heard the door click and quickly reached for a bar of soap, intending to wash and climb out.

'Just leave it on the bed, please, Jane,' she called out, convinced that the maid had returned with her gown.

There was no reply, but she heard footsteps, and then the creak of the bathroom door and she glanced over her shoulder, about to tell the maid to find her silk stockings and corset and lay them out, too, only to discover that it was not the maid standing there. 'Reid!'

Instinctively she sat forwards and hunched over as she drew her arms across her chest. From where he stood in the doorway, Reid could see no more than the smooth, wet curve of her back, her hair twisted up in a knot on top of her head and revealing the delicate slenderness of her neck.

'What do you want on the bed?' he drawled, leaning on the door frame, his voice soft and lazy as he looked at her in the bath, then raising his eyes to the lurid mural.

'Go away!' Sasha exclaimed, blushing hotly.

'Why? I'm rather enjoying the view.'

'Well, don't! I'm bathing.'

'I can see that.' He smiled, and added, 'I was talking about the ceiling.'

'Don't be a cad, and close the door!'

'A cad? Sasha, I don't think there is much of you that I haven't already seen.'

'That's different, I was ill then.'

His smile deepened into a grin as he levered himself away from the door and came in, unlinking the cuffs on his shirt sleeves. 'And now you are not ill. And we are, to all intents and purposes, husband and wife.' He looked at her for a long moment with his dark blue eyes. 'Or we will be as soon as we have the opportunity to, um…consummate.'

Sasha gasped, her eyes lifting to his. 'I thought we agreed that I would leave—'

'Did I agree, Sasha?' He finished unbuttoning his shirt, shrugged it off and then sat down on a small gilt stool as he removed his shoes and socks. 'It has suddenly occurred to me that really the best possible solution is for us to stay married.'

'What on earth are you doing?' demanded Sasha, suddenly finding it very difficult to breathe, her cheeks scarlet, distracted from what he was saying by his actions.

'I'm going to have a nice, refreshing bath before dinner.'

'But— But— I— I'm in the bath!'

His eyes scanned the huge enamel tub. 'Well, move over, then, and make some room.'

'I most certainly will not!'

'Why?'

Sasha heaved an exasperated sigh. 'Why do you always have to ask "why"?'

He shrugged, standing up to unfasten his breeches. 'Because like most males I cannot follow your female train of thought.'

Sasha averted her face as he peeled off his breeches, and then she looked back, convinced that he had not yet removed his under-drawers, only to find him standing there naked. She could not stifle a small exclamation of surprise, nor a discreet peek about the floor.

'I'm not wearing any,' he murmured. 'Spoils the fit.'

Sasha blinked, arrested by the stunning sight of Reid with no clothes on, her eyes skimming over the suntanned width of his shoulders, his broad chest covered with a scattering of bronze hairs that arrowed down the lean flat planes of his abdomen, his heavily muscled biceps a reminder of how easily he had carried her. Her eyes moved down to the male parts of him, her curiosity overriding her embarrassment, and she could see that he was as perfectly formed as any Grecian statue of a male god. She was still looking when, with an agile movement, Reid climbed into the bath. As two feet landed in the water between her ankles Sasha suddenly jumped up, in her haste slipping on the bar of soap she had dropped in the water.

'Steady.' Reid grasped her by the elbows and looked down at her, his glance sweeping over her small high breasts, her slender hips and the dark patch between her thighs.

Sasha had never, of course, stood naked with a man before in her life, and she looked up at him with huge eyes, her lips parted, swollen and red from the heat of the water and her sensual thoughts. The molten surge of arousal was a new sensation for her, yet warring with her blushing inexperience of such an intimate situation. She became aware that his body had reacted to her gaze and to her naked female body as much as she had reacted to his maleness.

He smiled, unabashed, amused by her awestruck glance, murmuring reassuringly, 'Don't be afraid.'

'Reid, I've never— That is, I— I…'

'Shh,' he murmured. 'I know.'

'I don't think I could…' Sasha gasped, with a nervous glance downwards at the much enlarged evidence of his arousal.

His hand gently stroked her hip, urging her closer, but just at that moment the bedchamber door opened and they heard the tap of heels and the soft voice of the maid as she idly hummed

'My Bonnie Lies Over the Ocean' under her breath, moving about the bedchamber as she laid out the freshly pressed gown and Georgia's underwear on the bed.

'Damnation,' Reid exclaimed under his breath, 'are we never to have any privacy?'

Sasha quickly climbed out of the bath and reached for one of the large fluffy white towels placed on a low marble-topped table, wrapping it around her, and backing away from him, averting her eyes from the sight of so much powerful and blatant masculinity. With a sigh Reid sank down into the water, and lay back for a moment, saying, 'Close the door on your way out, please.'

Sasha needed no second bidding and she did as he asked, then hurried to put on her underclothes. Jane helped her to dress, fastening the long row of pearl buttons at the back of the evening gown, the bodice made of lace and high-necked. The bustle supported a train that swept elegantly behind her as she walked, the very height of fashion, but just a little too long, the gown having been made for Georgia.

Once she was dressed she sat down at the ornate triple-mirrored dressing table and Jane set about brushing and sweeping her dark brown hair up into a smooth chignon, fastening a small, delicate pearl-encrusted tiara above her fringe, a box of jewellery being a wedding gift from Reid to his new bride.

'There, madam, looks lovely.'

'Thank you.' Sasha stared at her reflection, and then behind her at the door of the bathroom as it opened and Reid emerged, wearing nothing except a towel about his waist.

With a curt nod to Sasha, he walked past them to the adjoining dressing room, where his batman waited with his evening clothes. Sasha could not help but notice that the maid followed him with her eyes, and indeed, Reid was a beautiful sight to behold.

'Thank you, Jane, that will be all.' Sasha spoke a little more sharply than she had intended, and with a dipped curtsy the maid turned about and left the room.

For long moments Sasha sat and stared at her face in the mirror. It would be a very long evening, Sasha thought, another meal of many courses, the strain of making conversation with strangers, and a sense of loneliness that seemed to be unfurling within her now that the journey was over and they had arrived in St Petersburg. London seemed very far away indeed, and she wished so much that her papa and her sisters were all here with her. She had never in her life been apart from them, and their chatter and her father's strict sensible ways would at this moment be so very welcome. She felt very unsure about who it was that looked back at her in the mirror, and what she would become if she allowed Reid to persuade her to fall in with his plans. Why had he suddenly decided to keep her as his wife? She was sure he was not in love with her, for though they seemed to get along well enough as friends, and respected one another's minds, she feared there was little in the way of hearts involved, as far as Reid was concerned.

Chapter Six

At dinner Sasha enjoyed talking to Charlotte Hope-Garner, who sat at her left hand and chattered with light-hearted gaiety about her five children whom she so obviously adored; the eldest two boys, aged twelve and fourteen, were boarding at Eton, she explained with shining eyes, leaving her with the three young ones, two girls and another boy aged between seven and two. On her right sat a Russian guest by the name of Dr Alexei Bodanovsky, a physician commissioned to the royal court of Tsar Alexander. He complimented Sasha on her fluent skill with his native tongue and engaged her in an intense discussion about Russia. The food was excellent and the company interesting, yet her attention, her mind, her very heart and soul, wandered.

Reid was seated farther down the table, on the opposite side, and his dinner companions seemed to be equally amusing: a Russian princess on his left and her military husband on his right. Yet throughout the meal her glance often strayed and met his. By the look in his blue eyes she was left in no doubt that his thoughts strayed, too, into secret places that brought a blush to her neck and cheeks.

It was very late indeed when at last they retired. They took their leave of the few guests still lingering in the drawing room with their hosts and climbed the stairs to their bedchamber. As they traversed the thick carpet on the first landing, Sasha broke the silence by making a comment about the pleasant evening, and Reid nodded a reply. She glanced at him, from the corner of her eye. He seemed rather quiet and she wondered if there was anything wrong, if *she* had done something wrong.

'Dinner was excellent,' Sasha ventured as they climbed the next flight of stairs.

'Yes.'

'The chicken was delicious. I wonder what it was.'

'I think it is a dish from Kiev.'

'I didn't really enjoy that lumpy black stuff at the beginning.'

He smiled down at her. 'Caviar is an acquired taste.'

They came to their door and Reid opened it, stepping aside to allow her to pass first. Once they were inside he closed it behind him, looked for a key, but there was none, and then loosened his white bow tie and shrugged off his black tails.

Sasha kicked off her shoes, and removed the pearl tiara from her hair, sighing as she laid it on the dressing table. 'I'm so tired I could sleep for a week.'

She went to the bed and picked up the long-sleeved nightgown of frilled white cambric that the maid had left out for her, and then turned to Reid and asked for his assistance to unbutton her dress. He came to her side and deftly unhooked the long row of pearl buttons, unlaced her corset and then turned abruptly away from her, saying that he was going outside onto the balcony to get a breath of fresh air.

Sasha looked up, holding the bodice of her gown modestly to her chest. 'There is no need to leave, it's freezing out there. I will go into the bathroom and undress, if you wish.'

He stopped and turned back to look at her, with a quizzical frown. 'It is not my wishes that matter, Sasha. I am only think-ing of you, and your delicate…situation.'

His remark puzzled her, and she called out as he walked away. 'Reid?'

Again he halted and turned to face her. 'What?'

'Have I done something wrong?'

'No, of course not.'

'You seem very…cool.'

'Do I? I'm sorry.' He hesitated, and then seemed about to say something, and she waited expectantly, but he merely said, 'Get undressed and into bed.'

As the balcony door closed behind him, the white voile billowing on the icy draught, Sasha hurried to divest herself of the chiffon gown, her corset, petticoats and bustle. Then she went into the bathroom and washed quickly, brushed her teeth, pulled on her nightgown and returned, barefoot, to the bedchamber. For a moment she stared at the vast expanse of the bed, and then she dragged back the covers and arranged some of the pillows down the middle of the mattress. She had no idea why Reid had suddenly cooled in his ardour, but until he explained himself he was certainly not going to do any consummating of any kind tonight!

Out on the balcony, Reid gazed at the dark city of St Petersburg silhouetted by the pale light of a half-moon. There were a few boats out on the River Neva, their lanterns glowing yellow in the dark, and the glint of inky water rippling here and there at their passing by. It had been a very busy day; from what Sir Stanley had told him he knew very well that beneath the serene surface of this magnificent city lurked an undercurrent of evil. He had drawn the conclusion that the best thing for Sasha would be for her to return to London. Besides the danger of riots and bombs here in the city, he considered their encounter in the bathroom earlier in the evening.

He had never been with a virgin before and she seemed so delicate and vulnerable, so pure and innocent, that he could not imagine satisfying his carnal desires with her. She had seemed nervous and embarrassed and he wondered if she thought lovemaking only involved kisses and cuddling and not much else. With her strict upbringing, how could she be blamed for being innocent? Indeed, he knew well enough that it was no fault of Sasha's, yet when he compared her to someone like her sister Georgia—even though no doubt her nurturing had been just as strict, she was by nature earthy and voluptuous, a girl who would do anything, anywhere, and thoroughly enjoy it.

No, he sighed, he was not sure he could have a passionate relationship with Sasha. Yet to all intents and purposes the world now viewed her as his wife, so how could he do anything other than make her truly his wife, in every way? Her honour would be ruined if they now confessed, as well as his career, the effects rippling far and wide to tarnish both their families. Reid sighed, aware that Sasha had become a part of his life and his thoughts, and for her to leave both did not appeal to him. He went back inside, closing the door and glancing across the room at the small shape of Sasha lying in the huge bed.

Sasha lay curled up under the heavy bedcovers of eiderdown and sheets. She felt the cold draught as the balcony door opened, and then its click as Reid closed it behind him. She heard him move about as he undressed, the clunk of his shoes dropping on the floor, and then the room went very dark as he turned out all the lamps. She felt the mattress dip slightly as he climbed in, and the tug of the covers as he pulled them over his shoulder. Sasha held her breath, both of them aware of a tension as they settled into the comfortable bed. She stared into the darkness, at the vague shape of Reid's broad back, her heart suddenly pounding, wondering if he was going to turn to her and she would discover the secrets of passion between a man and a woman. As tantalising a thought as that was, Sasha suddenly swallowed nervously, realising that a man like Reid must have a great deal of experience of lovemaking, and she, as a virgin, had none. What if she made a fool of herself? What if he was not pleased with her? And just as swiftly came the stark reminder that their relationship was illicit and they should not be in this bed together at all! She wondered if Reid was having the same thoughts, as he made no move to turn around and touch her, but merely murmured a good-night.

'Good night,' Sasha replied, and then closed her eyes, her trust in him unwavering as she snuggled down and eventually slept.

It was still dark when a sound startled Sasha awake. She jerked, staring about the room, wondering where she was, a little confused and disorientated as she realised that this was not her Roseberry Street bedroom. And then it came again, several loud, staccato bangs. She sat up and threw back the bedcovers, exclaiming as she ran across the room to look out. 'What on earth was that?'

Reid had been wakened by the sounds, too, but he knew at once what they were. He jumped out of the bed and grasped her arm, pulling her back as she made to draw aside the curtains and peer out into the street. 'Sasha, come away from the window.'

'Did you hear that?' She half turned towards him.

He nodded his head. 'Yes. It's rifle shots.'

Sasha gasped, and made to rush to the window again, but he held her back. 'Who on earth would be out with a rifle at this time of night?'

Reid smiled as he replied drily, 'Not the sort of people you or I would care to meet, but don't worry, we are perfectly safe here in the Embassy. Come now, get back into bed.'

'But—'

'There is nothing to see.' He propelled her towards the bed, and bundled her into it, pulling the covers up over her before walking around and climbing back into his side.

Sasha lay there on her back, rigid, listening, but acutely aware that Reid had seemed very...naked. Before she could ponder on this interesting fact a sudden noise outside made her sit up, listening to the thunder of galloping horses on the rough cobbles, guttural shouts and shots that made the glass panes of the French doors rattle. With a squeal of alarm, and swift agility, Sasha leapt over her self-imposed barrier of pillows and all but flung herself against Reid.

'It's all right,' he soothed, his arm folding around her shoulders as she clung to him, trembling. 'There's nothing to worry about.' He repeated his earlier reassurance. 'We are safe here.'

Sasha groaned, turning her face into the smooth skin of his brawny shoulder, conceding that she did feel safe within the protection of his arms. 'Reid, what on earth have we got ourselves into?'

He grunted, but now was not the time to add to her fears by explaining that Russia was a turbulent nation on the brink of revolution. He moderated his response, merely stating, 'You should know well enough that the Russians are a volatile people.'

She gave a short, unamused laugh. 'Indeed they are, which makes me worry even more.'

His hand stroked her hair back from one temple. 'As long as we are careful, it will not affect us to any great degree.'

'Do you really think so?' In the dark she looked up at him, moving her head and body to face him. 'Will we be able to go about our normal lives, as we would in London?'

'Well, no. Some things will be different; we must be more careful and you must never go out alone, always take an escort.'

'Reid, you are scaring me.'

'I only want you to be aware, Sasha. Now, go to sleep. In the morning it will all seem much better.'

She smiled slightly. 'That's what my papa says.'

'Hmm.' Reid wasn't sure if he liked being compared to her father, but he said softly, 'Good night.'

She murmured a reply, but made no move to lie apart from him. He felt so warm and big, the solid length of his body beside her, a bastion that she could lean on. She closed her eyes and tried to go back to sleep, but she was far too aware of the bulk of his thigh and the wide barrel of his ribs, and the hairs of his chest, his skin, and his male, musky smell, and his breathing. She could tell that he, too, was not able to return to the depths of slumber, his breathing uneven, punctuated now and then by the workings of his throat as he swallowed. She felt tension in his body, and if she moved her legs against him, she could feel that he wore not a stitch of clothing. She remembered that earlier in the day he had been about to kiss her, and how much she wished that he had. Now, they lay awake, so much aware of each other in these intimate circumstances that it was impossible to sleep.

Impulsively she asked, 'Do you always sleep naked?'

Reid smiled in the dark, shifting slightly to accommodate her weight against him. 'That's not a very ladylike question, Miss Packard.'

'Mrs Bowen,' she corrected, with a mischievous smile.

His smile darkened to a puzzled frown, 'Now that's a question we certainly need to attend to.'

'We really should come clean and tell everyone the truth.'

He was silent, pondering, his fingers toying with the long strands of her hair as they lay in disarray about her shoulders.

When he made no response, Sasha poked him in the ribs with her finger. 'Reid?'

His fingers circled her shoulder. 'Don't worry yourself too much about it, I'll sort something out.'

'What do you mean?'

'Sasha, my little innocent, do you not realise that it is far too late for you to be leaving me? Thanks to your sister we are now husband and wife, or so everyone thinks, and to try to undo that and go our separate ways as though nothing has happened is, I fear, impossible. The scandal would be so great that you would become an outcast from society.'

Sasha listened to him in silence, and licked her lips nervously as she realised what he was trying to tell her. Not only would she be an outcast as a result of the scandal, but Reid, too, would not go scot-free. He might even be dismissed from the Army. With a sudden stab of alarm and fear for him, she asked in a very soft voice, 'So, what do you propose, then?'

He smiled above her. 'Propose is the operative word, my dear.

We must marry, in secret and in all haste. In name only, if that is what you wish.'

Greatly daring, Sasha pressed closer, moving higher up so that she could reach him. She lifted her hand and turned his jaw towards her. 'No, Reid,' she murmured, 'I want more than just your name.' She leaned forwards and pressed her mouth to his, in her first real kiss. His lips felt warm and smooth, the stubble of his chin rough against her face.

At first he did not respond, surprised by her boldness, and then slowly he turned towards her and his mouth opened. He rolled her over onto her back and kissed her with careful, tender expertise.

The broad width of his shoulders covered her body and Sasha's heart suddenly started beating very hard. Her lips parted beneath the pressure of his and she gave a little gasp at the firm wet thrust of his tongue stroking inside her mouth and instinctively she let her own tongue entwine with his. The sensation was delightful and unlike anything she had ever known. Her breathing was now quite rapid, though he seemed very much in control of his own, and she gasped and swayed her hips in a natural yearning towards his male body as they kissed.

She wanted to feel his skin against her own and she shrugged out of her nightgown, tossing it aside. When his hand touched her breast, and stroked down to her waist and hips, she gave a little moan of pleasure, pressing against him, yet drawing quickly away as she suddenly felt the solid bulk of his male arousal.

Through the hot haze of desire Reid remembered that she had never lain with a man before, and though it had been a long time for him, and the urge to take her was fierce within him, he restrained himself. His fingers stroked the length of her thigh with soft, soothing care. 'Sasha, much as I would love to, we mustn't, we shouldn't, we're not even properly married.'

'I know, but—' she moved her head in a little purr of pleasure, her eyes closed '—it feels so wonderful. I don't want you to stop.'

'I don't want to stop, either,' he murmured, hardly able to

help himself as he kissed the full curve of her breast, breathing in her delicate female scent; his senses were surrounded by the smooth silkiness of her skin, the womanly curves of her breasts and hips and thighs, her nipple so close he longed to take it in his mouth. 'We won't do…anything…just touching.'

'I— I don't know what to do,' Sasha confessed, melting at his touch, though her knees were still tightly clasped together.

'Do whatever you want.' His voice was a little rough, ragged with the effort of his self-control. 'Sasha, I am a soldier. I have had many experiences with women. I am not an innocent like you, but I would never do anything to hurt or frighten you.' He hoped his words would help her to relax and he very much wanted to touch her in her secret female place, but short of forcibly prising her legs apart he didn't think she was ready to yield. He asked carefully, 'What has your mother told you about… relations between a man and a woman?'

'Nothing.'

'Nothing? Surely she must have explained something.'

'I'm sure she would have, had she known that I was to be married,' Sasha replied in a small voice.

'Ah. I forgot.' He drew back then, and looked down at her as she lay beneath his body, so soft and trusting, so innocent, and suddenly his ardour cooled. How could he do with her the things he most wanted, when she had no understanding of it all and he had no right to be teaching her? It would be an insult to Sasha to indulge in an act that for him would be no more than a physical encounter.

'Reid…' Sasha reached up, her hands sliding over his shoulders, sensing his reluctance and pulling his body back towards her, her small hand moving down his chest and touching the hot, hard length of his manhood with curious yet clumsy fingers. 'I want to know. Show me, teach me. Please.'

He groaned. 'Sasha, please, don't touch me there.'

'Why? Do you not like it?'

His groan intensified into a growl as her fingers tightened.

'I like it very much. But you don't understand what will happen if you don't stop doing that.'

'Does it give you pleasure?'

'Yes.' His voice was strangled, his mouth reaching down to capture her lips in a sensual kiss.

'Then I don't want to stop. Show me, Reid,' she whispered against his mouth. 'Show me how to give you pleasure.'

How could he resist such a plea? And yet he knew he must proceed with caution; he whispered gently in her ear, telling her things that made her blush, and yet excited her in a way that she had never felt before. He encouraged her to explore his body, yet was careful with his own exploration of hers, never going too far, taking note of her reactions when he touched her here, or there, aware that she enjoyed his mouth sucking on her nipple, kisses on her ribs and shoulders and neck, but if his lips strayed below her waist she tensed. She was not ready for complete intimacy, and instead he urged her to do as she wished with his own body.

Sasha felt in control and curiously powerful, though he was physically much bigger and stronger than her. It was a new sensation as they lay side by side, and she kissed his chest, her other hand sliding over the strong muscles of his back and down to his buttocks. He groaned then, as his hips thrust beneath the squeezing pressure of her other hand. She felt an ache inside her, and yet was not sure where or why, or how to respond to the heat and urgency of his body. He showed her then how to grip him in her fist, his own hand closing over hers and guiding her, faster and harder. He could have made it last much longer, but with a hoarse growl he reached his goal quickly.

As their breathing steadied after a few moments, Sasha asked, in an awed, hushed tone, 'Is this how babies are made?'

He grinned at her naivety. 'Sort of. To make a baby I must do that inside you.'

She swallowed, and then whispered, 'Inside me where?'

His fingers touched the crisp dark curls of her Venus mound, his own voice no more than a warm breath as he murmured against her ear. 'I will show you, if you want me to.' She nodded, and his finger moved down, sliding gently into the warm silky folds of her sex, probing her entrance. 'Inside there.' She felt tight, and as he pressed a little deeper he could tell she was not particularly aroused, and he withdrew his hand as he felt her body tense. 'It's all right. I can understand that you are not ready.'

'Will I feel pleasure, too?'

'Of course. It would be very selfish and clumsy of a lover if you did not.' He leaned down and kissed her neck. 'Thank you, Sasha. A man takes pleasure in many ways, but often ladies are not very accommodating and easily shocked. I hope you are not too shocked.'

'I am a little, but I am glad that now I know.' She snuggled then against him, relaxed and eager for sleep.

As she settled down, Reid looked at her through half-closed eyes, through the hazy veil of satisfaction and sleep, realising that maybe his judgement of Sasha was in need of review.

The next few days were very busy days, with Reid taking up the reins from Major Hope-Garner as military attaché, and Sasha caught up in the social activities of Lady Cronin. On several afternoons they were taken for a carriage ride around the sights of St Petersburg. Sasha gazed in awe at the Winter Palace and Nevsky Prospekt, cathedrals, parks, monuments, and dozens of beautiful wrought-iron bridges spanning the River Neva. It was indeed a splendid and magnificent city, yet in dark corners and down alleyways she glimpsed the pinched and gaunt faces of shawled peasants shuffling along. She made enquiries about the lower classes and how she could be of help, perhaps if there were any missionaries in the city in need of benevolence, but these were quickly brushed aside and it was made clear to her that she was not to involve herself in such things.

'We are guests of the Tsar, my dear Georgia, and representatives of our Queen,' said Lady Cronin loftily. 'We must not be seen to be interfering.'

Sasha sat back as the carriage rumbled along the broad streets, silent, brooding on the unfairness of it all and determined that if she was to spend any great length of time here in Russia she would get to know her mother's people, and to help those in need of help if she could. And yet, she frowned, as the carriage rumbled along the wide cobbled streets, who was she to act the noble lady, when she was nothing more than a fake and a fraud?

It was only at night, when at last Reid and Sasha fell into bed and turned to face each other, that they had the chance for long murmured conversations, to shake off the cloak of secrecy and be their real selves. And then as their confidences and comments about the day petered out, Reid would draw her closer with one hand on her waist and kiss her. His kisses were sometimes deep and passionate, sometimes light and playful, but always Sasha sensed that he had a great deal of expertise in the art of making love. Yet Sasha held him back, sensing also that to indulge completely and surrender her virtue to him would be wrong in their present circumstances. There were moments when she felt quite robbed of any reason and all she felt was pure physical sensation. The temptation was strong to ease the deep, aching need within her, and again she voiced her opinion that they should tell everyone the truth.

As he kissed the side of her neck Reid murmured, 'I will make inquiries, discreetly of course. There must be a reverend of some kind, who administers to the poor—'

'A missionary?'

'Perhaps.'

'Where will you find him?'

Reid drew back, sighing impatiently and frowning at her. 'Sasha, stop interrupting. I don't know yet, but as soon as this damn ball is over and we've moved into our apartment, we will call on him, quietly marry, and then tell everyone the truth about who you really are.'

As he said the words, they both looked at each other, as it suddenly dawned on them the consequences of such an action.

It passed through Reid's mind that in all likelihood he would be relieved of his duties and sent back to London, for deception and misconduct—for being a liar. He swallowed, aware that his career was in jeopardy, and yet, what else could he do? He and Sasha could not continue indefinitely living a lie.

The same thoughts possessed Sasha and she whispered, 'I am so sorry, Reid, I never realised that—'

He pressed a finger to her lips. 'Shh. What is done is done, and now we must make the best of it. Go to sleep, Sasha, and tomorrow will soon be upon us. It will be our last day in the Residency and all we have to do is get through the ball, get married and move into our own apartment. All will be well, I promise.'

When Sasha awoke to the golden glow of a spring morning, Reid had already left in response to an invitation from the Russian Army to join them on manoeuvres for the day, accompanied by several other British and French officers. He had told her not to expect him back before the evening and in all likelihood would only meet her in the ballroom tonight. As she stretched languorously and turned her face towards Reid's pillow, still aromatic with his male odour, she smiled to herself. They had been in St Petersburg a week already, and tonight they would attend the grand ball that Lady Cronin had been planning and talking about ever since they had arrived. And then tomorrow she and Reid would be properly married, and they would begin their life together. Tomorrow night they would make love, truly, as man and wife, and Sasha rubbed the goosebumps of anticipation that flared on her forearms.

The maid brought her a tray set with hot chocolate and fresh bread rolls, butter and jam. They chatted companionably, mulling over the clothes in the wardrobe and choosing a pale blue outfit suitable for the morning's visit to an art gallery, the milliners, and one of Lady Cronin's English friends for luncheon.

After a busy morning, on their return Sasha spent the rest of the afternoon and evening lying on the bed, reading Sir Walter

Scott's *Ivanhoe*. As the shadows lengthened, she dozed, awakened by the apricot bloom of sunset deepening to darkest orange and then crimson, finally extinguishing into darkness. She heard the household rouse, the distant sound of voices, doors opening and closing. Jane came then, to light the lamps and run her bath. She hung up the freshly pressed ball gown upon a wooden dummy designed for such things, and Sasha rose from the bed, gazing at the elegant gown of cream silk, the bodice low cut and encrusted on one shoulder with rosebuds in a shade of ashrose pink, the train sweeping back in elegant folds over a high bustle. She went to bathe, and then, warm and freshly scented, she donned her underwear of petticoats, stockings and corset before Jane assisted her into her elegant cream gown. She sat down before the dressing table as Jane did her hair, fastening tiny, palest pink silk rosebuds into the mass of dark ringlets gathered at her nape.

Sasha stood before the cheval mirror, looking at her reflection and adjusting her gown here and there. A short knock on the door preceded Lady Cronin. For a moment she stood behind the open door and simply gazed at Sasha with sharp, shrewd eyes, and then she came in and gave her a most scrutinising examination from head to toe.

'You look quite charming, Georgia.'

Was it her imagination, or did she place undue emphasis on her sister's name? Sasha avoided her eye as she tweaked at a silk rosebud. 'Thank you, Lady Cronin.'

'Although I must say all your gowns do seem a trifle long in the hem. His lordship has still not yet returned, but the ball will begin at nine o'clock sharp, whether he is here or not.' She came into the room then and surveyed Sasha with a look that could only be described as icy. 'I would remind you, Georgia, that as the wife of a military attaché, a representative of the Queen's government, you have a certain reputation to uphold.'

Sasha felt the blood freeze in her veins, yet she merely answered demurely, 'Of course.' And wondered furiously what on earth Lady Cronin was leading up to, hoping that her guilt was not written plainly upon her face.

'This morning I received a calling card from a Countess Irena Sletovskaya.' She paused, perusing Sasha's face. 'She claims to be your mother's second cousin and was eager to call upon you.'

Sasha smiled, the name bringing to mind her mother's pleasure at receiving letters from this distant cousin, light-hearted and full of gossip that had brought a few moments of pleasure into her mother's somewhat dull world. 'How wonderful. Of course I would be delighted to receive her.'

'Certainly not! I must hasten to add that Countess Irena has the most lurid of reputations. She is well known to be the mistress of more than one *gentleman*.' Lady Cronin sneered the last word. 'You would do well to avoid her at all costs. I have returned her card and made it quite clear that you do not wish to associate with her.'

Sasha was taken aback at this high-handed interference in what was, to all intents and purposes, her own personal life, and the obvious insult to a member of her own family. Her reply was cool as she inclined her head in acknowledgement. 'I will discuss it with my—Major Bowen.'

'I am sure your husband will agree with me.' And with that rather curt observation and a slight nod of her head she departed, closing the door with a snap.

In the ensuing silence Jane murmured gently, 'It's only seven now, mum, I'll bring you up some tea and a bite to eat.'

'Thank you,' replied Sasha, and then stalled the maid with a hand on her forearm. 'Is Major Bowen back, do you know?'

'No, mum.' The maid shook her head, the ribbons of her little white cap fluttering as she bobbed a curtsy at the door. 'I don't think so.'

Sasha went to stand by the window, for the hundredth time that day, her figure reflected in the dark panes and the darkness of the city punctuated by yellow lamp lights. Her sense of foreboding had increased. The next two hours seemed both far too long and swiftly over. Her hand shook a little as she drank a cup of fragrant Earl Grey tea and nibbled on toast, ravenously hungry yet slightly nauseated by the anxiety of her thoughts. She tried to convince herself that she was worrying about nothing, and if Reid were here at this moment he would laugh aside her fears. At last the glass-domed clock on the mantel softly chimed the ninth hour and Sasha took a deep breath. As she descended the carpeted stairs, alone, and heard the distant strains of an orchestra, she wished more than anything that Reid was at her side, tall and strong and capable.

Sasha stood in the doorway of the ballroom, a solitary figure as she gazed upon the magnificent scene. The high ceiling was beautifully decorated with gold leaf and murals, and supported by six marble-and-onyx columns. Along the walls hung several vast mirrors in ornate gold frames, reflecting the colourful array of the guests. The silk and satin of the ladies' gowns contrasted with the dark coats of the gentlemen in tails, only the braided uniforms of the military officers outshining the beautiful ball gowns and sparkling jewellery of the ladies. An orchestra played in a gallery at the far end of the room, the poignant strains of a Strauss waltz filling the room with vibrant melody as couples on the dance floor swayed and whirled smoothly about.

She moved forward quickly, before anyone could take too much notice of her arrival unaccompanied; as she did so a familiar face emerged out of the crowd. She looked up at him with a smile of relief.

'Captain Turnbull, how very nice to see you.'

The Navy man, in full dress uniform, bowed to her and offered her a glass of champagne from a passing waiter, 'The pleasure is all mine, Mrs Bowen.' He winked at her. 'You look a bonnie lass tonight, I must say.' He looked about. 'And where is the Major?'

'I believe he is galloping about on the plains with Russian

Hussars.' She sipped golden liquid from the narrow flute glass, the bubbles tickling her nose.

He snorted on a laugh. 'Then we should not expect him back any time soon.'

'Oh?' Sasha looked up at him askance, with a sideways glance. 'Why is that?'

'My dear, they do like to drink, the Russians. Vodka, and plenty of it.'

'Well…' Sasha frowned. 'I hope he won't arrive in a—a foxed state.'

The Captain laughed. 'In the meantime—' he set aside his glass, and hers, offering his arm '—please do me the honour of the next dance.'

'Of course.'

Sasha smiled and spent a pleasant time dancing and chatting with Captain Turnbull, who then introduced her to friends of his, and she danced with the surgeon from HMS *Dorset*, and enjoyed conversations with several people, her fluency in French and Russian holding her in good stead and drawing much admiration and interest. Yet her glance frequently went to the door, in search of Reid. She so much wanted to share the pleasure of the evening with him. Despite being entertained by the company, the dancing and the champagne, she felt tension coiled in her midriff, her yearning for Reid increasing.

'Bonsoir, ma petite.'

A smoky, very low, yet strangely familiar female voice sounded close to her ear and Sasha turned to gaze upon its owner. It was as though she looked upon a twin of her mother, except this woman was slightly taller and her magnificent figure in its cream-and-gold gown the very perfection of tiny waist and voluptuous bosom. She had an alabaster swanlike neck and dark glossy hair coiled on her head, crowned with a diamond tiara.

'I knew at once that you must be Georgia,' the woman purred in English, her husky voice pleasantly accented. 'You are the spitting image of your mother.'

Sasha smiled, and inclined her head slightly. 'I could say the same, *madame*, although even my lovely mama could only claim to be a poor likeness.'

The woman laughed, an enchanting sound that drew glances from those standing nearby. 'Please, call me Irena.' She glanced covertly about and gently laid her gloved hand under Sasha's elbow. 'Come, let us find a corner where we can talk, before the Dragon Lady discovers that I have found you.'

'You mean Lady Cronin?'

'Of course.' Countess Irena wrinkled her delicate nose. 'I think she does not approve of me.'

Sasha merely smiled, realising that she could not possibly comment on Lady Cronin's true opinion of this very beautiful woman. Her curiosity was aroused, however, and despite the warning, she was eager to get to know the cousin who had grown up with her own mother and knew of her childhood. Judging from the many male glances that slid her way as they moved through the throng of guests, Countess Irena also had the allure and charm to attract admiration that every woman secretly longed for. Sasha glanced at her from the corner of her eye. Her face was a classic oval, the nose slightly aquiline, full ruby lips evenly shaped, and her dark black eyes fringed with thick, smoky lashes that Sasha suspected were outlined with a hint of kohl. No respectable woman would go about in public with a painted face, but Countess Irena seemed to be a law unto herself, and no doubt a very rich one. Sasha noted the glittering diamonds on her fingers, at her earlobes and sparkling in a delicate necklace upon her bosom, as well as the diamond-and-pearl tiara gracing her head.

They found two gilt chairs in an alcove and sat down.

'I am very surprised, Countess Irena, that Lady Cronin even let you in the door.' Suddenly realising how rude that must sound, Sasha held her fingers to her mouth. 'Oh, I'm sorry, I did not mean—'

Irena laughed, a throaty, husky sound. 'She could not very

well refuse. My escort is godson to the Tsar and a very influential young man.' She laid a reassuring hand on Sasha's wrist. 'Do not worry, I am quite sure that Lady Cronin has already made known to you her own strait-laced and narrow views on the entire population of Russia. Without even so much as leaving the Residency. Now, my darling Olga's darling girl, tell me all about yourself. I believe you are recently married to a British officer? Is he very handsome?'

Sasha's cheek dimpled on a smile, warming to this exotic cousin once removed. 'Oh, yes—' she sighed '—he is very handsome indeed.'

Countess Irena was no fool and she was quick to pick up on the wistful note in Sasha's voice, nor did she fail to notice the downcast expression in her eyes. 'A bride should be radiant and glowing after only a few weeks of marriage, but I sense this is not so, my dear?'

Sasha blushed and looked away, the restrictions of her English heritage far too ingrained to begin discussing personal and intimate matters in public. And yet, glancing again at Countess Irena, she realised that there was no one else to confide in and she was most certainly a woman who would have knowledge and experience of—Sasha blushed—*relations* between a man and a woman. Dare she ask her advice on how to win Reid, body and soul?

'Perhaps this is not the time or the place,' murmured Countess Irena, delving into the sequined reticule dangling from her wrist. She extracted a card and pressed it into her hand. 'We will talk when you call at my home.' She rose from her seat. 'I see my escort, it seems we are about to leave.' She leaned down, wafting a subtle scent of expensive perfume as she kissed Sasha upon her cheek. 'I am sure Olga said in her letters that her daughter Georgia was fair.' She stared hard at Sasha for a moment, and then smiled. *'Au revoir, ma chérie.'*

Chapter Seven

Sasha watched as Countess Irena swept away upon the arm of her escort, a Russian prince bedecked in the splendid regalia of a military uniform, his jet-black moustache matching his hair and eyes. He seemed quite a few years younger than Irena and Sasha envied the Countess her grace and beauty. She rose from her seat and glanced down at the card in her hand, about to discreetly slip it into her reticule when Lady Cronin barked, 'Georgia, I hope you have no intention of having anything to do with that dreadful creature!'

'I— I—' Sasha flushed, hiding her hand behind her back and desperately searching for a reply. Her first choice was a scathing one, but then it would not do to alienate the wife of a man Reid must work closely with. As her mouth opened and closed she suddenly felt warm fingers press into her waist, her slender back encircled by a scarlet-sleeved arm.

'And what dreadful creature would that be?' asked Reid. 'Don't tell me my wife has a roving eye already!' He frowned ferociously and said in a mock voice of deep anger, 'Wife, I shall beat you soundly!'

'Oh, no, not at all!' exclaimed Lady Cronin. 'I— I merely meant—'

Sasha glanced up and smiled with pleasure as well as relief at Reid, standing tall and very handsome in his dress uniform of scarlet-and-gold tunic, dark blue breeches and gleaming boots, a sword latched to his waist.

He winked at her and turned her away from Lady Cronin towards the dance floor. 'My apologies, ladies, for attending this magnificent occasion so late. Come, my little wife, I shall teach you to be obedient to your husband!'

Lady Cronin gasped, her eyes flashing with shock, for it was obvious from Reid's slurred tone of voice and the way he pulled Sasha close against his body, that he was well oiled and dancing was not the only obedience he had in mind. Sasha let him take command as they swept away into a waltz, the sensuous strains and Reid's surprisingly nimble footwork wheeling them about the dance floor in perfect rhythm.

'Look at her, the old trout.' Reid laughed. 'What's got up her nose, then?'

'Shh,' Sasha berated him, glancing about to see if anyone had overheard, and then looking up into Reid's face as he pulled her even closer against his chest, her slender body fitting between his legs as he manoeuvred her about. She gasped and shivered as his lips toyed with the curve of her ear. 'Are you drunk, Major Bowen?'

'As a lord, Mrs Bowen.' He groaned, his hand moving from her waist to clasp her bottom. 'Let's go upstairs.'

Sasha arched her neck away from his exploring lips and snatched his hand away from her bottom, placing it firmly on her waist. 'Behave yourself. People are beginning to titter.'

'Titter?' Reid threw back his head and laughed. 'Oh, my little virgin, how delightful you are!'

Sasha was now greatly alarmed and dragged Reid from the dance floor. 'For goodness' sake, do be quiet!'

Reid swayed, peering at her, his hair ruffled and grinning as he replied in a mock whisper, 'Sorry, old girl, almost gave the game away.' He took her hand. 'Come on, let's go to bed.'

Sasha thought it best to comply, fearing that Reid would blow their carefully constructed charade and bring disaster upon both their heads. Glancing about, she managed to catch Captain Turnbull's eye and with his assistance they led Reid up the stairs and to their bedchamber.

'Thank you,' Sasha said, as Reid began singing and tossing off his jacket, 'I can manage from here on.'

Captain Turnbull smiled, and made a swift drinking motion with his hand. 'It's the vodka, Mrs Bowen.'

'No doubt.' Sasha closed the door and then ran back to the bed as Reid began fumbling with the belt at his waist, singing a bawdy song at the top of his voice as he divested himself of his military trappings.

'Come here, you beautiful little thing.' He grabbed hold of Sasha about the waist and began to waltz her about the room. 'Where have you been all night?'

Sasha grimaced, clinging to him and trying desperately to stay on her feet as he whirled and dashed about. 'I have been here all the time. Where have you been, sir?'

'Oh, God!' Suddenly he stopped, holding a hand to his head as if the room spun in dizzy circles. 'Where's the bed? I think I'd better lie down.'

'Yes, I think you'd better.'

Sasha guided him to the vast bed and he sat down gingerly on the edge. 'Be a sport, sweetheart, and fetch me a glass of water.'

'Shall I ring for a pot of coffee?'

'No, water, please, got an almighty thirst.'

She went to the ornate bedside cabinet and poured a glass of water from the carafe left there by the maid. She gave it to Reid and he drank quickly, holding out the glass for more. After his second glass he handed it back to her and then flopped back onto the bed with a groan.

'God, what a day!' He lifted his head and looked up at Sasha, patting the space beside him. 'Come here, you're too far away and I don't have the energy for shouting.'

Sasha kicked off her shoes and climbed up onto the bed, kneeling beside him, her skirts billowing in a froth of silk gown and chiffon petticoats. She looked down at Reid as he lay on the bed, her eyes caressing the flaxen locks of ruffled hair that fell across his forehead, his straight nose and wide mouth, the very dark blue of his eyes, the strong column of his throat.

'Why are you looking at me like that?' he asked, his hand reaching out for her waist and pulling her down to lie beside him.

Sasha caught the whiff of alcohol on his breath and suddenly she became aware of the heat of his body and how big and powerful he was. She lowered her eyes demurely and shrugged, instinctively aware that Reid in this condition was an unknown quantity, and all her own anxieties of the day and their situation making her nervous.

His fingers grasped her chin and tipped her face up so he could see her eyes. 'For God's sake, don't go all prudish miss on me now,' he growled, raising himself up on one elbow and leaning over her, turning her so that she lay upon her back, beneath the heavy weight of his broad chest and shoulders. His eyes devoured the pink curves of her tender mouth, moving down to the pale skin of her neck and the arousing swell of her bosom. He groaned, and lowered his head to kiss her.

At the first touch of his lips on her own Sasha melted, her hands lifting to his shoulders and sliding down his back, her fingers digging into the hard strength of his muscles, her mouth opening. Yet as his kiss deepened and she felt the weight of his body, heard his heavy breath and felt his fingers fumble to lift the hem of her gown, she felt a cold sense of panic.

He became aware of her hands pushing at his chest and her mouth leaving his as she turned her head away from the deep plunging force of his kiss. 'Whar's wrong?' he slurred.

Her heart was pounding and her breath came in loud, ragged pants as panic flared through her. 'No, Reid, we agreed to wait until we are married.'

He groaned. 'I can't wait that long.'

'It's only until tomorrow.' She stared up at him with a dawning suspicion. 'You did arrange it with the minister, didn't you?'

Reid paused as his fingers pulled down the tiny sleeves of her bodice, considering the simple question with obvious difficulty. 'I think so. Damned if I can remember.'

'Oh, Reid!'

'Don't worry, sweetheart, if not tomorrow, then another day!' His hot mouth grasped at her smooth breast, his teeth gently scraping her soft skin as he felt the sudden urgent force of desire building inside of him, the sweetness and nearness of her body driving all thoughts from his mind except the need to be one with her, with sweet, generous, clever little Sasha. Suddenly it dawned on him how right it felt, how good it would be with her, yet he struggled with his ardour and the dull ache of too many vodkas to convey this fact properly to her, and he grasped her chin to kiss her more thoroughly, hoping that kisses would achieve more than muddled words.

Sasha gasped, and pushed at him, frightened now as her efforts failed to make him move away. 'No, Reid, not like this.' She struggled in earnest when his knee spread her legs and his fingers reached beneath her skirts to grasp the silk bow holding up her drawers. 'Stop it, Reid, you're drunk, I don't want you to.'

He laughed then, his mouth pressing rough kisses on her neck as he tugged at her drawers. 'Of course you want to, you've been eager for me to take you from the first moment we met.'

'Get off!' Outrage warred with embarrassment at the grain of truth amongst his words and Sasha lifted her hand, slapping him smartly across one cheek with her open palm. Her hand stung, the sharp sound ringing about the room, yet it had the desired sobering effect and Reid suddenly rolled away from her.

He rose from the bed and strode away, throwing over his shoulder, 'If you were Georgia, we'd be rolling around naked by now, with her on top, panting and enjoying every moment! She's the sort who knows what a man wants.'

His words cut her to the quick and Sasha turned her face away, closing her eyes at the sudden spurt of tears. She did not open them again until she heard the click of the door and looked up to find herself alone.

Just before noon the next day Jane brought a tea tray and a somewhat terse note from Lady Cronin. Reid did not stir when Sasha woke, roused by Jane's knock and the rattle of cups. With a sigh she sat up, pushing back the waves of her long dark hair as she unfolded the note, and greeted Jane good morning in a soft whisper, glancing at Reid as he continued sleeping, lying on his back with one arm stretched above his head. He had returned to their bedchamber some time during the night, but she had feigned sleep and remained in a curled-up position on her side of the bed, as far from him as possible.

'Morning, mum.' Jane poured her a cup of steaming tea and handed it to her, asking, 'Shall I run you a bath, mum?'

Sasha nodded with a grateful smile as she sipped her tea and read the note that summoned her to the drawing room as soon as she was presentable. Her heart fluttered a little; she was never one to enjoy confrontations and wondered if Lady Cronin intended to administer a lecture. Glancing again at Reid, she refrained from waking him. The note was addressed to her specifically and after last night's events she had no wish to see or speak to Reid any time soon. With a sigh and resolute straightening of her shoulders, she thrust back the warm covers and jumped out of bed. She bathed quickly in the deliciously hot water Jane had drawn for her, dressed with the maid's assistance in a modest skirt and jacket of warm burgundy wool, with a cream blouse buttoned to the throat, and her hair demurely swept up into a chignon at the nape of her neck.

Downstairs she knocked on the drawing-room door, opening it and peeking in. Lady Cronin sat in an armchair beside the fire hearth, a pair of pince-nez balanced on her nose as she gazed at a sheaf of papers in her hand. She looked up and imperiously crooked her finger at Sasha, indicating that she should enter.

Sasha walked into the room slowly, resisting the temptation to twist her hands behind her back like a naughty schoolroom chit about to be disciplined by her governess.

After a long moment of silence, Sasha said quietly, 'You wished to see me, ma'am?'

'Indeed.' Lady Cronin removed her pince-nez and fixed Sasha with a glowering stare. 'I feel most unhappy about having to speak to you in this fashion, Mrs Bowen, but far better that I should be the one, rather than involve my husband.'

Sasha felt pins and needles of alarm rush through her limbs. Her glance strayed involuntarily to the papers, perhaps letters, that now lay discarded in Lady Cronin's lap. Had they been found out? Was disaster about to fall upon their heads?

'Of course I realise that you are young, and that is why I am prepared to be lenient and grant you the benefit of ignorance. But last night I felt your behaviour was most—' she hesitated for a moment, searching her mind for the right word '—reprehensible.'

Sasha stared at her, trying hard to conceal her dislike for this cold and imperious woman, her anger lighting a slow fuse that she only hoped would not explode before she left the room.

'I did warn you that Countess Irena was *persona non grata* and I do feel that it is not in your best interest, or that of the British Embassy, for you to consort with such a woman. And in addition, I think you would do well to speak to Major Bowen and make sure that in future he…well, he restrains himself from making public shows of…affection. I realise that you are newly married, but I am afraid it is not at all dignified.'

For a long moment Sasha was silent, then she smiled tightly and asked, 'Are you finished?'

'I think that will do, for now.'

Sasha lifted her chin, 'Fortunately, Lady Cronin, we are to

leave this house today and my behaviour, or that of my husband's towards me, is none of your concern.' With that she turned sharply on her heel, ignoring the gasp that hissed from Lady Cronin's thin mouth.

She closed the door with a snap, her heart pounding uncomfortably hard in her chest as she began to hurry up the stairs with quick, sharp footsteps spurred by anger. Halfway up, though, she stopped, suddenly taken by an impulsive urge to thumb her nose at Lady Cronin. Why, she would go and see Countess Irena this very moment, while Reid was still sleeping. Indeed, she would spend the rest of the day with her and never return to this hateful house! She realised then that she would need her cloak and the card with the Countess's address printed on it. She returned to the bedchamber, opening the door quietly so as not to disturb Reid. But as she entered the room and closed the door, her swift glance to the bed found it to be empty. Disappointment was her first reaction that yet again Reid had gone, without even saying goodbye, and then relief as she remembered their tussle of the night before. His comment about Georgia had wounded her and still hurt even now in the bright light of day. There was a lump in her throat, holding in a well of unshed sorrow, as it dawned on her that whilst his thoughts and desires were all still for Georgia, they could never truly be man and wife.

She must go back to England. She must leave Reid and put this whole ludicrous charade behind her. But how? How would she get back to England on her own?

Then she remembered Irena, and went to the reticule she had discarded on the dressing table and fished out her card. She took down her cloak from the wardrobe and as she did so a small sound reached her ears and she turned to gaze at the door of the bathroom. From the familiar tap-tap noise and swish of water, she concluded that Reid must be shaving. The door was slightly ajar, and she peeked through it.

Reid stood with his back to the door, wearing nothing except a white towel draped around his hips. He stooped slightly to see his face in an oval mirror on the wall, and she watched fascinated at the play of muscles in his broad shoulders and arms, as they flexed while he shaved. His skin was smooth and honey-tanned, scattered with freckles across the shoulders bulky with muscle, his torso tapering down to lean hips and taut buttocks. She felt heat burn through her body, and an overwhelming desire to stand close behind him and slide her arms around his very masculine and appealing body, brushing the palms of her hands over the bronze hairs of his chest, sliding them down his flat stomach, pressing kisses to the strong, broad width of his back…

'Are you going to stand there all day ogling?'

Sasha jumped, startled that she had been caught out. 'I— I… How did you—?'

Reid smiled as he scraped a razor blade through the foam on his jaw. 'I can see you in the mirror, sweetheart. Come in.'

She pushed open the door, but stood on the threshold, acutely aware of the intimacy of watching a half-naked 'husband' attending to his early morning shave. Sasha swallowed, her eyes roaming everywhere except over Reid, yet wary of how easily her feelings for him could dissolve all sensible thought about leaving. And after what happened last night she felt indignant, and that he should be the one to speak first and apologise.

He smiled to himself, watching her with one eye in the mirror as he finished shaving. But the chill of her stare forced a sudden and alarming thought. 'Last night,' he asked hesitantly, 'did I… Well…did I behave myself?'

Sasha took a step forwards, folding her arms across her waist and cocking her head admonishingly to one side. 'No, you most certainly did not.'

Reid felt the hairs on his forearms rise. He quickly rinsed his face and reached for a towel to pat it dry, meeting Sasha halfway by taking a step towards her. His eyes swept the length of her slim frame. 'I hope very much that I did not hurt you. It was not my intention that your first time should be—'

'What?' Sasha stared at him with wide eyes, a blush suffusing pink beneath her pale skin.

'Well, I know that I was foxed, and you are—were a virgin.'

Sasha tapped her foot impatiently. 'We did not, well, I mean, I would not let you—'

'Oh? So you are still a virgin?'

Her cheeks flamed and she swung on her heels, departing from the intimate confines of the bathroom. 'Of course I am, you idiot!'

Reid followed, his bare feet padding soundlessly on the glossy parquet floors, a slight frown creasing his brows. He tossed aside the towel in his hand and quickly reached out to grab the cloak clutched in her hands like a shield, throwing it on the bed and then clasping his fingers around her wrist and pulling her to face him. 'Then what do you mean?'

'I mean that I have just received a brow-beating from Lady Cronin about your "public displays of affection", that's what I mean!'

His reaction was not one that she expected, or desired, as he laughed out loud and released her wrist from his clasp, his hand sliding to her waist and pulling her closer, his voice very soft and husky. 'I am afraid you will have to enlighten me, sweetheart, as I was very drunk last night and have no recollection whatsoever. What did I do?' His gaze lowered to the soft pink swell of her lips.

Sasha found it hard to breathe for a moment, and then she replied tartly, 'Why, you fondled and groped me as we were dancing!' With her hand flat against his chest, she pushed him away. 'And it's no laughing matter! The old dragon made me attend her in the drawing room and stand like a schoolroom chit while she administered a tongue-lashing!'

'Did she, indeed?' Reid grinned, his hold still upon her wrist, light yet inescapable.

'Yes! What are you going to do about it?'

'Nothing.'

'Nothing?' Her eyes flashed up at him.

'She is the ambassador's wife, there is little I can say.' He let her go then, and walked to his wardrobe to select a shirt and trousers. 'Don't let it trouble you. We leave today and will soon be installed in our own apartment. We can do as we please then.' Looking over his shoulder, he exchanged a very penetrating glance with Sasha. 'Is there…anything else I should apologise for?' He had a vague memory…

'Well…' Sasha glanced down at her shoes, reluctant to discuss the intimate complexities of the physical aspect of their relationship, and puzzled by her own wayward reactions to them, one moment aching with desire for him, and the next petrified of his advances.

'Come now, Sasha, spit it out.' He turned to face her, concerned by the pale stillness of her face.

'You…wanted me to—'

'What?'

'Let you… Well… I had to slap your face to make you stop.'

'I am sorry. I was drunk.' He frowned then. 'I can understand that you did not want your first time to be rough and careless with a drunkard, but do not make too much of it.'

'You said that if I had been Georgia she would have—' Sasha blushed, recalling his brazen words.

'She would have what?'

'Enjoyed it.'

He shrugged. 'Your sister is of a different nature.' As though to prove a point, he unwound the towel about his waist and laughed at her gasp as he stood naked before her.

'You might have warned me!' She looked away, quite astonished by the sight of such naked masculinity, the light from the tall wide windows clearly showing every detail of Reid's beautiful male body.

'No need to blush, Sasha. We are man and wife.'

'We are not, as you very well know.'

'I'll get hold of that minister today.'

'No, Reid, I really don't think—'

At that very moment the door opened and Jane entered, but seeing Reid standing naked in the middle of the room she exclaimed and quickly shut the door as she retreated.

Sasha sighed, her tone much aggrieved with both losing the moment to tell him she was going to leave, and for his lack of modesty, as she snapped, 'Now you have upset the servants, as well!' She glanced at the card in her hand and her cloak lying on the bed, snatched it up, and flounced to the door. 'I am going out!'

He strode after her. 'Sasha! Where are you going? We're supposed to be getting—' Suddenly sense prevailed and he bit back his words about getting married, heaving an angry sigh. He would have to find a minister himself, as soon as he could get away from the Embassy without anyone asking him where he was going or wanting to accompany him. Damn! How was he supposed to marry a woman who was already supposed to be his wife? And how could he convince that woman that he wanted her? His senses were starting to torment him as he yearned to make love with Sasha, her very presence and scent and the sound of her voice, day and night, seeping into his skin and her very self now firmly embedded in his heart. After the experience they had shared the other night, the thought of initiating Sasha into the pleasures of lovemaking were now far from being a daunting task, but one he longed to savour and enjoy. He made a move to the door, to run after her, but he was still in a state of undress and she was gone, only the sound of her footsteps tapping down the carpeted stairs left in her wake.

He hurried to dress, vowing that he would deal with Sasha later. He had an important meeting this morning with Sir Stanley and he had no time to wrestle with the problems of a wife who would not be a wife until there was a marriage.

Sasha ascertained directions to Countess Irena's home from a footman standing on the back stairs leading out to the courtyard.

Realising that she would not be deterred, the footman insisted on accompanying her, though it was only a few minutes' walk away. They let themselves out of the postern gate and into the street, a bitter wind howling about the tall buildings, elegant columns and many windows gracing the front façades of the palaces belonging to wealthy noble Russian families.

Countess Irena's palace was painted a pale pistachio green and boasted several white marble columns at the front, and long gilded windows brightly lit even at this time of the morning. Sasha hesitated on the steps, and then impulsively reached out and tugged the bell-pull. After a few moments the door opened and a tall, thin man wearing a grey wig and ornate liveried uniform greeted her with an enquiring expression upon his face. She gave her name and with a polite wave of his hand she was ushered into an anteroom, where the servant spoke to her in French and asked her to wait.

'You may go,' Sasha spoke to the Embassy footman, with an apologetic smile. 'I am sorry for keeping you from your duties. I will find my own way back.'

'No fear,' replied the young man quietly, who spoke in a broad London accent. 'Old man Cronin'd have me guts for garters if'n I left a lady here on her tod.' He squared his stout shoulders, stating firmly, 'I'll wait fer ya, ma'am.'

'What is your name?'

'Harry, ma'am.'

'Well then, Harry, I thank you for your trouble.'

She bit her lip as the servant returned and indicated that she should follow him. They crossed a hall lined with chequered marble and up a sweeping staircase of dark red carpet and ornate gilded balustrades that curved to the right and brought them to the first floor. For a moment she glanced down at the young footman as he waited on a chair in the hall below. She almost turned about and ran back, suddenly fearful of what was beyond the double doors they paused before. Then the servant opened one side and led her into a room quite unlike any place she had ever set foot in before.

The long salon was very brightly lit and seemed to be full of people. Small groups sat on chairs and gilt sofas, talking animatedly, laughing. At the far end someone played a grand piano, while several others leaned upon its glossy white surface and chatted with apparent indifference to the music rippling forth. The atmosphere struck Sasha as being thriving, bright and intriguingly sophisticated.

'Ah, my darling girl!' cried Countess Irena, striding towards her with both hands outstretched. She grasped Sasha's hands in hers and leaned down to kiss her on both cheeks. 'How wonderful to see you! Come, let me introduce you to my friends. Would you like a glass of tea? Or wine?'

Sasha declined both, her gaze noting the huge silver samovar that steamed on a linen-draped table, set with glass cups and trays of tiny sweet biscuits. On another table were several silver ice-buckets with bottles of champagne protruding from them and crystal glasses gleaming in orderly rows. Her mother's cousin obviously enjoyed entertaining, but this was nothing like the quiet half-hour sipping tea while they exchanged pleasantries that Sasha had envisaged!

Two hours later she begged her leave, guiltily aware that it was lunchtime and, despite her thoughts earlier of spending the day with Irena, she had stayed far longer than she should have. Her cheeks were flushed and she had enjoyed several interesting conversations and one heated debate with a variety of people, some of them impressive intellectuals and others simply charming and erudite. Of course, there had not been a private moment to discuss with her cousin the difficulties of her relationship with Reid, and in all honesty, she was not convinced that it would be at all appropriate. She decided to wait until she knew Irena a little better. After all, she could not totally ignore Lady Cronin's warnings and she could not risk courting any more scandal than they already held at bay. She declined Irena's invitation to stay for luncheon, but agreed that she would return again soon.

At the door, as she donned her cloak she turned to Irena with a smile. 'Thank you, it has been a wonderful time, and there have not been many of those lately.'

A slight frown creased the beautiful Irena's brow, and she purred softly, 'We will soon remedy that, my darling little one. You will be made to feel welcome here, always, and of course, your husband, too. I would like to meet him next time.'

Sasha hesitated, glancing away, wondering if now was the moment to ask for her help to escape from her 'husband', but instinctively she shrunk from the furore and shame of such an action. She was doomed, either way. Instead she demurely murmured, 'He is very busy.'

'But you are newly married. Surely he can spare time to spend with his new bride? I will send him a note, inviting you both to supper. It will be wonderful. Yes?'

Sasha merely smiled and inclined her head, then she glanced at young Harry. 'Let us be on our way.'

They walked back quickly, heads bowed against the biting wind, hugging the walls and making themselves unobtrusive. Harry grasped her arm as a party of horsemen clattered past, and he muttered something about Cossacks, leaning protectively over her slight frame. They had not far to go and though they both sighed with relief when Harry hammered on the postern gate of the Residency courtyard, and they were admitted at once, Sasha felt no sense of gladness to be 'home'. Climbing the stairs to her chamber, she was acutely aware of the silent and oppressive atmosphere of the household, strictly governed by a mistress who had no sense of gaiety, nor did she approve of the company of intellectuals, the so-called *literati*.

Sasha sat down at the writing bureau in her bedchamber and unfastened her cloak, intending to write to her parents at once and inform her mother of her meeting with Irena, and assure her that they were both well and her mother was not to worry about her. She drew out a sheet of paper and then sat staring out of the windows at the River Neva with a dreamy expression, and going over in her mind the people and conversations and music she had enjoyed that morning. At one point someone had told a rather risqué joke; it had been puzzling to her and she had blushed profusely, expecting Irena to reprimand the young man who had dared to utter such sauciness in the presence of ladies, but instead she had thrown back her head and laughed. Sasha smiled now, realising that she had enjoyed the stimulating company, and also that Lady Cronin's well-ordered drawing room was not the be-all and end-all of social circles.

While she sat there wondering what she could and could not write to her mother, the door snapped open suddenly and Reid strode into the room. He came to a halt beside her, with a thunderous frown upon his face.

'Where the hell have you been?'

With a little defiant tilt of her chin she looked up at him with raised brows. 'I have been to visit my cousin, Countess Irena.'

'Alone?'

'No, Harry the footman escorted me.'

'Who is this—this Countess Irena?'

'She is my mother's second cousin. Very beautiful, and very clever, and very rich.'

Reid swung away and went to stand before the window, staring out. 'And very Russian, no doubt.' He frowned, as he pondered on the vaguely familiar name. 'Do you mean Irena Sletovskaya?'

'Why, yes.' Sasha rose from her chair and went to stand beside him, an eager smile upon her face as she looked up enquiringly. 'Do you know her?'

He glanced down at her. 'No, but I have heard her name mentioned. She is a whore. I forbid you to go to her house again.'

'You have been listening to the malicious tongue of Lady Cronin!' exclaimed Sasha, stung by a sudden spurt of shock and anger at his harsh words. She moved away from him. 'It is nonsense and I will visit her whenever I wish! I had the most wonderful time with some very interesting people! Irena is going to send an invitation for us to sup with her. She wants to meet you.'

She did not go far before Reid's hand fastened on her upper arm and dragged her back. He pulled her up sharp against him, his voice very low as he spoke, his eyes holding hers as firmly as his hand held her arm. 'It is not from Lady Cronin that I have heard talk, but from officers in the Russian Army. Do not disobey me, Sasha. You will not go to this Irena's house again. It is for your own good.'

'Is it?' She glared at him, trying to shake free from his grasp. 'Or is it for your good and the British Embassy? Will you not at least meet her, just the once, and make your own judgement?'

He noticed her flushed cheeks, and the animated gleam in her eyes, and whilst he could understand the reasonableness of her request, his emotions, gradually being drawn closer and deeper towards her, were just as susceptible as her own and he felt a most unwelcome and unfamiliar stab of jealousy in his heart. 'I see these "interesting people" have made quite an impression upon you. Was there anyone in particular?'

'What do you mean?'

'A man, perhaps?'

She tossed her head. 'Don't be ridiculous!'

His glance fell to her mouth. 'Be careful. You are innocent and naïve, Sasha, you have no idea what men are capable of.' He let her go then, abruptly. 'This afternoon we are to visit the Hope-Garners and bid them farewell. Our belongings will be moved over and tonight we will spend our first evening in our new apartment.'

Sasha rubbed her arm and turned her back to him, staring in mutinous silence out of the window.

'Sasha?'

'I heard you.'

'Then come with me now, it is time for luncheon.'

'I am not hungry, and I must finish my letter to my parents. Let them know I'm all right.'

'You can do that after lunch.' With a sigh, he strode towards her, entwined his fingers intimately between the fingers of her left hand and pulled her with him to the door. 'I said, it is time for luncheon. We will not be late, and we will not eat separately and cause comment.'

As they moved down the staircase in apparent unison, Reid could not help but murmur softly by her ear, 'At times you are very much like your sister, quite determined. If this Irena is so wonderful, then perhaps I'd better come along on one of your visits to see for myself.'

Sasha stared straight ahead. 'If you wish.'

'She may be a whore, but I hear she is a very beautiful one.'

She snapped her head about to glare at him. 'Are you deliberately trying to pick a fight with me, Reid Bowen?'

He laughed, noticing again the resemblance to Georgia as an angry flush coloured her neck and her dark eyes flashed at him, amused by the similar trait of high spirits and courage, yet he defused her anger immediately as other guests sauntered along the hallway. 'No, sweetheart, of course not.'

They reached the dining-room doors and were ushered to their seats, forcing a postponement of any further debate upon the merits of the controversial Countess Irena.

Throughout luncheon the atmosphere felt unbearably false to Sasha's mind, as Lady Cronin prattled on with forced brightness. She concentrated on the plates of food placed before her that she had no appetite for, but at least it was a diversion. Once she glared at Reid and almost choked as he pinched her thigh, forcing her to pay attention to Lady Cronin and answer her question about whether she would like to take the maid Jane with her to their apartment. Realising that some effort was being made to cast oil upon the ruffled waters between them, Sasha smiled and accepted the offer with a few polite words of thanks. Appar-

ently they were also to have a cook, a butler and a footman, and
Sasha listened to Lady Cronin's expectations of how she would
entertain guests of the military attaché, the subtle implication
being that she would hold dinner parties and receive morning
callers whether she liked it or not.

From the corner of his eye Reid glanced at his 'wife', and
realised that Sasha was of course no schoolroom chit to be
ordered about, but a grown-up young woman very much in possession of her own mind. He noted the pursing of her lips and the
arched quirk to her brows as Lady Cronin all but laid down the
law, and he resolved there and then to extricate Sasha from what
had become an impossible situation. Apart from the fact that she
would be required to play hostess as his wife—difficult enough
considering that she was not his wife at all—it was becoming
harder and harder to resist the intimacies of their shared bed.
His yearning for physical pleasure with her became more intense
as each day passed, and he had two obvious choices—he could
either pack Sasha on to the next mail boat back to England, and
have done with the whole affair, or he could marry her and they
could begin to explore their relationship as a husband and wife
should, both physically and emotionally.

He turned to Charlotte, sat next to him, and asked carefully
and with great politeness, 'Ma'am, would you happen to know
whether there are any Anglican church services available to
us?' At his elbow he heard Sasha's swift intake of breath and
her spoon clatter into her glass dish of mint sorbet.

Charlotte dabbed a napkin to her mouth, and smiled shyly
at him. 'Why, yes, of course. There is a minister, a Reverend
Jones, who holds Sunday services at his house. But I do believe
he is away for two weeks, visiting friends in Moscow.'

'Ah…' Reid sighed. 'What a shame.'

Lady Cronin leaned forwards, catching the tail end of their
conversation. 'He's Welsh, but a fine enough fellow. I could
invite him to lunch when he returns and then you can both
meet him.' She peered at Reid across the table and frowned.

Major Bowen had not made the impression upon her of being a particularly religious sort, but she made no further comment.

That afternoon they all dutifully traipsed down to the harbour and waved goodbye to the Hope-Garners. Sasha was sad to bid farewell to Charlotte, who had been kind to her, if somewhat distracted by her many children and tasks involved with returning to England. They kissed each other goodbye and promised to write and keep each other informed of their new lives. She gave Charlotte a letter to be passed on to her parents, her guilt somewhat assuaged that soon her parents would receive news that all was well with her. Then Reid ushered her to a carriage and they set off for their new apartment.

It was situated in a grand building in a street behind the Residency. It had no view of the river, but overlooked the courtyard of the Residency from its rear windows, and the street from the front. Sasha was pleased to note that it had its own entrance, and a short yet elegant staircase rose from the hallway to the first-floor landing and the main salon, dining room, breakfast room and a study. On the floor above there were four bedrooms, two spacious bathrooms and a dressing room. Sasha made no comment when she discovered that her suitcases and trunk had been placed in a room opposite to one occupied by Reid's belongings, and though she felt relief that she would at last have her own room, there was a vague sense of disappointment, too. She wondered if Reid had given the order, or if the servants had naturally assumed the common custom that husband and wife would wish to occupy separate bedrooms.

The rooms were furnished in a more sombre style than that of the opulent luxury of the Residency, yet Sasha found there was some charm to the dark, heavy furniture, a solid old-fashioned sense of comfort with the large sofas and curved tables, the imposing sleigh beds and the heavy swags of brocade curtains that seemed so typical in Russia to dress the huge windows. There was little in the way of ornaments, which Sasha knew to be because of the Hope-Garners' many children, the presence of their boisterous little spirits lingering still.

That evening, after a quiet supper with Reid, she bade him good-night and retired to a hot bath and her solitary bed. She lay awake for a long while, listening for when at last Reid left his study and came upstairs. His door closed and she could hear nothing more. How she longed to lie in his arms again! Yet now they had assumed the correct proprieties, and she had no idea how to make her 'husband' fall in love with her.

Chapter Eight

~~~~~~~~~~~~~~~~~~~~~~~~~

Over tea and toast the next morning, at a round table in the cosy breakfast room, Reid made it clear that he would be out all day as he took up the reins for the first time in his sole capacity as military attaché.

'What will you do?' he asked, as he thanked Jane with a smile for the plate of scrambled egg and fried tomato that she placed before him. He picked up his knife and fork, then glanced keenly across the table. 'Sasha?'

She looked up from idly stirring sugar into her cup of tea, and shrugged. She felt out of sorts this morning, but could not really fathom why.

Reid ate quickly, mindful of the time, but he paused as he looked at her pale face and the shadows beneath her eyes. 'Did you sleep all right? Was the bed comfortable enough?'

Sasha smiled softly, a wistful look in her eyes. 'The bed was very comfortable, thank you. But it is a strange new house and I suppose I must get used to it.' It was on the tip of her tongue to tell him that she had missed sleeping with him beside her.

Reid rose to his feet, folded his napkin and laid it on the table. 'I will have luncheon at the Embassy, so I will not see you until this evening.' He bent and kissed her forehead. He, too, resisted the temptation to tell her that he had missed sleeping with her lying beside him.

They went their separate ways.

Later that morning Sasha rang for the footman and he accompanied her to Countess Irena's, the walk taking only a minute or two as the apartment was situated closer than to the Residency. She was greeted warmly, as before, and she passed several pleasant hours chatting and listening to music. At Irena's insistence she promised that she would soon bring Reid to visit her. Yet she did not dare to broach the subject with him, somehow sensing that it would create discord and in these weeks whilst they waited for the Reverend Jones to return and marry them, legally and with honour, she did not want to spoil the few moments she had with Reid.

By the end of May the weather had greatly improved, the sky turning from sullen wintry clouds to a clear blue, quite unlike an English sky in its intensity. On one afternoon she and Reid went riding in one of the many vast parks, and he confided in her that he had heard the Reverend Jones had returned and he would endeavour to visit him as soon as possible.

Holding the reins of her horse in one hand, elegantly attired in a green riding habit and top hat with black-spotted veil, Sasha glanced at him with a smile and mischievous light in her eyes. 'Does that mean we will be able to sleep together?'

Reid laughed, 'Why, yes, I think it would. Isn't that what a husband and wife usually do?'

'I don't know, I've never been married before. Not properly.'

Reid laughed. Glancing at her as she sat side-saddle, the teasing note in her voice and smile, Reid felt a flush of hot desire rush through him and he leaned over, pulling both her own and his horse to a halt. He deftly lifted the veil from her face and kissed her with passionate force. 'Is that what you want, Sasha?'

His face was very close to her own as he looked into her eyes.
'To sleep with me?'

She blushed, but she did not look away as she nodded and
lifted her mouth to his for another kiss. He obliged, and then
forced himself to let her go, moving his horse as he resisted the
temptation to gallop away with Sasha into the trees and find a
secluded spot to make love to her. They must wait, but the waiting was sweet agony!

They rode back to the house and in the heat of the moment
Reid agreed to Sasha's plea that he would go with her to her
cousin's for luncheon. He could very well do without the com-
plication of Irena Sletovskaya in their lives, but if it made Sasha
happy, then just the once would surely do no harm. It would
give him the opportunity to have a quiet word with the woman,
and make it clear that henceforth he expected her to keep her
distance from a young and impressionable Sasha.

They went on Saturday, Reid generally not expected to attend
the office, although Sir Stanley had warned that all manner
of things cropped up at odd and inconvenient hours and not
to expect too much of a routine. Most Saturdays Lady Cronin
demanded them to dance attendance on whatever social activities
she had planned, but this weekend they had to themselves, as
following a visit to Tsarkoe Selo in the pouring rain she had been
laid low with a cold and all had been cancelled. Reid resolved to
attend Reverend Jones's service on Sunday morning and ascertain whether he was to be trusted with the secretive and sensitive
task of joining himself and Sasha in holy matrimony.

At exactly twelve noon he knocked on Sasha's bedroom door
and she called for him to enter. He opened it and stood on the
threshold, watching as she settled a small pink hat atop her head,
a few feathers and bits of ribbon dancing to one side. 'Shall I
call for the carriage?' he asked, his eyes skimming over the
slenderness of her figure, a memory stirring in his mind of how

she had felt sleeping next to him and their pillow talk, and how much he missed both.

'Oh, no,' Sasha replied, picking up her gloves and reticule from the bed. 'Let's walk.'

He frowned. 'I don't think so, it's safer—'

'Nonsense, I often walk, it's only around the corner and it's such a lovely day, do let's.'

His frown deepened a little, and he realised suddenly that he actually had no idea what she did all day, alone, while he was at the Embassy, or out and about attending to his own affairs. It might well be prudent to keep a better eye on Sasha and her movements in future.

They set off down the wide street, a soft breeze blowing, fresh yet not biting, and Sasha walked happily with her arm slipped through the crook of Reid's elbow. It felt wonderful to be out of the house, just the two of them alone, together. In the last few weeks she had sensed that Reid was quite tense from the pressures of work. She chattered lightly, glad to see the smile return to his eyes as he walked at her side and responding in that steady, even tone of voice that she admired so much, at one point reaching with his left hand to squeeze one of her hands clasped about his arm. They were both smiling and relaxed by the time they reached the imposing white enamel-and-gilt portico of the Sletovskaya palace. As they mounted the steps Reid glanced up at the rows of brightly lit windows and marble columns, his eyebrows raised at the impressive opulence, but he kept any comments about how Irena had acquired her riches to himself, reluctant to spoil Sasha's naïve enjoyment. The door opened as soon as he rang the bell, and a liveried footman took their coats, hats and gloves. Sasha led the way up the curving staircase and they were met on the landing by her cousin.

'Ah, at last!' Irena threw up her hands in a dramatic gesture as she greeted them. 'You have brought your husband to me!' She moved with a rustle of gold silk and stood before Reid, quite obviously perusing him from head to toe, and then she winked at Sasha and held out her hand to him. 'I am delighted to meet you, Major Bowen.'

He leaned forwards and took her hand in his, pressing a light kiss upon the smooth, scented skin, but he refrained from the obvious courtesy of inviting her to call him by his first name. Instead, he bowed, and replied, 'Countess Irena Sletovskaya.'

Sasha glanced at him from the corner of her eye, suddenly wondering at the wisdom of this meeting. She had never known Reid to be deliberately rude to anyone; though his manner was polite and civil and was far from being rude, it was not as warm and cordial as she would wish from her husband towards a close member of her family.

Irena appeared unperturbed and linked arms with both of them as she led them along the carpeted corridor.

'You are looking lovely today.' Irena smiled at her. 'I do like the way you wear your hair, so natural. Don't you think so, Major Bowen?'

Reid nodded. 'Quite charming.'

'Of course, you are young, my dear, and it suits you, but if you wish my coiffeuse to show you some more sophisticated styles, she is at your disposal.'

Sasha smiled, delighted that Irena should take such an interest in her, but Reid had other views on the subject and he politely but firmly replied, 'That is very kind of you, Countess, but I like my wife's hair just the way it is.'

An awkward moment was avoided as they turned into a room to the rear of the palace, overlooking the formal and beautiful gardens just beginning to flower with the promise of spring. A fire flickered in the grate, surrounded by an ornate onyx hearth, the mantelpiece topped with silver-framed photographs and ornaments. A large black chesterfield was placed squarely in front of the hearth and Sasha and Reid seated themselves on this, while Irena sat in a gilt Louis XVI armchair beside the fireplace, facing them and the focus of their attention. A hovering servant offered glasses of champagne from a silver tray and several others busied themselves with making the final preparations to a square table, set with snow-white linen, silver cutlery and crystal glasses, the room richly scented by a centrepiece of lilies and orchids.

Sasha sipped from her glass and glanced away from watching Reid conversing with Irena to the table set for just three people. She had never known Irena to entertain less than a dozen to luncheon before, and she realised that they were to be the only guests. She lifted her eyes then to Irena and to Reid, who was twirling his glass between his spread knees as he sat on the edge of the sofa, while Irena talked about how much she had heard about him and how wonderful it was to finally meet him. She asked many questions about Reid's life almost from the time he was born, and these he politely if vaguely answered, while Sasha sat quietly at his side, hoping that Reid would soon thaw and show Irena his good nature that she herself found so charming. She observed the slender curve of her cousin's neck, the pale buttermilk glow of her perfect and unflawed skin, the ruby redness of her full, wide mouth, the dark glossy coils of her hair wound about her head in intricate and very becoming curls. Her voice was so soft and light, just a little husky, her scent almost as erotic as the flowers on the table. She was very beautiful, Sasha realised with a pang. No, she was more than that, more than just beautiful, she was... Sasha searched her mind for the right word and could not think of any that adequately described the mesmerising womanliness of Irena. How could anyone not admire her?

At Irena's urging they rose from the sofa and moved across the room to the dining table. They paused for a moment while she showed them a view of the garden from one of the three long windows, an elegant vista of terraced lawns, fountains, topiaries and lush shrub-filled borders. Then they seated themselves, with Irena at the head of the table, Reid to her left, the light shining on him, and Sasha to her right, with her back to the window. Once Reid had finished pulling out the ladies' chairs and they were all seated comfortably, the first course was served by servants who came and went with discreet silence. Sasha bent her head and stirred her spoon through the steaming chicken-and-noodle soup, watching Irena from the corner of her eye and copying the way she so elegantly ladled and sipped her soup.

'My dear—' Irena laid cool, slender fingers on her arm '—how is the esteemed Lady Cronin?'

They both chuckled at the private joke, as Irena always asked the question and usually Sasha would relieve her frustrations and angst by pouring out all her woes as far as Lady Cronin was concerned, but today, in front of Reid, she hesitated, glancing at him across the table. She replied with some reserve, 'I have not seen her this week, I believe she is abed with a cold.'

'Ah.' Irena dabbed at the corner of her mouth with a fine linen napkin. 'Please do give her my commiserations. She really should not go gadding about the countryside in inclement weather.'

'You are well informed.' Reid glanced keenly at his hostess, his soup spoon idle in the golden liquid, a thread of steel in his voice. 'I think it's admirable of Lady Cronin to make the effort to see as much of Russia as possible.'

'Of course,' Irena murmured, exchanging a glance with Sasha at his defence of a woman who only went where royalty and the British Embassy were best served.

For the main course they had beef fillets, accompanied by fine-shredded sautéed cabbage and light, fluffy dumplings. The food was delicious, cooked to perfection, and served with impeccable timing.

'My compliments to your chef,' commented Reid, as he cut into a tender piece of beef, darkly roasted on the outside, and pink in the middle, 'but I must confess that I am surprised by the menu, Countess. It's very much simple fare. No caviar or fancy French dishes, as I know the Russians do enjoy.'

Irena laughed, reaching for her glass of wine as she took a sip and eyed him over the rim with her dark, seductive eyes. 'Of course, Major, I always give my guests what they most enjoy and a man like you, a soldier, has simple yet robust tastes.'

'Indeed?' His reply was somewhat sardonic. He picked up his own wine glass, toying with the stem for a moment before taking a deep swallow of the rich red wine. 'And how would you know what I enjoy?'

'Oh, I have made it my business to find out!'

'Really? And might I ask, from whom? I trust my *wife* has not been telling tales.'

'Oh, no, not at all. But do tell me, Major Bowen, what was it like on the Hindu Kush and the Khyber Pass? Why, it sounds so romantic and very exciting!'

Deftly Irena changed the subject, and Sasha could say and do nothing as she sat there, watching them play a game, the one so determined to impress the other, who was equally determined not to be impressed. It was all she could do to stop herself from kicking Reid on the shins underneath the table!

Across the table Reid glanced at Sasha, and said gently, with all the concerned tones of a caring husband, 'You are very quiet, my dear, are you quite all right?'

Sasha felt the heat stain her neck as she flushed with her guilty thoughts, then she took a steadying breath, lifted her chin and replied, 'I am quite well, thank you, darling.'

His smiled broadened, for Sasha was not one to bandy about affectionate terms in public. He raised his glass to her. 'I am glad. Is the food to your taste, dearest?'

Sasha simply smiled, and inclined her head slightly, as though she could really find no comment worthy enough. Irena launched into a conversation about the merits of cavalry and infantry, and she spoke quite knowledgeably and intelligently about military affairs, yet still Reid failed to warm to her and would not be drawn into any discussion that Sasha knew he quite enjoyed.

Dessert was served, a Charlotte Russe and quite delicious with its layers of mocha mousse, cake and cream. After the meal they retired to the sofa while coffee was served and Sasha could not help but glance at the ticking hands of the blue porcelain French ormolu clock on the mantelpiece. How soon could they politely depart? she wondered. Just as she was beginning to feel quite annoyed with Reid, Irena suggested they leave Reid to enjoy his port in peace.

'Come and see the garden, I am sure Major Bowen has had quite enough of our female chatter.' She placed her arm about Sasha's waist and hugged her as they left the room.

From the doorway Sasha glanced over her shoulder at Reid, with a frown and significant glare, but he only stared back wide-eyed and with a shrug of his shoulders, as if to say, 'What?'

Arm in arm they went downstairs, footmen waiting at the door with velvet cloaks to ward off any chill. They stepped out into the garden and the bright sunshine was very pleasant, shining on the marble terrace and stone tubs of glossy-leaved miniature magnolia trees, and below that the lawns neat and elaborate as they wandered along shingled paths. They came to a fountain, rippling into a quatrefoil marble basin, rose petals bobbing on the surface.

Sasha could not help but chew her lip as she pondered on her thoughts as they walked in silence. Irena was quick to pick up on her mood.

'Have I bored you already, *ma chérie*?'

Sasha looked up, and smiled at Irena. 'No, of course not, it's just that…' She hesitated, reluctant to voice her disappointment with Reid; it seemed, somehow, disloyal. 'Well,' she murmured slowly, glancing shyly away, 'I must apologise for Reid's boorish behaviour.'

'Such men can be difficult, very proud and rigid about rules and etiquette.' Irena shrugged eloquently. 'And they are not ones to express sweet words of love. It is more…physical…for them.' She glanced at Sasha and smiled as her blush deepened. Then she stopped and turned Sasha to face her, with both hands on her shoulders. 'My dear, I can no longer keep it a secret, but I must tell you that I have had a letter from your mother.' She glanced about, and up at the windows of the palace, but they were quite alone in the garden. 'I know the truth…Sasha.'

At the mention of her name, Sasha's head reared up and suddenly her face flushed and crumpled as relief and alarm brought a rush of tears. Irena tutted, and patted her shoulders as she hugged her tightly. 'Now, dry your tears, enough of that nonsense.' She held Sasha away from her, lifting her bowed head with her fingers under Sasha's chin, her dark eyes holding an expression quite unlike any Sasha had seen on her before. 'We are the same, my dear, you and I. We are mistresses.'

Sasha gasped, suddenly realising the significance of her situation, and eager to make protest. She brushed the wetness from her eyes and cheeks. 'Oh, no, I am not Reid's mistress!'

Irena laughed, in disbelief. 'Well, you are not his wife. Do not be ashamed, my dear, sometimes it is far better to be a mistress than a wife. When you are bored with him and he no longer gives you pleasure and fine jewels, it is easy enough to move on to, shall we say, other delights.'

Sasha was shocked, and shrugged away from her cousin, and in the heat of an emotional moment she blurted out, 'I am not his mistress—indeed, I am still a virgin!'

For a moment Irena was silent, and then her eyes narrowed for a moment in a way that Sasha found quite unnerving, but the look was gone in a second and she smiled, patting Sasha on the arm as she said gently, 'Ah, I see. And now he is being noble and will not make love to you?'

'I— I suppose so.'

'And what will you do?'

'I must leave.'

'And pretend that nothing has happened? How very English!' Irena gave Sasha an assessing glance. 'No, my dear, you must bed him, as soon as possible. Mark my words, a man like that, if you do not make love with him, some other woman will.' Her fingers stroked over the skin of Sasha's delicate collarbone, her voice very soft and husky. 'Perhaps I can be of help, I can teach you how to please a man, show you, show both of you—'

'Whatever do you mean?' Sasha stared at her, moving away from her just a fraction and feeling most uncomfortable.

Irena smiled. 'Silly child, you know nothing of men, of their desires. Why, what I mean is that every man has a secret fantasy to make love to two women at the same time.' Her laughter was throaty and blatant. 'It is quite enjoyable.'

Sasha's shock turned to disgust, and she stepped quickly back, staring at Irena as if suddenly she did not know her at all. Was Reid right in his judgement of her? Was her mother's cousin more than just excitingly different and a little *risqué*, but perhaps immoral and wicked? Her first instinct was to pick up her skirts in both hands and run as fast as she could away from her, yet common sense and a keen instinct for survival reminded Sasha that Irena was party to knowledge of her circumstances that could bring disaster upon Reid. If the truth was made known about their relationship, he could be disgraced and dismissed from the Army. She could not afford to antagonise or alienate Irena, and so she said nothing, merely bowing her head and pretending her blush was one of embarrassment and not anger and disgust.

Seeing her shock, Irena made haste to apologise, equally aware of the risk of causing offence with one so closely connected to the British Embassy. 'My dear, I am sorry. It was inappropriate of me to speak of such things with such an innocent.' Irena linked arms with her as they walked back to the house. 'I am so glad we have had the chance to talk so frankly. At last the truth is out. It is so much better, do you not think?'

Sasha swallowed, with difficulty, but her voice was choked in her throat and she could do no more than nod.

'Don't worry, my little one, we will find a way to make Major Bowen your slave!'

Inwardly Sasha shuddered, but she said nothing as across the lawn strode the subject of their discussion. He waved and called out with a smile, reminding Sasha that he had an appointment with Sir Stanley and they must go if he was not to be late.

They kissed goodbye in the hall by the front door, Reid making polite thanks for the delightful luncheon as he bundled Sasha into her hat and gloves and coat.

'Goodbye, my dear.' Irena kissed Sasha's cheek and whispered by her ear, 'If you want to know anything, just ask me.'

Sasha nodded and smiled, yet her brow was creased in a frown as they walked back to the apartment. Reid's pace was brisk as he hustled her along, and it took her a few moments before she sifted through the chaotic thoughts in her mind and realised that no mention had been made of any meeting with Sir Stanley, and in fact she had thought they were going to the ballet.

'Reid—' She was about to question him about his altered itinerary when suddenly he stopped on the street corner and grabbed her by both arms, demanding her full attention.

'What was that all about?'

Sasha raised her face to him, eyes wide and lips slightly parted. 'What do you mean?'

'I was watching you from the window. What did Irena say? You're as pale as a ghost and your eyelashes are all spiky. What did she say to make you cry?'

Sasha heard the anger in his voice, and for a moment she did not know what to say. It was far too shameful to tell him about Irena's lewd ideas.

'Sasha! For God's sake, would you rather trust her than me? Tell me!'

She closed her eyes, sagging against him, as she sobbed a half-truth against his solid shoulder. 'She knows, Reid, she knows about us.'

'What! Sasha, how foolish to tell her—'

'I didn't! My mother wrote making enquiries, and told her all about Georgia and Felix, and how I took her place. She obviously put two and two together.'

'So she knows that you are not my wife?'

'Yes.'

'Then who does she think you are?'

'Your—' Sasha's voice sank to a whisper '—mistress.'

'I see. I hope that you did not go so far as to tell her we have never actually made love?'

'Well, um, she knows that I am still a virgin.'

'Oh, Sasha!' Reid growled, infuriated. 'You are so incredibly naïve.'

'What are we going to do?'

'There's only one thing we can do. Get married, pretty damn quick!'

He took her arm and marched down the street. They had arrived at their front door, and he lowered his voice as he told her, 'I will go over to see Reverend Jones this very moment, and ask him to perform a ceremony as soon as may be.'

He pulled the bell and the door opened within a few moments, and with a glance he warned her to keep quiet in front of the servants before turning away and going off in search of the Welsh minister. Sasha went indoors and spent an hour pacing the drawing-room floor, chewing her thumbnail and listening with every fibre of her being for the sound of the front door and Reid's return. At five o'clock Jane brought the tea tray and set it down, tentatively asking if she should run a bath and get Sasha's gown ready for the ballet.

Quite distracted by her thoughts, Sasha nodded, and wondered where on earth Reid could be. What was taking so long? She tried to steady her anxiety by sitting down and pouring a cup of tea. But it was not enough, and she found herself dwelling on Reid's words, his eagerness for the minister to 'perform a ceremony'. She felt a sense of disappointment that he had not said that he wanted to marry her, that their wedding would be because he loved her, but it seemed only to be out of duty, to save them from scandal and, no doubt, she thought with a vague and unusual sense of scepticism, to save his career from ruin. And then there was Irena, revealing a side to her character that Sasha had never suspected, and could not like. She sighed, realising that Reid was right and that from now on she would have to break all contact with Irena.

At last she heard the footman go to open the front door, and Reid's light, energetic step as he bounded up the stairs. She rose from her seat as the drawing-room door opened and he came into the room. Their eyes met, and she could tell at once from the grim set of his face that it was not good news. She sat down again and poured him a cup of tea, stirred in milk and two sugars and brought it to him as he stood before the hearth staring into the fire flames. He took the cup from her with a grateful smile, and Sasha asked, 'Did you find him?'

Reid nodded, and then shrugged his shoulders in a gesture of defeat, shaking his head at the same time. 'I am sorry to say that the Reverend Jones has made it rather difficult. He is not refusing to marry us, but rather insisting that the correct procedure be followed and the banns are read for three Sundays, and then we can be married, with all our friends and family in attendance.'

'Oh.'

'Indeed.'

'That would be rather…impossible.'

'Quite.'

'Do you think he will say anything? You know, make it known we are not actually married?'

He looked at her, his eyes scanning her anxious face. 'I hope not.'

Sasha turned away, pacing about for a few steps before turning to him anxiously. 'Oh, Reid, what are we to do?'

He shook his head. 'I don't know.'

'We can't just sit here and pretend that all is well. Too many people know already, the Reverend, and I-Irena— How can we be sure that either of them can be trusted to keep our secret?'

'Well, we can't.' He raked his hands through his hair and

then turned to her as an idea dawned on him. 'We will have to go back to England. We will have to do a Georgia and Felix.'

'Whatever do you mean?'

'Go to Gretna Green and get married, quietly and quickly.' As the idea took hold Reid began to make his plans. 'We will put it about my uncle in London is very ill, and as his only surviving relative, I have to be at his bedside.'

'Would it not be better if it was someone from my family? My mother.'

'No,' Reid replied quite emphatically, not at all keen to get the Brigadier involved in anything. 'Let me deal with this, Sasha; after all, it is my fault.'

'No, it's not, it is my fault; I brought this all upon you, Georgia and I.'

'To begin with, but it is I who have kept you here with me, sharing my life, and my bed, like a wife.'

'Reid—' she laid a hand on his arm, looking up into his strained face '—we can put an end to this. I will go, I will leave and we can pretend to get an annulment—after all, our so-called marriage has never been consummated. I could go to a physician to prove I am still a virgin.'

He gazed down upon her, and thoughtfully explored that possibility, but found it not to be to his taste. He shook his head. 'I could not put you through such an ordeal, Sasha. We will simply get married and that will solve everything. Captain Turnbull is returning next week and has been invited to accompany us to the Grand Ball at the Winter Palace. I will make the arrangements with him to convey us back to England.'

'Perhaps we could marry aboard ship if there is a chaplain onboard?'

He gave her an exasperated grin. 'I did suggest that once before, but you refused.'

Sasha had the grace to look contrite. 'Well, I did not think it a good idea at the time—after all, you were not particularly keen on—on—'

'On what?' he prompted.

'On…me.' She twisted her engagement and wedding rings on her finger, and stared at him, her eyes full of unspoken questions and doubts.

'Ah. I see.'

She could not bring herself to voice the words, to ask him if he really wanted to marry her, if he had any feelings for her, any love, because she felt sure that for him this was merely a practical arrangement.

He reached out and pulled her towards him, one hand on her waist, the other sliding to the back of her head as he brought her face closer. He leaned down, and she felt the warmth and strength of his body, and then he kissed her, and she responded, parting her lips, her hands resting on his chest as his mouth took possession of hers. He lifted his head, his eyes caressing her lips, her face. 'Sasha, I want you to be my wife. In a church on dry land, before God and the law.'

She smiled then, and refrained from spoiling the moment by demanding to know why. She would wait until he could tell her, without being forced, what his feelings really were.

'Now,' he said firmly, setting her aside, 'let us carry on as usual. I believe we are going to the ballet.'

At Reid's insistence, on Monday morning she went to visit Lady Cronin, and spent a dull few hours reading to her and listening to her blow her nose and moan about the harshness of Russian winters. She refrained from pointing out that they were well into spring now, but she tried to be kind and respectful, staying for a luncheon of soup and toast before departing for home. In the hallway of the apartment she searched eagerly for any mail from England—a letter from her mother, perhaps, in reply to her own—but seeing nothing, she surmised that perhaps Charlotte had been delayed in posting it.

For the next few days she waited, on tenterhooks, for some sign that they had been denounced, but life carried on very much as it had before. No one seemed to be any the wiser and she could only hope that her little tête-à-tête with Irena would have no consequences. She had hoped that Irena had turned her attentions elsewhere, until one morning midweek when the butler, Good, knocked on the drawing-room door and announced that a package had been delivered and where would madam like it?

Sasha beckoned for him to bring it in, and Good placed a large rectangular box on a table. Sasha found her sewing scissors and cut the string, pulling aside crisp brown paper and revealing a pink-and-grey striped dressmaker's box, tied with a wide satin ribbon. There was a note tucked into the ribbon and Sasha drew it out, unfolding the familiar thick, cream vellum with a sinking heart, her eyes skimming over the copperplate script in black ink.

Dearest Sasha, Please accept these, as a gift from one mistress to another. It will drive him wild! Love always, Irena.

Sasha crumpled the note in one hand, her teeth clenched, and then tossed it in the fire. She eyed the box as though it might contain a basket of snakes, and then decided to put it out of sight, and out of mind. She had no interest in anything Irena might send to her, and she did not write a note of thanks in reply. Carrying the box under her arm, Sasha went upstairs to her bedroom and stashed it in the back of her wardrobe. She promised herself that she would not look inside the box, and she went about her day, but it niggled at the back of her mind and that evening when she was preparing for bed she opened the cupboard door and stared at it. But no, she must resist, it was only Irena playing games and trying to tempt her into something that was bound to be... indecent. She closed the doors firmly and went to bed, listening for Reid, who was working late that evening at the Embassy, and only turning onto her side and settling to sleep when she heard him come in and go to his bedroom.

At breakfast the next morning, Reid ate poached eggs and perused a newspaper as usual, and then glanced over at Sasha as she picked at her toast, idly stirring a spoon through her tea as she stared out of the window with a glazed look in her eyes. He watched her for a few moments and then lowered his newspaper, saying gently, 'Are you all right, Sasha?'

'Hmm.'

'You'll wear a hole in that teacup.'

'Hmm.'

'Sasha!'

She started at his bark and looked up suddenly. 'What?'

'Please don't tell me nothing, when I ask what's wrong. What's wrong?'

She opened her mouth to say *nothing*, then snapped it shut with a smile. She shrugged her shoulders and murmured, 'I'm just bored, there's not very much for me to do all day.'

'I see.' Reid flicked back his wrist and glanced at his watch. 'Well, we can't have you moping around the house. I will make enquiries at the Embassy; maybe there is something you can get involved with.'

'Oh, no, please, not Lady Cronin and her sewing circle!'

Reid laughed, pushing back his chair as he leaned over to kiss her forehead. 'No, something more worthy of your intelligence and education. Maybe some translation work?'

She smiled, her eyes lighting up, and watched him go with a happy glow. How wonderful if she could have something worthwhile to occupy herself with each day. Humming softly, she finished her breakfast and reading Reid's newspaper, and then wandered out into the garden, taking a flat basket and snipping roses for the dining table. She thought of various menus that would please Reid and decided to ask the cook for his favourite roast beef and Yorkshire pudding. Taking the flowers indoors, she sent Jane to the kitchen for a vase and then went upstairs to wash her hands. In her bedroom she went to her dressing table and opened a jar of honey-and-almond hand cream, smoothing the sweetly scented lotion into her fingers and the back of her hands, wringing them round and round each other, and then glancing over her shoulder at the closed doors of her wardrobe.

She had thought of the box and its contents several times, and had congratulated herself on withstanding whatever it was that Irena was trying to tempt her with. Now, she wondered suddenly just exactly what it was she had sent. Why, it might well be something valuable, jewellery or a trinket that could be worth a fortune; in that case it would be best to return it at once and not be held to such an obligation. She crossed the room and opened the wardrobe doors, pulling out the box and giving it a little shake. It did not rattle, or feel particularly heavy. Then she sat on the bed and slowly lifted the lid on the box, burning with curiosity and wide-eyed apprehension all at the same time.

Between the folds of delicate tissue paper Sasha's fingers encountered soft black silk. She withdrew a pair of black lace-topped stockings, a black satin corset and a scrap of sheer black lace that must be a pair of drawers, but were the tiniest she had ever seen. Then she lifted out a book, turning it over, the lurid title inscribed in ornate gilt Russian lettering on the leather-bound cover. She opened the book and flicked through the pages, the colour suddenly rushing red hot to her cheeks as she gasped and looked at the drawings of naked men and women doing things that she had no idea a man and a woman could, or would, ever do! Part of her protested that she should fling the book away, and yet another part of her stared with burning fascination. Her heart beat very rapidly, and she felt sudden stabs of arousal in parts of her body that made her very aware of just where her passionate self was centred.

It was shocking, and yet suddenly she understood why Reid treated her with such polite distance. Is this what he wanted from a woman? No wonder he had been so hesitant! But surely not, Reid was such a gentleman, he couldn't possibly know of such things, or want them! Could he? Setting the book aside, Sasha picked up the black lingerie and went to stand before the cheval mirror. She held the satin corset against her, looking at her reflection. Feeling almost guilty, she unbuttoned her clothes until she stood naked, and then fastened on the corset, which was no easy feat without a maid, slipped on the gossamer knickers and rolled a stocking on each of her legs, fastening them to the straps dangling from the corset. Then she gazed at herself in the mirror, and gasped.

The exotic creature that gazed back at her seemed like someone from another world, and not at all like her normal self. Her cheeks were flushed, and there was a strange glow in her eyes. Slowly she raised her arms and pulled her hair free from its chignon, her movements causing the swell of her upthrust breasts in the tight corset to sway. She remembered Irena's words— *It will drive him wild.* How? Where? When? Did she even dare to put such a theory to the test?

While she wrestled with these thoughts, she suddenly heard Reid's voice on the landing below. She froze. What on earth was he doing home? Surely it was not time for luncheon already? But across the courtyard she heard the Embassy clock strike twelve. It seemed her questions would be answered far sooner than expected, as his familiar footsteps bounded up the stairs. With a gasp Sasha rushed to divest herself of her unusual garments, but in her nervous, guilty haste her fingers were all thumbs and she could not reach to unhook the corset. She was rooted to the spot as suddenly the door opened after a brief knock.

Chapter Nine

'Sasha, I thought we might—' Reid's swift entrance into her bedchamber came to an abrupt halt, as he stared with slack jaw and amazed eyes. 'What on earth—?' Kicking the door closed, he looked around swiftly, and felt his temper rise with violent fury. 'What the hell are you doing?'

'Reid, I— I—'

'Where is he? I'll kill him!' Reid rushed about the room, looking behind the curtains and flinging open the wardrobe doors. 'I might have known you'd get up to mischief the moment my back was turned!'

'No, no.' Sasha shook her head. 'It's not what you think!'

Suddenly she began to giggle, as Reid stomped about looking for her imaginary lover under the bed and behind the cheval mirror. She flopped down on the bed, rolling around with her knees drawn up, laughing so hard tears squeezed from her eyes, and quite unaware of how provocatively alluring her shapely bottom and legs were in that position.

Reid, realising there was no one else in the room, paused, catching his breath, unable to take his eyes from the sight of Sasha rolling around on the bed in black silk lingerie and looking quite amazingly seductive. Then his eye caught sight of the dressmaker's box and the slim leather-bound book. He picked it up and glanced through the pages, his voice quite strangled in his throat as he asked, 'Sasha, where did you get this?'

She sobered then and sat up, her hair disordered. 'Irena sent it to me.'

'Really? Might I ask why?' It was difficult to speak through his clenched teeth.

'Well, er, she thought we might be having difficulties in the bedroom, because I am still a virgin.'

With a snort of contempt he tossed the book away. It landed in a far corner and then he turned and looked down at Sasha, now sitting on her knees, the tight black corset provocative and revealing, her legs in the fine black stockings extremely pleasing to his male eyes. Considering how long it had been since he had made love to a woman, he was as easily aroused as a flame to tinder.

He leaned one knee on the edge of the bed and grasped a fistful of loose hair at the nape of her neck, pulling her gently towards him. Sasha looked up at him, her eyes wide, her mouth soft and pink. In a low voice he murmured, 'I don't think we need books.' He lowered his head, hesitated, but he could not resist the temptation and the deep aching need to touch her with his lips, his fingers, with all parts of his body.

Sasha felt the warm smooth caress of his lips on hers, and with a soft groan she reached up and slid her arms around his broad back, so that he lost his balance and they toppled together onto the bed. He rolled over her, his kiss deepening as his tongue outlined her lips in a slow sensuous movement, nudged at her teeth and then entered her mouth as she opened for him. His hands travelled down the length of her body, squeezing her buttocks clad in the briefest scrap of lace, and Sasha lifted her knee and stroked her stockinged leg along his thigh. Her fingers smoothed over the bulk of his shoulders, and he shrugged off his jacket, toeing off his shoes that fell to the floor with a clunk. The soft afternoon light shining through the voile curtains bathed them in an intimate glow.

As he rolled over she entwined her arms around his neck and they writhed together on the bed, groaning, gasping, panting, his hands kneading and stroking her bottom, her thighs, his mouth kissing her shoulders and the swell of her bosom encased in the black corset.

'Oh, God, Sasha, you are exquisite!' he growled, his teeth nipping at her hips, his hand running along the smooth length of her black-silk-clad calf.

The images she had seen in the book had already imprinted themselves on her mind and inflamed her senses. She looked at Reid with new eyes, sensual and inviting, and then she pushed at his shoulders and rolled him onto his back, straddling his hips as she ran her hands over his torso, pulling off his tie and unbuttoning his shirt, delighting in the feel of his chest hairs and muscles. She leaned back and closed her eyes, shaking her long hair and moving her hips in a tantalising sway. He groaned again, his fingers capturing her waist and encouraging her seductive movements. She opened her eyes then and looked down at him, leaning forwards so that her breasts tipped outwards in full mounds, and her eyes moved from the glory of his muscled chest to his male arousal, her fingers reaching out to boldly stroke him, feeling the hard bulk of him beneath the cloth of his grey trousers.

It was almost more than he could bear and his own fingers worked on the hooks and lacings of her corset, eager to free her body. It took some moments, but at last the stiffly boned satin fell away and he stared at her rose-tipped breasts, small but shapely and full. He sat up, cradling her back with his arms, and reached for her nipple with his mouth. Sasha gave a small cry, arching back as his fingers stroked along her spine, her body awash with waves of burning pleasure as he pressed hot open-mouthed kisses to her breasts, her ribs, her waist, before clutching at her hair again and kissing her mouth with frenzied passion. But she was still attached by her corset to her stockings and now with shaking fingers she unclipped them, and Reid slid the stockings from her slender legs, his fingers making such a simple task one that aroused and excited her. Reid grasped her hips and rolled her over again, until this time she lay beneath him.

'Sasha, Sasha,' he groaned, his fingers sliding over her soft thighs, stroking gently, his need so urgent and yet the waiting only making it more intense, as he gasped for breath and drew back. 'We must stop, not like this, we mustn't.'

Sasha gave a cry of frustrated desperation. 'Oh, Reid, don't stop, please, don't stop, I want you so much!' And she reached with one hand to tug away the final scrap of lace that was a barrier to their intimacy, spreading her legs and moving her hips against him.

His mouth returned to hers as his fingers kneaded her breast and then slid down the smooth curve of her waist and hips and down between her thighs, until he lightly brushed her in the one place where she longed for him to touch her, gasping with soft little cries as his finger explored gently. He could feel how swollen and moist she was, her warm skin sheened with a dew of sweat, and he had no doubt that she wanted this as much as he did, but still he would not yield to madness. He had to protect Sasha, even from herself.

'No, we must wait until we are married.'

'Reid, please don't be noble, not now. I will die if you don't… do something.' She did not know how to express the pulsating, urgent longing she felt inside her body, that she instinctively knew needed him, needed his body to satisfy it.

He kissed the side of her neck, murmuring gently, 'Sasha, it's too risky. I can't. But—' his fingers stroked the soft skin of her inner thigh, moving upwards to the soft down of her maidenhair and silky folds, feeling how aroused she was '—I can satisfy you in other ways.' He felt her quiver, her eager moans and the expression on her face arousing him even as his finger circled around her entrance, resisting the temptation to go any deeper into the hot, honeyed, virgin core of her.

Sasha closed her eyes, thrusting back her head as her hips moved to take the mysterious joy he offered. Confused, she opened her eyes and looked up at him. 'What do you mean?'

'I will do for you what you once did for me.' His fingers stroked delicately between her legs, his other hand caressing her breast, his lips nipping at hers, as he whispered soft words urging her to relax and enjoy the experience he was guiding her to.

'But…it is—' she struggled to speak between gasps of pleasure '—not fair.'

'Why? Are you not enjoying this?'

'Oh, I am, yes, yes, I am, but…it's…selfish.'

'No, I don't mind.' He kissed her neck with an amused smile. 'I am disciplined enough to abstain.'

'Oh, I wish you weren't! I wish you would take off your clothes and—'

He silenced her then, with his mouth, kissing her deeply, moving the focus of his finger's attention higher up and finding her nub, swollen and throbbing. She gave a muffled cry at the feel of him touching her there, and he watched her face as she closed her eyes and shuddered, her hips lifting off the bed, her legs spread and then closing together to press against his hand, until he parted them, stroking faster but very gently, building an erotic rhythm of pleasure, wave building on wave, shudder on shudder, pressing harder as he sensed her reaching a peak, and then she burst into the final clenching of pure ecstasy.

For long moments afterwards they lay entwined, their breathing slowly returning to normal, the creaking and shuddering of the bed now stilled in the sudden quiet of the room, where only moments ago all had been eager, desperate noise and movement. Sasha lay warm and glowing beside Reid as he slid to one side, lying beside her.

Then the sound of a bell chiming in the clock tower of the

Residency across the courtyard broke their intimacy. His hour for lunch had passed very swiftly, and in a most unexpected way.

'I must get back.' He rose on one elbow reluctantly, leaning over to kiss her soft, swollen mouth gently, his eyes searching her face, his fingers brushing back wayward strands of damp hair. His voice lowered as he asked, 'Are you all right? I hope, that is…'

Sasha smiled at his awkwardness, and stroked his forearm and then his jaw. 'It was wonderful.'

He smiled, rising to sit on the edge of the bed and button his shirt, tucking it into his trousers and pulling on his shoes. 'I am sorry to rush away. I hate to leave you like this.'

'It's all right, you must get back.'

He glanced at her over his shoulder. 'I will see you later.'

Again she nodded, and watched as he shrugged on his jacket and re-fastened his tie.

At the door he paused and glanced back again, nodding at the scattered black lace garments. 'Get rid of those.'

'Why?' Sasha sat up, modestly clutching the coverlet to her nakedness. 'Did you not like them?'

'They are very becoming, on a whore.' He paused, adding firmly, 'Not on my wife.'

He closed the door, leaving her to mull over his words. She lay back and closed her eyes, her thoughts roaming this way and that. At last another secret of the passion between a man and a woman had been revealed to her and she felt a glowing sense of awe. She closed her eyes, hugging the pillow that still held Reid's scent in her arms and drifted away into a warm, contented sleep. How wonderful it would be to finally make love with Reid, fully, completely!

Later, as the afternoon shadows crept across the room, Sasha woke, rose from the bed and bathed. She dressed in afternoon clothes, a caramel-and-cream striped silk dress, with a cameo brooch fastened to the ruffles below her throat. Then she collected the scraps of black silk, the book that really no lady should ever look at, and packed them all away in their box. She stood staring at the box for some time, chewing her thumbnail, remembering Reid's command about getting rid of them. Should she? Look at the effect the black underwear had had on Reid; despite what he'd said, she was sure that he had greatly enjoyed seeing her wear them, had certainly reacted most strongly! It seemed a shame to discard items that had given them both so much pleasure, and besides, how? She could hardly ask Jane to dispose of them; it would be far too embarrassing! She pondered for a moment on the idea of returning them to Irena, which would most definitely put her in her place and make it quite clear that neither she nor Reid were interested in her…persuasions.

But then, reflected Sasha with a worried frown, she could not afford to invoke Irena's displeasure; she was privy to their secrets and to anger or insult her by returning what she would consider to be gifts would be foolish. No, best just to put them away for now; she would dispose of them later, when a solution presented itself. She opened her bedroom door, peeked out, and seeing that there was no one about, she went downstairs to Reid's study and rummaged about until she found brown paper and string. Then she returned to her bedroom, wrapped the box and tied it up securely, then stowed it in the back of her wardrobe, beneath an old skirt with an unravelled hem.

At his desk in the Embassy building Reid surveyed the scattered paperwork and files, his mind quite distracted. The passionate encounter he had just experienced with Sasha had been unexpected in more ways than one. All he wanted to do now was return home, run up the stairs and take Sasha in his arms. He closed his eyes, stifling a groan as he thought of her naked body, how she had felt beneath him, her sweet soft breasts, her scent, her cries of pleasure, how she had felt while he'd touched her, how he longed to possess her completely, truly as man and wife… Was he being far too noble, as she had said? Did he dare to abandon his desk at this very moment and rush back to her? He had little enough to do—the role of military attaché was proving to be tedious—but even as he toyed with the scandalous idea, a knock on the door interrupted his thoughts. The Ambassador's secretary, Mr Hartley, came in, his face creased with concern, as was his usual manner.

'Reid, old boy, would you pop along to see Sir Stanley, please?'

'Of course.' He rose to his feet, his heart lurching for a beat or two, as his tanned complexion paled. Was he being summoned for a dressing-down? Had he and Sasha been caught out? Briskly he walked at John Hartley's side, as though nothing in the world could be of concern to him.

They entered the Ambassador's office, a large room appointed with luxurious curtains and carpets and heavy, ornate furniture. Sir Stanley was sitting at his desk, perusing several documents, and he looked up at once as Reid and his secretary entered the room.

'Ah, splendid.' He waved them both to sit down, and they seated themselves on the pair of matching chairs in front of his desk. 'Reid, I have just had a very disturbing report. It seems our Russian friends are moving men and armaments across the Caspian Sea. We are fairly certain that they are going to Afghanistan, to be used against British forces. Apparently there are several Afghan leaders here in St Petersburg, seeking to have an audience with the Tsar and further their ambitions.'

They discussed the situation for a few moments and then Sir Stanley said, 'We believe that the Sletovskaya woman has been entertaining them on behalf of one of her, er, um, a prince she consorts with.'

Reid sat up, his gaze hardening as he began to see in which direction this discussion was about to go.

'We need to know what's going on, especially as our own negotiations with the Afghans have stalled.' He gave a regretful sigh, then, 'I'm sorry, Reid, I do appreciate you are newly married and your wife is young, but her connection to Sletovskaya is too great an opportunity to be ignored. We want you to cultivate it, get yourselves invited to her house, keep your eyes and ears open and glean whatever information you can.'

Reid frowned. 'Sir, I have to say I am not at all keen on the idea; the woman has the morals of an alley cat and I am reluctant to expose Sasha—'

'Sasha?'

Reid flushed. 'I mean Georgia—Sasha is my pet name for her.'

'Indeed. But this is no time to be taking the high ground, old boy, and surely a few visits to attend supper and what have you would do no great harm? Besides, it's just a temporary assignment—the Afghans never stay away from home too long.'

'But, who am I looking for?'

'John's got the profiles, names, physical descriptions—he'll give you a briefing on exactly what the chaps look like. Obviously, it would be best if your wife knew nothing about this, she's young and naïve and goodness knows what might inadvertently slip from her tongue. Best if you accompanied her, seeing as you speak the Afghan lingo and can listen out for any interesting titbits of information. I am sure they will not be expecting anyone there to be able to speak their language.'

'I'm hardly a native speaker in either Pashto or Urdu, sir.'

'I'm well aware of that, Bowen, but you're fluent enough to understand a conversation, aren't you? That's one of the reasons we requested you be posted here.' Sir Stanley shot him a piercing glance, and then continued, tight-lipped. 'Just keep an eye out, get close to the Countess, win her confidence.'

'Is that really necessary, sir?' Reid shifted uncomfortably in his seat, not at all taken with the idea. 'I don't think my wife—'

Sir Stanley sighed, with more than a touch of exasperation and annoyance. 'Now look here, Bowen, in our line of work we quite often have to do things that we don't much fancy, that's what we get paid for. That's what we get medals and honours from the Queen for.' He ruffled some papers on his desk, picked up a fountain pen and pulled off the cap, a dismissive gesture as he pretended to turn his attention to a document, muttering gruffly, 'Just get on with it, there's a good chap.'

Reid exchanged a glance with John Hartley, who shrugged and rose from his chair, indicating with a discreet flick of his hand that Reid should do the same. He followed John to the door, where he paused as Sir Stanley called out to him, 'Good luck, and bring me something useful. By the way, where's that report I asked you for regarding your day out with the Russian Hussars? I expect details, Bowen, we want to know just what the Russian capabilities and intentions are.'

'I'm working on it, sir.'

Sir Stanley nodded. 'On my desk by the end of the day.'

'Certainly.'

Reid could do nothing more than utter that one word, before his clenched jaw prevented him from speaking. On the one hand, he was delighted at the prospect of getting out of the Embassy and doing something. These past weeks parked behind a desk had not been to his taste at all, and he did not think he would last long before asking for a transfer back to an active infantry unit. But on the other hand...Countess Irena of all people! He thought about the lewd book she had given to Sasha, about the exchange between her and Sasha in the garden after luncheon a few days ago that he had observed from the window. He was in no doubt that Irena had said something to upset Sasha, and that she had not told him the whole truth about that encounter, but he had swept it under the carpet, judging the association to be at an end. Obviously, now, it was not. As he returned down the corridor to his office, he murmured in an aside to John, 'What does he want me to do? Sleep with the woman?'

John considered the idea and asked, 'Would you? She's very beautiful.'

Reid snorted with disgust. 'No, I most certainly would not! What do you think I am?'

John laughed, patting him on the shoulder, as he poured oil on troubled waters. 'Only joking. Come on, let's go through those profiles and then you will have a good idea of who and what to look out for.'

'Right. Then I'd better get cracking and write up that report.'

'I hope your wife was not expecting to go out this evening? I doubt whether we will leave here much before ten.'

'No.' Reid's reply was terse, but he sat down at his desk and tried to put all thoughts of Sasha out of his mind as he concentrated on his work.

Sasha waited eagerly for Reid to return home. Darkness fell. It was not unusual for him to spend a good part of the evening at the Embassy, but on this occasion it seemed longer and more difficult to bear the waiting. She curled up in a chair beside the hearth, wondering if Reid felt any reluctance to return, or if it was merely pressure of work. Perhaps what had happened between them at lunchtime held no particular significance for him, whereas for her it was momentous and she longed to see him again and talk about it. Maybe Reid did not feel that way, maybe for him it had just been…a minor occurrence. Maybe he would carry on as usual, with his rather erratic hours and his devotion to his military career. She wondered if maybe what they had shared meant nothing to him; no doubt it was an experience he had often had before with other women and had very little to do with love. It had only been a desperate act of physical need, powerful and raw, the primitive responses of male and female. No words of love and devotion had passed between them. Sasha turned her face to one side and closed her eyes, as if that would block out her painful thoughts and they would not be real, causing her breath to escape sharply from between her lips, muffling the sweet agony against the palm of her hand as tears threatened to spill. How could she have been so foolish? How could she have thought for one moment that being intimate like that meant that Reid loved her?

She sniffed and dabbed at her eyes with a handkerchief tucked in her sleeve, hearing footsteps in the corridor. The butler, Good, came in, announcing quietly, 'Dinner is ready to be served, ma'am.'

Sasha glanced at the clock on the mantelpiece. It was eight o'clock already. With a sigh she rose from her chair, squared her shoulders and replied, 'I fear Major Bowen has been delayed yet again. Tell Cook to keep his meal warm, and that I will have mine on a tray upstairs.'

'Very good, ma'am.'

Upstairs in her bedroom Sasha sat down at the small table by the window, gazing pensively out at the inky dark sky studded with stars and a silver moon, as she wondered what Reid was doing at this very moment. He'd had no lunch and he must be ravenous by now. Was he eating with the Cronins? Had he given her no thought at all, not even to send a message round to say he would be late? Had he gone out? Was he enjoying himself somewhere, without her? Did he not feel eager to return to her, to her bed, and explore further the passion they had experienced so briefly? Had he even given any consideration to getting married? The only barrier to their complete fulfilment and satisfaction of their desires was his insistence that they be wed properly, husband and wife in holy matrimony. How? When? She could not stem the hot flush of frustration that coloured her cheeks, as her glance strayed to the still-rumpled bed. Oh, Reid, she thought, sighing, come home soon! Thankfully, she was distracted then by Jane knocking on the door and bringing in her dinner tray. It was so beautifully and carefully set with snow-white linen, gleaming silver, a rose in a crystal vase, that Sasha felt touched.

'Thank you, dearest Jane.'

The maid smiled, and retreated, pausing at the door, sensing that her mistress was deeply troubled. 'Anything you want, mum, just ring for me.'

'Thank you, but that will be all for tonight. You go on up to bed.'

Jane bobbed a curtsy and closed the door, leaving Sasha to eat her supper alone. The food was simple yet delicious as always, a hearty vegetable soup, followed by steamed trout and new potatoes, and a lemon sponge pudding. Afterwards, Sasha had a warm bath and put on her nightgown, pausing as she brushed her hair to stand at the window and peer across the darkened courtyard towards the Embassy. She could see the clock tower glowing, the black hands on the white porcelain background pointing to past nine o'clock. Surely he would be home soon? She got into bed and settled down to read *Jane Eyre*, leaving her door ajar and the lamp on, in the hope that Reid would not ignore the invitation when he came in. She needed to talk to him, to know what his intentions and feelings were, and that what had occurred between them in this bed was more than just lust.

By the time Reid had finished it was gone ten o'clock, but at last his work was done and he placed the twenty-page handwritten report on Sir Stanley's desk before he left. It was dark and cold as he walked briskly across the courtyard, taking a forbidden short cut that would bring him to the back of the apartment building, ringing the bell that would summon one of the footmen to open up the scullery door, and noting with approval that it was stoutly locked.

'Good evening, sir,' young Harry greeted him, opening the door and then thrusting the bolts and bars securely again as Reid came in. 'Can I take your coat?'

'Thank you. Is my wife still up?'

'Mrs Bowen retired some hours ago, sir.'

Reid stared around the warm kitchen, neat and tidy, a fire glowing in the range, sniffing at the scent of food. It had been a long day, with only tea and sandwiches, and as he gazed appreciatively at the range with its covered plates kept warm on top, the footman hurried to set out a tray with his meal.

'Shall I bring it to the dining room, or your chamber, sir?'

'No, I'll eat it here.' He didn't want to disturb Sasha, if she was asleep, with the commotion of servants and the clatter of cutlery. He pulled out a chair from beneath the scrubbed pine table, and then turned as Harry stood there staring at him, 'What's the matter, boy?'

'Um, er, nothing, sir, it's just that—'

'What?' Reid sat down with a weary sigh, as Harry placed before him a tray set with the same meal that Sasha had enjoyed earlier, now not quite so fresh as hers had been, but nonetheless hot food of any kind was welcome.

'Well, sir, it's just that upstairs folk don't usually eat, well, downstairs.'

Reid laughed, reaching for the salt and sprinkling some on the potatoes. 'I'm a soldier, Harry, I've had worse food in worse surroundings than this, I can assure you.' He eyed Harry speculatively, and then gestured towards the kettle sat on the range. 'Any chance of a mug of tea?'

'Of course, sir.' Harry dashed about getting teapot, cup and saucer.

'I said a mug.'

Hurrying to obey, Harry reached for one of the white china mugs used by the servants, found the sugar dish, and went to the pantry for milk. On his return, Reid gestured with his fork. 'Make yourself one, and sit down. I want to talk to you.' He smiled at the flash of alarm in Harry's eyes. 'Don't worry, you've done nothing wrong.' Reid concentrated then on eating his meal, enjoying every morsel, then laying down his knife and fork with a sigh, and nodding his thanks as Harry set down a mug of steaming tea in front of him. He waved him to a seat, took a sip from his mug, added two spoons of sugar, and then looked at Harry. 'I believe you've accompanied my wife to visit her cousin, Countess Irena, on a number of occasions.'

'Yes, sir.' Harry's eyes were wide as saucers, still fearing that he was about to be reprimanded.

'You know where the house is, and the servants who work there?'

'Yes, sir.'

'Good. I've got a little task for you, Harry. I want you to keep an eye on that house, see who comes and goes; if my wife goes there without me, I want you to stick very close to her. Understood?'

'Yes, sir!'

Reid rose from the table, throwing down his napkin. 'Tell Cook my thanks for an excellent meal.'

He went upstairs, treading softly, and paused outside Sasha's room. He could see through her open door that she was asleep, with a book clutched in her hand. He went in very quietly, and turned down the wick of the bedside lamp, until it gutted and the room was plunged into darkness. He resisted the temptation to lean over and kiss her. It was late, and after all the events of the day, he did not know what to say to her.

The glow of pre-dawn woke Sasha, and her first thought was the disappointing knowledge that Reid had not come to see her. She stirred restlessly, her ears tuned, but she could hear no sounds. Had he come home at all? Well, she would soon find out! She pushed back the covers and climbed out of bed, walking barefoot and on tiptoes as she left her own room and crossed the corridor. She paused in front of Reid's door, listening, but she could hear no telltale signs of movement. Slowly, carefully, she turned the handle and opened the door, peeping in. To her relief, she could see Reid sprawled on his back in the middle of the bed, bare-chested. She was so glad to see him that she had no thought except to be close to him, and she went in, closed the door behind her and padded softly across the carpet. She lifted the covers carefully and slid into the bed beside him, savouring the warmth of his body, the smell of his manliness. With a sigh she snuggled up against his side, her eyelids drooping as contentedly she settled down to sleep again.

Reid stirred, disturbed by the mattress dipping beneath his body and the awareness that he was not alone. He turned on his side, his hand sliding over her hip, sleepy still as he asked in a low, gruff murmur, 'What are you doing here?'

'I missed you.'

'Hmm.' He gathered her close, and whispered against her temple, 'I missed you, too.'

Then they both fell asleep, at peace in each other's arms.

The discordant bonging of the courtyard clock woke them again at seven o'clock. Reid groaned, and muttered, 'I'm going to get hold of some artillery and blow that wretched clock to smithereens.'

He made a move to get up, but Sasha pulled him back, her arms around his neck. She urged him closer and pressed her lips to his, parting them, inviting his kiss. He smiled, his hands fondling her hip and her bottom, and then he turned his attention to her mouth and kissed her deeply, but with distraction, aware that he must get up, that he must not give in to temptation. He pulled away, even as she mewed in protest, 'Don't go!'

'I must.' He turned to look at her, lying in his bed. 'You know I must. Come on, get up and we can have breakfast together.'

'Can't you take the day off?' She looked up at him, her eyes glowing with the promise of seduction.

'No.' He leaned over then, and hauled her up, despite her protests, swinging her up into his arms, kissing her lips soundly, before setting her on her feet, and playfully slapping her bottom. 'Get dressed.'

Sasha, relieved and delighted by his mood, her worst fears laid to rest by his kisses and playfulness, hurried away to her room and quickly washed. She dressed in a lace blouse and chocolate-brown linen skirt, brushed out her hair and pinned it up. She was just adding a cameo brooch to her blouse when Reid passed her open door, and stood there as he so often did, on the threshold. Why was he so reluctant to enter her bedroom?

She smiled at him, her eyes searching his face, questions on the tip of her tongue, but she held them back, reluctant to break the magic of these short moments she could spend with him before he would be gone for the day. His answering smile was no different from his usual expression, though what exactly she had hoped for she was not sure. Reid was not the type of man to be spouting poetry on bended knee, but she had hoped for… something, some acknowledgement that their relationship was closer and deeper than it had been before they had made love.

'Come along.' He took her hand and together they went down the stairs and into the breakfast room.

The servants appeared quickly, efficiently delivering tea and toast, and whilst they were present Sasha was careful about what she said, listening politely as Reid read his newspaper and pointed out some snippets of information about events going on in London, and then he laid aside his paper and asked her casually, 'Have you written a note to Irena yet? Thanking her for luncheon and…the gifts.'

Sasha almost choked on her tea, and quickly set down her cup in its saucer, glanced at Good as he hovered beside the door, awaiting a tray from the kitchen bearing Reid's bacon and eggs, and asked softly, 'Whatever do you mean?'

'Just that it would be politic to send her a note. Do it today, please.'

'But, Reid—'

'I thought we might invite her to accompany us to the opera tomorrow evening.'

Sasha lowered her voice as she stared at him. 'You can't be serious?'

'Why not?' He avoided looking at her, scraping butter on his toast and munching it with apparent devil-may-care. 'She's a woman of great influence. We have to be careful to keep her sweet.'

'Keep her sweet?' Sasha thought her eyes must be about to pop out on stalks, or else the Reid she knew and loved, yes, loved, must have disappeared in the night and been replaced by this…this lunatic. She took a deep breath, quite sure in her own mind that she wished to have nothing more to do with Irena, and could not imagine for one moment why Reid would want to, having told her only days ago to end all relations with her. 'Are you feeling quite well this morning, Reid?'

He glanced at her. 'Why?'

'Well, you seemed to have changed your tune as far as Irena is concerned. You were quite adamant only a few weeks ago that I should have nothing to do with her, and—' she lowered her voice, leaning towards him '—I have to say that you are completely right. Irena is not the lady we think.'

Reid smiled at her, seeing her tension, her outrage, and remembering, too, that scene in the garden, convinced now that something had happened between Sasha and Irena. He laid a reassuring hand over hers, his voice low yet firm. 'I am sure you are right, but, please, Sasha, just trust me and do as I ask.'

For long moments she stared at him, filled with misgiving, and then she inclined her head and succumbed with dignity. 'I will write a note this morning and send Harry round with it. Shall we meet her here tomorrow evening, or at the Opera House?'

'Excellent.' He paused as he finished a last mouthful of scrambled egg. 'I don't particularly want her here in our home; we'll meet her at the Opera.' He rose then, dabbed his mouth with his napkin, leaned over and kissed her forehead. 'I will see you later. Oh, and better invite John Hartley and his wife, too, it wouldn't be the done thing for Irena…' He waved his hand. 'Well, you know, we don't want to be viewed as a *ménage à trois*.'

Sasha watched as he left her side, and listened to his footsteps as he went down the stairs and the front door banged behind him. How very strange, she thought, mulling over their conversation. He wanted to continue fraternising with Irena, but he didn't want her in the house! Sasha shook her head, confused and puzzled,

and then left the breakfast room to go to the study, find pen and
paper and write a suitably polite note to Irena, however galling
it was to have to do so. She rang for Harry and despatched him
with it, and by late afternoon a reply came from Irena, saying
that of course she would be delighted to meet them at seven
o'clock at the Opera House.

The following day Reid was home by five o'clock, in good
time to prepare for their evening. They met in the dining room
to share a light supper before going out and her heart drummed
at the sight of him, so handsome in his black tails and white bow
tie. His jaw was scrupulously clean shaven and Sasha breathed
in the scent of him, a clean, masculine tang of sandalwood soap
and a subtle aftershave, and that elusive essence she could only
describe as eau-de-Reid.

He drew her to him, raising her hand to his lips and pressing
a kiss to the back of her gloved hand. 'You look lovely.'

'Thank you.'

Sasha glanced at her reflection in the mirror. She wore one
of Georgia's creations, an ivory and coral-pink off-the-shoulder
gown, with clusters of tiny rosettes on each shoulder. Her dark
hair was coiled up on her head and fastened with matching pink
rosebuds. She had done her best, but, as she feared, when they
met with Irena in the foyer of the Bolshoi Theatre, her cousin was
quite stunning and drew many a glance. Irena wore a dark red
velvet gown adorned with jet beads, her luxuriant hair swept into
ringlets, her pale marble skin and voluptuous figure perfectly
accentuated by the rich red velvet and *haute couture* design of
her gown.

Throughout the evening Sasha sat next to Mrs Emily Hartley,
a quiet, middle-age woman with greying hair who was quite
painfully shy and had little to say for herself. Irena sat between
Reid and John Hartley, seated to Sasha's left. It was an awkward
party, she thought, with three women and two men, and Sasha

was somewhat surprised that Irena had not brought a gentleman along as her escort. She tried not to pay too much attention to Irena, as she chatted with Reid. It was nothing, just a social occasion. She concentrated on the programme, on listening to the music, on smiling gently at Emily as she bent her head to try to catch her occasional murmur.

The magnificent Bolshoi was full, tiers of ornate boxes forming a curve around the stage, and it was also very hot, with ladies fanning themselves and sipping on glasses of iced pink champagne. Once the music began and the lights dimmed, Sasha glanced over to Reid and tried to catch his eye, but he seemed busy showing Irena how to use his opera glasses, leaning towards her, his arm as he held out the glasses almost touching her bosom. Sasha felt a wave of acute anger and jealousy surge through her, but resisted the urge to leap across the intervening space and haul Irena away from him. The music began, an opera entitled *Vakula the Smith* by a composer named Tchaikovsky. Sasha was not greatly familiar with his work, and it was somewhat dreary, but she sat with a smile politely fixed upon her lips and her eyes fastened upon the stage. It was a very long evening, and by its end she had the beginnings of a thumping headache. Irena invited them all to return home with her for nightcaps, but John Hartley, after one meaningful glance from his wife, declined, and Sasha, too, cried off, rubbing her temples delicately with gloved fingers.

Irena placed her arm around Sasha's waist, an intimate gesture. 'My poor little one, another time perhaps.' She laughed, a low, sultry sound as she glanced at Reid. 'Thank you for the evening, Major Bowen, you will of course let me return the kindness. I am having a little musical soirée on Wednesday evening. Please do attend.'

'We'd be delighted,' Reid replied, offering his arm as he escorted Irena to her carriage.

Sasha waited in the foyer with Mr and Mrs Hartley, and then bade them farewell as Reid returned and they went to their own waiting carriage, borrowed from the Embassy for the evening. Reid handed her up the steps and she sat down in the middle of one seat, spreading out her skirts, cloak and reticule, forcing him to take a place on the bench opposite. She sat silent and rigid as the carriage pulled away and rattled over the cobblestones homewards, her gaze turned towards the window of the carriage, although of course she could see little of the dark streets as they rumbled along.

Reid pinched his forehead with thumb and middle finger, as though he, too, had a headache, and then glanced at her, noticing her silence. 'Sasha?'

'Hmm?' Still she did not look at him.

'Are you all right?'

'Yes, thank you.'

He glanced at her profile and pursed lips, at her fingers clenched in her lap. 'You don't look it. Are you angry?'

'Yes.'

'Why?'

'Need you ask?'

'Well,' he said with a frustrated shrug of his shoulders, 'if I knew I wouldn't ask!'

'If you don't know, then I shan't say—'

'Sasha!'

She drew in a breath and said coldly, 'I'd rather not talk about it.'

'But…' He sighed then, and leaned forwards, hands dangling between his knees. 'Is it because of Irena?'

She was silent.

'Sasha?'

'Well, for a married man you were rather friendly.'

He laughed. 'Was I? Are married men not allowed to speak to women except their own wives?'

'You weren't just speaking to her, you were practically undressing her with your eyes and getting far too close.'

'Nonsense! It was the opera, in full public view.'

'You almost had your arm on her bosom.'

'When?'

'When you were showing her the opera glasses!'

'Ah. She did move rather closer than necessary, or expected.'

She glanced at him then. 'Reid…'

'Hmm?'

Sasha shook her head and then turned her face away. 'Nothing.'

'What? Tell me.' For some reason, into his mind flashed a replay of the scene he had witnessed from the upstairs window of the Sletovskaya Palace, of Irena and Sasha in the garden, and he added more gently, 'Please, tell me.'

She looked at him again, her lips and breath drawn pensively, in her mind a memory of exactly the same scene. 'Well…'

'Yes?'

'I think, well, I think Irena…wants you.'

'Indeed?' He could see the uncertainty and fear in her eyes, and reached out to draw one of her hands into his warm clasp, his voice very soft as he reassured her. 'As you pointed out, I am a married man, and you have nothing to be concerned about.'

'But that's just it, Reid, you're not a married man. You can do whatever pleases you.'

'It would not please me to—' he searched for polite words to use in front of a lady, in front of Sasha '—to be seduced by Countess Irena.'

'Why not? She is very beautiful.'

'No, she is not. On the outside maybe she has a certain structural perfection, but on the inside she has no beauty whatsoever.'

'You sound like you're assessing a building!'

He smiled, removing her glove and feeling the need to stroke his thumb over the soft, smooth skin of her palm. The gesture sent shivers through her body and their eyes melded together in a long look. 'Then if Irena's a building, she's a—' He thought for a moment or two and then said, 'She would be Newgate gaol, full of dirty, nasty things.'

Sasha shook her head and smiled at his silliness, her fingers flexing in his hand, her skin flaring with delight at his touch. 'And what sort of building would I be?'

'Hmm.' He leaned his head to one side, considering. 'You, my darling Sasha, you would be...the Taj Mahal.'

Sasha had no intention of relenting quite so easily, but she smiled, and was about to make a retort when the carriage suddenly lurched and she was almost thrown from her seat. The vehicle had been slowing as it turned a corner, now suddenly they came to a halt and she gave a small cry of alarm at the sound of the horses neighing and stamping, raucous voices shouting and strange thumping noises against the sides of the carriage. Amidst a sudden crack and smash of glass the shuttered window broke, scattering small shards of glass and broken slats of wood on the floor between them. Her gaze flew to Reid's in alarm, as he drew a small pistol from his pocket. They both stared at the shapeless forms crowding about the door, and the handle as someone on the outside tried to wrench it open. Reid reached out to try to hold on to the handle, but he was overpowered, the door flung open and several dark, bearded faces, capped with rough shakos, eyes wild and dark, crowded into the narrow aperture. Sasha yelped and drew back as rough hands reached blindly inwards, yet the only objects thrown at them were small square sheets of paper.

Reid pushed the nearest back with his foot, and fired a shot over their heads. He could hear the driver shouting at the horses, cracking his whip, urging them onwards, and the guard riding shotgun now followed Reid's example and fired a round from his rifle. The Russians stumbled back, having accomplished their aim of accosting the 'nobles' and forcing their propaganda upon them. The door swung wildly as the carriage hurtled away and Reid reached out to slam it shut. He moved to sit beside Sasha and pull her into his arms, prepared for hysterics and fainting. Though she was trembling and clearly shaken, her face pale, she indulged in neither.

Sasha reached down and picked up one of the pamphlets, squinting as she held it up to the flickering lantern light. 'Look—' she read the crude Russian words with ease '—they denounce the Tsar as a tyrant and demand freedom for the press, the nation and themselves!' She glanced up at him as he leaned close against her cheek, peering at the page she held. 'It's all very dramatic and not very good grammar, but how dreadful! These poor people are suffering so badly, Reid, is there nothing we can do?'

'We?'

'Why, the British government, the Queen!'

Reid looked at her, with an emotion half-mixed with admiration for her intelligence and half with amazement at her naivety. 'What would you have us do? Invade? Adopt every poor Russian and take him home to London?'

'No, of course not! But there must be something!' Sasha read the pamphlet again, exclaiming, 'I thought the serfs had been freed years ago. I remember Tsar Alexander issued an Edict of Emancipation—why, it must have been ten years ago, at least.'

'1861,' supplied Reid drily, having boned up on Russia and its affairs before leaving London. 'Somehow I don't think the Princes and Grand Duchesses of Imperial Russia have quite grasped the concept of paying their servants a decent wage.' His glance went to the window and with some relief he realised they had reached home. They descended from the carriage and hurried indoors, Reid pausing in the foyer as Sasha went upstairs, murmuring to Good that they'd had an unpleasant encounter and to be sure none of the household went out that night and all the doors and windows were securely locked.

In the drawing room Sasha went to the tea tray that Jane had left for them as soon as she had heard their arrival. She poured two cups of hot, fragrant tea, spooning in sugar, but as she stirred she wondered if Reid might prefer something stronger. Her glance strayed to the drinks cabinet, at the same moment as Reid came striding into the room. He went to the fire, lit even on this June evening, the sun never quite warm enough to reach into the huge dark rooms of the thick-walled baroque building. He warmed his hands before the heat of the flames, his expression thoughtful, as Sasha approached with their cups of tea.

'Would you prefer a brandy?' she asked, standing at his elbow.

'No, this will do nicely.' He drained the cup almost in one gulp.

He smiled down at her, rather absent-mindedly, she thought. She laid a hand on his forearm. 'Are you all right? I know it was a most alarming incident, but no harm came from it and we are home safe and sound.'

Reid laughed then, taking her cup and saucer away and placing it with his on the mantelpiece. His arms went around her slender frame and he stooped as he hugged her close against him, kissing her temple. 'My darling Sasha! It is I who should be reassuring you. In fact, you should be swooning and ashen-faced with shock and horror.'

'Well, I am not.' Her own arms slid around his broad back, and she savoured the scent and the warmth of him as she leaned against his chest, her voice a soft whisper. 'I had every faith in you, Reid, that you would protect me.'

He held her away then, and his eyes scanned her face, marvelling at how in just a span of a few brief weeks Sasha had matured into this—this amazing woman! He decided there and then to take her into his confidence, and, after kissing her for a long, enjoyable moment, he explained everything there was to explain about Irena.

Chapter Ten

'Do you really think Irena is a spy?' Sasha gasped, wide-eyed, leaning back in the circle of his arms.

Reid held her a little away from him. 'No, not exactly, but we think she's involved in intrigue of some kind—whether innocently or not is no concern of ours. She is, after all, a Russian citizen, not British. All we are interested in is what she knows and where she's getting that information from.'

Sasha frowned slightly, puzzled. 'Why are you telling me this?'

'Because...' Reid paused, not entirely sure himself why he had broken with protocol and disobeyed his orders. 'Because there is more to Irena than meets the eye, and I want you to be careful. And because—' he gathered her close and held her small, slim body gently against the hard bulk of his own '—I cannot bear to have you think my interest in Irena is more than just professional.'

Sasha sighed, and smiled, content, whispering against his ear as she stood on tiptoe, 'Shall we go to bed?'

Reid laughed, and then shook his head. 'Do you ever think of anything else, except to seduce me?'

'No,' Sasha answered with honest aplomb and an innocent expression.

'All in good time.' He kissed the tip of her nose, leading her from the drawing room.

Sasha pouted. 'Why not now?'

'You know very well.' Reid's voice lowered to a whisper, as they climbed the stairs together with arms linked. 'Not until we are legally wed.'

In the week following Sasha felt like an onlooker at a play, watching people moving about, even herself. They attended several suppers and a soirée at Irena's house. Reid paid a great deal of attention to her, and to her friends, and though Sasha quelled the jealous pangs with the knowledge that Reid meant none of it, the sophisticated gatherings and Irena's smug delight began to pall.

She missed the company of her sisters, and her mother, and even gentle Charlotte Hope-Garner, a quiet yet witty woman, and Sasha wished that she was still here, sure that the older, mature and motherly woman, experienced in the ways of the diplomatic world, would have sound advice. She realised that of course her father would be the most trustworthy and knowledgeable adviser, but she did not dare approach him! She resolved to write to her mother and to Charlotte, and she did both letters that very evening.

The next morning was a bright and beautiful day, the sun shining from a cloudless topaz sky, lilac trees now in bloom and the river busy with small boats as the citizens of St Petersburg enjoyed the good weather, gadding about to the various islands of the Neva delta to enjoy picnics on the shore, and to their country dachas on the outskirts of the city. Sasha resolved that she and Reid would see more of this intriguing and vast city before they returned to England. They so rarely had time alone to themselves—Reid worked long hours and at home there was always a well-meaning servant hovering. She thought a few sightseeing excursions would be a wonderful opportunity to spend time alone. Most nights Reid came in late and went straight to his own room and she would not see him until breakfast in the morning. At the first opportunity she broached the subject of seeing a little more than their small world of this apartment, the Embassy and Irena's palace.

'Reid, I thought we might pay a visit to the Hermitage.'

He looked up as he buttered a square of toast. 'Why?'

Sasha's lips curved in a slight smile. 'Does there have to be a reason for everything?'

'Of course.'

'Well, then, because I have heard from my mother that the Hermitage museum is magnificent. There are hundreds of paintings and sculptures, and also Roman, Asian and Oriental artefacts, just to mention a few out of the thousands of exhibits that have been collected since Catherine the Great, and it is reputed to be one of, if not *the*, best and largest art collection in Europe. Indeed, there are classical antiquities dating back to—'

'Whoa!' Reid cut in, with a laugh at her enthusiasm, but aware that he had to leave and make his way over to his office at the Embassy. 'Is there someone you want to take there?'

Sasha laughed. 'Yes, you!'

He looked at her sideways. 'Why? I don't know much about art.'

'Well, now's your chance to learn.' She smiled gently. 'And you are the person that I want to share the experience with.' Her eyes were warm as they studied his face, his mouth, promising things that had nothing to do with museums.

Reid swallowed his toast, catching the look in her eyes and thinking to himself that just in that moment how much more Russian Sasha seemed to be, the Russians being so flamboyant and extravagant, full of passion and soul one moment and ruthlessly intellectual the next. Her Englishness seemed to have diluted the less attractive traits, but he wondered how much

influence Irena had had in bringing out the more passionate side
of Sasha's nature. And whilst he was delighted, he did not want
that passion to be channelled in the wrong direction. Perhaps it
would be a good idea to spend some time together, just the two
of them.

'We will go tomorrow afternoon. Happy?' Reid rose from his
seat, bending to bestow his goodbye kiss on her cheek as usual.

'Very.' Sasha smiled back up at him, feeling that slight pang
in the region of her heart whenever he left her for the day.

They murmured their goodbyes and Sasha sat listening to
his footsteps fade down the stairs and the bang of the front
door behind him. She sighed, but then cheered herself up with
the thought that tomorrow they would share a whole delightful
afternoon, wandering around the Hermitage. She went to Reid's
study and sat down at his desk with pen and paper, making a
list of the Rembrandts, da Vincis and Rubens that she wanted
to see at the Hermitage, as well as the famous Kolyvan vase, a
huge bowl carved from jasper and long enough for three men to
lie down inside it toe-to-toe. She pondered on what its use could
have been, and then moved on to add other items of interest to
the list. She was aware that the Hermitage, part of the Winter
Palace, was so vast that it would take them several days, if not
weeks, to view most of it. Content that they would see the things
she really wanted to, Sasha folded the list and went upstairs to
her bedroom, tucking the list into her reticule and then browsing
through her collection of clothes to see what she could wear that
Reid would find enchanting. She selected a sea-green silk gown,
with close-fitting sleeves trimmed with lace and a sweetheart
neckline. The bustle was modest and the gown rustled with a
sensuous yet subtle swish against her legs as she walked. Cream
gloves and a matching tiny cream hat trimmed with silk mag-
nolias completed the outfit.

The weather held the next morning, and as soon as they had
finished luncheon Sasha rushed to fetch her hat and gloves. Reid

wanted to take a carriage, but Sasha was so impatient to be on their way she could not bear to wait for it to be summoned from the Embassy.

'Oh, do let's walk, Reid, it's such a lovely day!'

Reluctantly, Reid agreed and they set off, strolling down the broad avenue, dwarfed by the massive buildings and palaces of the Nevsky Prospekt. It was busy, with many people also taking advantage of the sunny afternoon to enjoy a stroll or carriage ride along the broad avenues. They crossed the narrow River Moyka over a gracefully arched bridge, its balustrade intricately wrought in filigrees of iron and gilded with gold. It was farther than Sasha realised and took them nearly an hour to reach the vast and open expanse of Dvortsovaya Ploschad—Palace Square. As they approached Reid pointed to the façade of a massive, flat-roofed building curving in a vast sweep as far as the eye could see and set with hundreds of small oblong windows on three floors.

'That's the headquarters of the Russian Army, the appropriately named, if rather dull, General Staff Building. I do believe that we will be watching the Russian Army on parade next Sunday, making their report to the Tsar.'

'Well, there's certainly nothing dull about the architecture.' Sasha eyed with some awe the yellow-and-white building, several times bigger than anything she'd ever seen in Whitehall.

In the middle a massive half-moon archway tunnelled into the depths. On either side the façade was decorated with ten white colonnades, supporting on the roof, rather incongruously set against the blue sky, a bronze statue of Victory driving her chariot, surrounded by half a dozen statues of people, but whether they were friend or foe Sasha couldn't tell.

'It's colossal,' she murmured. 'Amazing that it doesn't all come crashing down.'

They walked across the wide openness of the windy square and paused to inspect another monument set in its centre. Sasha craned her neck to gaze up at the thick red granite column soaring into the sky, like a giant stick of rock, and topped by another bronze statue, this time of a winged angel holding aloft a Christian cross.

She translated the inscription on the pedestal. 'To Alexander I, from a grateful Russia.'

Reid and Sasha exchanged a glance, but then without comment continued on their way. As they crossed the square, admiring their surroundings as they went, they heard the clatter of hooves and looked back towards the archway of the General Staff Building. Six horsemen rode out on black chargers, their manes shivering in long ripples, heads lowered with willing obedience. The sound of spurs and bridles jingling grew louder as the Russian Imperial Guardsmen trotted towards the Winter Palace. Reid's arm through Sasha's checked her and they waited for the Guards to pass them by, but the leading horseman held up his hand and the troop slowed to a stop. The horses snorted and stamped and Sasha caught a whiff of their pungent odour, and of leather and that indefinable smell of soldiers: sweat tinged with gunpowder and rifle oil, and a strong essence of alpha male. The leading horseman was a ranking officer and, though some might think him handsome, Sasha thought his features rather coarse, his moustache far too big and his eyes insolent as he looked her over from head to toe.

Reid recognised the horseman and greeted him, his face inscrutable, revealing nothing of his dislike of the man who was Irena's lover, or one of them, at least. He had been on manoeuvres with them on the plains some weeks before and was noted for his hard drinking and womanizing. Reid had been forced to come to blows with Kirovsky in order to free an unwilling gypsy girl from his advances and allow her to escape the tavern they'd been drinking in.

'Count Kirovsky.' He bowed slightly, with stiff formality.

'Major Bowen,' the Count replied in perfect English, having

spent some time at Sandhurst, his dark eyes roaming with undisguised interest over Sasha. 'And who is this enchanting young lady?'

Reid met his glance squarely, but without moving a muscle. 'This is my wife.'

'Your wife? I did not realise you were married!' He laughed, as Sasha turned her head to look at her supposed husband with a questioning frown. 'Your husband is very popular with the ladies—why, Irena has been talking about him non-stop. And does your beautiful wife have a name?'

Sasha parted her lips to deliver a retort, but the slight tightening of Reid's elbow against the crook of her own prevented her from doing so.

'Yes.' Reid's gaze was unyielding as he replied coldly, 'Her name is Mrs Bowen.'

Count Kirovsky smiled, his brows slightly raised as he recognised the signals from a fellow soldier protecting his territory, but he merely inclined his head towards Sasha. 'A pleasure to meet you, Mrs Bowen. And where is the delightful Irena—she is not with you?'

'No.'

'What a shame. But I will see her soon, perhaps.'

With that, he gathered up his reins, jabbed his horse with both spurs and trotted away, his troop jangling and clattering as they followed close behind as one body.

Sasha released her pent breath in a gust. 'What an odious man! Who is he?'

'No one you need worry about.'

They continued walking towards the Winter Palace and the entrance to the Hermitage museum to one side of it. Sasha asked, 'What did he mean, about being popular with the ladies? Have you met him before?'

Reid nodded. 'When we were on manoeuvres with the Russian cavalry.'

'Oh, yes, I do remember,' Sasha purred. 'You came back very drunk.'

'Well—' Reid cleared his throat and looked away '—drunk, but not *very* drunk.'

'You were *very* drunk.'

'I was not!'

'Well, never mind.' Sasha had no wish to argue and spoil the day. 'How does he know Irena? I have never seen him with her.'

Reid chose his words carefully—for all that Sasha was not a young schoolroom chit, she was still naïve and he did not want to shock her unduly. 'I think he is the sort of visitor that Irena receives in private.'

'Oh.' Sasha was silent for a few moments, and then she looked up and said brightly, 'Well, here we are!'

They stood before the entrance of the Hermitage, an impressive sight with its ten massive statues of Atlantes, sixteen feet tall and made of pure, gleaming granite, their arms crooked backwards as they appeared to hold up the portico of the entrance.

'Aren't they magnificent?' Sasha enthused as they mounted the steps.

Reid eyed the semi-naked torsos of the male Atlantes, displaying enviable muscles, taut, lean and massive, and replied drily, 'Quite.'

They entered the museum, their footsteps echoing on the marble floors as they wandered about the magnificent halls and rooms, richly adorned with marble pillars, gold-leaf cornices, elaborate crystal chandeliers, the floors inlaid with intricate designs in jasper, malachite and white marble; an opulence and grandeur that almost overshadowed the priceless paintings and ancient artefacts. There were few people about, yet even as she held her list in one hand and Reid followed at her side and they admired the art with murmurs to one another, Sasha could not concentrate. All she could think about was what Count Kirovsky had said. What did he mean about Reid being popular with the ladies? What had occurred when he had been away that day, or any day when he was not with her at home? Was there another woman? Was that why Reid no longer had any interest in making love to her?

'Sasha?' Reid gently whispered her name, as they stood in front of Leonardo da Vinci's *The Litta Madonna*. 'Shall we move on? We've been standing here for ten minutes already.'

'Oh!' Sasha shook her head, brooding inwardly on her thoughts, avoiding his gaze as they walked on down an echoing corridor with a dozen tall windows overlooking the Winter Palace canal, the walls adorned with frescoes copied from the Vatican, interspersed on one side with gleaming mirrors that reflected the light and the intricate artwork of the colourful, gold-edged frescoes.

Reid looked over her shoulder at the now rather creased and crumpled list in her left hand. 'What's next?'

He tried not to sound bored, to be interested for her sake, but he hoped that soon they would be done and they could go home. He wondered what Cook had prepared for afternoon tea and was quite looking forwards to sitting down in the drawing room with a hot cup of tea and a plate of sandwiches and cake. Glancing at Sasha, he noticed that she had become very quiet, and rather distant. Looking up and down, he made sure they were alone, before turning and catching her about the waist, pushing her into the deep recess of a doorway, the massive enamel-and-gilt doors closed.

'Reid!' Sasha exclaimed, glancing up at him as she felt the weight and strength of his warm body, pressing her up against the door. 'What are you doing?'

He held her firmly with one arm about her waist, the other above her head, leaning against the door frame, effectively penning her in and there was no escape. 'What's the matter?'

'Nothing!'

'Sasha, you have something on your mind, now spit it out!'

She bent her head back, aware of the feel of his body against hers, his hard chest and his muscular legs a delight to her senses, and the scent of him quite filled her nose and seeped into every pore of her body. Instead of speaking, she reached up and clasped his face between her two hands, her touch gentle and soft, her small fingers slightly splayed against the rough contours of his jaw. He looked at her, taken slightly by surprise, then standing on tip-toe Sasha reached up and pressed her mouth to his, in a rather awkward, inexperienced kiss, but one that made him groan with pleasure as he felt the sweet velvet of her tender pink lips against his own firm male ones.

His hand slid to the back of her head, supporting her delicate neck as he stooped over her and parted her mouth with the force of his own, taking control and guiding her into the sweetest kiss of passion she had ever known. His tongue swept within, tasting, possessing, and their breath came in sharp gusts from their noses as they clung to each other. Sasha's hands slid around his broad, strong back, moving upwards and pulling him tight against her, so that she could feel his body and his arousal, delighted with the effect that she had on him, and the pleasure of his deep, intimate kiss.

They were lost in their own little world as time passed by, and neither of them wanted to end the intimacy of their locked mouths, but then they heard the tap of heels and the murmur of voices at the far end of the corridor, and Reid pulled away. His glance lingered on her flushed face and swollen lips for a moment, with a slight smile, as Sasha hurried to straighten her bodice and the little hat perched on the side of her head amidst loosened hair. Then he took her hand and led her away, his fingers laced intimately between her own.

They did not speak until, by mutual accord, they had left the museum and were walking homewards across Palace Square. Reid glanced sideways at Sasha, who had her head down and was walking briskly at his side.

'What was that for?' he asked gently, watching the blush flare on her cheeks.

She shrugged, turning her head away slightly.

'Sasha?' He stopped, pulling her to a halt in front of him. 'Is something wrong?'

She bowed her head, considering what to say to him, and then lifted it quickly. 'Reid, do you still want me?'

'What a strange question!'

'Do you?'

He studied her face for a moment before replying, realising that something must have upset her. 'Has Irena said something to you?'

'About what?' she gasped, a frown creasing her brows as she gazed up at him in alarm.

'I don't know, about, well…' He shrugged, slightly embarrassed. 'About being a virgin.'

'It's not that, it's not about me, it's you I am wondering about. Have you— That is…?' Sasha floundered, stumbling on unknown words for a subject she didn't know very much about. 'Perhaps you have become bored, and there is someone more… experienced, like Irena, except not Irena because I know you don't want her, but—'

'Sasha, what on earth are you talking about?' Reid took hold of her by both shoulders, forcing her to stand still and look at him.

'Count Kirovsky said you were popular with the ladies.'

'Ah.' At last Reid understood, and he smiled wryly with a little shake of his head, lifting her chin with a crooked forefinger. 'I haven't been to bed with other women, if that's what you are wondering. Yes, there were girls in the tavern, and they were all over us, but I did not get intimate with anyone. Why would I, when I have you waiting for me at home?'

'Well, we've never—'

'Not yet. But we will. When the time is right.'

They smiled at each other, knowing that waiting for that moment, when the time *was* right, would only make it all the more sweeter. They linked arms and walked homewards, Reid expressing how ravenous he was and how he hoped there was a good tea waiting for them. Sasha laughed, looking up at him, at this handsome, charming man who had come into her life so suddenly and filled it with this strange unknown feeling of… happiness.

That evening they were sitting comfortably in the drawing room, at peace with one another's company as Reid caught up with some work that he had missed while spending his afternoon at the Hermitage, reading reports on the political situation. There was a lot to digest with the Russians now at war with Turkey and still meddling with the Afghans, as well as unrest in their own backyard, particularly from a revolutionary group called Narodnaya Volya, the People's Will, who would like nothing better than to murder the Tsar and do away with all aristocracy. He glanced across to where Sasha sat curled up in the corner of the sofa, next to him. She had taken her shoes off and leaned her cheek on one palm as she read a periodical, and had been quietly absorbed for a good half-hour.

'What are you reading that's so fascinating?' he asked, stretching out a hand to slide it under the hem of her skirt, absently caressing the delicate bones of her ankle.

Sasha looked up, shivers of delight tingling from her ankle all the way up her leg and into her body. 'It's *The Russian Messenger*—they have another instalment of Leo Tolstoy's *Anna Karenina*. It's quite fascinating—have you read it?'

'No,' Reid replied drily, 'not quite to my taste.'

'And those boring reports are?'

'They are not boring.'

'Neither is Tolstoy.'

'Then we must agree to disagree.'

She met his smile with one of her own, and bent her head, eager to discover whether Anna would succumb to the charms of Vronsky and allow herself to be seduced, but it was very difficult to concentrate on anything except the feel of Reid's fingers moving on her ankle and her own desire to be seduced!

She shifted slightly, and smiled to herself as she studied his face from the corner of her eye, but he was once again engaged in reading the reports scattered about on the sofa and the floor. She sighed and was about to ask him to stop when Good knocked on the door and announced that they had a visitor. It was John Hartley from the Embassy. He hurried into the room, panting slightly as though he had just been running, which he had. His normally impeccable grooming was all out of sorts, his hair and tie askew and Sasha noticed the cloth of his trousers over one knee was torn and dirty. With one accord both she and Reid rose from the sofa.

'John, are you all right?' Reid enquired politely.

'Oh, yes, thank you, it's not me you have to be concerned about.'

'What's happened?'

'It's the Ambassador, or should I rather say, it's the Tsar—well, actually, it's both!'

Reid turned to his colleague and ushered him to a chair, nodding to Good, who left the room and closed the door. Reid went to the drinks cabinet and poured John a shot of brandy into a crystal glass. He handed it to him and Sasha wondered whether to ring for some tea, but stood quietly as the two men talked in earnest tones.

'Someone has tried to assassinate the Tsar—' John took a swig of his brandy '—and damn well nearly got us, too!'

John went on to explain how he and Sir Stanley had been visiting the Pavlovsky Barracks to finalise arrangements for the Sunday parade when, quite out of the blue, Alexander II had arrived.

'He does like to do that, you know, turn up unexpectedly and mix with the troops, although there were so many Imperial Guardsmen that you could barely squeeze anyone else in the room. We had tea and a rather good evening, the Russians singing and in good humour for a change, but then as we were going down the steps to make our way home, some lunatic lunges out of the dark and starts firing shots!' John paused as he took a handkerchief from his pocket and wiped his forehead, before taking another sip of his brandy. 'I tell you, it was mayhem! People were ducking and diving all over the place. I pushed Sir Stanley to the ground, but not quite quickly enough—he's taken a shot in the shoulder.'

'You could have both been killed!' exclaimed Sasha, aghast.

'Indeed, but fortunately it wasn't us he was after. The Guardsmen grabbed the Tsar and hauled him back inside, a few of them gave chase after the gunman, but the devil was gone quick as a ferret down a rabbit hole. If they'd got hold of him, I wouldn't like to imagine his fate.' He glanced at Sasha then, remembering the presence of a lady. 'Well, suffice to say, it was all over very quickly.'

'Damn, I missed it all!' Reid growled, rising impatiently to his feet and pacing about, before swinging to face John. 'Where is he now? Sir Stanley, I mean.'

'He's back at the Embassy; they wanted to take him to the Palace to be attended by one of the Tsar's own physicians, but I thought it best to bring him home and get our own Dr Watts to take care of him.'

'Good. Well, we'd better get over there. Sasha, would you come, too, and be of assistance to Lady Cronin?'

'Of course,' Sasha murmured, and hurried to fetch her coat and gloves.

It was very late by the time they returned home again from the Embassy, secure in the knowledge that Sir Stanley had received nothing more than a grazing wound and that Lady Cronin had not gone to pieces at the thought of her husband almost being murdered. Indeed, she had been quite calm and collected, and insisted that there was nothing more either Reid or Sasha could do by staying all night. Several burly Household Cavalry men accompanied them on their return journey, a mere few minutes' walk, but no one was taking any chances.

* * *

In the next few days a palpable tension was to be felt in the city, with soldiers and policemen on every street corner, hunting for the man who had dared to point a gun at the Tsar. A description and rough charcoal drawing of the wanted assassin was distributed on printed leaflets by the police, but, as on previous occasions, the culprit had melted away like snow on a spring morning.

The excitement died down, and life carried on as before, and Sasha wondered whether the assassin would be aware that he had accomplished nothing and be ready to make another attempt. She asked Reid if the Tsar would not appear in public for a while and the Sunday parade would be cancelled, but Reid assured her that the Russian Emperor would not skulk behind locked doors and the Sunday parade was a spectacle not to be missed by anyone. It was to be held on the Field of Mars, adjacent to the Pavlovsky Barracks, situated in the heart of the city between the Summer Garden and Court Quay.

On Sunday morning Sasha travelled in a carriage with Lady Cronin and other ladies of the Embassy and took her place in the Royal Pavilion overlooking the massive parade ground. There were thousands of people present, not to mention thousands upon thousands of soldiers from all parts of Russia gathered on the Field itself. There were several ranks of Imperial Guard mounted on their magnificent horses and looking very proud and fearsome, as well as Cossacks from the Steppes in their bright red tunics, baggy black pantaloons and fur shakos. There were noble princes from Georgia, Mongols on sturdy ponies, Tcherkesses and Persians and foot soldiers from every regiment.

Sasha stared in awe from where she sat with all the guests, ambassadors from most European countries and Russian aristocracy. She searched for Reid, who was mounted and on the Field, along with other members of the British military waiting to pay their respects to their host, Alexander II, but she could

not find him amongst the seething mass of horses, lances fluttering with flags, and the many-coloured uniforms. She looked
about to see if she could spot Irena, but either she could not see
her or she was not attending. Sasha had noticed that Irena very
rarely attended any public functions, particularly functions in
honour of the Tsar.

The Tsar arrived mounted on a grey stallion, followed in an
open landau by the Empress Maria. The many bands of each
regiment thundered into the national anthem, the whole Field
a quivering mass of waving flags as the Tsar thundered past at
a slow gallop, his escort riding alongside in haphazard fashion
as the Tsar darted about, pausing to speak here and there to his
soldiers.

It was a magnificent and unusual spectacle, a day that Sasha
would never forget, but at the same time it was almost overwhelming and a little frightening. She was glad when at last it
was over and their carriage came to collect them. She climbed
inside and seated herself beside Lady Cronin with a small sigh
of relief.

Lady Cronin glanced at her, and smiled gently, patting her
on the knee. 'Home for a nice cup of tea, I think, my dear.'

'Oh, yes—' Sasha smiled in reply '—that would be lovely.'

They smiled and sat back as the carriage pulled away on its
journey homewards to the safe familiar world of the British
Embassy.

Sasha realised that the Grand Ball was only two weeks away,
so she went to visit Madame Dieudonné, a French seamstress
very popular with the ladies of St Petersburg. She wanted to
impress Reid by wearing a new ball gown, one that was made
especially for her, and not for Georgia. She chose a ruby-red
creation, with a pleated satin bodice decorated with diamanté
and a swirling skirt of criss-cross layered chiffon. It suited her
dark hair and eyes, the low neckline and tiny sleeves showing

off her delicate shoulders and creamy skin perfectly and with feminine allure.

The ball was to be held at the Winter Palace in the presence of Tsar Alexander II and his wife, Empress Maria. The Ambassador sent a note to say that Captain Turnbull would be visiting in the next week and would the Bowens be kind enough to provide him with overnight accommodation and include him in their party to be transported to the ball? Sasha replied that they would be delighted.

She was happy to receive the Navy man when he called upon her on Friday afternoon, a week before the ball.

'Captain Turnbull.' Sasha held out both her hands in warm greeting, which the Captain took in his, and stooped to kiss her on the cheek, his beard rather scratchy. Then she waved him to a chair, but her countenance soon turned to shock as she looked up, aware of another person as Good still stood at the drawing-room door, ushering in a young woman. Sasha stared, her mouth gaping open.

'Georgia!'

Chapter Eleven

For a long moment all Sasha could do was stare, and then she saw the uncertainty, almost fear, in Georgia's blue eyes. There were shadows beneath them and she appeared so much thinner than the last time Sasha had seen her. Thinner, and not at all glowing with happiness. Despite everything, Georgia was still her sister, her little sister whom she had loved and adored and cared for all her life. Without a word, with tears in her eyes, she held open her arms and Georgia ran into them with a small sob. Despite being taller, she leaned her head on Sasha's shoulder and clung to her.

'I'm sorry. I'm so sorry!'

'Shh.' Sasha patted her back, soothing her, waiting until Good had departed and closed the door before straightening and holding Georgia a little away from her. She glanced sideways at Captain Turnbull, hesitating, wondering how much he knew about whatever predicament Georgia had fallen into this time. Or was her presence here in St Petersburg still part of the same charade?

Intercepting the glance, Georgia blurted, 'He knows everything. Well, almost everything.' Georgia blushed then, and Captain Turnbull stared discreetly at his boots.

'Well…' Sasha guided Georgia to a chair, seeing that she was distraught, a state she had never witnessed her bright and confident sister in before. She sat her down, with a small, reassuring squeeze of her hand to Georgia's shoulder. 'You had better tell me what's happened and why you are here.'

Sasha, her hands trembling, terrified of the sudden chasm of truth that had opened at her feet, knew that everything was about to change. She seated herself in front of the tea tray, pouring them each a hot fragrant cup and piling small plates with delicacies—Dundee cake and oat biscuits with slices of cheddar cheese—handing these out and taking a sip of her tea before looking across the table. She could find no further excuse to delay the inevitable.

Georgia was obviously reluctant to speak, but the awkward moment was soon covered by Captain Turnbull as he reached into his jacket pocket and drew out two sealed envelopes, one cream manila and the other blue. 'Before I forget, lass, here are some letters for ye.'

'Oh, how wonderful.' Sasha set aside her cup and took the letters, glancing at them and pleased to see that one was from her parents, and the other was from Charlotte, which had no doubt crossed with her own in the post. With due regard for her visitors, she placed them in the pocket of her skirt, resolving to read them later when she was alone.

'I hear I am a lucky man, Mrs Bowen.' The Scottish man smiled. 'I am grateful fer yer offer of a room, but I can just as well stay on the ship, if it is more convenient?'

'Not at all, Captain, we are pleased to have you stay with us, Reid will enjoy the company. When did you arrive?'

'Early this morning. I brought…your sister ashore just as soon as I was able.'

'Thank you, it is very kind of you to take the trouble. Have you come from London?'

Captain Turnbull shook his head, setting aside his plate, now covered with just a few crumbs. 'Direct from Edinburgh.'

'Oh.' Sasha glanced askance at Georgia, 'So, Papa does not know you are here?'

Georgia bowed her head and replied in a small voice, 'No. We have not spoken since.'

Sasha involuntarily fingered the envelopes in her pocket, her anxiety growing, but her thoughts were interrupted by Georgia blurting, 'Sasha, darling, I'm afraid I must prevail upon you for some funds. I have not yet paid Captain Turnbull for my passage.'

Sasha digested this information for a moment or two, and then replied as casually as she could, 'Of course, I will let you have the monies in the morning, if that is all right, Captain Turnbull?'

He nodded, finished his tea and then rose to his feet, sensing that the two girls had much to discuss. 'If you would not mind, Mrs Bowen, I will take myself off to my room, and then I have a few errands and calls to make about town.'

'Of course.' Sasha rose and hoped there was not too obviously a note of relief in her voice as she pulled the bell-rope to summon Good, and when he arrived quite promptly, she asked him to show the Captain to his room. 'We will see you at dinner, then, Captain Turnbull. Eight o'clock?'

He nodded and left the room. As soon as the door closed Sasha turned to Georgia, her eyebrows raised and her face quite clearly demanding answers to a dozen questions. She sat down again and asked Georgia gently, as she made no move to explain herself, 'What is it, Georgia dearest? How have you been these past, what is it, two months? Where is Felix?'

'Oh, Sasha!' At that Georgia rose from her chair and flung herself at Sasha's feet, her face buried in her silk lap, overcome by a storm of weeping. 'I am such a fool!'

'Shh,' Sasha soothed, stroking her hair, so fine and fair, such a contrast to her own straight dark locks. 'Tell me. What has happened?' Her glance strayed to Georgia's left hand as she clutched at Sasha's skirts, and she noticed that there was no gold wedding band on her finger. 'Please tell me, Georgia, tell me the truth.'

Georgia sniffed and hiccupped, wiping her nose with the back of her hand, but keeping her face turned away from her sister, as she began to tell her the events of the past two months. 'Oh, it was horrid, Sasha, quite horrid. Felix baulked when we got to Gretna Green.' She began to cry again, silent tears running from her eyes. 'After we—we, well, you know, it was a long way, we had to stop overnight at various inns. And then, afterwards, he said he did not wish to get married quite so soon, and we went to the Westfaling estate near Perth, and stayed there for a week or so, until Felix got word that his mama was on her way and—and—'

Sasha could well guess. 'The little rat made all haste to get rid of you.' At Georgia's nod Sasha resisted the urge to curse Felix very rudely and in a most unlady-like way, her fingers convulsing, and then she murmured gently, 'And then? Did you go home to London?'

'No. How could I? Papa would have been livid, after all the shame. I could not believe that Felix had turned so horrid, I thought he would change his mind, and then realised that he did not love me at all, and how could I love someone so—so callous? Who had no regard for my feelings, and—and—' here Georgia sniffed and blushed '—really, it was most disappointing, not at all how I thought it would be.'

'Running away from home so rarely is,' Sasha commented drily.

'No, I don't mean that. I— I mean, you know...' Her voice trailed away.

'What?'

'Being with a man. Making love. It was most unpleasant.'

'Ah.' Sasha could think of no wise comment to comfort her sister with, her mind straying to the exquisite pleasure she had experienced with Reid. How could she contradict her sister on that subject? Of course she could not, could not possibly tell her that the man who should have been her husband was now her lover, and a wonderful one at that. But then, she mused, had not Georgia encouraged her to take Reid for her husband, when she had not wanted him, had in fact, discarded him like ill-fitting shoes? She returned her attention to Georgia, and asked, 'So, what happened? You left him?'

'Not exactly. He drove me to Edinburgh and left me there.'

'What! Alone?'

'He gave me some money, so I could find lodgings.' Georgia straightened her slim shoulders then, with a slight toss of her head reminiscent of the old Georgia. 'I felt very angry when he did that, like he was paying me, like I was a—a—'

Sasha cut in hastily. 'The cad! I will shoot him myself if I ever set eyes on him again!' She returned to the puzzlement of where exactly Georgia had spent the last few months. 'So, where have you been living, in a hotel?'

'For a few days, and then with friends I met some years ago. You remember Emily Stuart, and her brother Donald? They were quite surprised to see me, but most welcoming, but after a month even her generous parents tired of a permanent house guest. And then Captain Turnbull came to dinner one evening, and when we got chatting and I realised he was sailing to St Petersburg and he realised who I was, he offered me a passage, and it seemed like the best thing to do. I wanted to go home, to Mama and Papa, but how could I? After all that has happened, I am a disgrace to the family, and will be shunned by society.'

'Papa would be forgiving, he would not turn you away.'

Georgia shook her head, doubting the truth of that. 'No, not now. I—' she lifted her head then and glanced up at her sister '—I am...with child.'

Sasha gasped, her hand clutching at Georgia's wrist. 'Oh, my dear! Is it Felix's?'

Georgia almost glared at her, recovering some of her spirit. 'Of course it is!'

'Then he must do the honourable thing and marry you! I shall write to Papa at once and ask him to make all the arrangements.'

'No!' Georgia leapt to her feet. 'I do not wish to be tied for the rest of my life to a—a lying, heartless, spineless wretch like Felix!'

'But, Georgia, think of your child, he must have his father's name or he will be shunned by society as a bastard.' She, too, rose to her feet and tried to take hold of Georgia by her elbows, but her sister flounced away.

Georgia shook her head with a mulish pout. 'Not necessarily. Well, that's why I came here, I thought, maybe, seeing as everyone thinks I am married to Major Bowen, that I could, well, you know, just—'

Sasha stared at her, the light suddenly dawning as all became clear. Her blood ran cold in her veins as she realised that Georgia had come to take her place as Reid Bowen's wife, rightful or otherwise. She suddenly felt quite faint, and sat down with a bump upon her chair. She had realised that the status quo was about to change with Georgia's arrival, but she had not imagined quite how drastically! Beneath her shock she felt a small spark of anger, at the thought that Georgia considered she could just walk in and take Reid away from her, take him to be the father of her child, another man's child, and Sasha would merely smile and let her. As though her feelings counted for naught, her wishes and her desires meant absolutely nothing to Georgia!

But, no, she must not be so harsh on her sister. Sasha frowned, and then rose from her chair and paced to the window, overlooking the courtyard. She glanced towards the windows of the Embassy. Somewhere behind one of them Reid would most probably be working at his desk. Her heart lurched and she felt a physical pain at the thought that tonight, when he came home, it would not be to her, Sasha, his wife, but it would be to Georgia. What would he say? How would he react? Would he be pleased that Georgia had at last decided to take up her position as his wife? After all, as far as the world knew, vows had been spoken before God by Reid Bowen and Georgia Packard. But quite how they would substitute one Georgia for another, when they were quite unalike in looks and height, she did not know!

It was all too much, too suddenly. She needed some time to think and consider the best way forwards. All her instincts were screaming at her that she must not let Reid find Georgia here when he came home. But she could hardly hide her away in the attic, nor could she ask her to return to the ship, or send her to stay in a hotel. What on earth could she do with Georgia? Where to put her, just for tonight, until she could think properly, organise things? Somewhere safe, and yet in a place where she would not cause undue comment, and where she would feel comfortable and welcome. Sasha continued to stare for some long moments, and then suddenly she realised there was only one place that she could take Georgia to—their cousin, Countess Irena, whose house was nearby and always busy with guests coming and going, and she was sure that gregarious Irena would only be too delighted to have a relative to stay.

Later that evening, as she joined Captain Turnbull in the drawing room before dinner and poured him a whisky, she asked, as she handed him the cut-crystal tumbler, 'Captain Turnbull, I hope you don't mind if I ask you to please not mention to Reid about, um, my sister's arrival. He's been very busy and under a lot of strain lately; I think it's best, just for tonight, if we refrain from adding to his worries.'

'Of course.' Captain Turnbull swirled his whisky about in its glass, and then fixed her with a gimlet stare as he said in his soft Scottish brogue, 'I would not wish to interfere in private family matters that are none of my business, but remember, "O what a tangled web we weave…"'

Sasha smiled and finished the quotation for him. '"…when first we practise to deceive." Have no fear, I do not intend to deceive my hus—Major Bowen, it's just all come as a bit of a shock and I merely seek to protect my sister from any further folly. She is quite happily ensconced with our cousin, the Countess Irena, and tomorrow we will sort it all out.'

He bowed, accepting her explanation, and then gruffly added, 'Should you need any further assistance, please, I would be honoured.'

'Thank you.'

At that moment the drawing-room door swung open and Reid strode in, freshly washed and changed for dinner. He greeted Captain Turnbull warmly, shaking hands with him, and asking how his voyage had been, turning to Sasha as they conversed and kissing her on the cheek as he accepted an aperitif from her, his arm lingering around her waist for a moment in an affectionate gesture. Being part of such a scene of domestic bliss almost caused Sasha to burst into tears, but she was saved from disgrace as Good announced that dinner was served.

If Sasha seemed quiet and somewhat strained as she picked her way through the meal, Reid made no comment, though he did notice. After dessert she pleaded a headache and left the gentlemen to their port and conversation, taking herself off to bed. In her chamber she sat in her nightgown, curled up in a chair by the window and staring out through the curtains, her heart heavy and her mind quite blank. Far from coming up with solutions to their predicament, she had no idea what to do. She remembered the letters from home that Captain Turnbull had given to her, and went to rescue them from the pocket of her lavender day gown. She opened first the letter from Charlotte, who rambled pleasantly about their new home in Ireland and her husband's new post advising and liaising with the military and the local civilians in Dublin.

...the Irish are a friendly people and many have made us most welcome, but they have a depth of strength and passion that makes me think them most like the Russians! Being from a Catholic family myself, I can quite understand they are disgruntled at the moment. I do hope Anthony can help. The coun-

*tryside is very pretty and green, and though our house is quite
modest it is in a pleasant cul-de-sac and the children enjoy the
gardens and the paddock for their ponies. It is such a relief to
be in a place where everyone speaks English! Do come and visit
me, it would be wonderful. Your most loving and devoted friend,
Charlotte.*

With a smile Sasha folded the letter away, and then opened
the one from her father. Her eyes skimmed over the words, for
this was no warm and friendly missive, but a curt and frank
command that demanded obedience. Her father insisted that
she return to London at once.

*...it is all well and good that no one knows of the appalling
deception that you and your sister have perpetrated, but it is
not one that can continue indefinitely. It is merely a matter of
time before it is discovered. Not only will your reputation be
ruined, but that of Major Bowen, who no doubt will face court-
martial for disgraceful conduct. My dearest Sasha, I implore
you, return home at once. We will arrange for the marriage
between Georgia and Major Bowen to be annulled, for I know
you, my virtuous daughter, and I am fairly sure that I know
Major Bowen, too, as an honourable man, and that neither of
you have been rash enough as to commit adultery...*

Slowly Sasha let the paper fall into her lap, frozen, and yet
dully aware that her father spoke as clearly as if he had been
in the same room with her at this very moment. And she must
obey. Her sense of guilt and anxiety lifted as she contemplated
the future, where at last she could be herself and the truth would
be known. Although, not the whole truth. Some things must
remain a secret for ever. Like the fact that she and Reid had been
intimate, and that she loved him. And that she was not his wife.
But Papa was right, the only way forwards now was to return to
London, and have the marriage annulled, wipe the slate clean,
and somehow she and Georgia would pick up the pieces of their
shattered lives, and start again.

Somehow.

Sasha chewed on her lip, staring into space. But how?

How would Papa's plan work for Georgia? She would be an unmarried girl bearing a fatherless child. She would be disgraced and shunned. No doubt Papa would pack her off to their country estate, and the child would be given away for adoption. Then Georgia would return to London and…and what? She did not think Georgia, for all her faults or failings, would so readily abandon her baby, yet how on earth could she keep it?

For some long while Sasha pondered on their problems, her mind darting this way and that as she sought a solution whereby everyone could be happy and free from scandal. But whatever way she looked at it, it was not possible. Someone would have to suffer, someone would have to make a sacrifice, and she had the dreadful feeling that that someone was going to be her. Had she not always protected Georgia, and taken the blame for every little escapade that she had ever tumbled into? She loved her sister, and her loyal nature would not allow her to fail her in any way. And in a different way she loved Reid, truly and deeply, and she could not fail him, either. She could not allow anything to happen that would tarnish or hinder his career or reputation. A plan began to form in her mind, and she knew that it was the only solution.

Sasha had mulled things over, and listened for Reid's tread on the stair, but she had dozed off long before he came up to bed. She awoke when his arms lifted her from the chair and carried her to the bed. He sat down on its edge, cradling her on his lap as he nuzzled her neck, breathing in the soft, feminine scent of her sleep-warm skin.

'You were very quiet tonight, Sasha, and I think I can guess why. It's all gone on far too long, I know, but don't worry.' He kissed her gently, savouring the velvet softness of her lips. 'I have spoken to Captain Turnbull about a passage to England. We sail with him next Sunday morning, after the ball. And then, as soon as I can arrange for a special licence we will be married.' His hand slid inside her nightgown and fondled the warm, smooth weight of her breast. Sasha stiffened in his arms, and he looked at her, with a plea and dark desire in his eyes. 'I can't wait any longer, Sasha, I want to make love to you, now.' His voice lowered to a persuasive whisper, as he gently nibbled her collarbone. 'What difference will it make? We will soon be wed.'

Sasha smelled brandy on his breath. She had no doubt he and Captain Turnbull had consumed a fair share of alcohol and all Reid's defences were down. She stared at his blond head, lowered to her breast, his lips caressing her nipple through the thin cotton of her nightgown. She suppressed a groan, her thighs melting at his touch. She should resist him, insist that he return to his own bedroom, but everything had changed and she greatly feared that tonight would be all she would ever have with him, for in the next few days she must give him up, and let him take his rightful place as Georgia's husband.

Her fingers lifted and caressed the nape of his neck, smooth and tanned from recent mounted cavalry exercises with Russian officers. She closed her eyes, breathing in his masculine aroma, a clean mixture of soap and musky-male and brandy.

'Sasha?' He sensed something was awry; she was so silent, almost pensive. 'What's wrong?' He stroked her cheek with tender fingers, his thumb dwelling on the swell of her lower lip, a puzzled frown on his brows. 'I will leave, if that is what you truly wish.'

For a reply, Sasha gazed at him for a long moment, and then wrapped her arms around his shoulders and pressed him down onto the bed. He laughed, nuzzling her neck as he rolled over on top of her, delighted by her passion. She was quiet, but then so was he, as quickly she helped him to strip off his clothes. He lifted the hem of her nightgown and pulled it up and over her head, freeing her completely. Naked, they rolled into the middle of the bed, Reid stroking his hand down the length of her body, kissing her gently, tenderly, his lips and fingers brushing and nibbling and teasing her, and she reached up to explore his back and his buttocks and his chest with her own fingers, her kisses inviting and eager. She savoured the broad width of his muscular shoulders and the weight of his body as he lay half on top of her. She felt so warm beneath him, and fluid, as if all her nerves and muscles had melted into a puddle of chocolate. He licked and tasted and consumed, until the moment came when the wanting and the aching could not be contained any longer and she parted her thighs for him. Reid opened his eyes and looked at her. Sensing it, she opened her eyes, too. With her body and her eyes, she silently told him what she wanted, and he gave it to her.

It was the most exquisite sensation she had ever known, and she gave herself up to it completely. She wanted it to go on and on forever, feeling him inside her, the strength of his body, his heat and his passion as he moved, sweeping her along on a tide that was at first slow and languorous, mounting and rolling, gathering them up on to its crest until finally the peak crashed and wrapped them together as one, gasping and panting, her cry smothered by his shout, and at last they gave each other the ultimate pleasure, satisfying the primitive needs of their desire in one final thrusting burst of energy.

Gasping, his skin damp with sweat, Reid groaned softly with satisfaction, and eased his weight off her slender frame, rolling to one side, and turning her to lie beside him. He stroked back her hair, his forearm resting between her firm, swollen breasts, where he could feel her heart pounding, gradually slowing to a more moderate rate as her breathing slowed, too. He kissed her gently, willing her to open her eyes and look at him, his glance admiring her supine body, which had given him such intense pleasure. He was sure she had felt it, too, but this was her first time and he hoped that he had not hurt her.

'Sasha,' he murmured gently, 'are you all right?' And then he felt tears squeezing from between her eyelashes, and he raised himself up on one elbow. 'Sasha, sweetheart, I am sorry! I'm sorry if I hurt you, I tried not to.'

She shook her head then, and opened her dark eyes, gazing up into his eyes as she lifted her fingers to his face and gently stroked his cheek. 'You did not hurt me, Reid. It was…wonderful. Thank you.' It was indeed the most wonderful experience, one that she would treasure within her memories for the rest of her life.

'Then why are you crying?'

She opened her mouth to speak, to tell him about Georgia, about her plan, but she could not. She shook her head and drew him closer, snuggling up against him, her fingers stroking the hairs on his chest. 'It's nothing.' She would have this night, just this night, if nothing else and she could not bear to spoil it. She would tell him in the morning.

They slept, with Reid curved about her back, his arm draped over her waist.

Before dawn she woke him with kisses and they made love again. This time, her body knew the pleasure to come; their lovemaking took only moments before she was climbing on top of him, taking him with a glorious, abandoned passion, her long dark hair swirling about their naked bodies as she straddled him and arched her head back, her breasts swaying before his fascinated gaze as he watched her moving on top of him, the early morning light casting a golden glow on her body. His teeth clenched, panting with a warring sensation of intense pleasure as he enjoyed their union, and self-discipline as he tried to restrain himself from reaching the end too soon. His hands gripped her waist, guiding her, feeling the hot sweat of her skin and then as she gave a cry he joined her in mutual release.

'That was nice,' he murmured, surprised at her wantonness, kissing her neck as she tumbled down to lie beside him. 'I would never have guessed.'

Sasha gazed up at him with a soft, loving smile.

Reid drew back a bit and stared down at her. 'Something is wrong. I can feel it. There is something you are not telling me, Sasha.'

Now was the moment; she had to tell him about Georgia. But she could not. How could she speak the words that would destroy such sweet happiness? And how brief it was! Her lashes lowered, avoiding him.

'Don't do that. Don't shut me out. You can trust me, Sasha, you know you can. What is it?' His fingers under her chin lifted her head, but her continued silence now angered him, and he turned away, thrusting back the bed covers, not realising that as he left her bed their lives were about to change. 'Very well! You can be just as stubborn as Georgia sometimes! I am going to bathe and get dressed.'

Sasha half-rose on one elbow and stretched out a hand towards him, her lips parting to call him back. But she did not. Still some unseen force kept her quiet, in check, dreading the moment when finally they must part. Tears came to her eyes then, as she watched her love walk away. She felt sure that he would never come back, and she held a hand to her mouth, muffling the soft sobs, turning into the pillow and pulling the blankets over her head as she wept.

She did not go down to breakfast, but waited until Reid had departed for the Embassy before rising from the bed. She ran a bath, and lay in the hot water for a long while. Her body ached, pleasantly, a reminder of what she had shared with Reid. She felt languorous, as though she could lie in this bath all day and keep the world and its tragedies at bay. But eventually she had to get out, and pat her body dry with a white, fluffy towel. She stared at her body, at the faint pink marks from Reid's fingers, feeling within her the ache that could not be seen, where he had possessed and pleasured her with his own male body. With a sigh, Sasha dressed and then went downstairs to the breakfast room, suddenly feeling hungry. She ate a lot more than her usual tea and toast, and then she called for Harry, knowing that she could no longer delay going to see Georgia, and telling her of the grand plan that would restore her to respectability and make their lives once more decent and honourable.

When Irena greeted her, still dressed in her negligee, albeit opulent lilac satin that was remarkably modest with its billowing folds and thick material, Sasha responded with quiet confidence, no longer afraid of this woman, who was not a threat to her any more, knowing full well that Reid's motive for paying her attention was not from infatuation or lust. She sat down at the table when invited to by Irena and accepted a cup of tea.

'Darling, your sister is still asleep. I looked in on her just moments ago.' She smiled at Sasha, rather like a cat contemplating a mouse. 'What on earth are we going to do with her?'

'That's a very good question.' Sasha smiled at her, seeking to make an enemy into an ally by taking her into her confidence. 'What do you suggest?'

'Well—' Irena shrugged, artfully '—I don't know. It must have come as quite a shock for you. What does your—?' She paused delicately as she cut a piece of melon. 'What does Major Bowen say?'

'I have not told him.'

Her brows arched in surprise. 'Why ever not?'

'There has not been an…appropriate moment.'

'Perhaps…you do not wish to give him up.'

'Perhaps…I don't.'

They stared at one another, and then Irena chuckled. 'Perhaps it would be best if Georgia stayed out of sight, and then returned to England. No one needs to know that she is here.'

'Perhaps you are right.' Sasha caught her breath for a moment, realising that she was putting herself into Irena's power, and wondering what price would have to be paid for her assistance. And her silence. But for her plan to work, no one must know about Georgia, or see her, until they got back to London. Sasha rose from her seat. 'If you do not mind, I would like to see my sister now.' As Irena rose to accompany her, she held out a hand. 'I can find my own way, thank you.' She softened her words with a smile. 'I need to speak to her alone, find out what has happened to her in the last few months.'

'Of course.' Irena inclined her head.

Sasha departed and walked along the landing and up a flight of stairs, remembering the way from when she had brought Georgia here yesterday afternoon. Was it only yesterday? she mused. So much had happened in such a short space of time, and it all felt quite unreal. Reaching Georgia's bedroom door, Sasha knocked discreetly, but when there was no reply she opened the door and peeked in.

The curtains were drawn and in the gloom she could only make out the vague shape of Georgia asleep in the bed. She hesitated, wondering whether to leave her, but it was mid-morning and the day could not grow old without Georgia being aware of her part in The Plan, and the need for her to stay out of sight. She stopped a passing maid and asked her to bring a breakfast tray of tea and toast. The maid bobbed a curtsy, her eyes wide and greatly impressed by the English lady's perfectly spoken Russian.

Sasha went into the room and opened the curtains, daylight flooding in, but still Georgia did not stir. She crossed to the bed and leaned over her, gently shaking her shoulder and calling her name. With a groan, Georgia shrugged away, and then at Sasha's insistence she rolled onto her back and peered up, her hair a tangled blond mass on the pillow and her face creased as she squinted at Sasha.

'God, is it morning, already?'

Sasha snorted. 'It's very well near afternoon!' At the sound of a knock on the door, Sasha retrieved the tea tray from the maid and then firmly closed the door. She set the tray down on the ornate cabinet beside the bed and poured a cup for Georgia, who now struggled up into a sitting position, ran her fingers through her hair and then yawned.

'Oh, isn't it lovely here, Sasha? I do like Cousin Irena, she's so beautiful.'

'Indeed.' Sasha handed her the cup of tea and then sat down on the bed near Georgia's feet, looking at her pensively. 'How are you feeling?'

'Well enough.' Georgia sipped from the cup, and then grimaced, turning to the tray to add two teaspoons of sugar. 'And isn't this house wonderful? I've never been inside a palace before. I think I shall enjoy staying here very much.'

Sasha shrugged. 'It's only a small one. There are many more palaces in St Petersburg, and much bigger than this.' She watched as Georgia helped herself to a bread roll, spreading it liberally with butter and jam. 'Georgia…' She hesitated, wondering how best to delicately frame her question. 'Georgia, when—that is, how far along are you? You know how erratic you can be.'

Georgia shrugged. 'I have missed at least one of my monthly times.' She brushed crumbs from her nightgown. 'What time do you think Reid will come to see me today? How did he react when you told him I was here?'

Sasha swallowed, and picked at a loose thread on the hem of her skirt. 'Well—' she glanced at her sister '—the thing is, Georgia, it's not going to be as easy as that. You can't just walk in to Reid's life and suddenly become his wife.'

'Oh?' Georgia seemed genuinely puzzled. 'Why not?'

'Because I am his wife! Or at least everyone in St Petersburg thinks so.'

Georgia nodded. 'Yes, I see what you mean.' And then she looked at Sasha, with all blind faith. 'What shall we do?'

Sasha sighed, her voice constrained. 'Well, if you are to become his wife again it will have to be back in London. Reid and I had planned to sail home next Sunday morning, after the Grand Ball—'

'Why?'

'To—to see his Uncle Percy. He's not been well.'

'Oh.'

'I thought that you could sail with us. I will speak to Captain Turnbull and arrange for you to have a cabin alongside ours. And once we are underway, we will tell Reid and swap places. When we reach London, you will step off the ship as Mrs Bowen, and no one in London will be any the wiser.'

'Providing, of course, that we do not bump into anyone from St Petersburg that could tell the difference.'

'Yes. And providing you stay out of sight between now and when we sail.'

'What!' Georgia groaned. 'You mean stay in this house for a whole week? I really wanted to explore!'

'Not only stay in this house, but stay inside this room. No one must see you.'

'Oh, Sasha, no!'

'Yes!'

'I could wear a veil.' Georgia pouted.

Sasha shook her head and leaned forwards to grab Georgia by both wrists, giving her a little shake. 'Do you want to sort this mess out or not?' She climbed down off the bed. 'Believe me, Georgia, I have no more desire to do this than you do, but it's the only way. Papa has written to say I must come home at once, that the marriage will be annulled, and if I do not comply I will not be at all surprised if Papa does not turn up on our doorstep! And then where will we be? No,' she said firmly, 'you are going to have to do as you are told and not go gadding about. Just for once, don't be selfish and—and think of your child. Do you understand?'

Silently, Georgia nodded. 'But you will come to see me? You won't leave me here completely alone?'

Sasha went to her then, and hugged her, seeing the forlorn expression on Georgia's face. 'Of course, dearest, I will be here every day for as long as possible. It's only a week; the time will soon pass.'

Having secured Georgia's promise to remain within her bed-chamber, Sasha prepared to leave. She promised to call again soon and to bring Georgia whatever she might need.

'Now remember—' Sasha stood in the doorway '—you are to stay exactly where you are.'

Georgia nodded with a glum expression, and Sasha closed the door. As she turned towards the staircase she caught sight of a flick of lilac satin disappearing behind one-half of the double doors leading to Irena's private apartment and bedchamber. She thought it prudent to impress upon Irena that under no circumstances must Georgia leave her room or be seen by anyone, and followed after Irena. She opened the door, the air fragrant with Irena's exotic scent, but at the sound of low voices Sasha paused on the threshold. She gazed across the richly furnished room to where Irena languished on a sofa, a man perched on its edge and stroking her throat with the back of his hand. Irena had such a look of bliss upon her face, unlike any expression Sasha had ever seen her present to the world before.

Catching sight of Sasha, Irena pushed him to one side and the man instinctively glanced over his shoulder, before turning away and taking great pains to keep his back to her. How odd, thought Sasha, he was a rather rough-looking character, his clothes dark grey and black coarse linen, his lank brown hair unfashionably long and his face, though not ugly, weatherbeaten and tanned. He looked like a farmer, or a railway worker, Sasha mused, but already Irena was at her side, taking her by the elbow and ushering Sasha from the room.

Out in the corridor, with the door closed, Irena murmured, 'You should not be here, my little one.'

'Who is that man?' Sasha asked with frank curiosity.

'Just a friend.' Irena did not elaborate, but steered Sasha away and down the corridor, 'Your sister is well? She is settled in her room?'

'Yes, thank you. Please, Irena,' Sasha pleaded earnestly now, 'please make sure she stays there. We will be leaving in a week's time to go back to England, but it's absolutely imperative she stays out of sight.'

Irena nodded, with a slow smile. 'Of course, I will see to it.' Suddenly she leaned forwards and gathered Sasha close to her in an embrace, whispering against her ear, 'I hold your secret safe, but I must ask you to hold mine, too.'

'What do you mean?' Sasha was puzzled, and then, as enlightenment dawned, she nodded her head towards the closed double doors of Irena's apartment. 'Do you mean that man?'

'Yes.'

Sasha gave a low chuckle. 'Irena, I can assure you that I am not concerned with your gentlemen friends, nor would I gossip about them.'

'It is more than that, but promise that you will speak of this to no one?'

Sasha nodded. 'Of course, I promise.'

Irena kissed her cheek and they bade each other farewell, but Sasha pondered as she walked down the stairs to the hall below. Who was he? Someone else's husband? He looked vaguely familiar, but she thought it best not to pry any further, for curiosity almost certainly killed many a cat. She donned her cloak with Harry's assistance and made her way home.

As she walked, a puzzled frown creased her brow. It was a windy day, storm clouds gathered and she thought they might have some rain before evening. She couldn't stop thinking about the man in Irena's apartment. What was so odd about him that he had stuck in her mind? Was it his dark, shabby clothes? Or… something else? She thought she might have seen him somewhere before and while at first she thought his rough appearance indicated that he was a servant of some sort, she somehow did not think she had ever seen him in that role in Irena's household before.

The wind churned up dust and litter, and it was a scrap of paper blowing across her path that suddenly jolted Sasha's memory. She skipped and hopped as she chased after the leaflet, clutching at it in triumph and turning it over to examine the crude head-and-shoulders drawing of the man who was wanted for the attempted assassination of Tsar Alexander II. With a gasp, Sasha stared at the face of the man she had just seen! She broke into a run, eager to get home and speak to Reid at once.

'Ma'am,' called Harry, breaking into a trot at her side, 'is everything all right?'

'Oh, Harry, I don't know, but I have a horrible feeling that it's not!'

When they reached the apartment, both gasping for breath from the run, Sasha dashed up the steps and inside, throwing off her cloak and hat as she asked almost hysterically of Good, 'Is the Major in?'

'Yes, ma'am, he's in the drawing room with Captain Turnbull.'

Sasha made haste to hurry up the stairs, but then, halfway along, she suddenly stopped, and paused. She realised all at once that she could not possibly say a word about the man she had seen at Irena's, not in front of Captain Turnbull. Why, she was sure that she should not even mention it to Reid. Would he not be honour bound to report it to the authorities? She could not do that to Irena. Whatever her faults, she was still her cousin and reporting that she harboured a suspected revolutionary and assassin would mean almost certain death for her. She had made a promise, to keep Irena's secret, but some promises could not be kept, not when they meant harm to others. Sasha chewed on her lip with a worried frown, and then proceeded more slowly, and quietly. She greeted Reid and Captain Turnbull with a graceful smile, and said nothing about Irena, Georgia or anyone else. No one could have guessed the anxiety she felt, nor the war that was waging inside her head as she wondered whether this was one secret that would prove to be too heavy a burden.

Chapter Twelve

On the evening of the ball Sasha held up her skirts with one hand, and placed her other arm through Reid's elbow. He smiled at her as they stepped from their carriage and onto the scarlet carpet lining the Jordan staircase inside the Winter Palace.

'You look…ravishing,' he murmured close to her ear, his breath warm on her delicate skin.

Sasha smiled in response, delighted that the very expensive gown had achieved its desired effect, but her attention was diverted by the magnificence of their splendid surroundings. The ornate baroque twin staircase swept in marble grandeur up to a landing where three double pairs of grey marble pillars supported a vaulted ceiling encrusted with gilt cornices, voluptuous golden caryatids and frescoes of the gods on Mount Olympus. It all quite took her breath away, yet there was no time to stand and stare as the many guests filed up the carpeted stairs to the state ballroom above. Dutifully she and Reid followed in the wake of Lord and Lady Cronin as they climbed upwards.

In the Nicholas Hall a vast sea of people assembled around the sides of the ballroom, and Sasha caught her breath at the splendid sight. She thought there must be several thousand guests at least! All the men were elegant in black tails and white bow ties, or dashing in military uniforms. Even the plainest of women seemed beautiful and glamorous in their sweeping gowns in fashionably muted hues of cream, oyster-pink and white, glittering ruby, sapphire and emerald necklaces adorning their throats in dazzling rainbow hues, tiaras twinkling and flashing as only diamonds can. Sasha was one of the few women to wear a brightly coloured gown and she thought she detected a slight frown of disapproval from Lady Cronin, who wore cream satin, but she straightened her shoulders and lifted her chin, her pleasure taken from the fact that Reid was delighted with the way she looked.

They were offered glasses of champagne from a passing footman and Sasha sipped hers carefully, aware of the watchful eye of Lady Cronin. Away from the dance floor, in a bronze-and-malachite pavilion, tempting delicacies of caviar and smoked salmon and a vast array of other hors d'oeuvres were served, prior to a sumptuous buffet that would begin at midnight. The guests nibbled whilst talking and the champagne was continuously served while they all awaited the entrance of the Tsar and Tsarina.

Their Imperial Majesties made their appearance at the far end of the ballroom, but Sasha could see little from where she stood. It was not long after their arrival that the dancing began and when Captain Turnbull politely invited her onto the floor she accepted with a gracious smile and nod of her head, while Reid turned to Lady Cronin. They whirled into a mazurka, joining many of the other dancing guests, yet Sasha only had eyes for Reid and longed for the moment when duty was done and they could dance together.

He looked even more handsome than she had ever seen him before, but it was not because of his uniform, which emphasised the broad width of his shoulders, slim hips and blond good looks. It was because she was in love with him, and as they danced, he with Lady Cronin, she with Captain Turnbull, their eyes found each other across the intervening couples, and she could not look away. Their intimacy had created a bond, for far from not returning to her bed, Reid had made love to her every night for the past week, and she had made love to him every morning as the dawn broke. She could not wait to be in his arms, to dance a waltz with him, knowing that they would be perfectly in tune.

At last, duty done, Reid turned to Sasha and held out his arm. He escorted her onto the dance floor and placed his hand on her waist, his other hand clasping her gloved fingers firmly. They swept away, the music seductive and sensuous. As they whirled and stepped back and forth, they spoke not a word, and yet they were not silent. His eyes spoke as they dwelled on her lips, on her cheeks and ears and neck, and down to the swell of her breasts rising above the low curve of the ruby-red gown. She answered him, her own eyes lingering on his mouth, remembering how his lips had kissed her, how his tongue had caressed the most secret and sensitive parts of her body. She smiled, and felt the heat of him as he pulled her closer, stooping a little so that his jaw rested against the softness of her smooth cheek.

Then Reid whispered close to her ear, 'Tell me.'

'What?' she whispered back.

'The secret that you are keeping from me.'

She stiffened, and shivered a little. 'How do you know I have a secret?' Her voice was a mere breath against his cheek.

'I can see it in your eyes. You are always so open and expressive. I know you, Sasha, intimately, and there is something you are guarding. Tell me, sweetheart.'

She sighed, and then relaxed against him. She could not lie to him, not when she loved him so much. 'I can't tell you, not now.'

'Why? Is it something that will make me angry?' He was smiling, not at all concerned that it might be anything that was going to rock their world.

'I don't know. It might.'

'Have you spent too much money? I notice that you have cashed several of the banker's drafts that you have shown no interest in before. That gown must have cost a fortune.'

'No, it's nothing to do with money.'

'Then tell me.' His grip tightened with frustration.

'I will.'

'When?'

'Later.'

'Tonight?'

'Yes.'

'Promise? Promise me we will not go to sleep until you have told me this secret?'

'I promise.'

'Good.'

He settled back to enjoy the dance with her, and the evening passed far too quickly for Sasha. The ball was a wonderful occasion, and it was not until the early hours of morning that they returned home. But they did not sleep, for their trunks were packed, ready and waiting in the hall, and they only had to change their clothes before a carriage drove them down to the docks and they boarded HMS *Dorset*.

They had been shown to a cabin, the same one Reid and Sasha had shared before. As the door had closed, she wondered if Georgia had followed her instructions and was safely ensconced in the cabin next door.

As the tide turned at dawn the crew cast anchor and gently the naval ship slid away from the dock. Sasha went to the porthole and stared at the palaces and buildings of the city as they passed by, silently saying goodbye to a magical city and the most wonderful and magical time of her life that would never be repeated again. She drew off her gloves slowly, aware of Reid behind her, slipping his arm around her waist and nuzzling her neck.

'Don't forget your promise,' he murmured, his fingers straying to the buttons of her gown. 'But first, it's dawn, Sasha—have you forgotten to do something?'

She blushed, remembering her passion for making love to him

as the sun broke on the horizon, but now, instead of encouraging his fingers to disrobe her, she pushed him away and took a step towards the door. He turned to face her, his expression serious, and rather stern. He folded his arms over his chest, head to one side.

'Right, that's enough, Sasha, I want to know what's going on. And don't even try to pretend that there is nothing, because I know there is!'

To his surprise she replied meekly, 'All right. Just wait there for a moment.'

She opened the door and stepped out, and he gaped after her, wondering what on earth she was about. Was it a surprise of some kind? Or something else, something more worrying? He could hear a cabin door open farther along the corridor, and the low murmur of voices. Female voices. Then he heard footsteps approaching, and Sasha said quietly, as she appeared in the doorway, 'Close your eyes, Reid. And promise me that, no matter what, you won't shout.'

'Very well. But there is no need for all this palaver, you know very well that you have me wrapped around your finger and I would not dream of shouting at you, how could I when I—'

'Now, you can open your eyes.' Sasha ushered Georgia in, and closed the door, tensing as she held her breath and awaited the eruption of Reid's fury, her eyes half squeezing shut.

But there was only silence, and she looked up to see Reid standing there staring with his mouth open, hands on hips.

'Hello, Major Bowen.' Georgia smiled at him.

'Uh…' Reid stared at her. 'Um, hello, Georgia.' His glance went at once from her to Sasha, standing just behind her sister. 'What… What on earth…are you doing here?'

'Well, it's rather a long story, and I am feeling very tired—do you mind if I sit down?' Georgia made a move to go past him and take a seat in the tub chair placed in a corner beneath the porthole.

He moved quickly aside to let her pass, raking one hand

through his hair. 'Er, no.' He glanced again over his shoulder at Sasha, and noticed now that she had made no move to take off her coat and was standing by the door with her travelling case, as though she was about to depart. 'Sasha? What's going on?'

Sasha swallowed the huge lump that was in her throat, watching Reid and Georgia, so close together in this confined space, watching them as soon other people would be watching them, as a couple, man and wife. Tears began to crowd in her throat, and her voice was watery as she explained, with Georgia adding little bits here and there, and Reid listened in silence as the grand plan to make Georgia Packard truly his wife was unfolded. But at its end, he reacted most unexpectedly, in a way that neither girl had anticipated.

'No!' He paced about; in the confined space he did not have far to go. 'God damn it! Are you both mad? What the devil do you think you are playing at? And what do you think I am, some sort of monster, to go from one sister to the other—' he snapped his fingers '—just like that!' He stared at them both and then shouted, 'No, damn it! No, I will not do it!' And with that, in high dudgeon, he wrenched open the cabin door, stepped out, and slammed it behind him.

'Oh, dear,' murmured Georgia, staring at her lap, and then she glanced accusingly at her sister. 'You did not mention that he is in love with you.'

Sasha gasped, staring at her, and then she shook her head. 'No, no, of course he's not, he has never said anything of the kind to me.'

'He might not have said it, but that's what he feels.' Georgia looked at her sister curiously. 'Have you… Has he…taken you to bed?'

'No, of course not!' Sasha blushed hotly, both at the lie and the question. Then she turned and opened the cabin door. 'I'd better go and find him, talk to him.'

'Yes, I think you'd better.' Georgia looked at her solemnly, then, just as Sasha was about to leave she called out, 'Oh, before

I forget—' she rummaged in the pocket of her gown '—Irena asked me to give you this.'

With a sigh, Sasha held out her hand and took the note in a sealed envelope that she recognised as being from Irena personally.

'She was very particular about it. Said I was to give it to no one except you.'

Silently, Sasha took the note and went out of the cabin. She paused in the corridor and tore the thick cream paper open. Penned in Irena's black, bold writing were only three words, undated and unsigned: *We have fled.*

Sasha stared at it, but it was more than she could deal with right now. She folded the note carefully and slipped it into her pocket, for a brief moment wondering where Irena had gone to. But right now she had other more important matters to deal with; besides, she was beginning to learn that people like Countess Irena Sletovskaya invariably landed on their feet. Sasha hurried along the corridor, and up the metal rung of steps to the deck above. The horizon was now a golden slash of bright light as the dawn broke in a blaze, splashing its brilliant colours over the city, now receding in the distance against a backdrop of sea and sky. There was only a gentle breeze to fan her hot cheeks, as her feet echoed on the wooden planks, hurrying as she searched for Reid, her heart aching for him, for them both. She found him aft, leaning on the railings with his hands clasped together and staring at the churning white foam of the ship's wake. Seagulls wheeled and screeched, but his attention was not drawn by them.

Her footsteps slowed as she approached him, but he did not look up even when she stopped at his side. She laid one hand gently on his arm. 'Reid?' Still he was silent, and she pleaded, 'Please, Reid, talk to me.'

He looked up then. 'Why?' His eyes were a dark, tormented blue as they bored into her own. 'What am I except a prize stallion to be shifted between mares?'

'Don't say that!'

'Well, it certainly sounds as if you and Georgia have got it all planned down to the last detail, our lives rearranged according to the whims of Georgia Packard.' Suddenly he swung round and grabbed her arms. 'Tell me, Sasha, tell me truthfully that this is what you want? To swap places with your sister, to let her be my wife?' She hesitated, looking away from him, and he seized on the moment like a triumphant prizefighter. 'I thought as much. You don't want this any more than I do! It's barbaric! It could never work!'

'Reid, it has to. Can't you see, this charade cannot go on forever! My papa has written insisting that I return home and the marriage be annulled. I cannot pretend to be Georgia for the rest of my life!'

'No, of course not! But we could start again. Your father is right, best to get the original marriage annulled and start again. With the right woman.'

'But we can't! It's too late. People will find out. You'd be disgraced, dismissed from the Army, court-martialled, even.'

'Nonsense!' But his voice wavered a little; he could not be entirely certain that any of that could be avoided.

'Please, listen to me,' Sasha pleaded. 'It's been wonderful, but now it's over. We must go back to the real world.'

'What? Thanks for the roll in the hay and now let's move on? Sasha, I don't believe you mean that. You're not like that! I don't want Georgia, it's you I want!'

'No!' She struggled from his grasp. 'It's only lust, Reid, you'll get over it. Remember, it was Georgia you chose in the first place.'

'I didn't know you then. I— I love you, Sasha.' There, he had said it, but still it was not enough and he felt like he was drowning, trying to hold on to Sasha as she wriggled from his grasp and covered her ears with both hands.

'Don't say that!' she gasped, her heart slamming hard in her chest. 'It's not love. You will forget me—'

'No! Never!'

'Please, Reid, try to understand—'

'Understand what? That we made a mistake? That I married the wrong girl in the first place? I know that, and we can put that right. We can—'

'No, we can't!' Sasha shouted then, frustrated, aching with her love for him and jealousy that she could not have him, and fury with Georgia for ruining their happiness. 'She's with child!'

'What?' Reid stilled and stared down at her.

'Georgia is expecting a baby.'

For a moment he just continued to stare, and then he let her go and laughed out loud, but it was not a happy sound. 'This just gets better and better! Now I'm expected to give my name to another man's child, and take on the mother when she left me in the first place for that man!' He glowered out to sea. 'I am beginning to think that I want nothing more to do with either of you!'

Sasha was silent, gazing down at her boots, ashamed at how badly they had manipulated him. She whispered, 'I'm sorry.'

His voice was hard as he replied, 'You will be. Believe me, you and your bloody sister will be very sorry!'

He began to walk away and Sasha called out, running after him, 'Reid! What do you mean? Please, don't do anything rash.'

But he would not listen and strode away. He went to see Captain Turnbull and requested a third cabin, as far away from the Packard sisters as he could get. A steward moved his luggage and, though eyebrows were raised, no questions were asked.

Throughout the five-day voyage Reid did his best to avoid both Sasha and Georgia, and when he could not, at meal times, he was icily polite when speech was necessary, but otherwise ignored them.

Georgia and Sasha each had their own cabin, and though Georgia suggested they move in together, Sasha refused. She wanted to be alone—she did not need an audience to her weeping every night into her pillow. She could feel very little compassion towards Georgia at the moment, who indeed did not seem to need her sympathy and support as she set about charming various officers, languishing in the common room and notably taking many a turn about deck with Captain Turnbull. Sasha was grateful for the Captain's escort, his stalwart presence a buffer, yet she wondered how Georgia could smile and laugh so gaily when all around them disaster and heartache loomed.

The night before they were due to dock at Tilbury in London, Sasha lay awake, staring at the riveted ceiling above her bunk. How cruel was fate! How could she protect Georgia from the shocking scandal that was about to break and ruin all their lives? How could she let Reid walk away, with all this horrid ill feeling and confusion between them? She felt a sudden and urgent need to talk to Reid, if only to convince him to take Georgia back. But as she lay there another thought came to her mind, and she could not bring herself to move. He had said he loved her, and she smiled at the thought, turning on her side to face towards the end of the corridor where his cabin was, wishing so much that he would change his mind and forgive her, that she could lay with him now, curled up against his warm bulk, safe and loved and cherished. Sasha closed her eyes, sighing, reliving the nights of tender lovemaking with Reid, and then suddenly she began to cry, stifling the aching sobs with one fist in her mouth. It could not be. She would never kiss him, or hold him, or feel his warm body moving against hers ever again.

What they had done, she and Georgia, was unforgivable.

A fire crackled in the hearth of the drawing room, even though it was July. The house on Roseberry Street was unusually quiet and before the fire sat the Brigadier, idly perusing a copy of the *The Light Dragoon's Journal*, though his thoughts often wandered. On a chaise longue opposite, Olga dozed beneath a tartan rug, a fluffy grey cat purring against her side. He regretted at times like this, when it was so quiet, sending the two younger girls, Philippa and Victoria, abroad with his sister, ostensibly on a tour of Europe's art and history, yet removing them from the ugly repercussions of scandal. A scandal that as of yet had still not broken, nor would it, he considered, until Georgia decided to surface, and Sasha was exposed.

On the mantelpiece a clock ticked gently...*tick-tock...tick-tock...*

Time, that was all it would take, just the passing of time.... The Brigadier cursed silently within the confines of his mind, cursing the likes of Felix Westfaling and Reid Bowen to all the fires and damnation of hell!

He wondered if Sasha had received his letter, and for the tenth time that day he wondered where on earth Georgia could be. A terse interview with Lady Westfaling had only evinced that she was not with Felix, who apparently was spending some time preparing for the grouse in August on their Scottish estate. Why had they not heard from her? Surely he had not raised a daughter who could be so selfish and so immoral as to just disappear into the blue like that, leaving in her wake a trail of devastation? And on her wedding day! He was sure that Major Bowen could not be at fault; he seemed like a gentleman and he could not imagine any reason why Georgia should so detest marrying him that she chose to run away. Although, of course, it had taken him a few days to realise that, and to realise that it was not Georgia who had walked up the aisle, married, and sailed away to Russia with Major Bowen, but Sasha. And that Georgia had run away from home. The Brigadier sighed heavily.

Olga stirred, murmuring, 'Is it time for tea?'

'It's a little early, my dear, but I'll ring the bell, if you wish.' He rose from his chair, and then paused by the window as a carriage drew up in front of the steps. It was a hansom cab, and he frowned, puzzled, for he was not expecting any guests.

Shifting on the chaise longue, Olga sat up. 'Who is it?'

'I don't know. Were you expecting anyone?'

Olga shook her head, with a frown and shrug of her shoulder, and the Brigadier strode to the door just as he heard Lodge open the main entrance, and his exclamation, followed by the sound of female voices, had the Brigadier rushing to open the drawing-room door long before the butler. As he pulled it wide, he stopped on its threshold and stared at Georgia and Sasha standing in the hallway amidst piles of luggage and shrugging off their coats and hats.

Both girls froze as they saw their father, and exchanged nervous glances. But it was their mother who screamed, throwing aside her rug and moving faster than anyone had seen her move in years, her slippered feet pattering across the marble hall, arms thrown wide as she cried, 'My girls! Darlings!'

'Mama!' cried Sasha and Georgia in unison, rushing to embrace her.

'You are home at last!' Olga purred, and, arm in arm, led her daughters into the drawing room.

It was a tearful yet joyous reunion, as though they had been away on holiday, and no explanations were asked until much later that evening, when the Brigadier dismissed the servants after dinner and the family sat down in Olga's bedroom as they tucked her up for the night, and any further conversation could not be heard by anyone except the four of them.

The Brigadier sat in a striped upright chair by the window, while the two girls lay on the bed as close to their mother as possible without squashing her delicate, slender frame. She held hands with each of them, one on either side, Sasha resting her cheek against her mother's shoulder and Georgia leaning back against the padded brocade headboard.

'Well?' The Brigadier fixed them both with a stern stare. 'You needn't think that all will be well, because I can assure you both that I am very angry, and deeply shocked by your disgraceful behaviour. And there's no use looking at your mother like that, you have caused her a great deal of distress. I should beat both of you soundly with my strongest riding whip.'

Sasha and Georgia both avoided his eye, biting their lips and feeling heat flare up their necks and cheeks as his withering harangue continued, but at the end of it, their father fell silent and neither of them spoke.

'Georgia?' he barked at her, and she jumped. 'I have no doubt you are the instigator of it all, you usually are, leaving poor Sasha to clean up your mess.'

'Oh, Papa!' wailed Georgia, 'please don't be mean.'

'Then tell me where the hell have you been for the past two months?'

'Well…' She glanced at Sasha, but there was a dark warning in her eyes. 'I— I can't really say.'

'Try.'

'Well…'

'We know for one thing you have not been with Major Bowen. Where have you come from today?'

'From St Petersburg,' Georgia answered promptly, in an injured tone, relieved to be able to tell her father at least one item of truth.

'Alone?'

'No, of course not. I was with Sasha. And Major Bowen.'

'Indeed!' The Brigadier snorted, finding that hard to believe, glancing to Sasha for confirmation.

'It's true, Papa, we have sailed from St Petersburg in the company of Major Bowen.' The sisters exchanged a glance, for they had cobbled together an explanation that might, just might, scrape them through this, if Major Bowen kept to his side of the bargain. 'Papa, Georgia was so nervous about getting married that she begged me to go with her, so you see it was not she who ran away from home, but me. I went with her to St Petersburg.' Sasha glanced away, hoping that he would not detect this lie.

Georgia chipped in then. 'When we got to Russia, Major Bowen and I realised that we just would not suit and—and, well, you see, we never, well, that is—'

'The marriage was not consummated,' Sasha supplied.

'You did not mention this in your letter, Sasha. And why did you not write yourself, Georgia, and tell me all of this?'

Both girls fell silent.

'And where is Major Bowen now?'

'He has gone to his Uncle Percy.'

'He's not well,' added Sasha. 'But he said that he would call upon you tomorrow to discuss an…annulment.'

'Who? Uncle Percy?'

'No, Major Bowen!' the two girls sang in unison.

The Brigadier made an inarticulate sound, having the most uncomfortable feeling that his girls were pulling the wool over his eyes, but he was so relieved to have them home, and apparently unscathed and with the minimum of scandal, that he felt it difficult to further berate them.

Olga interjected, 'Please, Conrad, I am very tired and so happy to have the girls home at last. Can we not talk about this in the morning?'

'Of course, my dear.' He rose to his feet. 'Now, you two girls go along to your rooms.'

Georgia and Sasha kissed their mother good-night and slid off the bed, halting at the door as their father called out, 'And you had better both still be there in the morning!'

At eleven o'clock sharp the next morning, the earliest permitted hour for visitors to call, Lodge went to open the door, summoned by a resounding and urgent rapping of the brass knocker.

Sasha was descending the stairs at that very moment, as Major Bowen was admitted in to the entrance hall. He glanced up at her, and for a moment their eyes dwelled on each other. Sasha felt an ache of yearning in her chest. She had missed him so! Yet it had been less than a day since she had last seen him. But he did not speak to her, and he looked away as he followed Lodge down the corridor to the rear of the house and the study.

The Brigadier sat behind his desk and he looked up as Lodge opened the door and announced, 'Major Bowen, sir.'

'Thank you, Lodge.' He rose from his chair. 'Close the door. And we are not to be disturbed.'

'Very good, sir.'

Reid was dressed in military uniform, for after his call upon the Brigadier he had an interview in Whitehall with his superiors.

For a moment the Brigadier and Reid stared at each other, uncomfortably, and then Reid removed his hat, standing upright as he spoke formally. 'Sir, I have come to ask you for your daughter's hand in marriage.'

The Brigadier gave no sign at all of the shock that inwardly made him flinch, for this was not what he was expecting, but he answered coolly enough, 'Indeed? And which daughter would that be?'

'Why—' Reid smiled '—Alexandra, of course.'

The Brigadier did not respond with a smile of his own. A muscle twitched in his cheek and his piercing blue eyes narrowed. 'You consider this to be a laughing matter, do you?'

'I— I, no, sir, of course not.'

'God damn it!' The Brigadier lost his temper then, and slammed his fist down on the desk. 'How dare you! Get out! Get out of my house!'

Reid was taken aback by the Brigadier's reaction and failed to see why, but he stood his ground. 'Sir—'

The Brigadier advanced on him then, casting his eye about for a weapon and wishing he had his riding crop to hand with which to give the blackguard a thrashing. 'I don't know what you think you're playing at, Bowen, but I can assure you I'm not having any of it!'

'But, sir, let me explain—'

'Explain? What, that you intend to go through my daughters until you find one to your liking, or, having ruined them all, move on to some other unfortunate family? Good God, man—'

'It's not like that at all, sir!'

'Indeed?'

'I've had nothing whatsoever to do with Georgia; it's Sasha I want, and Sasha I love.'

'Really? Then why didn't you marry her in the first place?'

'Well, I didn't know her then—'

'And now you do?'

'Yes, very well.'

'How well?' The Brigadier stared at him with lips pursed, his eyes like blue lightning.

'Well, um, er…' Reid hesitated, wondering at the wisdom of telling the truth here, and how it would affect Sasha.

'Bowen, I don't know if you've spent too much time out in the sun whilst you were in Afghanistan, but I can assure you that you are quite deluded if you think that any relationship with any of my daughters is ever going to happen! Let me spell it out for you—having married and cast aside one daughter, I, and society, and your superior officers, would take a very dim view of you suddenly marrying her sister. I will take in hand all the arrangements for the annulment of your marriage to Georgia, and that is all I have to say to you, Bowen. Now, get out!' He swung sharply about and went to stand by the window, with his elbows akimbo and his back to Reid. He did not turn to look around until he heard the click of the door as it opened and closed.

Sasha, who had been listening at the keyhole, now quickly whirled away behind the library door. But seeing that Reid emerged alone, and that he stood there in the corridor looking quite perplexed and furious, wiping the sweat from his brow before replacing his hat, she dashed out and grabbed him by the hand, one finger to her lips, urging him to be quiet. Reid looked guiltily about, but allowed her to lead him into the library and close the door. She took him over to the window, away from the door and being overheard.

'Reid—' she looked up at him '—you were not supposed to

come here and ask to marry me! You were supposed to arrange for an annulment!'

'From Georgia.' He bent his head to look at her, his eyes skimming over her face and lips, his nose assailed as he breathed in her scent as she stood so close to him, his senses at once flaring. He put his arms around her, pulling her close, murmuring against her hair, 'I have missed you so much in the last week, Sasha. Please, say you will marry me.'

Sasha sagged against him, feeling in her heart the same as he did, but knowing in her mind that any union between them would be impossible. 'How can we? I cannot go back to St Petersburg with you as your wife, not if the marriage is to be annulled. I cannot pretend to be Georgia any longer, and you cannot marry me whilst everyone thinks you are still married to her!'

Reid sighed, stroking her back, holding her close against him. 'Damn!'

'You must go back to Russia.'

'Not without you. I couldn't bear it.'

'You have to, Reid, you will be court-martialled if you don't!'

'Maybe I could resign my commission, buy myself out.'

'Because of me? I would not be responsible for such a thing— you love the Army!'

'I love you more!'

She gazed up at him then, and he leaned down to kiss her. She closed her eyes and surrendered herself to the feel of his lips moving warmly on hers. Then the chiming of the clock reminded him that he had to get to Whitehall and he drew back, his eyes dwelling on her face as though he might never see her again. His mind was darting this way and that, seeking a solution, and then he murmured, stroking the side of her face, 'There is another way.'

'What? How?'

'We let the scandal break.'

'What on earth do you mean?'

'You come back to Russia with me and we tell the Ambassador the truth.'

She gasped. 'No, Reid, we couldn't!'

'Why not?'

'You will be disgraced and dismissed!'

'Isn't that what we want? We can come home, make a life for ourselves here in England, as husband and wife. I have an estate in Dorset, we could manage comfortably enough.' His hand slid from her back and over her hips, to rest on the flatness of her stomach. 'Your sister might not be the only one expecting a baby. Have you thought about that? How can I leave you here, alone, knowing that you and I might have created a child?'

Sasha felt her cheeks burn. She shook her head, fearing the enormity of what he proposed, the repercussions, how her family would be shocked and furious, and how his military career would be ruined.

'No, Reid, I cannot let you do such a thing.'

He straightened then, glancing anxiously at the clock. 'Do you not love me, then, Sasha? You have never said so. Is it only a…physical… attraction that you have for me?'

Sasha felt her heart contract, and she closed her eyes for a moment before turning away from him and staring out of the window at the garden, in full summer bloom. She had to lie, she had to make him go. 'Of course.' She forced a light laugh. 'It was only lust, Reid. You will get over it soon enough.'

Reid swallowed, his jaw clenched, and then he stepped back from her, slowly and carefully placing his hat on his head. He bowed. 'Good day, then, Miss Packard.'

She turned and offered him her hand, saying brightly, swallowing hard to shut back the tears that sparkled at the back of her eyes like silver splinters, 'Goodbye, Major Bowen, and good luck.'

Chapter Thirteen

Over the next few days a succession of lawyers, a physician and a clergyman all paraded through the hallway of the Packard mansion, spending some hours closeted with the Brigadier in his study. These gentlemen were all well known to him, the lawyers having been family retainers for many years and handsomely paid, and Dr Mattheson and Reverend Albright had been at school with the Brigadier, and passed through Sandhurst with him. The result was that Georgia's annulment from Major Bowen was soon underway, with discreet swiftness and on the grounds of non-consummation. No one challenged it.

Sasha wondered how Georgia's innocence was going to be affected when evidence of her increasing state became apparent, but her fears on these grounds were demolished when Georgia sailed into her room early one morning before breakfast, and nonchalantly announced, with a sigh of relief, 'False alarm, Sasha, darling. My monthly has started at last.'

Sasha stared at her, open-mouthed, as she sat brushing her hair before her dressing-table mirror, while Georgia helped herself to tea and biscuits from Sasha's tray. 'Are you quite sure?'

'Oh, yes. I think it's because I am home and feeling relaxed and happy. Don't you?'

Sasha felt numb, lowering her hairbrush and sitting there quite still. How typical of Georgia! She had no idea how her news affected other people. Why, to think that she had been prepared to do the noble thing and give Reid up so that Georgia's child, her non-existent child, could have a name! At the thought of Reid she felt that searing ache in her chest again, and wondered where he was at this very moment, what he was doing, how he was feeling. In a few weeks' time he would sail back to Russia, and she would never see him again.

Their father thought it best, under the circumstances, that they lead a quiet life and not take part in the social whirl of summer functions. He sent word to their housekeeper in Shropshire and asked her to open up the house and prepare for their arrival, just as soon as he could clear the decks of his own obligations and depart from London. They would spend the rest of the summer, and most probably the winter, too, in the country, returning to the capital in the spring, and a fresh start.

Georgia huffed and sighed, bored, longing to be out riding her horse in the park, to attend dances and luncheons, to meet with her friends, but the Brigadier forbade it. His two eldest daughters were a source of great concern to him, the one being far too gay and giddy, and the other far too quiet. He thought he might have well resolved the problem of what to do with Georgia when a most unexpected suitor came calling. At first, none of them had any idea his intentions lay in that direction and he was welcomed merely as a family friend. Then one afternoon he appeared to join them for tea and a game of croquet on the lawn, and his appearance caused Georgia to gasp.

'Why, Captain Turnbull, you have shaved off your beard!'

He looked years younger, and he had rather a pleasant face, not handsome in the way of Reid, thought Sasha, looking at him carefully as she handed him a plate of biscuits, but certainly not at all ugly and his eyes were a sea-green, most appropriate for a Naval man. He was, of course, a good twenty years older than Georgia, but they seemed to enjoy each other's company, she laughed when he was about and the Brigadier had no doubt that his maturity, his quiet sense of strength mixed with just a dash of Scottish no-nonsense attitude was just what she needed. Captain Turnbull's proposal, much to everyone's surprise and relief, was accepted by both the Brigadier and Georgia.

Sasha questioned her sister as they made ready for bed that evening. 'Are you sure, Georgia? Captain Turnbull? You're not toying with him, are you? He's a very decent, kind man and I would not like to see you hurt him.'

Georgia stared at her sister for a moment, and then smiled, with a little shake of her head. 'No, of course not, it's not like that.'

'I would never have guessed.'

'What do you mean?'

'Well, I didn't think he would be the sort of man you would want to be romantically involved with. He's not exactly young and dashing, like Felix.'

'No, thank God, he's not!' exclaimed Georgia. 'I know he's much older than me, but I like that. He makes me feel safe, and I know he won't hurt me or run away because he's so upright, and I know that when he kisses me, he knows what he's doing and I feel a tingle from head to toe.'

The engagement was to be a long one, as the Captain was soon to depart for sea again and would be away in the Mediterranean for six months. It was not to be made formal and public knowledge until Georgia's annulment from Major Bowen had been through the courts. It could well take some time, but neither Georgia nor Captain Turnbull felt any need to rush things.

Now that the question of Georgia was settled, he hoped, the Brigadier turned his attention to Sasha. There seemed little he could do to help bring the smile back to her face. There was an air of grief about her, and sometimes he would come upon her unexpectedly, in the library or in the conservatory, and he noticed that her eyes were red from crying. She seemed to find solace in reading and drawing, spending hours on overly romantic charcoal sketches of dashing soldiers and writing poems. There seemed to be a sense of anguish in Sasha that found release in poetic expression. He was glancing through her sketch book one day when a poem fell out from between the pages and he could not help but read it.

The Fusiliers

With pride and grace he did wear
Dark beret and hackle of a Fusilier
Pristine white tipped with scarlet
Hard won against a foreign foe

Across the plains they did gallop
Swords drawn, muskets primed
Their battle cry to the four winds cast:
'For England and St George!'

While the Colonel's lady watched
As she sat and waited upon a drum
And fought to still the fear in her heart
That her brave Colonel was only hers
'Until death us do part'

The poem seemed unfinished, and when he looked for another page he found only sketches of a Fusilier—Major Reid Bowen. He could understand now that what she felt was grief, for if Bowen was declaring love for her, then, no doubt, Sasha had returned his feelings. He felt a guilty stab as he thought of the letters and notes that Bowen had sent to Sasha over the last few weeks, all of which he had destroyed. But no, damn it, he could not encourage the match! The man was a scoundrel. She would get over him, sooner or later. As the thought passed through his mind, Lodge appeared at the conservatory door and announced, 'The Earl of Clermount has called, sir.'

The Brigadier muttered under his breath, his old friend being the last person he wanted to see, purely because of his connection to Bowen. 'Tell him we are not at home.'

'Her Ladyship and Miss Alexandra are already entertaining him in the front drawing room, sir. I was sent to fetch you.'

'Oh, damn!'

With ill grace he marched down the corridor and arrived in the drawing room just in time to overhear his wife say, 'Oh, please, let us not be so formal. Do sit down, Percy. Tell me all your news. What is going on in London nowadays?'

'My dear, very little that you would find surprising,' Percy replied, lowering his ample frame into the armchair alongside Olga's. 'The Queen has gone to Balmoral again, it seems there will be no end to her mourning and the nation must manage without her—' He stopped, catching sight of Conrad as he came striding through the doorway, hesitating and rising to his feet as he greeted his old friend, who did not seem particularly friendly towards him at the moment.

The Brigadier nodded and busied himself with accepting a cup of tea from his wife, plunking a finger of shortbread in it as he mulled over the best way forwards and just how friendly or unfriendly he should be to someone as influential as the Earl of Clermount.

'I have had a letter from my cousin, Irena,' her mother said. 'You remember her, don't you, Percy? At one stage, a long time ago, I think you were quite smitten with her.'

The Earl coloured beneath his collar and muttered gruffly, 'Er, perhaps.'

'Well, it seems she is now in Paris—goodness knows what she's doing there and who with! She has bought a house near the Bois de Boulogne; she says it's very pretty and she is enjoying the French way of life. Shall we invite her to join us for Christmas?'

This last sentence was directed at her husband, but he merely muttered that they would discuss it later and sipped his tea.

To fill an awkward moment the Earl carefully engineered the

conversation in another direction, and while they conversed, and
her father silently observed, Sasha moved to the armchair beside
the fire and folded away her embroidery frame. She sat down,
accepting a cup of tea from her mother, and gazing politely and
yet with little expression at her parents and their guest, making
no comment as they talked. She turned her attention to her tea
and while she sipped, unbidden into her mind came the sudden
memory of a lurching ship's cabin, and being offered a cup of
tea from a strong, suntanned hand, a deep voice urging her to
drink as she suffered the throes of seasickness. The prick of
tears stabbed sharply behind her eyes, and she struggled within
herself, as she often did, to blink them back and give no outward
sign of the sadness and terrible sense of loss that afflicted her.

Time, that was all she needed, just let time pass by and she
would forget. Or so she had thought, weeks ago, but not a day
went by when she did not think of Reid, or wonder where he
was, and what he was doing. How she longed to hear his firm,
steady voice, see the smile in his eyes, and feel the touch of his
hands on her skin. Here she forced her mind to cease its futile
thoughts, for the memory of Reid's fingers on her body was a
memory she could not, must not, ever think about.

Summoning up every ounce of her will, Sasha listened to the
conversation. Tea cups rattled, Uncle Percy commented on the
cook's excellent pastry, her mother murmured that the weather
had been quite warm for this time of year, and the Brigadier
mentioned that Philippa and Victoria were currently enjoying
Venice before sailing for France and then home for Christmas.
Conversation petered out and they were all silent, with bowed
heads, brushing crumbs from their laps, clinking teaspoons in
cups, and thought of the one person who was not there, and how
he had affected all their lives.

'Well…' the Brigadier murmured, glancing at the clock on
the mantel. The obligatory half-hour for calling had well passed.

'Indeed.' Uncle Percy's gaze also strayed to the clock, but
he made no move to rise. He cleared his throat, and said in a

strained tone, 'There is one matter, that I, um, wished to mention. My nephew, Reid—'

'Percy…' growled the Brigadier as his brows lowered in displeasure.

'Hear me out, please, Conrad.' He turned in his chair towards Sasha. 'Please, my dear, Reid has implored me to speak on his behalf.'

'There is nothing—' Sasha began, her fingers twisting the pale grey silk of her gown, but then her taut voice caught on the emotions that threatened to burst from the confines of her throat.

'You'd better leave, Percy.'

With one hand raised, Percy rose to his feet, and said in a firm, loud voice, 'Just listen for a moment! Please…' He gazed about, imploring in a softer tone. 'No one regrets what happened more than Reid. It was not his fault—'

'Huh!'

'Just listen, Conrad, for God's sake! Sasha…' He took a step towards her, drawing her to her feet as he clasped both of her hands in his. 'Please listen to what I have to say. I cannot believe that a girl with a good and kind heart as I know you to have would not give anyone a second chance. Hmm?'

Sasha inclined her head slightly, the ache in her chest rippling out from somewhere deep within her heart.

Taking a steadying breath, Uncle Percy rushed on, before the Brigadier decided to throw him bodily out of the house. 'In two days Reid will be returning to St Petersburg—his ship sails on Friday evening.'

Sasha winced. 'Please, don't. We made a terrible mistake and now we must make the best of it. I— I am quite happy to carry on as if—'

'Sasha, you do not strike me as a happy girl, gaily carrying on with her life. I sense your sadness, and I can assure you that Reid is in no better state.' He glanced keenly at her eyes, lowered and avoiding his. 'This situation needs to be resolved one way or another.'

The Brigadier took a step towards them, his voice quite firm. 'As far as we are concerned, it's all done and dusted. Nothing more to be considered and we are making the best of it.'

'Indeed?' Percy's tone was quite sceptical, and he pressed his case further, urging Sasha, 'Please, my dear, before the poor boy goes away for God knows how long, just see him, please.'

'I— I...'

Sensing her hesitation, he continued, 'He is staying at my house until Friday, on his last few days of furlough before departing for his ship. He could call upon you whenever—'

'That's quite enough,' barked the Brigadier sternly. 'Percy, despite our years of friendship, I must insist that you leave.'

'Oh, Conrad, do shut up!' Percy snapped, severely annoyed by this display of parental control. 'Let the poor girl make up her own mind. Sasha, what do you say?'

Her mind was whirling, with a heady mixture of hope and fear and pain. It was all too much to bear, and with a small sob she snatched her hands from Uncle Percy's clasp, picked up her skirts and ran from the room, ignoring her father's frowning disapproval, the soft plea from her mother, and the gaping servants hovering in the hallway.

In her bedroom she closed the door and flung herself down upon the comfort and safety of her bed. There were no tears, only her ragged gasps for breath and her racing heart, and the haunting, ever-present memory of Reid. She closed her eyes for a moment, yearning suddenly, as though by the mere power of her thoughts she could reach out to him. How empty her life had been without him!

All that night she lay sleepless in bed, going over and over what Uncle Percy had said. She spent hours talking herself out of the growing insistence at the back of her mind that she must see Reid.

* * *

She awoke on Friday morning feeling overwrought, her head aching and eyes heavy from lack of sleep. She rose from the bed, dressed apathetically and went downstairs. Her father was already seated at the dining table, reading *The Times*, and not a word was said as she sat down, and a maid brought her a teapot and toast. They ate in silence, and then her father snapped his newspaper closed and departed, the atmosphere thick with tension. She sighed as the door banged behind him, and she poured her tea and sipped slowly from the cup.

Later that morning she went shopping on Oxford Street, purchasing new gloves and sketch paper, and chocolate peppermint creams from the confectioner's, returning home for an early lunch with her mother upstairs in her boudoir.

'Your papa has gone out,' Olga murmured, dipping a crust of bread in her soup. 'He is most distressed.'

'Why?' Sasha asked with little interest, staring out as they sat at a small round table set in front of the window overlooking the green leafy chestnut trees of the square.

'You know why, of course, Sasha dearest.' Olga waved her hand expansively. 'All this—this commotion with Uncle Percy about Major Bowen.'

Her tone of voice reflected the dullness of her eyes as Sasha replied, 'I doubt that, Mama. It's more likely he is worrying about a campaign somewhere.'

'Sasha,' Olga reproved in her smoky voice, reaching for the peppermint creams and popping one in her mouth, 'that is not a kind thing to say. Your papa worries very much about all you girls.' For a moment she studied her daughter, who sat so still and silent, gazing out at nothing, at least nothing that Olga could see, as she, too, glanced at the street below and the blue summer sky. After several considering moments, she spoke softly. 'My dearest, darling Sasha, my beautiful girl, it hurts me to see you like this.'

Sasha turned her head to look at her mama. 'Whatever do you mean?'

Olga smiled, her dark eyes fluid with emotion. 'Do you think that no one sees? That *I* do not see? The light has gone out of you, ever since you came back from Russia with your Major Bowen.'

Sasha fiddled with a silver knife, her eyes downcast as she murmured, 'He is not mine, Mama.'

'What happened, Sasha?' Her mother spoke gently. 'I thought it best not to ask, for you are a grown-up young woman and have the right to privacy, but I cannot bear to see you so alone and unhappy. Did he make love to you, Sasha?'

Sasha frowned, her head jerking up at this intimate enquiry. 'Mama, what kind of question is that?'

'Did he?'

Sasha sighed, her cheeks blushing rosy pink. 'Yes.' As her mother gazed at her expectantly, she added, 'And it was wonderful.'

'You were alone together for many weeks, and Major Bowen is a very handsome and, ah, what is the word—?' She waved her hand about, even after all these years in England still occasionally struggling with the language.

'Kind?' Sasha prompted.

'No, no.' Her mother shook her head.

'Strong?'

'Yes, almost…virile!' Her dark black eyes snapped as she smiled, pleased to have grasped the right word. 'A virile man, a manly man, as your papa would say. He would want more than just kisses, eh?'

'Oh, Mother!' Sasha blushed even more, her eyes downcast.

'What?' She shrugged with the expressiveness of her culture. 'It is the truth. I think a man such as him, alone with a beautiful girl like my Sasha—'

'I am not beautiful.'

'You are, my dearest, not like Georgia, but beautiful in your own soft, quiet way. He has a place in your heart, has he not?'

She could not hide the truth from her mother, simply nodding her head.

'I knew it! And you are in love with him?'

Tears suddenly spilled down Sasha's cheeks, as a surge of emotion, long suppressed, suddenly rose from within her heart and overflowed. She nodded again, unable to speak as the tears crowded hot and burning in her throat.

'Then go,' her mother urged. 'Go and see him. You could walk to Uncle Percy's house in ten minutes.'

Sasha shook her head. 'No, I cannot.'

'Why?'

'He— He would be ruined. Disgraced. Court-martialled.'

'What does that matter? Is not love more important? Love will always find a way. Go, quickly, before it is too late.'

Sasha looked up then, hesitating, yet in her mind's eye already seeing herself donning her cloak and running down the road, knocking on the door of the Earl of Clermount's mansion, being shown to the room where Reid would be, perhaps reading the paper by the fire, and he would rise and turn towards her... But then she shook her head, fearing the consequences of such an action. What would he say? How she regretted ever pretending to be Reid Bowen's wife! And now her penance would be to shun all thoughts of love and happiness, to live a quiet life and make amends for her disgraceful behaviour. She could never be with Reid. It was best just to let it go, let Reid go, and the memory would fade.

'I can't, Mama.' Sasha rose from her seat and turned away, halting as her mother's hand clasped her wrist and stopped her in her tracks.

'Why not, my love?'

'Because—' Sasha hesitated, searching for the right words '—it would not be right. We behaved very badly, and now we must pay the price.'

'Oh, pish!' Olga's elegant nose tilted to the ceiling. 'Why, if I had not run after your father in the middle of a Russian winter as he was about to leave for England, we would not be married now. We would not have had all these wonderful years together, madly in love and blessed with our four beautiful girls.' She shook her daughter's wrist with insistence. 'Go, Sasha, go to him. Quickly.'

With a regretful sigh Sasha freed herself from her mother's clasp. She went downstairs to the drawing room and forced herself to sit down at her embroidery frame. Carefully she opened her basket of threads and needles and selected one of each. It soothed her mind to concentrate on a matter that did not come easily to her. Several times she pricked her finger and had to undo untidy stitches. On the mantel the clock ticked gently, and chimed the hour with a delicate ting-ting-ting-ting-ting. Five o'clock. She glanced at the window—the light was still bright and clear. Just a few more stitches, she promised herself, then she would go upstairs and change for dinner. Yet her eyes flew constantly to the clock, and it seemed that each minute ticked by with agonising slowness. Would it never reach the half-hour? Why must time pass by so slowly? When she needed it to flash by with such speed that soon, quickly, she would be free from this torment that gripped her! The needle pricked her finger again, and this time she did not patiently grit her teeth.

'Oh...damn!' Sasha exclaimed.

Suddenly she could bear it no more. She jumped to her feet and ran from the room. She wrenched open the heavy front door, quite forgetting her cloak, even her hat and gloves. Her soft leather slippers pattered on the stone steps leading down to the street, as she flew down them with a whirl of green skirts. She ran, as quickly as her legs would carry her, gasping for breath, all the way along the street and around the corner and down the next street, across the small garden in the middle of the square, across the rough cobbles of the street, until at last she came to the shiny black front door of Uncle Percy's house. Raising her hand, she grasped the brass lion's head and rapped it firmly.

Her breath tore raggedly from her heaving ribs, and she waited, her heart pounding with more than just the exertion of running. She knocked again, several loud raps in quick succession, and then the door opened and she pushed past the butler, and into the hall.

'Why, Miss Packard, good afternoon.' He closed the door, a little taken aback by the impetuous behaviour of this usually sedate young lady. 'His lordship is not at home at the moment.'

'I wish to see Major Bowen,' Sasha burst out, adding, 'Please.'

He shook his head, with a regretful grimace. 'I am sorry, Miss Packard, but both the Earl and Major Bowen have departed for Tilbury Docks.'

'They've gone?'

'Yes, miss.'

'Already?'

'Well, yes, miss.' He was a little puzzled by her question but stood politely and attentively. 'Would you care to leave a message?' He indicated the pen and writing paper laid on a bureau.

A hot wave of colour suffused Sasha's cheeks and she turned back to the door, biting her lip with embarrassment. 'No, thank you.'

The butler quickly moved to open the door for her, and watched with a slight frown as she descended the steps with shoulders bowed in defeat. He closed the door and stood pensively for a moment, deep in thought. Then, despite Sasha's denial, he stooped to the notepaper and wrote, *Miss Packard called.*

Unbeknownst to him, those three small words would change everything.

Returning home, Sasha went upstairs to her room and sat down on the edge of the bed, facing the window and staring blankly into space. The light was fading now, the shadows stretching from the trees and across the street, casting her in their bleakness. Reid was gone. She would never see him again. And yet he was never far from her mind. Tears ran silently down her face, but she did not sob. It was over. She must face the truth of it and turn her thoughts, her feelings, her very life, elsewhere. For a wild moment she thought of what she could do to escape from the pain and desolation of her loneliness, envisaging herself following in the footsteps of Florence Nightingale and nursing sick soldiers in desperate conditions. Or perhaps going to Africa and bringing the Bible to the poor people there. Surely in those conditions, far from home, she would be able to forget?

Her father insisted the family always sat down to eat dinner together, and though she would have much preferred a tray in her room, Sasha dutifully descended the stairs and took her place at the table. Her parents conversed quietly, trying not to make it obvious that she was their cause for concern, but failing to hide the numerous glances that came her way. The fish had just been served when there was a sudden commotion, raised voices in the hallway, and the dining-room door burst open. The Earl of Clermount brushed aside Lodge as he rushed in, black cape whirling, still wearing his top hat and carrying his ebony walking cane in a most decisive manner.

'Sasha!' He came at once to her side and with one hand grasped her upper arm, lifting her from her chair. 'If we hurry, we may just make it in time!'

Her knife and fork fell from her hands, clattering with a jarring noise onto her plate. The Brigadier rose from his seat, exclaiming loudly at just what the hell was going on?

'No time now, Conrad, old boy, got to get Sasha to Tilbury.'

'But—' Sasha gasped, watching her starched white napkin flutter to the floor as Uncle Percy dragged her bodily from the dining room and into the hallway.

Here Lodge was ready with her cloak and helped her to don it whilst in motion.

'Don't worry,' Uncle Percy called over his shoulder to the astonished onlookers of family and servants, 'I'll look after her.'

Sasha hurried alongside him as they rushed down the steps, fearing that if she did not she would fall and injure herself, and then he was urging her into his carriage, one hand in the small of her back. She barely had a moment in which to sit down before he rapped his cane on the ceiling and with a lurch, a crack of the whip and a shout from the driver, they set off at great speed and Sasha clutched at Uncle Percy's arm, both in alarm and consternation.

'Where are we going?' she gasped.

'To the docks at Tilbury. With any luck we will get there before the ship sails.'

As the coach rattled onwards Uncle Percy frequently poked his head out of the window to harangue unfortunate pedestrians, coal-carts and hackney cabs, urging his coachman to hurry.

Sasha raised her voice above the noise of the thundering wheels. 'Uncle Percy, I really don't think this a very good idea.'

'Oh?' He glanced keenly at her from the corner of his eye, half hanging out of the window. 'Why do you say that? You did come to the house to see Reid, did you not? I am sorry we were not there, but I had an unexpected invitation to the opera, so we left early.'

'Well, yes, I did, but—'

'Just as I thought.' He turned back to the window, raising his voice to bellow, 'You there, get out of the way, can't you see this is an emergency?'

Sasha cringed, blushing with embarrassment and hoping that no one would recognise them. The Packards' reputation was hanging in the balance at the moment and she hated to think what her father would say if he knew about this mad dash through London. As they drew closer to their destination, Sasha, too, began to peer out of the window on her side of the coach, but it was not with eagerness, her emotions leaning more towards anxiety and wide-eyed terror. It had been several weeks since she had last seen Reid, pretending a callous disregard for him and sending him away. What on earth would he say to her now?

The carriage drew to a shuddering halt, the coachman jumped down to unfold the steps, but Uncle Percy had already flung the door open and leapt out, urging Sasha to follow him and firmly grasping her elbow as they plunged onto the crowded quayside. The vast side of a ship loomed above them, and the quay was a dangerous obstacle course, the poor lighting from paraffin lamps making little impression on the gloom of dusk. More than once she bumped into the sharp corner of a trunk or knocked against the ankles of an urchin perched artfully on a bale or barrel. There was a dank smell of water, rotting timber and other odours she did not care to identify.

'There!' shouted Uncle Percy triumphantly. 'There he is!'

Sasha craned her neck, peering upwards in the direction that he pointed with his cane, but all she could see were a throng of shapes leaning against the rails of the ship, only vaguely discernible as human beings. It was not a naval warship, but a civilian vessel, a fast cutter carrying mail and supplies and a half-dozen passengers.

'Damn, they've taken down the gangplank!' Pulling her along in his wake, Uncle Percy began to shout, pushing his way through the crowd of people waving goodbye to the passengers, trying to attract the attention of just one amongst many. 'Reid! Over here!'

As they hurried they came to the edge of the dock and could go no farther. Sasha watched as the vast bulk of the ship moved and inched back, slipping slowly away from them. With alarm she leaned back, bending her neck painfully as she peered upwards in a desperate attempt to see where Reid was.

'Sasha! Up here, to your left!'

She heard his voice and took several paces backwards to get a better view. And then she saw him, his tall, broad-shouldered frame even more bulky enshrouded in a heavy military coat.

'Sasha!'

'Reid!' She waved, her soft voice quite unable to reach across the widening gap between them. It was surprising how quickly the ship departed, one moment close to hand and the next sliding out into the waters of the Thames. 'Goodbye!' she called, waving her arm back and forth. 'Take care and God bless!'

He shouted something in return, but the wind and the distance snatched his words away. Just at that moment the sun broke through a gap in the clouds and glowed orange, revealing Reid more clearly. She watched, frozen to the spot, as he ran along the deck towards the stern, bringing him a fraction closer to where they stood on the quay and he raised his voice to shout, but all she heard was 'Wait…' and the rest was beyond her hearing. Within a few moments the ship was gone, sailing away down the river and to far-off, foreign places. Quite suddenly, much to her consternation, she burst into tears.

Uncle Percy put his arm about her shoulders, patting her upper arm clumsily. 'There, there.' And then he stopped and stared. 'Wait a minute, what—?'

There was a general buzz of consternation from the quayside as they watched the ship lean to one side and then make a slow, awkward turn and chug slowly back towards the dock. Sasha sniffed and wiped the tears from her eyes, watching with hopeful, bated breath. As soon as the great bulk of the sides had touched the wharf, ropes were thrown and the gangplank lowered.

'Look!' exclaimed Uncle Percy. 'It's Reid. He must have asked them to turn about.'

With a sob Sasha tore from his grasp and was running down the quayside, reaching the end of the gangplank just as Reid descended. For a moment they stood still, gasping for breath, staring at each other, the question in each other's eyes. Then Reid held his arms open to her and she flung herself into them with a cry, her hands tightening about his neck.

'Sasha, my love, I cannot bear to go! These last few weeks have been hell without you!' He rained kisses on her cheeks, and forehead, her nose and chin, finally kissing her mouth and then gasping, 'I will ask the captain to unload my trunks.' He half-turned towards the anxiously hovering captain on the deck of the ship, but Sasha pulled him back.

'You must go, Reid, you cannot desert your post like that!'

'I won't go back without you, Sasha.'

'You must!'

'Sasha—' his voice became low and serious as he held her close to him, looking deep in her eyes '—do you love me?'

'Yes!' she cried. 'Of course I love you, so very much!'

'Then come with me, and to hell with everything!'

She laughed, and shook her head, and then turned back towards Uncle Percy, torn between her love for Reid and the desperate, aching need to be with him, to love him, and the duty that forced them to order their lives according to the rules and regulations of society. As she took a step away from him, her sense of duty well ingrained, with it came another sensation, one of being utterly bereft, and she knew that she could not do it. She could not continue to live without him.

Sasha laughed then. 'I don't have any clothes.'

He smiled, too, taking her hand, tugging her up the gang-plank. 'I will lend you some of mine, or maybe one of the other passengers has a wife who can lend you some. And then I will buy you a whole new wardrobe in St Petersburg!'

'What on earth will Lady Cronin say?' she gasped, breath-less, as she ran behind him, the sailors on the deck shouting and cheering, urging them to hurry. 'Reid, this is madness!'

'I don't care!'

They reached the deck and Sasha turned to wave back to Uncle Percy, calling, 'Tell my father how sorry I am, and ask him to write to all the generals he might know so that Reid doesn't get into trouble!'

'Goodbye!' Uncle Percy yelled, waving. 'Don't worry, I will make sure that no one stands in the way of true love!'

Laughing, feeling like naughty children stealing cakes from

the kitchen, Reid and Sasha embraced, kissing in between smiles, as the ship began to inch its way back out into the Thames again, the last glowing ruby embers of the evening shining on their faces. They stood entwined together, waving goodbye, and then when the quay was out of sight Reid took her by the hand and led her below decks to his cabin. Sasha followed him, and as he closed the door behind them and drew her into his arms, she leaned her head against his chest and sighed with relief. Happy in the knowledge that at last all her days of anguish and grief were over and she had come home to the only place she ever wanted to be, with Reid.

For a moment they didn't speak, and he stroked her hair and her back with a warm, caressing hand, savouring the feel of her small, slender body against his, content at last to have her back where she belonged. Gently, he pushed her a little away from him and lifted her chin with his fingers, raising her face so that he could see into her eyes.

'I have missed you so much,' he murmured.

Sasha looked up at him, her glance sombre, yet a smile upon her lips. 'I have missed you, too. It was agony sending you away like that. I thought I would die from the pain of it.'

'Thank God you did not!' He hugged her tightly, kissing the side of her neck. 'Now you are here with me and I will never let anyone come between us again, not even the Brigadier or, worse, Lady Cronin!'

They both laughed, then he stooped and covered her mouth with his, kissing her deeply. The heat flared between them, fingers fumbling with buttons and fastenings in their desperate haste and need to feel the intimate joy of each other's skin and be as close as a man and a woman could be. They stood locked together as they kissed, naked, their clothes gathered in little heaps about the floor. Sasha clasped the lean hardness of Reid's body, running her palm over his back and his taut buttocks, pressing against him. He stooped farther, his head lowering to her breast, gently exploring her nipple with his tongue. She groaned and they staggered down upon the narrow bunk bed, kissing with frantic need.

'Sasha, will you marry me?' he gasped, lifting his head for a moment.

'Yes,' she answered at once with a sultry, breathless grin, her legs and arms wrapped possessively around his body. 'Yes, my dearest, darling Reid, again and again and again!'

Epilogue

Christmas Day, 1878

A late dawn broke across the wintry, snow-dusted Dorset hills and glinted amber on the window panes of Appledene Manor. The light strengthened and smoke rose from the chimneys, but this morn, on the one day of the year eagerly awaited and enjoyed by most families, the Appledene servants trod softly, aware that their household was perhaps an exception.

They had taken the liberty of putting up festive decorations; Mr Shaw, the butler, and Mr Rudd, the estate manager, had gone out into the woods and cut down a pine tree, dragging it homewards through the first flurry of powdery snow ten days ago. They'd put up red ribbons and orange pomanders and Mrs Blake, the cook, had made gingerbread stars with which to decorate the tree, as well as other Christmas delicacies in an effort to tempt the appetite of their pale and wan young mistress. The maid, Dolly, who came up from the village five times a week to help clean the big rambling stone house, could scarce hold back her glowing admiration for the quiet woman who had risked all in the name of love.

'It's ever so romantic,' Dolly was heard to murmur often, her voice hushed as Mrs Blake frowned at her. 'She's ever so brave, don't you think?'

Mrs Blake would cluck her tongue and tell her to be quiet, that her betters' business was no business of hers. But everyone knew, from the highest lords and ladies of the land to the lowest scullery maid. The scandal a year ago could scarce be contained, and though it had been dealt with, in a quite ruthless yet swift manner, the aftermath was one that the two people at the centre of it had to live with.

'It's so unfair,' Dolly muttered, lower lip pouting. 'They can't help it if they love each other.'

'Go and take her tea up.' Mrs Blake added two mince pies to the tea-tray and a sprig of holly, before handing it to Dolly. 'And don't you be waking her if she's still asleep, poor lamb.'

In her bedroom, dark still as the pale sun glowed behind the closed curtains of heavy blue brocade, Sasha lay in a ball in the middle of the imposing four-poster bed, her knees drawn up, and her cheek pillowed beneath the palm of one hand. She had cried herself to sleep, as she often did, and even the joy of Christmas could do nothing to stir her heart, not when it was so leaden, when every day Reid did not enjoy the comforts of his own home, but a rough cell in a military prison. She did not know where, as Reid had insisted that she not be told, as he did not want her to visit him in such a dire place. She suspected that Uncle Percy knew, but he had refused to divulge any information, insisting that this secret was for her own good and the least they could do to respect Reid's wishes. She wrote letters, twice a week, and he wrote back to her, though less often, their letters travelling via Uncle Percy. It was he who saw to Sasha's welfare, providing her with a generous housekeeping and personal allowance, and administering all of Reid's affairs and investments, so that Reid rested easy in the knowledge that she was not suffering for want of anything, except his freedom, and the desperate need to be together again.

On returning to St Petersburg, Reid and Sasha had decided that it was best to admit the truth at once, and from the ship they had gone directly to the Embassy and an interview with Sir Stanley Cronin. He had been shocked, and then coldly angry, at their deception, yet his reaction was one that neither Reid nor Sasha had anticipated. Sir Stanley had called for the guard and had had Reid arrested, and told Sasha in no uncertain terms that she was to leave the Embassy immediately and never return. With nowhere else to go, she had gone to Irena's palace, and though her cousin was no longer in residence, the household was still maintained and the servants relieved to have someone to serve. She had stayed for two weeks, and then followed Reid back to London on a separate ship, where instinctively she had directed her hackney carriage to take her to Roseberry Street, to her home and her family. Here, too, her father had closed the door in her face, outraged at this second act of deception and betrayal, and refused to speak to her. In despair, Sasha had gone to Uncle Percy, and there she had remained, all during the most bitter and distressing weeks of their lives.

Reid was stripped of his rank at court-martial, and sentenced to two years in a military prison for gross misconduct, deception and improper use of government funds and privileges. She had not been present, although Uncle Percy had, and he assured Sasha that he would do everything possible and in his power to see that Reid would soon be released. The newspapers had printed lurid and only half-true tales of the story, much to their consternation, but there seemed little anyone could do to refute them. Reid refused to be interviewed by a newspaper editor and had to be forcibly restrained from punching the gentleman senseless.

At Reid's insistence, Sasha had gone to his family home in Dorset, Appledene Manor, there to hide away from the cruel judgements and harsh punishment of society and her own family. She wrote secretly to her mama, who wrote back to say that she must be patient, and wait until her father and the scandal had cooled, and all would be well again.

That was more than a year ago, and Sasha had led a quiet, comfortable yet lonely existence in the Dorset countryside. The servants were kind, obedient yet wary, and the village she rarely ventured into. She had missed Georgia's wedding to Angus Turnbull, the annulment at last finalised, and Reid's letters were full of plans for their own wedding. But Sasha had missed out on life as it seemed to pass her by. But life had not missed out on her, and had given Sasha a very special gift to sustain her, a precious gift that Reid knew nothing about and every day she had to bite her hand to stop herself from writing to tell him. But Sasha believed that for Reid to know about it now would be torment and unbearable for him, so she kept this secret from him, for his own good.

Sasha was not asleep, but did not stir when Dolly came in, hesitating by the door and walking softly and setting the tray down on the bedside cabinet. Sasha kept her eyes closed, and felt guilty, but she did not want her day to begin, and the aching pain of it, not just yet. She lay a little longer, and then with a sigh, as a small sound in the room next door roused her, she rolled onto her back and stared up at the canopy of the bed. It was Christmas Day, and she should get up and give thanks and be grateful.

She lay for a while longer, and then the sound of carriage wheels rumbling and crunching on the gravel driveway roused her. She pushed back the covers and padded barefoot to the window, tweaking the curtains an inch as she peered out, squinting against the glare of light, convinced that it must be Uncle Percy. Though she was greatly fond of him and his care, he was not the one person in the world she longed to see the most. But as she looked out and the carriage came into view from behind a stand of yew trees, she gave a gasp, recognising the Packard family crest emblazoned on the door, and behind there followed a second carriage. Could it be? Sasha gave a little cry, half-wonder, half-joy, and reached for a plaid shawl, throwing it around her shoulders as she tucked her feet into slippers and then ran from the room.

The carriages came to a halt by the front portico as she descended the stairs, and Mr Shaw walked with slow dignity across the chequered hallway and opened the door. Sasha was almost at the bottom stair when the hallway seemed to fill with people, and she wondered if she should pinch herself, because surely she must be dreaming!

Her mother came in first, assisted by Philippa, and then came Victoria, carrying a rosy-cheeked infant dressed in a sailor suit, followed closely by Georgia and Angus, and then came her father. Sasha ran across the hall and all was noise and confusion as she kissed and hugged her mother and her sisters, and then turned, with a frightened look upon her thin and pale face, to her father.

With a choked and gruff cry the Brigadier strode briskly towards her and opened his arms. She flew into them, sobbing against his shoulder as he kissed her temple and held her tightly, stroking her hair.

'My child, my dearest child, can you ever forgive me?' He wept, and his wife and daughters looked on in amazement, never in their lives ever witnessing tears from the stern and unyielding Brigadier.

Sasha cried out, 'Oh, Papa, there is nothing to forgive! It is I who have done such wrong!'

'No, you have done nothing, except fall in love.'

For a long few moments, father and daughter hugged one another and then with a laugh they linked arms and no more was said. There was an inaudible sigh of relief from the rest of the family, and then much chattering as they went into the drawing room, as though the past year had never been, no rift and no partings and no sorrow. Georgia was proud to introduce her baby son, George, to his aunt and Sasha was happy to meet him. Then she quickly excused herself and went upstairs to dress and see to her own responsibilities.

Dolly was kept busy lighting the fires in the bedrooms and the dining room, and rushing up and down the stairs with tea and cake for the guests, while Mr Shaw and the Packard grooms carried in the luggage and the hampers of food they had brought from London. Mrs Blake was relieved to behold these and took delight in preparing a delicious luncheon of turkey and ham and plum pudding.

It was a wonderful Christmas day, and Sasha was flushed with happiness as her family gathered around her, but throughout it all her heart was heavy as she thought of Reid in prison and wondered how he fared and what he was doing. Uncle Percy might still have come down to Dorset to see her, but she hoped that instead he was spending the day with Reid, and keeping him good company with a bottle of port and some nourishing food.

The daylight had almost gone and the lamps lit when, for the second time that day, Sasha heard the sound of carriage wheels on the driveway. She wondered who it could be, sure that it must be Uncle Percy after all, and indeed she could hear the sound of his voice as he greeted Mr Shaw, and she glanced nervously to her father, who looked somewhat grim. Then the drawing-room door opened and Uncle Percy came in, greeting them all jovially.

'Happy Christmas, my dear Sasha.' He stooped and kissed her cheek. 'Forgive me that I have not had time to wrap your Christmas gift, but it was far too large and cumbersome!'

He swept his arm towards the door and through it walked a man she had been thinking about only moments before.

'Reid!' With a shriek she ran to him, and he grinned as she flung herself at him. 'Reid, my darling! I can't believe it!'

Reid laughed and clasped her tightly in his arms as he whirled her around in a circle and then bent his head and kissed her lips. They embraced, and kissed, and embraced again, Sasha stroking her palm over his much-beloved face, noting that he was thinner and in need of a shave and a good hair cut, but at least he seemed well enough.

She glanced over his shoulder at Uncle Percy. 'How on earth did you manage it?' And then her face paled and she frowned with sudden fear. 'Is it only for today? Must you go back—?'

'No, no, my dear,' Uncle Percy rushed to reassure her. 'I have been petitioning the Queen for Reid's release all these months, and at last she has listened. There were a number of non-violent, high-society prisoners released today and we were fortunate that Reid was one of them.'

'Can you bear to have me?' Reid laughed as he held her face between the palms of his hands and his eyes devoured her, noting every curve and colour of her soft, flushed face. 'An ex-con?'

Sasha tisked and frowned at him. 'Nonsense, you are no more a criminal than—than anyone else here!'

Angus echoed her sentiment with a hear-hear, repeated in various degrees of volume about the room.

Reid returned his gaze to Sasha, tilting his head to one side and looking at her with a slightly puzzled air. 'You are even more beautiful than I remember,' he whispered, 'yet somehow different, I can't quite—'

Sasha smiled, and reached up to lay her forefinger on his lips, taking his hand and leading him to where her mother lay upon a sofa, with a young baby wrapped and sleeping peacefully upon her lap.

With tears in her eyes Sasha whispered, 'She is three months old, and she is ours.'

Reid caught his breath and then dropped to one knee as he knelt down and gently moved aside the soft fold of the blanket his daughter was wrapped in, to see her sweet and tender face, so like her mother's. He thought for the first time in his life he would not be able to hold back the tears that spiked the back of his eyes, and he was right.

His voice was choked as blindly he reached for Sasha's hand

and kissed her knuckles, with reverence and awe and shame that for his pleasure she had borne this child, alone and outcast. After a moment he composed himself and asked, 'What is her name?'

'Her name is Hope.' Sasha stroked his fair hair as he knelt and stared at his daughter.

Her grandmother moved and lifted the small bundle, offering Reid his daughter. He stood up. Gently he placed his large hands beneath the baby and cradled her to his chest, before shifting her into the crook of his arm and with his other arm drawing Sasha in close to his side. They gazed at their daughter in wonder, and then at each other, and then suddenly Uncle Percy and the Brigadier were breaking open bottles of champagne; the noise woke the baby and startled young George, who both started to cry. Everyone was laughing and talking, while Reid and Sasha stood as though they were alone on a deserted beach, their eyes only for each other, until glasses of champagne were handed to each of them and they all turned to the Brigadier as he called for attention.

He raised his glass. 'To Reid and Sasha!'

The salute was echoed by everyone, and though it was not yet their wedding day, it was only a few months later that they stood amongst spring blossoms and sunshine at the altar of the Church of St Ann, and before God and all their family and the cream of London society made their vows to become husband and wife.

* * * * *

REQUEST YOUR FREE BOOKS!
2 FREE NOVELS PLUS 2 FREE GIFTS!

Harlequin®

American ★ Romance®

LOVE, HOME & HAPPINESS

YES! Please send me 2 FREE Harlequin® American Romance® novels and my 2 FREE gifts (gifts are worth about $10). After receiving them, if I don't wish to receive any more books, I can return the shipping statement marked "cancel." If I don't cancel, I will receive 4 brand-new novels every month and be billed just $4.49 per book in the U.S. or $5.24 per book in Canada. That's a saving of at least 14% off the cover price! It's quite a bargain! Shipping and handling is just 50¢ per book in the U.S. and 75¢ per book in Canada.* I understand that accepting the 2 free books and gifts places me under no obligation to buy anything. I can always return a shipment and cancel at any time. Even if I never buy another book, the two free books and gifts are mine to keep forever.

154/354 HDN FEP2

Name _____ (PLEASE PRINT) _____

Address _____ Apt. # _____

City _____ State/Prov. _____ Zip/Postal Code _____

Signature (if under 18, a parent or guardian must sign) _____

Mail to the **Reader Service:**
IN U.S.A.: P.O. Box 1867, Buffalo, NY 14240-1867
IN CANADA: P.O. Box 609, Fort Erie, Ontario L2A 5X3

Not valid for current subscribers to Harlequin American Romance books.

Want to try two free books from another line?
Call 1-800-873-8635 or visit www.ReaderService.com.

* Terms and prices subject to change without notice. Prices do not include applicable taxes. Sales tax applicable in N.Y. Canadian residents will be charged applicable taxes. Offer not valid in Quebec. This offer is limited to one order per household. All orders subject to credit approval. Credit or debit balances in a customer's account(s) may be offset by any other outstanding balance owed by or to the customer. Please allow 4 to 6 weeks for delivery. Offer available while quantities last.

Your Privacy—The Reader Service is committed to protecting your privacy. Our Privacy Policy is available online at www.ReaderService.com or upon request from the Reader Service.

We make a portion of our mailing list available to reputable third parties that offer products we believe may interest you. If you prefer that we not exchange your name with third parties, or if you wish to clarify or modify your communication preferences, please visit us at www.ReaderService.com/consumerschoice or write to us at Reader Service Preference Service, P.O. Box 9062, Buffalo, NY 14269. Include your complete name and address.

HARI1B

REQUEST YOUR FREE BOOKS!
2 FREE NOVELS PLUS 2 FREE GIFTS!

red-hot reads!

YES! Please send me 2 FREE Harlequin® Blaze™ novels and my 2 FREE gifts (gifts are worth about $10). After receiving them, if I don't wish to receive any more books, I can return the shipping statement marked "cancel." If I don't cancel, I will receive 6 brand-new novels every month and be billed just $4.49 per book in the U.S. or $4.96 per book in Canada. That's a saving of at least 14% off the cover price. It's quite a bargain. Shipping and handling is just 50¢ per book in the U.S. and 75¢ per book in Canada.* I understand that accepting the 2 free books and gifts places me under no obligation to buy anything. I can always return a shipment and cancel at any time. Even if I never buy another book, the two free books and gifts are mine to keep forever.

151/351 HDN FEQE

Name	(PLEASE PRINT)	

Address		Apt. #

City	State/Prov.	Zip/Postal Code

Signature (if under 18, a parent or guardian must sign)

Mail to the **Reader Service:**
IN U.S.A.: P.O. Box 1867, Buffalo, NY 14240-1867
IN CANADA: P.O. Box 609, Fort Erie, Ontario L2A 5X3

Not valid for current subscribers to Harlequin Blaze books.

Want to try two free books from another line?
Call 1-800-873-8635 or visit www.ReaderService.com.

* Terms and prices subject to change without notice. Prices do not include applicable taxes. Sales tax applicable in N.Y. Canadian residents will be charged applicable taxes. Offer not valid in Quebec. This offer is limited to one order per household. All orders subject to credit approval. Credit or debit balances in a customer's account(s) may be offset by any other outstanding balance owed by or to the customer. Please allow 4 to 6 weeks for delivery. Offer available while quantities last.

Your Privacy—The Reader Service is committed to protecting your privacy. Our Privacy Policy is available online at www.ReaderService.com or upon request from the Reader Service.

We make a portion of our mailing list available to reputable third parties that offer products we believe may interest you. If you prefer that we not exchange your name with third parties, or if you wish to clarify or modify your communication preferences, please visit us at www.ReaderService.com/consumerschoice or write to us at Reader Service Preference Service, P.O. Box 9062, Buffalo, NY 14269. Include your complete name and address.

HBI1B

REQUEST YOUR FREE BOOKS!

2 FREE NOVELS PLUS 2 FREE GIFTS!

ALWAYS POWERFUL, PASSIONATE AND PROVOCATIVE

REQUEST YOUR FREE BOOKS!

2 FREE NOVELS PLUS
2 FREE GIFTS!

PASSION
GUARANTEED
SEDUCTION

YES! Please send me 2 FREE Harlequin Presents® novels and my 2 FREE gifts (gifts are worth about $10). After receiving them, if I don't wish to receive any more books, I can return the shipping statement marked "cancel." If I don't cancel, I will receive 6 brand-new novels every month and be billed just $4.30 per book in the U.S. or $4.99 per book in Canada. That's a saving of at least 14% off the cover price! It's quite a bargain! Shipping and handling is just 50¢ per book in the U.S. and 75¢ per book in Canada.* I understand that accepting the 2 free books and gifts places me under no obligation to buy anything. I can always return a shipment and cancel at any time. Even if I never buy another book, the two free books and gifts are mine to keep forever.

106/306 HDN FERQ

Name _____ (PLEASE PRINT) _____

Address _____ Apt. # _____

City _____ State/Prov. _____ Zip/Postal Code _____

Signature (if under 18, a parent or guardian must sign) _____

Mail to the **Reader Service:**
IN U.S.A.: P.O. Box 1867, Buffalo, NY 14240-1867
IN CANADA: P.O. Box 609, Fort Erie, Ontario L2A 5X3

Not valid for current subscribers to Harlequin Presents books.

**Are you a current subscriber to Harlequin Presents books
and want to receive the larger-print edition?
Call 1-800-873-8635 or visit www.ReaderService.com.**

* Terms and prices subject to change without notice. Prices do not include applicable taxes. Sales tax applicable in N.Y. Canadian residents will be charged applicable taxes. Offer not valid in Quebec. This offer is limited to one order per household. All orders subject to credit approval. Credit or debit balances in a customer's account(s) may be offset by any other outstanding balance owed by or to the customer. Please allow 4 to 6 weeks for delivery. Offer available while quantities last.

Your Privacy—The Reader Service is committed to protecting your privacy. Our Privacy Policy is available online at www.ReaderService.com or upon request from the Reader Service.

We make a portion of our mailing list available to reputable third parties that offer products we believe may interest you. If you prefer that we not exchange your name with third parties, or if you wish to clarify or modify your communication preferences, please visit us at www.ReaderService.com/consumerschoice or write to us at Reader Service Preference Service, P.O. Box 9062, Buffalo, NY 14269. Include your complete name and address.

HP11B

REQUEST YOUR FREE BOOKS!
2 FREE NOVELS PLUS 2 FREE GIFTS!

Harlequin
Romance

From the Heart, For the Heart

YES! Please send me 2 FREE Harlequin® Romance novels and my 2 FREE gifts (gifts are worth about $10). After receiving them, if I don't wish to receive any more books, I can return the shipping statement marked "cancel." If I don't cancel, I will receive 6 brand-new novels every month and be billed just $4.09 per book in the U.S. or $4.49 per book in Canada. That's a savings of at least 14% off the cover price! It's quite a bargain! Shipping and handling is just 50¢ per book in the U.S. and 75¢ per book in Canada.* I understand that accepting the 2 free books and gifts places me under no obligation to buy anything. I can always return a shipment and cancel at any time. Even if I never buy another book, the two free books and gifts are mine to keep forever.

116/316 HDN FESE

Name	(PLEASE PRINT)

Address		Apt. #

City	State/Prov.	Zip/Postal Code

Signature (if under 18, a parent or guardian must sign)

Mail to the **Reader Service:**
IN U.S.A.: P.O. Box 1867, Buffalo, NY 14240-1867
IN CANADA: P.O. Box 609, Fort Erie, Ontario L2A 5X3

Not valid for current subscribers to Harlequin Romance books.

**Are you a subscriber to Harlequin Romance books
and want to receive the larger-print edition?
Call 1-800-873-8635 or visit www.ReaderService.com.**

* Terms and prices subject to change without notice. Prices do not include applicable taxes. Sales tax applicable in N.Y. Canadian residents will be charged applicable taxes. Offer not valid in Quebec. This offer is limited to one order per household. All orders subject to credit approval. Credit or debit balances in a customer's account(s) may be offset by any other outstanding balance owed by or to the customer. Please allow 4 to 6 weeks for delivery. Offer available while quantities last.

Your Privacy—The Reader Service is committed to protecting your privacy. Our Privacy Policy is available online at www.ReaderService.com or upon request from the Reader Service.

We make a portion of our mailing list available to reputable third parties that offer products we believe may interest you. If you prefer that we not exchange your name with third parties, or if you wish to clarify or modify your communication preferences, please visit us at www.ReaderService.com/consumerschoice or write to us at Reader Service Preference Service, P.O. Box 9062, Buffalo, NY 14269. Include your complete name and address.

HRI1B

REQUEST YOUR FREE BOOKS!

2 FREE NOVELS PLUS 2 FREE GIFTS!

 Harlequin®

SPECIAL EDITION

Life, Love & Family

YES! Please send me 2 FREE Harlequin® Special Edition novels and my 2 FREE gifts (gifts are worth about $10). After receiving them, if I don't wish to receive any more books, I can return the shipping statement marked "cancel." If I don't cancel, I will receive 6 brand-new novels every month and be billed just $4.49 per book in the U.S. or $5.24 per book in Canada. That's a saving of at least 14% off the cover price! It's quite a bargain! Shipping and handling is just 50¢ per book in the U.S. and 75¢ per book in Canada.* I understand that accepting the 2 free books and gifts places me under no obligation to buy anything. I can always return a shipment and cancel at any time. Even if I never buy another book, the two free books and gifts are mine to keep forever.

235/335 HDN FEGF

Name		
	(PLEASE PRINT)	

Address		Apt. #

City	State/Prov.	Zip/Postal Code

Signature (if under 18, a parent or guardian must sign)

Mail to the Reader Service:
IN U.S.A.: P.O. Box 1867, Buffalo, NY 14240-1867
IN CANADA: P.O. Box 609, Fort Erie, Ontario L2A 5X3

Not valid for current subscribers to Harlequin Special Edition books.

Want to try two free books from another line?
Call 1-800-873-8635 or visit www.ReaderService.com.

* Terms and prices subject to change without notice. Prices do not include applicable taxes. Sales tax applicable in N.Y. Canadian residents will be charged applicable taxes. Offer not valid in Quebec. This offer is limited to one order per household. All orders subject to credit approval. Credit or debit balances in a customer's account(s) may be offset by any other outstanding balance owed by or to the customer. Please allow 4 to 6 weeks for delivery. Offer available while quantities last.

Your Privacy—The Reader Service is committed to protecting your privacy. Our Privacy Policy is available online at www.ReaderService.com or upon request from the Reader Service.

We make a portion of our mailing list available to reputable third parties that offer products we believe may interest you. If you prefer that we not exchange your name with third parties, or if you wish to clarify or modify your communication preferences, please visit us at www.ReaderService.com/consumerschoice or write to us at Reader Service Preference Service, P.O. Box 9062, Buffalo, NY 14269. Include your complete name and address.

HSE11B

The moment had come to make her choice.

Alexandra stood still, poised in between two lives, two futures. She could speak up now and tell Captain Bowen the truth, and go back to her life as the lonely Miss Packard with no suitors. Or she could keep quiet, not say a word, until the ship sailed and they left England's shores. She could step into Georgia's shoes and the role of Mrs. Reid Bowen.

A memory of his face came to her mind. His blue eyes, his fair hair, tanned skin, the set of his broad shoulders, his warmth, his smile and his voice—even his smell had already melted into her skin, her blood, into her heart, and she could not, however sensible it might be, do anything to part herself from him.

CATHERINE MARCH

was born in Zimbabwe. Her love of the written word began when she was ten years old and her English teacher gave her *Lorna Doone* to read. Encouraged by her mother, Catherine began writing stories while a teenager. Over the years her employment has varied from barmaid to bank clerk to legal secretary. Her favorite hobbies are watching rugby, walking by the sea, exploring castles and reading.